SINS, & NAU
GAMES

NEW YORK TIMES BESTSELLING AUTHOR
J. KENNER

BLACKWELL-LYON SECURITY

Lovely Little Liar
Pretty Little Player
Sexy Little Sinner
Tempting Little Tease

THE STARK SAGA
novels
release me
claim me
complete me
anchor me
lost with me
damien

novellas
take me
have me
play my game
seduce me
unwrap me
deepest kiss
entice me
hold me
please me
indulge me

STARK SECURITY
Shattered With You
Broken With You
Ruined With You

MAN OF THE MONTH
Down On Me
Hold On Tight
Need You Now
Start Me Up
Get It On
In Your Eyes
Turn Me On
Shake It Up
All Night Long
In Too Deep
Light My Fire
Walk The Line

For all of JK's titles,
please visit www.jkenner.com

Praise for J. Kenner's Novels

"Kenner always knows how to deliver a man to swoon over ..." *The Read Report*

"I could not be more enamored with these characters. What an amazing new series J.K. brings us!" *Crystal's Book World (on Blackwell-Lyon)*

"I have read many J. Kenner's books, but this one has to be in my top 5. It was fast paced, suspenseful and HOT." *Read.Review.Repeat Blog (on Shattered With You)*

"With enough emotion to rip out your heart and the right amount of sexiness and intrigue to ramp up the excitement, *Broken With You* has to be one of my favorite J. Kenner novels to date." *Harlequin Junkie Blog*

"It is not often when a book is so amazingly well-written that I find it hard to even begin to accurately describe it . . . I recommend this book to everyone who is interested in a passionate love story." *Romancebookworm's Reviews (on Release Me)*

"A sizzling, intoxicating, sexy read!!!! J. Kenner had me devouring *Wicked Dirty* ... With her sophisticated prose, Kenner created a love story that had the perfect blend of lust, passion, sexual tension, raw emotions and love." *Four Chicks Flipping Pages*

SINS, LIES & NAUGHTY GAMES

NEW YORK TIMES BESTSELLING AUTHOR
J. KENNER

M&O

Sins, Lies & Naughty Games © 2019 by Julie Kenner

Sins, Lies & Naughty Games is a compilation/collection of the following copyrighted titles:
Lovely Little Liar Copyright © 2017, 2018 by Julie Kenner
Pretty Little Player Copyright © 2018 by Julie Kenner
Sexy Little Sinner Copyright © 2019 by Julie Kenner

Cover design by Michele Catalano, Catalano Creative
Cover image Lovely Little Liar by Annie Ray/Passion Pages
Cover image Pretty Little Player by Annie Ray/Passion Pages
Cover image Sexy Little Sinner by Perrywinkle Photography

Digital ISBN: 978-1-949925-57-9
Print ISBN: 978-1-949925-58-6
Published by Martini & Olive
v-2019-11-10P

All rights reserved. No part of this book may be reproduced, scanned, or distributed in any printed or electronic form without permission. Please do not participate in or encourage piracy of copyrighted materials in violation of the author's rights.

Lovely Little Liar, Pretty Little Player, and *Sexy Little Sinner* are works of fiction. Names, places, characters and incidents are the product of the author's imagination and are fictitious. Any resemblance to actual persons, living or dead, events or establishments is solely coincidental.

LOVELY LITTLE LIAR

CHAPTER ONE

I DON'T BELIEVE in relationships, but I do believe in fucking.

Why, you ask? Hell, I could write a book. *The Guy's Guide to Financial, Emotional, and Business Success*. But honestly, why bother with a book when the thesis boils down to just four words: Don't Date. Just Fuck.

Hear me out.

Relationships take time, and when you're trying to build a business, you need to pour every spare hour into the work. Trust me on this. In the months since my buddies and I launched Blackwell-Lyon Security, we've been busting ass twenty-four/seven. Working assignments, taking meetings, building a rock solid client base.

And our commitment's paying off. I promise you our roster wouldn't be half as full as it is now if I was spending chunks of prime working time answering texts from an insecure girlfriend who was wondering why I wasn't sexting every ten minutes. So skip the dating and watch your business flourish.

Plus, hook-ups don't expect gifts or flowers. Drinks or dinner, maybe, but a guy's gotta eat anyway, right? There may be no such thing as a free lunch, but you can come close to a free fuck.

But it's the emotional upside that's the kicker for me. No walking on eggshells because she's in a bitchy mood. No feeling trapped when she demands to know why poker night was more appealing than watching the latest tear-jerker starring some tanned metrosexual sporting a man bun. No wondering if she's banging another guy when she's not answering her texts.

And definitely no falling into a deep, dark pit of gloom when she breaks your engagement two weeks before the wedding because she's not sure she loves you after all.

And no, I'm not bitter. Not anymore.

But I am practical.

The truth is, I like women. The way they laugh. The way they feel. The way they smell.

I get off on making a woman feel good. On making her shatter in my arms and then beg for more.

Like them, yes. But I don't trust them. And I'm not getting fucked over again.

Not like that, anyway.

So there you go. Q.E.D.

I don't do relationships. I do hook-ups. I make it my mission to give every woman who shares my bed the ride of her life.

But it's a one-way street, and I don't go back.

That's just the way I roll. I walked away from relationships a long time ago.

So as I pull up in front of Thyme, the trendy new

restaurant in Austin's upscale Tarrytown neighborhood, and hand the valet my keys, all I'm expecting is business as usual. Some causal flirting. A few appetizers. A solid buzz from a little too much liquor. And then a quick jaunt back to my downtown condo for some mid-week action.

What I get instead, is *her*.

CHAPTER TWO

"WELL, then, I need you to make an announcement." The leggy brunette's voice belongs to a woman used to giving orders. "He must be here by now."

Legs is standing in front of me at the hostess stand, her back turned so that all I can see is a mass of chestnut brown waves, a waist small enough for a man to grab onto, and an ass that was made to fill out a skirt. In front of her, a petite blonde clutches a stack of menus like a lifeline as she gnaws on her lower lip.

"Well?" Legs' voice is more demand than question.

While the hostess explains to Legs that the restaurant really isn't set up for announcements, I glance at my watch impatiently. The traffic on Sixth Street had been more of a bitch than usual, and I'm running five minutes late. An irritating reality considering that I'm habitually prompt, a remnant from my military days. I'll cop to a lot of vices, but tardiness isn't among them.

Legs, however, is going to make me even later, and I frown as I glance toward the bar area to my left, looking for any unaccompanied woman who might be "J" from the 2Nite app. But there's no one sitting alone who looks like she's waiting for "PB" to join her.

It's my first time using this particular app, and its schtick—because they all have a schtick—is that all contact is anonymous until you actually meet your date. That's fine and dandy, but it makes connecting difficult. After all, would she really have left her name as J at the hostess desk? Because I'm going to feel like an idiot if I have to call myself PB.

Then again, I'll be lucky to have the chance to call myself anything at all, because Legs is spending so much time harassing the hostess that the restaurant will be closed before I can ask about J or claim a table.

"—except I already told you that I don't have his name," Legs is saying as I tune back into their conversation. The corporate warrior tone has faded, replaced by frustration and, I think, disappointment.

As for the hostess, she now looks even more frazzled.

"All I know is that he works for a security company—"

Ding, ding, ding. Folks, we have a winner.

"—and he should already be here."

"J," I say confidently, stepping up beside her. "I'm Pierce Blackwell." I pull a business card from my wallet and hand it to her when she turns to face me.

"Of Blackwell-Lyon Security. *PB*," I add, just in case that's not absolutely clear. "I'm very happy to meet you in person."

And that, frankly, is one hundred percent true. Because while the rear view might be amazing, from the front, my date for the night is even more stunning. Her dark hair frames a pale face with skin so perfect I have to force myself not to reach out and stroke her cheek. She has a wide mouth that was built for naughty things, and the kind of curvaceous body that lets a man know he has a real woman in his arms.

"Oh." Her voice is a little startled, and her amber eyes are wide with surprise. She's dropped the stern tone she'd used with the hostess, and I see relief in her eyes. I guess she thought I was going to stand her up, despite the fact that she doesn't look like the kind of woman who gets stood up often.

And her obvious relief that I've arrived suggests a vulnerability I wouldn't have guessed from listening to her interrogate the hostess.

Honestly, I like the contrast. It suggests a strong personality wrapped around a soft, feminine core. In other words, a woman who knows what she wants from a man, but isn't afraid to let him take control.

Did I mention I like taking control?

My card is still in her hand, and she glances down as she reads it, her thumb softly rubbing over the raised lettering in what I think must be an unconscious motion, but still makes me imagine the brush of that thumb over my hand, my mouth ... and other much more interesting places.

She lifts her head. And in the moment she meets my eyes, I'm certain that I see a familiar spark. The kind of heat that means we skip the appetizers, slam back a quick get-to-know-you drink, then barely make it back to my condo with clothing intact.

I know women like the way I look. Dark blond hair, a body that's in prime shape at thirty-four thanks to military training and my current job's requirements, plus blue eyes that have been known to draw compliments from strangers.

So the heat I see on her face doesn't surprise me. But then I blink, and damned if that fire doesn't disappear, her eyes going completely flat. As if someone flipped a switch.

What the hell?

Was I hallucinating? Fantasizing?

Or maybe she's just doing her damnedest to fight an intense, visceral lust.

But why would she? She came here tonight wanting the same thing I did. One night. A good time. And absolutely no strings.

Honestly, it makes no sense. And right now, the only thing I'm certain of is that the desire I saw on her face is gone. *Poof.* Just like a magic trick.

No heat. No fire.

No goddamned interest at all.

"So, will that be two for dinner?" the hostess asks brightly. "The wait's about forty-five minutes in the dining room, but there are a few tables open in the bar."

"That'll be fine," I say, determined to get this evening back on track. "We'll probably stick with drinks and appetizers." I look to her for confirmation, but she's frowning at her phone and doesn't look up again until we're seated.

"The drinks here are good," I say as the hostess leaves us with the bar menus. "I live downtown, so I've been coming here a lot since it opened. How about you? Been here before?"

One perfectly groomed eyebrow arches up in a way that I find incredibly sexy, despite the fact that she's obviously annoyed. "I've only just arrived in town. When would I have had time?"

"Right. Good point." Now I'm just being conciliatory, because how am I supposed to know when she moved to Austin? I read her profile and there wasn't a single word in there about her being new to town. But my only other option is to tell her flat out that tonight is a bust, and then get the hell out of there.

Except I'm not ready to give up on her yet. Because despite our off-kilter start, there's something intriguing about J. And I know damn well that I saw a spark of interest in her eyes. And so help me, I intend to get it back. Because, hey, who doesn't love a challenge?

"Speaking of time," she says. "Under the circumstances, I feel I need to be completely honest."

"Go for it."

"It's just that I didn't appreciate being kept waiting," she says. "Punctuality is extremely important to me."

"Me too." That's true, but I'm surprised she's getting bent out of shape for a mere five minutes. Still, at least we've found one tiny patch of common ground. "I'm almost always early. I'd blame the traffic, but honestly I should have left the office earlier."

I flash my most charming smile. It hasn't failed me yet, and thankfully tonight is no exception. She relaxes a bit and leans back in her chair, her finger tracing the leather edge of the menu.

"I'm glad to hear it. You've seemed lackadaisical about the whole thing so far. It's not the attitude I'm used to."

I reach across the table and take her hand. It's soft and warm, and my cock tightens in response to a fresh wave of lust. She may be prickly and inscrutable, but she's also fiercely self-assured, and the combination is seriously hot.

"Sweetheart," I say. "I may be flippant about a lot of things, but never about this."

"Sweetheart?" She tugs her hand free of mine, and I couldn't have gone limp faster if she'd dunked me in a barrel of ice water. "And you called me J, too? I mean, what? Are we starting a hip hop band?"

"We could," I quip, trying to regain my balance. "PB and J. You have to admit it works."

I laugh, because it *does* work. And why the hell is she griping at me, anyway? If using initials irritates her that much, she should have picked an app other than 2Nite.

"Just call me Jez," she says. "Or Ms. Stuart if you prefer to be more formal." She's sitting up straight now, and I'm thinking that she couldn't be more formal if she tried.

"Jez," I say. "I like it."

"It's short for Jezebel, obviously. And of course our parents named my sister along the same theme." She leans back, clearly expecting a response.

"Parents will do that," I say, since I've got nothing else. Let's just say that talk of parents and siblings isn't usually par for the course on these kinds of dates.

Still, it must have been the right thing to say, because she smiles, and it's the kind of smile that lights her whole face. And even though I don't do full nights—not ever—I can't help thinking that it's the kind of smile I'd like to wake up to.

"Listen," she says, "I know I may seem formal and demanding, and that can be a little off-putting for some people. It's just that I take all of this very, very seriously."

"I get that." I mean what I say. After all, I know that I'm a nice guy, but a woman has to be careful who she goes home with.

"I'm glad you understand," she says as the waiter comes up to take our order.

I hand the waiter my menu. "Angel's Envy. On the rocks. And the lady will have...?"

"Club soda with lime." She meets my eyes as the waiter walks away. "I like to keep a clear head."

Okay, sparks or not, this woman is exasperating. "Honestly, right now, I'm thinking I should have ordered a double."

Her mouth tightens with disapproval. "Fine. But I hope you have a clear head when it counts. I expect complete attention to detail."

I hold her gaze for ten full seconds. And then—because at this point I have nothing to lose—I slowly let my eyes roam down. Her usually full lips, now pressed together in a thin red line. The soft curve of her jaw. The tender slope of her neck.

Her top button of her silk blouse has come open, and I can see the curve of her breasts spilling out over the cups of her pale pink bra. I pause just long enough to imagine the taste of her right there. The feel of her soft skin against my lips. And the way her bossy, severe voice will soften when she writhes beneath me and begs for more.

Slowly, I raise my eyes. "Sweetheart," I say. "I'm all about the details."

I watch, satisfied, as a pink stain colors her cheeks. She exhales, then swallows. "Right. Well, that's good."

I bite back a smile. I'm not sure what kind of game

we've been playing, but there's no doubt in my mind that the score is currently in my favor.

She draws a breath, and I can tell she's trying to gather herself. "So if you're all about the details, then you already know my problem."

I lean back, grateful when the waiter returns with my drink, as that gives me time to think. *Problem?* The only problem I remember her mentioning in her profile was that she'd been working such long hours she hadn't been properly laid in months. I'd assured her I could remedy that, and she'd promptly accepted my RFD—which is 2Nite speak for "request for date."

"Well, you've been going a hundred miles an hour," I say, and she nods, looking pleased that I remember.

"And all this drama with my sister is adding a whole new layer of insanity."

"Your sister?"

She looks at me sharply, and I immediately, regret my words.

"I thought you'd done your homework." There's a challenge in her voice, but I barely notice it. I'm too mesmerized by the way her lips now close over her straw.

I shift, my jeans feeling uncomfortably snug. And honestly, what the hell? Because I can already tell this woman is bad news. Intriguing, maybe. Challenging, definitely. But way, way too much trouble.

Apparently, the parts of me below the table aren't nearly as critical, however. But I'm going to attribute that to a general desire to get laid, and not necessarily to Jez.

"Well?" she presses.

"Are you always this..." I trail off, thinking better of saying what I was thinking. *Bitchy*.

"What?"

"It's just that this smells remarkably like a job interview. Which seems a bit like overkill for just one night."

"One night? Oh, no. I'm looking for something for at least three weeks. After that, we can decide if a long term commitment would make sense."

"Wait. What?"

"I was with Larry for over five years," she says, which explains why she's been so awkward tonight. I'm guessing this is her first time to even use a dating app.

"That's quite a while," I say.

"It is. And honestly, I prefer the continuity that goes with a long-term arrangement. With someone I can trust, of course. That's what I'll be evaluating with you, of course. Assuming you check out and can prove yourself. Which, frankly, I'm starting to doubt."

I wince, suddenly picturing a panel of Olympic judges at the foot of my bed as I attempt a double rolling dismount with a flip.

I shake my head, dismissing the thought.

"Right. Okay. Let's back up." I slam back the rest of my bourbon. "Now it's my turn to call you out for being unprepared. Because my profile is crystal clear. No long term commitments." I flash that charming smile again. "Forget marriage. I'm all about the one-night stand."

"That's absurd. You're seriously considering doing this for just one night? And you think that would be okay with me? That I want to do this repeatedly?" She gestures at the table, as if having a man buy you a drink is the most hideous torture imaginable. "Are you insane?"

"My shrink doesn't think so."

She stands, then hooks her purse over her shoulder. "I wish your policy had been made clear. This has been a complete waste of time in a week when I don't have any time to waste."

"Jez—" I stand and reach for her, but she steps back. I have no idea why I want her to stay, but I do.

She, however, isn't giving me the chance to convince her.

"Thank you for the drink." She draws a breath, and I can see her effort to settle herself. "I really am sorry for the misunderstanding. Despite everything, I think it would have been... *interesting* working with you."

And then she turns.

And then she's gone.

What the hell just happened?

"Another?" the waiter asks, as I sink back into my chair.

"Yeah. A double this time. I think I need it."

I sit there for a minute, a little shell-shocked, and I'm not sure why. I damn sure shouldn't be disappointed she walked, because that one would have been trouble for sure. The last thing I need is a woman who wants to cling.

But still, I've sat in a bar and had a drink by myself on several occasions. But never before has the empty seat across from me seemed quite so empty.

I sigh, then lift the drink the waiter slides in front of me. I savor the bite of the whiskey, wondering if it's the alcohol that's messing with my head. Making me think that maybe two dates wouldn't be the end of the world. Hell, maybe even three.

Because the truth is, even though I never quite figured her out, I haven't been that entertained by a woman in a long time.

My phone chirps, signaling an incoming message from 2Nite.

I snatch it from my jacket pocket, certain it's a message from Jez.

But it's not.

Oh, it's from J, all right. But as I read it, I get a dark, twisting feeling in my gut.

Sorry I missed our date. Work blew up and I had to fly to Dallas. Rain check?

J

I read it twice, just to make sure that the bourbon isn't making me hallucinate.

But, no. The message is clear. J—the woman I was all set to meet here tonight—isn't in Austin. She's two hundred miles away.

Which means that she didn't show.

Which means that Jez isn't J.

Which means that I have no idea who Jezebel Stuart is.

And I damn sure don't know what the hell we spent the evening talking about.

CHAPTER THREE

I SIT in the bar and nurse my drink for a full fifteen minutes before lightning finally strikes, and I get it. And, yeah, maybe I should have made sense of the whole convoluted mess faster, but my head wasn't in the game. Instead, it was on those never-ending legs. That soft skin. Those sultry, penetrating eyes.

Not to mention a mouth that was made for both sin and sarcasm.

I'd been distracted, yes. And more than a little slow on the uptake. But I give myself credit for pulling it together at the end. And the moment I do—the moment I finally understand the complete and total clusterfuck that was our conversation—I bolt out of my chair and head for the door.

Jez, of course, is long gone.

Damn.

I head back inside and drop into the chair I'd abandoned. My watered down drink is still there, although the bus boy's about to grab it. I practically growl at him, like an alpha lion claiming the last scrap of a downed gazelle, and he backs away, eyes wide.

I slam back the dregs of my drink, then chew on the ice as I tap my phone thoughtfully.

Now that I see the big picture, the real scenario is painfully obvious. I'd come here expecting to meet my hook-up. She'd come expecting to hire some unreliable cop-in-a-box who hadn't showed.

Or had he?

I frown, pondering the coincidence. Had he? More specifically, had *I* showed?

With a groan, I lean back in my chair, and take a deep whiff. Because right now, I'm afraid I smell a rat.

I pull out my phone, dial Kerrie's home number, and wait for her to pick up.

"Don't I get enough of you at work?" my sister says.

"You can never get enough of me, and you know it."

She snorts. "Seriously, what's up? I'm running a bath, and there's a sexy Scottish laird waiting for me to join him."

"Anticipation," I say. "Makes everything all the sweeter." Our mother had a collection of Barbara Cartland novels that my little sister discovered when she was eleven and I was twenty-one. She was my parents' surprise-it's-not-really-menopause-yet baby, and because of that she spent more time hanging around the house as a kid than I had. My parents were older and working and less inclined to drive her all over creation, and I was in the Middle East for my first tour, and not around to play big brother.

Apparently Dame Cartland is a gateway drug, because I'm pretty sure that Kerrie has now read every romance novel ever written. All of them, that is, except for ones featuring ex-Special Forces heroes. She says she pictures me and that it's just too weird.

"Especially since you're hardly romance hero material," she once quipped. And considering that a romance requires more connection than a late night hook-up, she's probably right.

Now she sighs dramatically. "What do you need?"

"Did you schedule a meeting between me and a woman named Jezebel Stuart?"

"Wait—what?" Her voice is sharp now, interested, and I'm certain that she's my culprit.

"Dammit, Kerrie. If you schedule an appointment, you have to push it through to the calendar. That's about as basic as your job gets."

"I know how to do my damn job, and I didn't schedule an appointment with you. But—"

"With Cayden? Connor?" I rattle off my partners' names.

"No. No appointment. Nada. Zip. Now do you want to drop the bullshit and tell me what's going on?"

"Are you at your computer?"

"Yes, I have a computer in my bathroom." I can practically hear her roll her eyes. "What do you need?"

"I want some background on this woman. Jezebel—"

"Stuart. Yeah, I know. You said. I don't need a computer for that. She's from Phoenix, but she's lived in LA for the last ten years. She's in Texas right now, though. Her sister's filming a movie. And why am I telling you all this?"

"Are you already online? How do you know all that?"

"Um, maybe because I have a life and read things other than *Tactical Weapons* and *Security Magazine*."

"And *Peanuts*," I add dryly. "I never miss Snoopy in the Sunday paper."

"Her sister's Delilah Stuart," she continues, ignoring me. "And Jezebel's her manager. Is that why they're hiring us? Because of all the harassment Delilah's been getting since she cheated on Levyl with Garreth Todd?"

"Not exactly." I have no idea who Levyl is, but I'm familiar with Garreth Todd. Mostly because all of my spare time isn't spent buried in my magazines, despite what my sister thinks. I also have a deep affection for any movie with a high body count and at least one kickass car chase, and Todd has starred in three of my recent favorites.

As a general rule, I'd rather shove bamboo under my fingernails than read, discuss, or think about Hollywood gossip. But now that Kerrie's brought it up, I do remember a conversation a while back. A date of mine kept droning on about some former child actress who'd recently skyrocketed to superstardom as an adult. At first, she'd been beloved by fans. Not only because of her breakout role, but because she was dating the lead singer of a popular boy band. The kind of band whose songs send tween girls into convulsive fits and have grown women secretly buying unauthorized biographies in the grocery store checkout line.

Apparently, the actress and the singer's romance played out in the tabloids, with the two being a sugary-sweet power couple that everyone rooted for.

But then the actress was awarded a plum part in a major movie opposite Garreth Todd. When the news broke that the actress had slept with Todd—thus breaking the singer's heart—she immediately went from being America's sweetheart to being a soulless harpy who shredded men's lives. She was still making the front page of entertainment magazines, but now it was because she was reviled and hated by females the world over, all of whom were taking the singer's broken heart way, way, way too personally.

As far as I know, there were no death threats against the actress, but considering my date's vitriol when she relayed the whole soap opera to me, I wouldn't be surprised.

My date had ended the story by saying the actress got what she deserved. Apparently, she'd been fired from some big franchise movie, and was pretty much a pariah as far as getting a job was concerned.

Like I said, a soap opera.

At the time, the actress's name meant nothing to me. Now, I'm certain it was Delilah Stuart.

Before I get the chance to ask Kerrie for more details, she plows on. "This is going to be great. I bet Delilah has all sorts of security assignments coming down the pipe. And if we have her business, we can get more entertainment jobs. There's so much film and music work in Austin, and even with all the controversy, a recommendation from Delilah would be golden. We could totally plug the hole left by Talbot, you know?"

I did know. Blackwell-Lyon is still a relatively new business, and when the guys and I broke off from our old firm we'd anticipated a steady stream of contracts with Reginald Talbot, a Silicon Valley billionaire who moved his family and his business to Austin about ten years ago. But five months after Blackwell-Lyon opened its doors, Talbot decided to retire, sold the entirety of his operation to some huge corporation, and headed to the Mediterranean with his wife.

In other words, he's working on his tan, and my partners and I are scrambling to fill the gap in our client base.

"So what exactly happened?" Kerrie asked. "You had a meeting with her? How?"

"Irrelevant," I say, because once Kerrie knows the real story, I'll never hear the end of it. "Right now, I just need to find out where she's staying." I'm a security expert, not a PI. But over the years, I've cultivated some resources. "Call Gordo and tell him I have a rush job."

"Please would be nice."

"Please."

"Well, since you asked so nicely..."

"Kerrie." There's a warning in my voice.

"I'm just messing with you. I don't need to call Gordo. Delilah's staying at the Violet Crown. So I bet Jezebel is, too."

"And you know this how?" I ask, already mentally calculating how long it will take to drive there. The Violet Crown is a high-end boutique hotel in central Austin. And, conveniently, just a few miles away from Thyme.

"Twitter. Someone at the hotel snapped her picture and posted it. *Hashtag Delilah Stuart.*"

I frown. "When was it posted? Are there others?"

She's obviously at her computer now, because I hear her tapping keys. "Um, the post went up about fifteen minutes ago. And it's got a couple of dozen likes." There's more tapping. "But I don't see any more posts. Lots of retweets, though. Why?"

I ignore the question. "I'll call you later." I've left a fifty on the table, and I'm already on my way to the valet stand.

"Pierce," she presses as I pass my ticket to the valet. "What's going on?"

"Nothing, I hope."

"But—"

I hang up, then drum my finger on the ledge of the valet stand. I want my car, and with every second that passes the knot in the pit of my stomach cinches just a little tighter.

I may not have the full story yet, but I know enough.

I know that Jez came to Thyme because she was looking to hire a security detail. I know she mentioned her sister in our conversation.

I know that Delilah's still reviled by fans.

And I know that her location is now public.

Call me paranoid, but that doesn't sit well with me.

CHAPTER FOUR

"I NEED you to connect me to Jezebel Stuart's room." I'm racing down Fifth Street toward Lamar Boulevard, my phone hooked up to the Range Rover's audio system.

Hopefully, I'm worrying about nothing. Surely the current production company has security on Delilah. But if so, then why was Jezebel looking to hire me? Or, rather, why was she looking to hire the guy who was supposed to have shown up instead of me?

I don't know, and at the moment, I don't care. Bottom line, Jez may think I'm a total incompetent prick, but I can't walk away until I'm certain she and her sister are safe.

"I'm sorry, sir, but there's no one by that name registered here." The girl doesn't sound like she's old enough to legally drink, and I know that I'm ruining her day. But better hers than Jezebel's.

"Excellent," I say, adding a little charm to my voice. "That's exactly how you were supposed to respond. I'll be sure and let your manager know that you've stuck with protocol."

I pause long enough to let her tell me that she has no idea what I'm talking about. When she stays silent, I know I guessed right: Jez and Delilah are guests, management is fully aware, and the staff has been ordered to protect their privacy no matter what.

"I'm with the studio's publicity department. Jezebel's expecting my call."

"But I'm not supposed to put anyone through."

"No, you're not," I say. "And I commend you for being so diligent. You were informed of the call in protocol, I assume?"

"Um—"

"My apologies, you should have been made fully aware. Obviously we have to be able to get through to the Stuarts, even if they've turned off their cell phones. So you just put me on hold, then call up. Tell Jezebel that Pierce Blackwell needs to speak to her. *PB*," I add. "Be sure to tell her it's PB. And tell her it's important."

I'm pretty sure my name isn't going to win any points with Jez. But I'm hoping she'll pick up the call out of sheer curiosity.

"But—"

"That's the designated procedure," I insist as I make a right turn onto Lamar and head toward the bridge. "Once Ms. Stuart accepts, you just need to patch through this call."

"Oh. Okay. Hold please."

Elevator music starts to play, and I give myself a mental high five.

My victory fades quickly, however, as my time on hold extends. I'm at the bridge. I'm on the bridge. Now I'm stuck at a light. I glance to my right at the moon reflecting on the surface of the river that we locals called Town Lake until the city renamed it Lady Bird Lake about a decade ago. It's a dammed off section of the Colorado River, and why we don't just call it that is one of life's little mysteries.

I let my eyes travel up to the low, rolling hills on the south side of the river. I can't see it from this angle, but I know the Violet Crown's up there. And Jezebel.

By the time I'm over the bridge and making a right turn onto Barton Springs Road, I'm still on hold, and I'm thinking that Jez has shut me down entirely, and I'll never get through.

I'm about to end the call, re-dial, and try again, when the clerk comes back on the line. "I'll connect you now," she says, before I can ask what happened.

And then it's Jez's voice. "How did you find me? For that matter, why are you calling? Did I leave something at the bar?"

"I'm about three minutes from your hotel. I'm going to pull in behind the hotel and park by the service entrance. A black Range Rover. Get your stuff. Get your sister, and meet me back there."

"In case it escaped your notice, you and I don't work together."

"If you're always this argumentative, I'll take that as a good thing. But right now, you need to trust me. I'm moving you to a different location."

"Trust you? I don't even know you. For that matter, I'm pretty sure I don't like you."

"Only pretty sure? Glad to know there's a small window I can crawl through."

"Pierce—"

"And maybe you don't like me, but you do trust me," I continue. "If you didn't, you wouldn't have taken my call at all. So I'm betting you checked me out. Went to my website. Googled my company, my background."

She says nothing, which I take as confirmation.

"Where's Delilah?" I ask, careful to keep my victory smile out of my voice.

"I thought you didn't know anything about my sister?"

"I'm a quick study. And I know that someone tweeted your hotel."

"*Shit.*"

Her tone makes it clear that she didn't know. "You should have some sort of set-up for alerts," I say mildly.

"I do—or I did." She curses softly again. "It's just that lately there's been so much on the Internet about Delilah that my phone never stopped dinging. Now our publicist pulls it nightly and emails it to me every morning."

"Look, the Crown's a great little hotel, but it's not secure enough for you. Get your sister, meet me, and let me take you someplace safe."

"Why is this even your problem?"

And that, I think, is a very good question. And one I'm not sure how to answer. Primarily because the real answer —that she's filled my head, and not helping her is simply unacceptable—is something I don't want to acknowledge. Much less share.

So instead I go with an honest lie. Something true, but not my reason. "Because I think you and I have something in common," I say.

"I sincerely doubt it."

"I have a younger sister," I say. "And I'd move heaven and earth to make sure nothing bad happened to her."

For a moment, she says nothing. Then she says very softly, "She's not here. They had a late call tonight. One of the guys working set security is bringing her back. But she texted me a few minutes ago. They're close."

I've reached the Crown now. It's low and sprawling and shaped like a U, the interior of which sports a popular —and public—open-air bar that surrounds a pool.

All of the rooms have patios that look out over either the pool or the greenbelt. A valet stand is at the apex of the circular drive, right at the access point to the bar area. I'm guessing that Delilah made the mistake of stepping onto her patio or in front of a window, and a fan snapped a picture from the bar area.

The valet stand is also right by the main entrance to the hotel's interior, which is accessed by a short covered walkway that runs in front of the bar area to a door at the end of one of the U's prongs. Which means that anyone coming into the hotel has to walk past the bar. Which is great for generating business. But not great for privacy or security.

As I drive slowly forward, I can see that the bar is teeming. It's always been popular, but right now it's so full of bodies it looks like Dante's version of hell.

I'm hoping that the place instituted a really amazing Wednesday night Happy Hour, and that accounts for the crowd. But I'm thinking that some of those people came not for the drinks, but for the entertainment. And Delilah, I'm afraid, is the star attraction.

"Text your sister. Have the driver take her around back."

"Too late," she says. "She says they just pulled up."

Sure enough, a black Lincoln Town Car has rolled to a stop right past the valet stand. The bellboy must recognize the car, because he scurries to open the back passenger side door. The driver gets out, and starts to circle around to the passenger side as well.

I can't see who's in the car, but the crowd in the bar has a clear view, and as soon as the door opens, a throng of them stand. I've rolled down my windows, and the catcalls and cries of *bitch* and *slut* and *Levyl deserves better* ring loud and clear.

I slam the car into gear and plow forward just as the crowd starts throwing rotten tomatoes. And half a dozen cameras flash intermittently, illuminating the scene.

The tomatoes splatter on the sidewalk, and Delilah dives back into the car, slamming the door shut behind her as a hail storm of little red bombs explode against the side of the car.

I bring the Rover to a squealing stop beside the Lincoln. "What's happening?" Jezebel cries, her voice tinny through the speakers.

I don't bother answering. I'm out of the car and pulling open the left-side passenger door on the Lincoln. Delilah, looking young and scared, cowers away from me. I hold out my hand. "I'm with Jez. Come on."

She hesitates, and I'm thinking that I'm going to have to dive in the car and forcibly scoop her up, when Jez's voice blares from the Range Rover's speakers. "Do what he says, Del. I'm coming."

Immediately, Delilah lunges for me. I grab her hand and pull her toward me, then load her into the back seat of the Range Rover.

"Hey!" the security guy calls, solidifying my assessment of him as an incompetent prick.

On the hotel side of the Lincoln, a group of women are surging forward, their eyes filled with an anger I don't understand, but certainly can't deny.

"Bitch!"

"Levyl was too good for you!"

"How could you hurt him like that?"

"Whore!"

They're getting closer, and I'm on my way back to the driver's side, yelling for Jez to meet us at the service entrance.

But right as I'm about to get into the car, she bursts through the hotel door, then skids to a halt, just a few feet from the boiling crowd. *Shit.*

Her phone's at her ear, and I can hear her cry of, "Delilah!" in stereo—from the sidewalk a few yards away, and through the rolled-down window of my Range Rover.

"Jez!" Delilah calls. "Please, mister!"

I hesitate only a second, debating whether it would be faster to get in the Rover or sprint to the sidewalk.

I sprint.

The crowd's not interested in her at first, but then someone calls out, *Jezebel,* and they move *en masse* toward her, shouting questions about Delilah. A surge of furious energy rips through me—they are *not* touching her—and I push myself to get to her faster, only taking an easy breath when I finally grab her outstretched hand.

"Come on," I order, even though there's no need. She's right beside me and we race toward the car together, fingers twined, while young women grab at my jacket, shouting curses and questions and swearing that Delilah will pay for the way she hurt their sweet, wonderful Levyl.

"In," I say, opening the door so she can get in behind me and be next to her sister. I slam the door, climb into the car, and burn rubber getting back to the street.

I don't stop until we're well away from the hotel. Then I pull into one of the lots at Zilker Park, cut the engine, and relax, my eyes going immediately to the rear view mirror. To *her*.

The women are right next to each other, Jez's arms around Delilah, who's cuddled up against her, crying softly. After a moment, Jez lifts her eyes and meets mine in the mirror. *Thank you*, she mouths, and I look away, my chest tightening with emotion. I tell myself I'm only thinking about Kerrie. Putting myself in Jez's shoes, and empathizing about how she's feeling now that her sister's safe.

It's not true, of course. What I'm feeling is the shock of this woman's gratitude. That soft, grateful look from a woman I know is strong and competent, but who still needed me. And the pride of coming through for her.

For her.

Because it's not about the job. It's about the woman. And that's not something I've felt in a long time.

Frankly, it's not something I want to feel at all.

Suddenly, the huge interior of my Range Rover is feeling claustrophobic. I grab the handle and open the door, then step out, shutting it behind me. They need privacy. And I need space.

But after a few minutes, I hear the door open, then slam shut. I'm leaning against the front of the Rover, looking out toward the soccer field and the river. My condo's on the other side, and from this angle, I can see the rise of my building blending in with the downtown Austin skyline.

Home.

"It's a pretty view," Jez says, easing up beside me.

"Your first time in Austin, right?"

I'm still looking at the city lights, but I can see her in my periphery. The way she turns toward me, her head tilted just slightly, as if I'm a knotty puzzle she has to solve. "Why were you at Thyme? It wasn't to meet me."

"Blind date," I say, turning toward her. "Mistaken identity." I nod toward the car. "We should write it up. It could be one of those romantic caper films. Your sister could star."

Immediately, her expression shuts down and she wraps her arms around herself as if cold. It's March, but it's Austin, so there's barely a chill in the air. Even so, I take off my jacket and put it around her shoulders. She flashes me a quick smile, looking both sheepish and vulnerable. "I'm starting to wonder if there's going to be anything to star in."

"What are you talking about?"

For a moment, I think she's going to answer. Then the wall slams back in place, and she just shakes her head. "Nothing. Never mind."

"Jez..."

"Honestly, it's not your problem." She pushes away from the car. "Thanks for your help—really. But we'll be fine now. When you take us back, you should probably go to that service entrance, though."

"We're not going back," I say.

"Excuse me?"

"It's South By Southwest right now," I tell her, referring to the well-attended Austin conference and festival. "We're talking fans, reporters, the whole nine yards. They're all in town. And the Violet Crown isn't secure. You think the photographers are going to stay away from that bar just because you ask them nicely?"

"You're right," she says, surprising me. "I'll take care of it tomorrow."

"How about we take care of it tonight?"

Her lips press tight together. "I appreciate what you did," she says. "But I'm not hiring you. I need a firm that can provide a long-term solution, not a one-night fix."

"Tonight's working out pretty well for you," I say with a wry grin. "But just to be clear, in work, I'm all about long-term relationships."

"So it's just your personal life that's truncated?"

Something about the way she says it stabs me in the gut. As if she's stripped me down to the essentials and found me wanting. "Yeah," I say. "I've slipped on the relationship suit before. It's a little too tight for my taste."

She nods. "Well, I don't suppose it matters either way. We're not in a relationship, we're not having a one-night stand, and I already have a new security team lined up for the rest of the shoot."

"Led by the same guy who didn't show up at Thyme?"

"Actually, yeah."

I nod. "Seems reliable and solid. Good choice."

"The studio vetted him," she says tightly. "They just got the date wrong when they set up the meet. He's flying in tomorrow."

"And Larry?"

Her brow furrows. "What about Larry?"

"He's your former security detail, right? The one you were with for five years?" I make a spinning motion with my finger beside my head. "I reran our conversation in my head. It makes a lot more sense now that I know who you weren't."

"What about him?"

"He approve of your new guy?"

"I—I wouldn't know." She draws a breath and looks down at the ground. "He died over a year ago. A drunk driver in Newport Beach."

My blood pounds through me—this story is too familiar. "Larry?" I say. "Laurence Piper? Colonel Laurence Piper?"

Her eyes widen. "You knew him?"

"I spent six months under him. I went to his funeral," I add.

"You were in Special Forces."

I nod. I don't like to talk about my time in uniform. I don't regret it—I have my job and my training because of the skills I learned in the military—but the things I saw can haunt a man. And I learned a long time ago to turn my back on the pain.

"I think Larry would want me to make sure you're safe," I say now. "To get you out of the Crown." The wind's blown a strand of hair over her lips, and I brush it away without thinking, surprised by the shock of awareness that jolts through me as my fingers brush her cheek.

She feels it, too. I'm certain of it. I hear her shuddering breath. I see the way she drops her gaze, then starts to take a step back. She stops herself, pulling my jacket tighter around her. When she looks up again, she's all business. "We'll never find a room. It's the festival, remember? And all of our stuff is at the Crown."

"In other words, if I can get your things delivered to you and set you up in a room, you'll move hotels, no argument?"

"Well, hell," she says. "I walked into that one."

I fight a smug grin. "Right straight into the fire."

Her lips are pressed together, but this time it's not with irritation, but because she's trying not to laugh. And the effort is making her eyes light up, giving her a glow that's both sexy and sweet ... and really not the direction my thoughts need to be traveling.

After a second, she pulls herself together. "Okay. Fine. You win. But you'll never get a room. It's insanity."

"Shall we bet?" Now I'm the one playing with fire. But I can't help it. I want to feel the heat, even at the risk of being burned.

Her eyes narrow. "What are the stakes?"

"I thought you were my date earlier tonight. Let's make it official. Have dinner with me tomorrow."

A single brow rises in that way she has. "When you thought I was your date, we were having drinks."

"Fair enough," I say. "Drinks and appetizers. Deal?"

"Deal," she says. "But you're not going to win."

"Watch me." I pull out my phone, hoping my confidence isn't misplaced, then dial a friend I haven't spoken to in years. "Ryan Hunter," I tell her. "He used to own his own security business, but now he's the Security Chief for Stark International," I continue, referencing the huge international conglomerate owned by former tennis-pro turned billionaire entrepreneur, Damien Stark.

"And that's helpful how?"

"The new Starfire Hotel on Congress Avenue is a Stark property. So if management is holding back a room, I'm ninety percent sure Ryan can snag it for me."

He answers on the fourth ring, and after some quick catching up, I cut to the chase. "Ideally a suite," I say after explaining the situation. "But I'd be grateful for anything you can wrangle."

"Hang on," he says, then puts me on hold. "You're in," he says when he returns. "Ask for Luis when you get there. He'll get them set up."

"I owe you."

"I'll remember that."

I chuckle, then hang up. A lot of the security business is run on traded favors. Today, that practice worked well for me—and for Jez, who's eyeing me with curiosity.

I flash a victorious smile. "Never bet against the house."

"Let's go," she says, and though her voice is stern, I hear the humor underneath.

As promised, Luis takes good care of Del and Jez, providing them with pseudonyms for check-in, a suite on a floor with private key access, and a floor plan that consists of two bedrooms that connect from opposite sides to a huge living area.

"I hope this is suitable?" Luis asks.

"It's great," Jez assures him.

"So you're all set," I say after Luis leaves. He's promised to personally act as a liaison with the Crown to arrange the delivery of both women's things. "Tomorrow night. I'll pick you up at eight."

"I'll meet you at Thyme," she says, then smiles innocently.

"Fair enough. But no club soda with lime."

"Deal," she says.

"You two need to shake on it," Delilah says, walking in from the bedroom she'd claimed.

I hadn't gotten much of a look at her earlier, but it's easy to see why she'd shot to stardom. At eighteen, she has a maturity about her that seems much older. But there's an innocence, too, suggesting a life that's just a little too sheltered.

She's shorter than her sister, and thinner. Almost too thin, at least for my taste.

Her face is classically beautiful, but a smattering of freckles gives her an approachable quality. She's full of laughter, despite the harassment by the fans, and it's easy to tell which is the more serious of the sisters.

"Thank you again," Delilah says to me, for what must be the thousandth time. "For the rescue and for the room."

"You're welcome again," I say, and she grins.

"He was good, wasn't he?" she says to Jez.

"Bossy and arrogant," Jez says, her eyes flickering to me. "But, yeah. He was good."

I smile, more pleased than I should be by the compliment.

"Of course, he's also an ass," she adds, making Delilah burst into laughter.

"Watch it, or I'll make another bet. I think we both know your track record."

"I'm quaking with terror."

Delilah's head moves, her eyes wide as she watches the two of us like a tennis game. "So tomorrow, right? I'll just hang out here."

"You'll definitely hang out here," Jez says. "No late shoot tomorrow. So no repeat of tonight." She glances at her watch. "You have a five a.m. call. I'll wake you at four. Go." She nods toward the bedroom.

Delilah looks at me, her expression exasperated. "She forgets that it's been five years since I was thirteen."

"You forget what a bitch you are when you don't get enough sleep."

That's her, Delilah mouths, holding up a hand to shield the finger she's pointing at Jez.

"I heard that."

"I'm going, I'm going." Delilah pauses in the door of her room. "Thanks again, Pierce. For everything."

"My pleasure," I say. And then she closes her door, and I'm alone with Jez, and this palatial suite seems suddenly too small.

I clear my throat. "I should let you get to sleep, too."

She nods. "Yeah. It's late."

"Tomorrow," I say.

"Tomorrow." She steps toward me, and my heart pounds in anticipation of her touch—and then with mortification when I realize that all she's doing is walking to the door.

"Lock it behind me," I order.

"Of course."

Then I'm outside, and she smiles, and the door closes in my face.

And that, I think, is the end of that.

Except it's not. I'm going to see her tomorrow.

And right then I realize that I made a mistake with that bet. I should have kept my mouth shut.

I should have just walked away.

Because Jezebel Stuart is the kind of woman who gets under your skin.

But I'm not the kind of man who sticks.

CHAPTER FIVE

"THIS IS MY FAVORITE SHOT," Kerrie says, holding up her tablet so that Connor can see what she's looking at. Then she turns it to me, as if I'm just an afterthought. "I like how everything's in focus except you and Delilah. You're both just a little blurry."

"Nice," I say, leaning back against the break room countertop and sipping my second cup of late-afternoon coffee. After a day reviewing blueprints in prep for an upcoming job, I need the caffeine. "Way to be kind to your big brother."

The image is from the Crown, and it shows Delilah and me hurrying from the Town Car to my Range Rover.

"An action shot," Connor says, flashing a wide grin. "And with a movie star. I don't know, Blackwell. Could be the start of a whole new career for you."

"Nah," my sister says to Connor. "You're the one with the movie star looks."

"Hey." I hold up my hands, pretending offense. "What am I? Dog food?"

She sets the tablet down and eyes me critically. "You'll do," she says. "Empirically you're pretty hot, even if you are my brother. It's the eyes that do it. You have bedroom eyes."

By the fridge, Connor snorts.

"I'm serious," my sister says. "I mean, he's got the body for sure—thank you Uncle Sam— and a solid jawline. Extra points, by the way, for the beard stubble."

"I try."

"But it's those pale blue eyes that get him laid. I mean, basically he got what I was supposed to have. The bastard."

My sister has dark hair and brown eyes, and she knows damn well that she's stunning.

"But *you*," she continues, looking to Connor, "you have that mysterious dark thing going on. It's seriously hot."

"You just want in my bed," Connor teases.

"Been there, done that," she says airily.

As always whenever their past fling comes up, I eye both of them, searching for signs that their short-lived relationship is going to somehow blow up—and blow back on the business. But they both seem fine with having moved on. And although that surprises me—Kerrie's had a crush on Connor since she was thirteen and I brought him and Cayden home with me when we were on leave—I also know that the fourteen-year age difference between them is something that Connor was never comfortable with.

Since they didn't bother consulting me when they broke it off, I don't know all the reasons. But I do know they've stayed friends.

Which works out well for the business, because my sister's doing a stellar job as our office manager, a role she took on after she confessed to me that she was bored out of her mind with her previous job as a paralegal. Now, she runs the office and is going to school part time for her MBA.

She picks up the tablet again. "There are dozens more pictures like that one. Maybe hundreds. Want to see?"

"No," I say firmly, as Connor says, "Hell, yes."

"Fine," she says, putting the tablet down with a smirk. "I'll show Connor later, when Cayden's here to share your humiliation."

"That's why you're my favorite sister. You treat me so well."

"I'm amazing," she chirps. "But seriously, your fifteen minutes of fame could be good for our bottom line."

Cayden slides into the room, then leans against the wall, his arms crossed. "Well, that's something I like to hear. What did our Mr. Blackwell do?"

Kerrie passes him the tablet, then gives him a rundown of last night—her version, at least. Cayden listens, amused, his expression much the same as Connor's. To be expected, I suppose. They're identical twins. But it's easy to tell them apart these days. Cayden wears a patch over his left eye— the injury being the reason he'd been discharged three years ago despite intending to stay in the game until retirement.

He still does some fieldwork at Blackwell-Lyon, but mostly he's the face of our organization. And he's damn good at the job. "The patch makes me look tough," he often says. "And that's a baseline requirement when I'm asking folks to put their lives in our hands."

He hands the tablet back to Kerrie. "So all this coverage is bringing in new business?"

"Not a flood," she says. "But I must have fielded at least a half-dozen calls today. I guess folks figure if Pierce is watching out for Delilah, then he can watch out for them, too."

"She hired us?" Cayden asks, which was a very Cayden-like way to cut to the chase.

"No," I say. "That was a one-off."

"You never did tell me how you met them," Kerrie says.

"I met Jezebel at Thyme. We'd both been stood up."

"Mmm." I can tell she doesn't believe me. I can live with that.

"All that good work and she didn't hire you?" Connor asks. "What kind of a rainmaker are you?"

"The kind who's not." It's no secret that my skills are in the field. Cultivating new business is Cayden's specialty. "But all things considered, I think I did all right." I point at Kerrie. "Didn't she just say the phone's been ringing all day? I've done my job."

I keep my tone light. A *nothing to see here, move along folks* kind of attitude.

But the truth? The truth is I do want the job. Because without it, tonight's going to be the last time I see Jezebel Stuart. And that small fact isn't sitting well with me at all.

"Okay, enough about my brother. Are we gonna have this meeting or not?"

Connor nods toward the round table in the middle of the break room, Kerrie puts out a bowl of jelly beans—her personal vice—and we settle down for our Thursday morning meeting where we review all current assignments and go over the budget.

Kerrie's in the process of giving us the bad news about

how much our firewall upgrade is going to cost when an electric chime signals someone entering the reception area.

"And that's on the budget wish-list, too," Kerrie says, as she rises. "I'm the office manager, not the receptionist. We need to hire somebody, stat."

She disappears through the door, heading the short distance to the reception area. I can hear her speaking with someone, but can't make out words. Not that I'm really trying. We get a few walk-ins, but most clients come through referrals. Usually when someone walks in the front door it's because they're delivering a package or dropping off fliers for a new take-out restaurant.

So I'm not surprised when Kerrie returns quickly. But I am surprised by who I see with her.

Jezebel.

CHAPTER SIX

"RIGHT," Kerrie says, looking between me and Jez. "So, Connor? Could you and Cayden come with me to the file room? I'm having trouble, um, rebooting the server."

She heads out, and they both follow, but not before shooting me a half-dozen curious glances. I can't provide much insight, though. The fact is, I'm curious, too.

I gesture to the table. "Jelly bean?"

"Um, sure." She sits and pulls out a pink one.

"I guessed wrong," I say. "I would have pegged you for licorice."

She holds the candy between two fingers. "You think I'm not feminine enough for pink?"

"Not hardly," I say. I take the seat next to her, my knee brushing hers as I sit. "I just don't think it's you."

"Is that a fact?"

I reach for her hand, my fingers caressing her skin as I pluck the light pink bean out of her grip, then pop it into my mouth. "Sweet," I say, as her brows rise.

"And I'm not sweet?"

"I didn't say that."

She looks up at me, interested, as I pull a black bean from the bowl. "But you have a kick, too. Not to mention a classic pedigree." I put the candy in my mouth, and suck for a moment, noting with pleasure the way she squirms a little on the chair. And the way she doesn't meet my eyes. "And the truth is, I never think I'm going to enjoy the black ones, but each time I actually give them a whirl, I realize I can't get enough of them."

"Oh." She swallows, then licks her lips. "I always assumed they were an acquired taste."

"Nothing wrong with that, is there?"

She holds my gaze. "No. I suppose not."

"Maybe tonight I'll order you a glass of Sambuco. Like jelly beans with a buzz."

Her smile flickers, then dies.

"Okay, bourbon it is. Or wine." My quips don't reignite her smile, and I lean back in my chair. "All right, tell me the truth. Where did my banter go off the rails?"

I've obviously surprised her, and a laugh bubbles out. She presses her fingers over her lips and shakes her head. "Sorry. No, you're fine."

"Fine?" I study her. "Aren't you a lovely, little liar."

"No, really. I'm sorry, and you're banter's fine. I just mean that we won't be having that drink tonight."

The words are like a kick in the gut, but I hold it together. "Not a problem," I say. "We can jump straight to the sex."

She lifts a single brow, and for a moment I think it's arched in disapproval. But then I see the quick flicker of amusement in her eyes before she tilts her head and focuses on the jelly bean bowl.

She takes two of the mottled yellow ones. "These are you. Popcorn jelly beans. Sweet and salty, and very unexpected."

I tilt my head. "That sounds remarkably like a compliment. But it can't be." I lean back in the chair, resting my head against my intertwined fingers. "Because if it were a compliment, you wouldn't be canceling our date. A date that I won, remember? I'm thinking we're facing a pretty serious rules violation here."

I mentally cringe. With such lame jokes, it's no wonder she's blowing me off. And although I'm tempted to give my groveling skills a run for their money, I'm not sure I'm ready to turn in my Man Card just yet.

"The compliment's coming," she says. "I'm cancelling our date because I want to hire you. To be Delilah's security detail, I mean. Well, not just you. Your whole shop as needed."

"Oh." I stand and go to the coffee maker, mostly because I don't want her to see the expression on my face. Honestly, I'm not entirely sure what she'd see on my face. Disappointment about tonight? Excitement about the job? Surprise that she'd offer? Especially considering she already had someone lined up...

"Why?" I ask, turning back to her. "I thought the studio had already arranged for someone?"

"Yeah, they had."

"And from your expression, I'm guessing that they're agreeing to the switch only because you took them off the hook for paying the bill."

"We're good for it, Mr. Blackwell. In case you were worried about the check bouncing."

"Never doubted it for a second. Coffee?" I grab a mug and hold it out for her. She shakes her head, and I put the mug back in the cabinet. "Larry," I say, and when I turn back to her, it's clear from her expression that my guess is dead-on. "This is about Larry."

Her shoulders rise and fall. "He trained you," she says, as if that's a full explanation. "And I don't know anything about the group that the studio hired."

"You don't know much about me, either."

"Like you said, I did some homework. And last night I saw you in action. And you're right."

"I usually am," I quip. "What am I right about now?"

"When you called my hotel room last night, remember? You said I trusted you." She tilts her chin, her eyes defiant. "You were right. I do. And so does Delilah."

I like the sound of those words more than I want to admit.

"And if I say that we don't have room on our docket? That we're serving our clients at capacity right now, and don't have the resources to take on someone new?"

She stands up and crosses to the counter, then leans back against it as she studies me cooly. "Is that something you're likely to say?"

I shouldn't, dammit. Hell, I shouldn't even be considering turning down this job, especially when just fifteen minutes ago I was standing in this room wishing that the job was mine, just so I could see her again.

And now here she is, offering me that very carrot. I should be ringing a damn Klaxon and letting Kerrie and the guys know we have a new client, and telling them we're about to celebrate by paying down some debt and balancing our ledgers.

I *should,* but now that she's here and I'm faced with the very reality I wished for, I can't quite conjure the enthusiasm, much less the words. Because this woman has gotten under my skin, and the temptation to have her in my bed is just too damn much. How the hell am I supposed to work side-by-side and not touch her?

And what if I do give in? What if I break all my rules and let myself succumb to this walking, talking temptation named Jezebel?

Either she'll slap my face—in which case I've fucked up our working relationship right there—or she'll melt in my arms.

Good in the moment, maybe. But I'm afraid that once she's in my bed, I won't want her to leave.

And that's the kind of complication I really don't need in my life.

"Pierce?"

"Yeah, right." I draw a breath. "Sorry, but we really are all booked up."

Her hips sway as she crosses to me in two long strides. She uses both hands to grab my collar, then levers herself close, her lips brushing my ear as she whispers, "Liar."

The words shoot straight through me, making my cock stiffen. And, yeah, forcing me to fight the urge to thrust my fingers in her hair, hold her head in place, and kiss her senseless.

Did I mention I find competence extremely sexy?

And she's either done her homework ... or she's an extremely good poker player.

Frankly, a woman who can bluff is pretty damn sexy, too.

She takes a few steps back, her mouth curved down into a frown. "Look, I know our first meeting was a little off the wall. I mean, I pretty much thought you were an incompetent ass."

"If you're trying to convince me to take the job, you're not doing a stellar job."

Her mouth twitches. "What I'm trying to say is that my perception has changed."

I take a step toward her, my eyes locked on hers. "So you don't think I'm an incompetent ass anymore?"

She's standing beside a chair, and her hand tightens on the back of it. But her eyes never leave my face. "You're still an ass," she says. Her voice has gone a little breathy. Just a little. Barely even something you'd notice if you weren't paying attention.

I was paying attention.

I take one more step closer. "But?"

She licks her lips, and damned if I don't crave that mouth. "But I think you're a competent ass."

"You're right. I am."

I'm standing in front of her, just inches away. I can smell her perfume, a subtle vanilla. I can feel her heat. I can see the way her blouse rises and falls with the quickening of her breath.

This is my chance.

I can slide my hand behind her neck and hold her still. I can crush my lips over hers and pull her body tight against mine. I can lose myself in the softness of her body, and feel my cock harden against her curves.

It would be so simple to pull her close. To claim her mouth, my tongue demanding and hard as we give in to one wild, ravenous kiss that leaves us both as breathless as sex.

I could do it all so easily.

I could ... but I don't.

Instead I slide my hands in my pockets. I turn away and face the table. And then I draw one deep breath.

"Pierce?"

"Let's go get a drink."

"A drink," she repeats, her voice flat. "I don't know if that's such a good—"

"It's almost five. I've had a long day. And we can talk about Delilah's schedule, your concerns, the job parameters. All that good stuff."

"So it's a business meeting." There's no intonation in her words at all. It's as if she's deliberately trying to strip them of any emotion. And as a result, I have no idea if she's relieved or disappointed.

"There's a bar a couple of blocks down. The Fix on Sixth. A friend owns it, so we should be able to score a table in the back, even during South By."

She's silent for a moment, obviously considering. Finally, she nods. "All right, then. Lead the way."

Kerrie's working on the computer in the reception area, and her brows rise as we enter the room from the hall.

"We'll be back in a few hours," I tell her. "Can you put together a standard client contract and leave it on my desk? Ms. Stuart can review it when we get back."

"Of course, sir." Her tone is entirely professional, but I

know her well and can tell she's dying to ask me a thousand questions.

I open the door for Jez and guide her out into the elevator bank before Kerrie's overcome with curiosity, breaks protocol, and starts firing away.

We're waiting for the elevator when Jez says, "Your receptionist seems..."

"What?"

"Competent," she says, although it's obvious that wasn't her original thought.

I regard her curiously. "Really?" Kerrie *is* competent, but that isn't the vibe she's been projecting since Jez walked in. On the contrary, I'd say rampant curiosity was the emotion of the day.

"Actually, yes. But I was really going to say that she seemed curious." The elevator doors slide open, and she steps on, then glances back at me. "Is that because of me or you?"

"Both, I'm guessing. You, because of your sister. Me, because my sister's habit is sticking her nose into my business."

"Your sis—*oh*. So is this a family business?"

"Not in the way you mean," I say. "Kerrie started working for us when she got disillusioned with her last job. And as sisters go, she's not too much of a pain in the butt."

"You're older than she is."

"Ten years," I tell her. "She's twenty-four."

Jez nods. "I'm nine years older than Del. So there you go." She smiles up at me, and I'm struck by how much I like seeing her smile. "We both have younger sisters that we work with."

The elevator glides to a stop on the first floor, and I hold my hand over the door, ushering her out. "With that much in common, you may end up actually liking me."

She brushes my arm as she passes. "I like you," she says, and her soft words just about slay me. I want her. That's pretty much the bottom line. Because there's something about Jezebel Stuart. Something snarky. Something funny. Something sexy.

Sometimes even a little bitchy.

I don't know her well, but I've already seen that she's complicated and loyal, smart and committed.

She's a woman with layers, and so help me, I want to peel away each and every one of them.

And that's a dangerous way for a man like me to feel.

CHAPTER SEVEN

"PIERCE?"

It's not her voice, but her hand gripping my elbow that pulls me from my thoughts.

We're outside now, standing at the southeast corner of Sixth and Congress, just outside my office building.

"Sorry. I was thinking." *About her.* "About security. Transportation. Everything."

"Glad to know you're on the ball. But which way?"

"Turn right," I say, pointing that direction. "We're just going a few blocks down."

Sixth Street is to Austin what Bourbon Street is to New Orleans. Only cleaner and classier and without the strip clubs. And usually without the drunk revelers vomiting in the street. During the SXSW festival, though, the distinctions between the two streets are minimal, and even this early, there are already packs of college students moving along the already crowded sidewalks.

The festival isn't limited to one location—in fact much of it takes place off Sixth Street at other venues and at performance tents set up along the river. But Austin hasn't dubbed itself the Live Music Capital of the World for nothing, and even when there's no festival in town, there's a lot of live music. Especially downtown.

The Fix is a few blocks from my office, an easy enough walk even in this crowd, and I expect it's going to be crowded since it's set up with a stage in the main room. Sure enough, I can see a band playing through the window, and there's a line of people, all wearing festival wristbands, waiting to get in.

"Maybe we should try somewhere else," she says, frowning at the line.

"Trust me." I take her hand to lead her toward the door, then feel a bit like a teenager when she doesn't pull away.

"Sorry," the door guy says. "We got a line. And you don't have a wristband."

"Tell Tyree it's Pierce Blackwell. We're not here for the music. I want to take the lady to the back."

The guy's young and skinny and pale—he's either a vampire or he's spent too many hours inside the university dorms—and he's making the most of his power over the door. He takes his time looking us up and down, then pulls a walkie-talkie out of the pocket of his jacket and signals for Tyree. For a moment, I consider that my friend might not be on site, in which case, I'll have to find someplace else to take Jez where we can get a seat despite the festival madness.

But then I see him approaching through the glass, a huge bear of a man whose beard and gold earring give him a pirate quality. Today, he's wearing a short sleeved black T-shirt with the Fix on Sixth logo, and the muscles under his dark cocoa skin flex as he reaches out to shake my hand.

"Haven't seen you in a week," he says, ushering me and Jez inside. "Where've you been?"

"Avoiding the crowds," I admit. "But I thought Jez should see some of South By. And she can't visit Austin without getting her fix."

His teeth flash as he smiles. "Got that right. Nice to meet you, Jez," he says, his voice loud enough to hear over the R&B band. "I'm Tyree. Call me Ty. I own this dump."

"Hardly," she says, looking around. "It's great."

"It's got potential," he admits. To me he adds, "Renovations and repairs are kicking my ass. But I'll get it done."

"Ty and I served a tour together," I tell her. "Right before he traded in his uniform for a barman's apron."

"And a shit-ton of debt," he says. "This week we're in the black, though. So things are looking up. You here for the music?"

I shake my head. "Just the atmosphere. Jez and I need to talk. Thought I'd take her to the back."

"You know the way, my friend. Tell pretty boy back there I said to treat you well."

He's grinning, and I know he's talking about the new bartender, a grad student from the University whose name I can't remember.

"He's nice," Jez says. Her mouth is close to my ear, and I know that's only so she doesn't have to yell, but her proximity has the side effect of kicking my pulse up a notch. "I like him."

"Just don't cross him," I say, and she laughs.

"I'll remember."

We grab the only empty table and order two glasses of bourbon on the rocks. "So what do we need to talk about?" she asks, after the drinks come and she's taken her first sip. "Or did you just want to get me liquored up?"

"Would you think less of me if I said the latter?"

She hesitates only a second, then shakes her head. "No," she says, in the kind of low, sultry voice that runs over a man's skin like a ripple of fire. "But we both know it's a bad idea."

"You might be surprised how many bad ideas turn out to be very, very good."

Her smile fades, and she glances down at her drink, her finger tracing the rim.

"Jez?"

"Sorry." She looks up with a slow shake of her head. "It's just that we're here because of a bad idea that was just plain bad."

It takes me a second to parse the comment, but when I do, I say, "Levyl."

"Are you familiar with the whole story? Him and Delilah?"

"Yesterday I wasn't. Today, I have the basic Internet search version of the scandal."

"Scandal," she says, making the word sound as harsh as a curse. "A teenager should be able to make a few mistakes in her love life, but when hers blew up, it had to play out all over the tabloids and social media."

"Levyl's about her age, right?"

She nods. "He's a year older than Del. They started dating when she was seventeen. They did a movie together —he's the lead singer for Next Levyl."

"It's a boy band that won that TV show, right?"

"Exactly. And when the band hit, they were everywhere for a while, especially Levyl and the drummer. They got movies, TV shows, you name it."

"It wasn't on my radar," I admit. "But I vaguely remember hearing about him and the band."

"If you weren't dead, you heard about them. They were that popular. Still are, really, though it's settled into a more controlled insanity. But those first couple of years..." She trails off, shaking her head. "At any rate, Del and Levyl met when he was really exploding, and the world took a shine to them. Like the romance of the century. It was crazy—especially when she turned eighteen and the public started pressuring them to get engaged."

"Pressuring?"

"Fans on social media mostly," she explains. "But even talk show hosts would bring it up. It was crazy. And I think it was a little too much for Del. She adored Levyl—she still does—but when she went on location, and Garreth Todd was her co-star..."

I nod. "I read about that. Sounded to me like he seduced her."

"He did. Hell, he's admitted that much. And it didn't last—Garreth dumped her. But she's still the one who's vilified, because she broke Levyl's heart." Her voice is rising, and she takes a deep breath, obviously so that she can rein in her emotions. "Like I said, only eighteen and the whole world knows her private affairs."

"That's got to be horrible. I don't even like my sister nosing around in my life."

As I'd hoped, that makes her smile. "Yeah, well, that's the backstory. As for your part in all of this, you—"

"I think I got a sense of that last night."

"The crazed fans? Yeah, that's part of it. But the rest is all about my sister." I must look confused, because she goes on. "Levyl's coming here on Tuesday. I guess he's performing during the festival."

"And you think Delilah's going to want to see him?"

"Yeah. She's hurting. Those two together were combustible. Besides, it if was me, I would. If I'd hurt the man I loved? If I wanted to at least try to explain what happened and apologize? Yeah, I'd be all over that."

"They haven't talked since—"

"Just by phone. She cried for two days."

"Poor kid. What a mess." I rake my fingers through my hair, thinking. "We can get her to his concert. Get her safely backstage."

She shakes her head. "No, no you can't. Anything like that will leak. Right now, it's starting to die down—last night was nothing compared to what it's been. But if she goes there—if she sees him and it gets leaked—it's going to blow up again. She'll be vilified in the press again. Harassed on the set."

She signals for another drink, her expression harried. "Look, there can't be any scandal here, not even a hint of it. We can control her access to fans to keep it at a minimum, but if it blows up again—if what happened last night happens on a bigger scale—then my sister is pretty much out of a career."

I lean back, surprised by such a bold statement.

"I'm serious," she says, obviously seeing my confusion.

"The studio's already fired her from one job—she was supposed to have a lead in a popular action franchise. And that would have been a huge payoff in terms of money and her clout in the industry. But when the scandal broke, they wouldn't touch her.

"But she has a contract," she continues, her words spilling out. "And so they put her in this. It's small and has next to no budget, but even so, they're just waiting for a reason to kick her off. And if the scandal kicks up again, they'll have their justification. I'm not supposed to know, but a friend who works in the executive offices told me. The lawyers have pretty much said that if the mess blows up, the producers can fire her and not be in breach of the contract."

"But she's in the middle of making the movie."

She shakes her head. "No. We've only just started. They could fire her and bring in someone else, easy."

I don't know what to say to that, and she must realize it, because she continues. "So that's what I need you for. That's the basic job parameters. You're protecting my sister from the fans, yeah. But mostly you're protecting her from herself. And if you fuck it up—if you lose her and she sneaks off to see Levyl or gets herself caught up in some sort of fan riot—I will fire your ass so fast it will make your head spin."

I study her, and it's easy to see that she's entirely serious. "And here I thought we were becoming friends."

"Competence impresses me, Mr. Blackwell. From what I've seen so far, you and your company fit the bill. Hopefully I won't be kicking my ass Wednesday morning."

"What's Wednesday?"

"The Austin part of the shoot is just a week. We fly from here back to Los Angeles. Everything else is on backlots and in the studio."

"I see." It's Thursday, and I'm more disappointed than I should be to know that she's leaving in just under a week.

"So that's pretty much it," she says, as the waitress delivers a fresh round of drinks. "Your typical teen celebrity security detail. Plus angst and scandal."

"I've got your back."

"Good," she says, lifting her drink. "Because if you fuck it up, I promise it won't be pretty."

I raise my drink as well, then hold it out to toast. As soon as she clinks her glass against mine, I take a sip, then put it back down, studying her.

"What?" she demands.

"You're not as tough as you pretend to be, Jezebel Stuart."

Her brow creases, and she glances down. I'd meant the words as a tease, but it's clear I've struck a nerve.

When she looks back up at me, there's a new kind of ferocity in her eyes. "I am," she says. "I didn't used to be—hell, I didn't want to be. But this job, this life…"

She trails off with a shrug. "Just don't fuck with me, okay?"

I want to reach across the table and take her hand. I want to pull her into my arms and hold her and tell her that I might not understand all the demons she's had to fight over the years, but that I will slay any that come near her now. I want to tell her that I'll keep her safe, whatever it takes.

But I know that this swell of emotion rushing up inside

me is about the woman and not about the job, and so I push it back. Hold it in. And all I say is, "I wouldn't dream of it."

She swallows the rest of her drink and lets out a heavy sigh. "So I guess this job's not as sexy as what you usually do. Protecting state legislators or whatever."

"It's sexy enough." I take her glass from her hand and raise it to my lips.

"Oh," she says as she watches, her eyes on my mouth, as I take the last piece of ice. Then I reach for her hand. It's warm except for the chill on her fingers where she'd touched the glass, and I fight the urge to kiss those fingers to warm them.

She clears her throat, then tugs her hand from mine and puts it in her lap. "So, um, what else do you do?"

"A lot of basic protection, like you said. And since Austin's the capital, you're right about providing security to politicians. And we work with a lot of performers. Usually not with Del's Hollywood pedigree, but we've done security for some Grammy award winners who've performed at the Long Center and Bass Concert Hall."

"Any teen clients?"

"A few. One about a year ago stands out. I was still with my old firm then, but I took the job on my own, off book."

"What happened?"

I take a deep breath and think of Lisa. "Beautiful girl. Bubbly. Lots of fun. And very smart. Had a full ride at the University," I say, referring to the University of Texas, the prestigious, well-endowed institution that has helped shape Austin's culture.

"She was nineteen, and a stalker put his sights on her." It's a case I don't usually think about, and I take a long swallow, letting the bourbon burn down my throat, as the memories well up.

"What happened?"

"He attacked her—she was lucky. Got away with her life, but he slashed her face. Deep cuts with a jagged blade. And then he made clear that he intended to finish the job."

"She hired you?"

"She did. Well, her father did." Hire is a relative term. I met Lisa through Kerrie, who'd met her in Gregory Gym, where they both took a spin class. Since neither Lisa nor her dad had the money for the fee, I took the case as a barter, in exchange for her dad doing some custom cabinet work for my condo.

"What happened?"

"The stalker tried again." I start to raise the drink, then put it back down. "He's dead."

"You killed him."

I pause, then tilt my head in acknowledgement. To be honest, his death still haunts me. Not that I killed him—I'd do it again in a heartbeat—but what I saw in his eyes. I'd seen a lot of things during my time in the military, but I don't think I truly believed in evil until I looked at that man's face.

Jez is watching me, and I know she can feel the weight that's settled over our conversation. She says nothing, but she reaches out and takes my hand. My instinct is to pull away, but instead I hold on, surprised by how much the contact soothes.

But it only lasts a moment. Then, I gently pull away. "Sorry."

"No, it's—"

"I don't expect to be killing anyone on this job," I say, intentionally trying to add back some levity. "Unless of course the producer's an asshole. Then we can talk bonus."

A tentative smile touches her lips. "Fair enough." She tilts her head, looking at me. "So I guess you understand teenage clients. And it sounds like you're good with high maintenance clients from the entertainment world, too."

"Absolutely," I say, appreciating the tease in her voice. "But I have a feeling this assignment is going to be my favorite."

"Because of my sister?"

I meet her eyes, and the heaviness that had been in the air is finally brushed completely away, replaced by something equally dangerous. "No."

For a moment, we just look at each other, a faint pink rising in her cheeks. Then she finishes off her drink and reaches for the small wallet-style purse she'd left on the table. She slides the strap over her arm, then flashes an awkward smile. "We should probably go. I bet your sister has the contract ready."

"Sure." I stand, a little disappointed. I don't know why—it's not as if this were a date. As if we were going to leave the bar and head down Sixth Street, popping into various venues to drink and dance, her body pressed close to mine in the throng.

That wouldn't happen. But so long as we sit here, I can nurse the fantasy. And I hate that Jez has thrown reality back in my face.

She's three steps away from our table, and she looks back. "Coming?"

That's when I realize she's flustered, too. She hasn't

given a thought to paying, and right now, she looks like a rabbit who's looking back at a hunter.

But this rabbit looks like she'd be happy to be devoured.

At least it's not just me.

I toss a hundred on the table—I happen to know the waitress, Melanie, is struggling to come up with the balance of her tuition—and follow Jez to the doorway into the main area.

The bar is coming to life, along with the street. And as in my fantasy, the crowd pushes us closer together. I take her hand, ostensibly to lead her to the door, but really because I just want to touch her, and by the time we reach the exit and step out into the cool night air, I'm breathing hard and sweat is beading on the back of my neck. Not from the exertion of getting out of there, but from the effort of fighting the urge to stay.

She's still holding my hand, and when I glance down and see our intertwined fingers, that's it. It's all over. I say a silent prayer and lift my head so that I can see her face, and there's so much heat reflected back that it almost melts me.

"Pierce," she says, but I just tug her toward me.

"Come on," I say, urging her down the street, faster than I should since she's wearing heels, but I can't wait. And when we've gone two blocks down the street, I pull her into the service alley by my office and press her against the wall, caging her in my arms.

"I'm sorry," I say. "But I have to." I thrust my fingers into that rich, dark hair, hold her head steady, and claim her mouth with mine.

It's probably the most wonderful, terrifying moment of

my life. Jez, soft and warm in my arms, juxtaposed against the fear that she's going to shove me back and slap my face.

But she doesn't. Instead, her lips part more, and she leans into the kiss, her mouth as hot and wild as my own. She tastes of alcohol and desire, and my head swims, intoxicated by her surrender as much as by her touch.

One hand cups the back of my neck, pulling me closer. The other presses against my back, giving her leverage to arch up against me. Her hands are the most potent of aphrodisiacs, telling me without words that she wants this moment as much as I do, and my entire body tightens in response, need coiling through me. A wild craving. A desperate longing.

I'm hard as steel, and it's taking all my self-control not to slide my fingers through the slit of her skirt and tear the damn thing right off of her. I want to thrust my hands between her legs, then slip my fingers beneath the hot, wet silk of her panties. I crave the slippery heat of her desire on my fingertips. That sweet, slick evidence that proves how much she wants me.

I imagine bending my head and tasting her breasts. In my fantasies, I strip her bare and fuck her hard, our overheated bodies writhing together on cool, smooth sheets. My cock and fingers working a primal magic, sending her up and over and into the stars, until she explodes in my arms and begs me to do it again.

But I can't do that. Not really. And so this kiss—this single, wild kiss in a filthy alley—is our stand-in for clean sheets and wild sex, and I thrust my tongue in deeper, making the most of it. She tastes like bourbon and sex, and as our tongues war and our teeth clash, I fear that this is so wild and so frantic that we're going to draw blood.

But I don't care. All I want is this moment. All I want is *her*.

She's practically melting against me, and I'm losing my mind. My thoughts reduced to basic, primitive needs, so powerful I can barely stand it.

My condo's only a few blocks away. I could step into the street. Grab a taxi, and take her home.

It would be a bold move. But then again, so was kissing her in an alley.

But, of course, we can't.

"Jez," I say, regretfully breaking the kiss. She opens her eyes, and by some miracle I grow even harder when I see the wild, blatant desire heating her eyes.

"We can't," she whispers, and though the words are like a knife, I know that they were inevitable.

"I know."

Her brow furrows. "Then why—?"

"Because I don't get involved with clients," I say, silently damning my own stringent rule. "But I had to taste you—just once—before we sign the contract."

CHAPTER EIGHT

ANYONE WHO'S EVER SAID that watching a movie being filmed is exciting is a goddamned liar. It's exciting for about the first fifteen minutes, when you've just arrived, and the crew is busy setting up lights or dressing the set or doing whatever it is that movie crews do.

Then you see how much sitting around it involves. Sitting and waiting and being quiet. And take after take after take.

I'm sure it's scintillating if you're in the cast or on the crew. But as an observer? Honestly, it's mind-numbing.

And yet here I am. Not because I think there's an immediate threat to Delilah—it's a closed set with its own security team—but because she's Blackwell-Lyon's responsibility, and this is my shift, and I need to understand her routine if I'm going to do my job.

So I'm sitting and watching and learning. I've seen three takes of Delilah's current scene, and while I don't know much about acting, I have to say I'm impressed with her skill. It's an angst-filled scene, and she's managed to kick me in the emotional balls all three times she's run through it.

But that's about as exciting as it gets, and since the entire scene is under four minutes and I've been sitting here for almost three hours, I'd say the return on investment is low.

"You do this every day?" I ask Jez, when she approaches my chair between takes. It's a director-style folding chair with a canvas seat and back. It doesn't, however, have my name on it.

"Exciting, isn't it?" she says dryly, and once again I'm struck by how much I like this woman. We're simpatico, she and I.

"As much fun as watching grass grow."

"Watching action scenes is fun, though," she tells me. "When the stunt double comes in, especially."

"Now you're talking," I say, willing to hold out for this tiny thrill. "When are they shooting that?"

"They're not." A hint of a smile flashes. "That was in the movie she got fired from. This one's all deep emotion and torment." She pats me on the shoulder. "Enjoy."

"Where are you off to now?"

"Back to the hotel. I can't get a decent signal here, and I have a video call scheduled with Delilah's agent, then her publicist, and then her accountant. I'll be lucky if I survive the day without my head exploding. You're good?"

I want to tell her I'd be better if she stayed. I've barely seen her since we arrived, and while I'm here to work, the truth is I missed her last night.

After we got back to my office and finished the paperwork, I'd planned to go back to the hotel with her. But Jez shut me down. "Del's already tucked away in her room and the floor is secure, right?"

"Right," I admitted. And that was all well and good, but I knew the real reason was that she wanted time away to clear her head. And as much as I regretted the distance, I had to admit that was probably smart.

"Fine," I say now. "Del and I will see you at the hotel after the shoot."

She heads out, and since the cast and crew are pulling long days, I settle in for another nine hours of soul-crushing non-excitement.

Fortunately, I only have to wait an hour before Delilah comes by and flops on the ground beside my chair. "I am *so* wiped out," she says. "But I have forty-five minutes until we start up again." She passes me a wrapped sandwich. "Want? The powers that be are making me eat salad."

From the tone of her voice, you'd think they were making her eat gruel.

She's wearing skinny jeans and a *Keep Austin Weird* T-shirt. Her damp hair is pulled back into a ponytail, and she's wearing no make-up. I assume she showered in her trailer before heading my way. Presumably, there's another hair and make-up session scheduled for after lunch.

All in all, she looks like she could be a freshman at UT, and she's at least as laid back as any local Austin girl. She crosses her legs then peels open the lid from her salad. "I'm ravenous. Tonight, when we get back to the hotel, I'm going to actually eat." She looks at me. "How about you? Gonna stay for room service? I'm thinking we need to order all the fries. Like, *all* the fries."

"No salad and quinoa for you tonight?"

She wrinkles her nose. "Don't rat me out, okay? I'll have a hard enough time when I get back to LA and my trainer kicks my ass. But while I'm here, I'm eating when I can. Besides, I'm fully clothed in this movie. No love scenes. No showers. No slow-mo shots of me in a bikini running on a beach. Honestly, it's nice to just act, you know?"

"Not really," I admit. "But I'll take your word for it."

Del smiles, and that's when I can really see her star power. It's bright and photogenic and lights up the set.

"You like her, don't you?"

"Who?" I ask, though I know perfectly well who she's talking about. And like Pavlov's dog, my pulse has sped up just at the mention of Jez.

"My sister. She's not really a bitch, you know."

"Sure she is," I quip, making Del laugh.

"Okay, fine. Maybe she is. But you like her anyway."

"Yeah," I admit. "I do."

"Good." She sounds smug. "And just so you know, Jez has reasons."

"I don't think she's a bitch," I say, though I don't mention that I've definitely witnessed some bitchy moments. "But what are the reasons?"

"That stupid book, of course."

I frown. "What stupid book?"

"That tell-all book that my old bodyguard wrote."

"Larry?" That can't be true.

"Oh, no. The guy who came after. Simpson. The prick. He called the book *The Stuarts of Beverly Hills*. It was total trash—one of those things they published superfast to get in on all the drama with me and Levyl and Garreth—

but he said some pretty shitty things about Jezebel in it, too."

She lifts her shoulder. "They got pretty close, if you know what I mean. So now she's careful. That's why we've only had a series of rent-a-guards since she fired him. But it's hard not really knowing the guys who are watching over you, you know?" Her words are flying fast, and I wonder if it's because as an actress she's usually scripted, so she's taking advantage of being off book.

"At any rate," she continues, before I can get a word in, "sometimes she comes off as bitchy, but it's only because she's protecting us."

I'm gripping the wooden arms of the chair so tight I'm probably leaving dents. And I swear if this asshole Simpson was on the set right now, he'd be a dead man.

"Anyway," she says, standing up and brushing the dust off her jeans. "I just thought you should know. In case she seems, you know, distant."

"I'm just working for her, Del. There's nothing going on."

"Of course not," she says, but right then I doubt her acting skills, because she really doesn't sound convincing.

As soon as she heads off to the trailer to get in make-up for her next scene, I pull out my phone, open a web browser, find a digital copy of the book, and settle in to read.

Immediately, my blood starts to boil. He talks about how their parents died, and how Jez stepped in as head of the family and manager of Del's career, which was already on track, as the girl had been discovered at age six. He gives details about Del's dating and how she met Levyl and her interactions with fans. He runs though arguments between Jez and Del. Reveals their conversations, their habits, the details of their lives.

It's not skanky, but it's invasive as shit. He's told the world things that only someone close and with access would know.

In other words, he broke their trust.

Bastard.

I finish the book about an hour before Del wraps for the day, which is good, because that gives me a chance to quit seething before we get into the Range Rover and head for the Starfire.

"I ordered some food," Jez says when we arrive at the suite. She points to the spread laid out on the suite's dining room table, and Del squeals and claps her hands.

"These are for me," Del says, taking the entire basket of fries. "I'm going to go gorge myself in my room and watch bad reality television." She flashes me a mischievous smile, and I can't help but think that she's leaving us alone on purpose. And not so that we can talk business.

"Hey," I say, after Del's gone. "How was your day?"

Jez presses her fingers to her temples. "Crazy."

"Bad crazy?"

"No," she says, "just busy crazy." She glances at the table. "We're going to talk shop, so does that mean you're still on duty?"

"If you're asking if I can have some of that wine, I think I can go for it."

"Good. Because I don't want to drink alone, and I need one." She passes me the bottle and a corkscrew. "I didn't think to have the waiter open it. You'll do the honors?"

I take the bottle, and open the wine, then pour us each a glass. "Cayden texted me as we were pulling in. He's gone over security with the staff, and the other two guests on this floor checked out this morning. Blackwell-Lyon now holds those rooms through Thursday." Which means no one outside of our team and the hotel staff can access this floor. And as far as security goes, that's a very good thing.

"Really? That's going above and beyond."

"Nothing's beyond if it keeps you safe. And Cayden's one hell of a negotiator. You won't find a surprise charge for those rooms on your bill—from us or from the hotel."

"If paying for those rooms keeps Del out of the middle of the kind of melee you saw the other night, I'd happily pay for them."

"I know." I take a seat on the sofa, then indicate the cushion next to me. "You've proven over and over again how much you're willing to sacrifice for your sister."

"I have," she says, sitting beside me without hesitation. She's wearing a white V-neck T-shirt and a gray skirt made out of some sort of stretchy material. Her feet are bare, and I get the feeling this is Jezebel's typical work-at-home uniform. Still professional, but not as buttoned up as the pantsuit she'd been wearing on set this morning.

"Not that I think of any of it as a sacrifice," she continues. "It's just—"

She cuts herself off sharply, then turns to look at me, frowning. "I've *proven over and over again*. That's what you said."

"Yeah."

For a moment, she's silent, her brow furrowed as if she were trying to solve a knotty math problem. Then it clears, and she says, "*Fuck,*" so softly I almost don't hear her. She puts her glass on the table, then stands, then turns to look at me.

"You read the book." The words are an accusation, and she doesn't specify *what* book. Clearly, she knows she doesn't need to. "Del shouldn't have told you about that," she says, not waiting for me to answer.

"I read it today," I admit. "And I think Del was trying to help."

"Help?" Her brows rise. "Help how?"

"Help me," I clarify. "She realized that I want to get to know you better."

"Great. Just great. Because that book's certainly the way to do that. *Fuck,*" she repeats, and this time I hear her just fine.

"He was an ass," I say. She's turned away from me, and now I gently take her elbow and urge her back to face me. "Simpson was an ass who broke your trust."

"Isn't that the truth?" She thrusts her fingers in her hair, lifting it up before letting it fall back in waves around her face. I know the gesture came out of frustration, but the look is sexy as hell, and it's all I can do not to gather her close.

"Do you want to talk about it?"

She shrugs, then goes over to the table and plucks a tortilla chip out of a ceramic bowl. She dips it in salsa, then takes a bite. I assume that's her way of saying no, so I'm surprised when she carries the chips and salsa to the couch and puts them on the coffee table. She sits again, this time tucking one foot under her so that she's facing me.

"I didn't have my guard up," she says. "I'd gotten so used to trusting someone, that I just let down all my walls."

"Larry," I say, and she nods.

"He was like a dad to me. It was easy, you know? And then he retired and moved to Orange County, and I hired Simpson. And I guess I was primed to trust." She licks her lips, then takes a sip of wine. "I let him get too close."

I nod. I'd guessed as much.

"And then when the book came out—" Her voice breaks, and I take her hand. I'm not sure if I should, but right now, I need to touch her, not just for her, but for me. "I wanted to go cry to Larry, but the accident—he was already dead. And—" Her voice breaks, and she visibly gathers herself. "And I thought, *well, at least he can't see my humiliation.*"

"Jez..."

"I complained to him. Simpson, I mean." She laughs harshly. "Isn't that a nice way of putting it? I lost my shit. I ranted and screamed and I think I threw a book at him." She closes her eyes and takes a deep breath. I squeeze her hand, and when she squeezes back, she looks at me gratefully.

"He flat out told me that since everything in the book was true, I couldn't do a thing about it. And then—" Her breath hitches. "And then he said that I was lucky he didn't talk about how lousy I was in bed."

She makes a noise like a gasp and leaps to her feet, her hand going over her mouth. I stand behind her, my hands on her shoulders. "If I ever meet him, I swear I'll put him in the ground. He doesn't deserve to breathe the same air as you."

Her shoulders start to shake, and I gently turn her so that she can press her face against my chest and cry while I hold her.

"I'm sorry," she says after a while, as she pulls away. "And oh, man, I got your shirt all wet."

"It'll dry."

She flashes a watery smile. "You're—unexpected."

"Am I?" I turn the word over in my head. "In a good way or a bad way?"

"Good." She brushes a finger under her eyes, drying her tears. Then she nods, as if reassuring herself. "Yeah, good. Although why the hell I'm telling you any of this, I don't know."

"Because I brought it up," I suggest. "Because you need someone to talk to. Because Simpson's bullshit was part of the price you pay for celebrity, and so was that mess we ran into at the Crown the other night."

"All true," she says. "And all so goddamned unfair."

I take her hand and urge her back to the sofa. "Stretch out," I say, and when she does, I put her feet in my lap. Her toes are painted a pale pink, and she looks like she hasn't gone a day without a pedicure. And when I rub my thumb along her arch, she tilts her head back and moans.

I want to hear that moan again—and not because of a foot massage.

"Why unfair?" I ask. "I mean, other than the obvious."

"Nothing. I shouldn't even—Hey," she snaps when I take my hands off her feet.

"Truth," I say. "Or no massage for you."

She scowls at me, but nods. Then she tilts her head back and closes her eyes. "You read the book, so you know what happened. Our parents died in an accident, and instead of starting college, I stepped in as Del's manager. I didn't trust anyone else, and my mom had been doing it for years, so I sort of knew the ropes. And I knew Mom would want me to. Plus, I love my sister. I do."

"But?"

"But I never had the chance to figure out what I want to do. And all I know is that I don't like this life. I don't like living in LA. I don't like being in the spotlight."

She opens her eyes and shrugs. "So that's it. That's my guilty secret."

"Why don't you stop?"

"I will, but not until Del's ready. In a lot of ways she's mature, but she's also been incredibly sheltered. Leaving her now would be a recipe for disaster."

"She might surprise you."

"She might. But that's not a risk I want to take. She's too important to me."

"So you have a plan," I say, taking my hand from her foot and moving to massage her calves.

"That feels amazing—you're *so* hired. And yes, I have a plan. And until then, I'll just suck it up and live with the drama."

"You can manage." I'm barely paying attention to my words. Instead, I'm sinking fast into the feel of her. The smoothness of her skin. The heat of her body.

"And it's crazy," she continues, "because as much as I hate it is how much Del loves it. She thrives on this life. Even the scandal doesn't bother her. She just wants to act."

"What about you? What do you want?"

She sits up, then pulls her legs back and tucks them

under her, as if the question has made her uncomfortable. "I honestly don't know."

Her voice is soft, barely a whisper. But I hear the truth in her words, and I want to pull her into my arms and hold her close.

"No? Not even a little thing?" I tease. "Dark chocolate with sea salt? More tortilla chips? World peace?"

"Honestly, right now I just want—"

"What?"

She sighs. "I just want to take a shower and crawl into bed. It's been a long day."

Her words shred me. I didn't realize how much I wanted to stay until she yanked the possibility out from under me. "Sure," I say. "Of course."

I rise. "I'll let you rest. Tomorrow's a night shoot, right? I'll call you in the morning and we can talk time and logistics. In the meantime," I add as I head for the door, "you know the protocol. Don't leave this floor without coming to get me. I'm going to crash in the room on the end."

"Pierce?"

I hesitate, my hand on the knob. "Yeah?"

"I lied."

I turn, something in the tone of her voice firing my senses and making my cock grow hard. "Did you?"

She stands up, then takes a step toward me. "I don't want to sleep."

I take a corresponding step toward her. "No? Then what do you want?"

I hear the tremor in her breath. Then I watch as she comes one step closer. Then another and another, until she's just inches away from me. She meets my eyes, and her gaze never wavers. "I want you to kiss me," she says.

Her words ignite inside me, and I have to shove my hands into my pockets to keep from yanking her into my arms. And it just about kills me to say what I have to. "I told you. I don't sleep with clients. And you don't sleep with anyone on your payroll, remember?"

"I'm not asking you to." She comes closer, and I can smell her vanilla scent. And that's not good, because right then, I want to devour her. "I just want a kiss."

"Jez…"

"Here," she says, pressing her index finger to the corner of her mouth. "Just one little kiss."

Her eyes are locked on mine, and right then I'd swear she had super powers, because I have no will to fight. I can only lean in, my lips brushing softly over the corner of her mouth.

"Good?" I ask.

"Yes," she says, but she's shaking her head no. And her eyes tell me that she wants more.

I lean back, my pulse pounding as I look at her. Her parted lips. Her heavy lids. Her tousled hair.

Her chest rises and falls with each breath, and I'm certain that she's as turned on as I am. She swallows, and I watch the way her throat moves, fighting the urge to lean in and kiss that little indentation at the base of her neck.

I let my gaze dip lower, taking in the curve of her breasts and her nipples, hard beneath the thin material of her bra and T-shirt. It's hemmed at the waist and not tucked in, and I know that if I were to reach out, I could press my hand against her abdomen and feel her muscles tremble as she sucks in a breath.

And if I went lower...

Well, I can't help but wonder what she's wearing under that skirt. A thong, I imagine, or nothing at all, because the material clings smoothly to her hips and legs. And if I slip my hand between her thighs, would I find her already wet?

I think I would, and the thought makes me hard.

I should walk away—I know that. But when you get right down to it, I've never been one to follow the rules. And sometimes, doing the right thing is highly overrated.

"Jez," I whisper, and then I don't even give her time to respond. Because, dammit, I can't risk her saying no. So I swoop down, claiming her mouth, holding her close. She tastes like wine and sin, and I want to get drunk on both. Intoxicated by her touch. Her taste.

"Kisses," I murmur, holding her chin as I look deep in her eyes. "That's what you want? Like this?" I ask, brushing my lips over hers. "Or like this?" I demand, trailing a line of kisses down her neck to the soft indentation at her collarbone.

She trembles under my touch, and the only sound she makes is a soft, breathy, "Yes."

"Jez," I murmur, but her name is muffled by my mouth on her breast, over her bra and shirt. She arches back, her shoulders resting on the wall behind her, the angle of her body now giving me better access. But I want to taste her, not the shirt, and I slide my hands up, taking the shirt with me, until I've exposed her white, cotton bra.

It's unlined, and her nipples are like pebbles against the thin material. I close my mouth over one breast and suck, then use my teeth to tease her nipple. She cries out, then whimpers when I pull back, releasing her.

But I'm not letting her off that easily. On the contrary, I'm still on my quest for skin, and I use my teeth to pluck up the edge of the bra and yank it down, freeing her breast.

She's gasping, her fingers sliding into my hair as she presses me closer, forcing my mouth where she wants it, and I use my tongue to tease her nipple until I feel her start to tremble and I know that there is no way—no way—that I am going to let her come without tasting her sweet pussy.

She whimpers when I pull away, then blow a stream of air on her now-wet breast. "Please," she begs as I brush a line of kisses right at her bra line. "Pierce, please."

"Shhh." I lift my mouth from her skin long enough for a single command. "Not a word," I order as I slide my hands down to the waistband of her skirt. It's a pull-on style, but I don't push it down over her hips. Instead, I inch the material up—higher and higher until the skirt barely covers her, and I press my hand against her inner thigh and slowly stroke my way up.

She's trembling, and her soft noises are making me crazy, and I'm so fucking hard it's painful. But right now, all I care about is touching her. I want to feel her, hot and slick on my fingers, and I'm so, so close.

Mostly, I want to taste her. To flick my tongue over her clit. To suck and kiss and tease until she explodes against my mouth.

Just a kiss, just like we said.

But it's the most intimate kiss of all.

Slowly, my fingers rise. She's wearing a barely-there thong, and I impatiently yank it down, uncovering her slick heat. And at the same time, I keep my kisses coming, lower and lower, until there's no more skirt, just flesh, just *her*, and she's waxed and smooth and wonderful.

"Please," she begs as I close my mouth over her. As my tongue finds her clit. As my fingers thrust inside her in time with my intimate kisses, my tongue laving her. My lips tormenting her.

Her hips start to move, and she's riding my mouth, her hands in my hair guiding me. And I'm getting harder and harder as I hear her raw, passionate noises. And all I want to do is make her come. Make her explode.

And know that I'm the man who took her over the edge.

"Yes!" she cries, and her body trembles, her pussy clenching tight around my fingers.

I'm already on my knees, but now her legs give out, and she tumbles to the ground, pulling me down with her.

My hands are all over her. Touching her. Stroking her. Listening to her soft sounds, her needy murmurs. "I can't get enough of you." And it's true. I've tasted her—now I want to claim her. Hard and hot and fast, then softly. Tenderly. I want to feel her break into a million pieces, and I want to be deep inside her, her body tight around my cock, when I come.

"Good," she says. "Because I want more, too." Her face is buried against my chest, but now she rises, her face and torso lifting as she meets my eyes. "I want so much more."

She unbuttons my shirt, then brushes a kiss on my breastbone. She starts to kiss her way down, lower and lower until my already stiff cock is so hard against my jeans it's almost painful. Her hand cups me through the denim, and I arch back, trying to steady my breathing. And when her fingers unbutton my fly, it's a goddamned miracle that I don't come right then.

She shifts her position, and I know she's about to pull out my cock and take me in that hot little mouth, which sounds like a slice of heaven. Except it's not enough. Dammit all, it's just not enough.

I reach down and cup her face. Her eyes flicker in confusion. "*More*," I say.

She licks her lips, looking so damn tempted. "We both have rules."

"I think we've bent those rules so much, they're twistier than nautical knots."

Her teeth drag over her lower lip, and I chuckle.

"A woman with integrity," I say. "I can't fault that."

"Pierce?"

"Hmmm?"

"You're fired."

CHAPTER NINE

YOU'RE FIRED.

I don't think I've ever heard such magical words.

The kind of words that set me free. That open up all sorts of wonderful, decadent, intimate possibilities.

The kind of words that fire my blood and make me hard.

The sound of her voice has barely faded when I have her arms above her head, her wrists crossed, and my hand holding her in place. Her T-shirt is still awry, her bra all twisted up. Her skirt is around her waist, and her panties are around one ankle.

She looks wild and ready and absolutely beautiful.

"I'm a free agent now," I say. "Imagine the possibilities."

"I want to do more than imagine," she says. "I want to be so sore I can barely walk tomorrow. I want—"

"What?"

"I want tonight. I'll hire you again in the morning, but dammit, Pierce, right now, I want you inside me."

I'm still mostly dressed, too, but I don't care, and from the way she's begging me, neither does she. "Now," she demands. "Pierce, please. Now."

I release her wrists so I can unbutton my fly, and it's only then that I realize I don't have a condom. Which is ironic, since I *always* use a condom.

"I don't either," she says when I tell her as much. "But I'm clean, and I'm on birth control."

"I've been tested," I tell her. "I'm safe. Do you trust me?"

I watch her eyes as she answers, and damned if her soft, sincere "yes" isn't the most erotic sound ever.

"Good," I say, "because I can't wait."

"Me neither." She reaches for me, pulling me on top of her and claiming my mouth with the kind of intensity that makes a kiss feel like a fuck.

"Baby," I say. "I don't think I can go slow."

"Don't," she begs. "Don't you dare go slow."

I meant what I said. I couldn't go slow if I tried. I've wanted her since I first saw her at Thyme, and now that she's half-naked and beneath me, I can't hold back. Not the first time, anyway.

I ease my hand between her legs, stroking her. Opening her.

She arches up, meeting my movements, body lithe and warm and ready.

She's slick and beautiful, and I ease over her, then tease her pussy with the head of my cock, just to make us both a little more crazed.

But Jez is having none of it, and she reaches down, her hand closing around my shaft as she guides me to her center. "Now," she demands. "Dammit, Pierce, I want you inside me," and her words are so hot and desperate that I can't hold back. Can't even take it easy. And I thrust inside her. Once, twice. Deeper each time, until I'm so deep and tight that it seems like I'm going to lose myself.

I piston inside her, my weight on my hands against the floor, her hips rising up to meet me. And her eyes—her eyes are locked on mine.

I'm close, so damn close, but I'm not ready to come yet. "Over," I say on a gasp. "Get on top."

With my hands on her waist, I roll us over, and it's so fucking sexy watching her ride my cock that I still may not last.

"Clothes off," I order, flicking my eyes over her clothes as I reach between our bodies and tease her clit with my fingertip. "There you go," I say, as her core clenches around me, tightening with her coming explosion.

She rips her shirt and bra off, then yanks the skirt over her head as well. She's fully naked now, and I'm still completely dressed except for my open fly, and it's so damn sexy that I know I'm going to lose it soon. "Come on," I urge her. "Come with me."

"Yes," she says as I stroke her. "Oh, God, yes, don't stop."

But I wouldn't dream of stopping, and I play with her pussy as she rides me—and then, as she cries out that she's coming, and she clenches tight around my cock—I empty myself inside her, the orgasm rolling over me with the force of a goddamned tidal wave.

And then, when I'm spent, she collapses on top of me,

her breasts against my shirt, her lips brushing just above my collar.

I take her chin and guide her mouth to mine, then kiss her long and deep. "Baby," I say, when we come up for air, "you feel like heaven."

"Funny. I thought that was you."

I chuckle, then slide out from under her. "Come here," I say, as I pick her up. She curls against me, naked and soft, and I carry her to the bedroom, only then realizing how lucky we were that Del didn't decide to leave her bedroom to go get a snack.

I put Jez in bed, then strip and slide in next to her. She's wiped me out, but unlike my usual encounters, I'm not inclined to leave. On the contrary, I want to stay. I want to spoon against her. Which, right there, tells me something about the way I feel about this woman. Because I'm not a guy who spoons.

Except with Jezebel, apparently I am.

She's warm and her ass is nestled against my crotch, and despite the fact that I'm both spent and exhausted, I want her again.

I can wait, though. It feels too good just holding her.

I know I should move. Should get up and go to my own room. Make a cup of coffee. Do something.

But I can't quite manage, and the longer I stay like this the deeper I slide down toward sleep.

"Pierce?"

The sound of my name pulls me back with a jolt. "Sorry, sorry. I didn't mean to doze off." I sit up, groggy and confused, and kicking myself for not having gotten out of here sooner.

"I'll get out of your hair," I say, as I push myself upright and sit on the edge of the bed, my back to her as I try to locate my clothes in the dark.

"No, no, wait."

Something in her tone worries me, but when I twist around to face her, I can't read her expression. "Jezebel? Baby, what is it?"

"You're not—you're not dating anyone, right? I'm not being the other woman?"

I almost laugh. I'm about as far away from attached as a man can get. And at least until I met Jez, that was fine by me. Now—well, I'm not exactly looking to pop the question, but I can't deny that she's made me reconsider my one-night-then-move-on *modus operandi*. Because I could definitely handle two nights with this woman. Frankly, three would be just fine, too.

"Pierce?" There's worry in her eyes, and I realize my hesitation made her doubt.

"I'm not," I say hurriedly. "Not by a long shot."

"Oh." The relief in her voice is palpable. "Good. I mean, I'd assumed you were single. Because you'd said you were meeting a blind date that night we met. I'm guessing Kerrie set you up."

"Not exactly." The words spill out automatically, and I immediately wonder what the fuck I'm doing. Just say *yes*. Just agree and be done with it, because what does it matter?

"Not exactly a blind date? Or not exactly Kerrie?"

"It wasn't a blind date. And Kerrie had nothing to do with it." *Idiot*. I'm an idiot who has no control over the words that come out of his mouth.

Except I'm not. Not really. Because for better or for

worse, I don't want to pull my punches with this woman. This is new territory for me—but there's no denying the way I feel.

"Not a blind date," she muses. "But you didn't know what she looked like and—*Oh!* The initials. I read about that somewhere. That new app." She grins at me, and thankfully she looks amused and not scandalized. "You had me confused with a hook-up."

"Which was a horrible mistake," I say, then lean in to brush a kiss over her lips. "Because you are so much more than that."

Once again, I hear my words and can't believe I'm saying them.

At the same time, I can't deny that they're true.

Del had it wrong—Jez isn't a bitch, she's a witch. And somehow, she's completely enchanted me.

"So why no girlfriend?" she asks.

"Complaining?"

"Hardly. I'm curious." She shifts to sit up in bed, pulling the sheet up to cover her breasts, which seems a damn shame to me.

I lie down again, my arm up over my head. I consider ignoring the question. Changing the subject or, better yet, distracting her by pulling her on top of me and taking her again, hard and fast.

But there's the problem of that spell she's cast. I want to talk to her. I actually want to stay here in bed with her and have a conversation about my past. Seriously, it's the damnedest thing.

"So?" she presses. "Are you about to tell me to mind my own business?"

"No," I say, and manage to bite my tongue before I say that I'd like to make it her business. "Just gathering my thoughts."

She clicks on the bedside lamp, then slides out of bed, and I enjoy the view of her naked back disappearing into the living room. Then I enjoy even more the full frontal view when she returns with two glasses of wine.

"Just fyi," I say. "Wandering around naked tends to not be conducive to talking. For future reference."

She hands me a glass as I prop myself up in bed, then puts hers on a side table. She slides back in and wraps the sheet around her. "Noted. You were saying? About your pathetic lack of a girlfriend or wife?"

I shake my head, amused, then take a sip of wine, still not sure how to begin. Finally, I cut to the chase, "I survived the military," I say. "I didn't survive my engagement."

"What happened?"

"I loved her. I thought she loved me. And then three hours before the wedding she told me that she couldn't go through with it. That she didn't love me. That she wasn't sure she ever had."

She presses her hand over mine. "That bitch. Oh, Pierce. I'm so sorry."

"I'm over it." I shrug like it was no big deal, even though of course it meant everything. I meet her eyes. "But I don't do relationships."

Her brows rise. "You're looking at me as if that's an issue. It's not."

"Right," I say, and though that's exactly what I should

want to hear, the words still hit me hard before sitting in my stomach like a ball of lead.

"I'm only here for a few more days, remember? And until Del is ready to run her own career, my focus is on her, not relationships, not dating, not any of it."

The hint of a smile blooms wide as she gestures between us. "I don't regret this at all, but I'm not a shrinking violet of a girl who's been suddenly mesmerized by your magical, mystical cock."

"It is pretty spectacular, isn't it?"

"I'm not about to say anything to add to that ego," she says. "What about these women on the app? Aren't they looking for relationships?"

"It's not that kind of app. Plus, I make it clear. I'm just in it for the night."

"Really? How mercenary."

"It's worked for me so far." But even as I say it, I can't shake the feeling that my brick wall of one-night stands is about to come crashing down.

"Hmm."

"You don't approve."

"On the contrary, it's pretty smart." She lies back down, then props herself up on her elbow. "Maybe I should follow your lead."

I frown, not understanding. "What are you talking about?"

She stretches out, her head now on the pillow so that she's facing the ceiling. "It's just a good way not to be alone, right?"

"Sure," I say automatically. But that's a lie. I'm always alone with those women. And as much as I hate admitting it, being here with Jez—touching her, talking to her—has only driven that simple fact home.

For a moment, we're both quiet. Then she sits up again and pulls her knees to her chest and wraps her arms around them. "We're getting far too maudlin. So here's what I was thinking. About tomorrow, I mean. Del and I are scheduled for a full day at the spa, and then at seven she has to be on the set for the night shots."

"Right," I say, more disappointed than I should be that I won't be seeing her during the day. "And I'll be here at six to pick you two up."

"Well, yeah. I mean, unless you have time during the day."

"Of course I do. This is a full-time gig, remember? But if you're suggesting I get a pedicure, I think I'll pass. But Connor's scheduled to be with Del tomorrow until five. Maybe he'd like a facial."

"Very funny. No, it's just that I was thinking."

"About?"

"Del. And how she might have more fun doing a spa day with someone closer to her own age."

"Uh-huh."

"Right," she says, then clears her throat. "You told me Kerrie's twenty-four, right?"

"Kerrie? Yeah."

"That's close. Do you think she'd be up for it?"

"A spa day with a movie star who also has a wicked sense of humor? Yeah, I think she'd be on board." I do my best not to anticipate where else this is going. But I'm seeing a long, lazy day stretched out in bed with Jez, while Connor watches over the girls at the spa.

"And I was thinking that maybe you and I could—"

"Yes."

"—do Austin," she finishes.

I sit up. "Wait. What?"

She frowns. "What did you think I was going to say?"

"Nothing. Backgammon. Something like that."

Her laugh fills the room like music. "Well, I think *backgammon* can be on the menu. But I've only been to Austin once before, and I was hoping you could show me around."

That sounds remarkably like a date to me. And while I would be enthusiastically on board with spending the entire day naked and in bed, the idea of a date causes a chorus of *Danger, Will Robinson* to ring in my head.

Because I don't do relationships. I don't.

But somehow when I'm around Jez, I have to keep reminding myself of that.

Then again, she's already pointed out that she's leaving in less than a week. And I have no real indication that she's reading anything more into spending the day together than simply spending the day together.

Which I want to do.

More than I probably should, actually.

"Pierce?" She's frowning at me. "I didn't think it was that hard a question. Are you—"

"I'm in," I say, because I'll be damned if I'm going to let someone else show her around town. "Just thinking about where we'll go."

"Great. Good." She breathes deep, then yawns.

I slide out of bed and scan the room, looking for my pants. "I'll let you sleep. I'll go text Kerrie and Connor, and then tomorrow after we get them settled at the spa, you and I will hit the town."

"Okay," she says, but I can hear the hesitation.

"Problem?"

"It's just that at six o'clock tomorrow I have to hire you again. I was thinking that so long as you're not on payroll right now..."

"Are you asking me to sleep here, Ms. Stuart?"

She sits up, letting the sheet fall away. "Actually, Mr. Blackwell. I'm not asking you to sleep at all."

CHAPTER TEN

"THIS PLACE IS AWESOME," Jez says to me, glancing up at the toy pterodactyl hanging from the ceiling. "And these pancakes are amazing. I've never had gingerbread before."

"Never?"

"I've led a sheltered life," she says, her voice totally deadpan.

I laugh and hold my cup up for a coffee refill as our waiter passes by. We're on South Congress at Magnolia Cafe, my favorite restaurant in Austin, second only to the original Magnolia Cafe on the other side of the river. It has a laid-back atmosphere, tons of character, and food that I'm willing to go out of my way for.

In this case, it's not out of the way at all. Not only are we just a couple of miles from the Starfire Hotel, but we're also right at the south end of the SoCo shopping area. And since Jez told me that she wanted to buy a souvenir for Del today, I figured we'd spend some time window-shopping our way back toward the river.

"We're lucky we got in," I say. "This place is usually jam-packed on Saturdays, especially during South By." I glance around—it's crowded, but not crazy busy.

"It's not yet ten," she says. "Anyone who was out late last night is probably still asleep." Her teeth graze her lower lip as she looks up at me through her lashes. "I know I'd still be asleep after my very late night if it weren't for having to get my sister out the door."

"Is that so?" I ask, as her foot rubs my ankle from across the booth. "If you're tired, we can always go back to the hotel and spend the day in bed while our sisters do the spa."

"Tempting, but no." She takes a sip of her coffee, and I get hard just watching her mouth on that white ceramic cup. "You promised me a day out." She puts the coffee down, her eyes never leaving mine. "I'm looking forward to whatever you have in mind."

"You, Jezebel Stuart, are a tease."

"Maybe a little," she says, then pulls her foot away. "But I can be good." She sets her fork down and leans back. She's managed to eat half of her short stack. Which, considering the size of the pancakes, is pretty impressive. "So tell me about this place. How'd you find it?"

"I've been coming here since I was a kid. I always got a kick out of the *Sorry, we're open* sign, and when Kerrie was little, I used to tease her by telling her that the whole restaurant was part of a time warp."

"Because of the sign that says they're open 24/8?"

"She never believed me," I say. "My sister is far too cynical."

Jez laughs. "Yeah, she looked pretty cynical this

morning when she was jumping up and down and clapping about a spa day."

"She hides her cynicism well," I retort, and Jez throws her napkin at me.

"When are you going to tell me the plan for the day?"

"Never," I say. "You're just going to have to trust me and go along for the ride. Think you can handle it?"

She crosses her arms and narrows her eyes. "No," she says. But her smile says yes.

Half an hour later, she's already bought Delilah three souvenir T-shirts from Prima Dora, a local shop next door to Magnolia, along with five packs of kitschy cocktail napkins. "Del loves this kind of stuff," she says, grinning as we walk hand in hand, the shopping bag tight in my free hand. "Where to now?"

"Now we wander."

"I like it here," she says after we've walked a few more blocks. "Definitely trendy, but it's colorful and fun and most everything seems local. Oh—"

She stops at the corner and points to Allen's Boots. "*That* I need." Her smile is wide as she turns to me. "Cowboy boots for when I'm back in LA. Authentic ones, don't you think?"

"Who am I to argue?" I say, and we cross the street and head inside. Unlike some of the stores on South Congress, Allen's Boots has been in this location forever, and the guys in there know what they're doing—even going so far as to tell Jez that she'll be better off if she breaks the red boots she's chosen in slowly. She, however, insists on wearing them for the rest of our jaunt.

"I like them," she says, kicking her foot out as soon as

we're back outside in the sun. She does a sort of hop-step, then leans against me as she laughs. "I saw that in a movie once. Well, not *that*. But some sort of dance step."

"We'll start with the two-step and let you work your way up."

"You know how?"

"I've managed once or twice."

"Show me," she insists, taking my hands as if we were waltzing.

I laugh and back away. "Trust me. It's better if I don't try to teach you in public. My skills aren't that good."

"On the contrary," she says, letting her hand slide down my T-shirt, and pausing just below my belt. "I think your skills are excellent."

"Jez..."

I'm sorely tempted to blow off the rest of our excursion and teach her a few horizontal dance steps. But she just laughs and skips back. "Later," she whispers. "Promise?"

"Oh, yeah," I assure her.

She takes my hand and we head down the street again, and we talk about everything and nothing. The knick-knacks in the windows, the shoppers passing by. The weather. Books. Even Irish poetry, although how we got on that subject, I have no idea.

When I ask, she just shrugs and laughs and grabs my hand, looking more carefree than I've ever seen her. And right then, I think that there's not a single thing I want more in the world than to keep her looking that way forever.

It's a dangerous thought ... but somehow, it's not as terrifying as it should be.

"Thanks," she says later, as we leave Lucy In Disguise

with Diamonds, both sporting funky pairs of retro sunglasses. "I needed this."

"Who doesn't need neon sunglasses?"

"Good point," she says. "But not what I meant. Seriously," she adds, putting her hands on my shoulders and rising up on her tiptoes to brush a soft kiss over my lips. "Thank you."

She starts to pull away, but I cup her head, and keep her close, deepening the kiss until she moans, and I feel the reverberations all through my body.

"Where to now?" she whispers.

"Well, I have a whole day planned. After SoCo, I thought we'd rent a paddleboat and spend an hour or so on the river. Then we could grab lunch at one of the food trucks on Barton Springs Road, then head to South Austin and check out the Wildflower Center before heading back downtown for a sushi happy hour."

"That sounds amazing."

"Or we could skip all that, and I could show you my favorite view of the river."

"Where's that?"

"My condo."

Her eyes widen almost imperceptibly. "So, I'm guessing that the view of the city is a euphemism?"

"It might be," I admit. "I know you said you wanted your day out. But Jez—"

"Shut up, Pierce," she says, silencing me with a finger on my lips. "And let's go. I'd hate to miss an exceptional view."

CHAPTER ELEVEN

IT'S A GORGEOUS MARCH DAY. The afternoon sun sparkles on the river. The trees are green, a few of them even starting to bud.

It's truly a beautiful view.

None of that, however, compares to Jezebel.

We're in my living room, and she's at the window that opens onto the balcony and overlooks the scenic river view. But it's the woman who truly takes my breath away.

She's already taken off her boots, but now I want to do away with the rest of her clothing, and I step up behind her, determined to make that happen. "Close your eyes," I say, and I'm gratified when she does. "Arms up." Once again, she complies, and her willingness to trust me is as much of a turn-on as her soft skin and delicious scent.

I grab the hem of her shirt and pull it up over her head. She makes a little whimpering sound, but doesn't object.

"Next the jeans," I say, as I peel the bra off of her and toss it aside. "Take them off for me. Underwear, too."

The windows are slightly tinted in defense against the sun, and at this time of day, there's a bit of a reflection. She looks up, then meets my eyes in the glass. I wait for her to protest, but she says nothing. She just unbuttons her fly, then wriggles out of the jeans, her underwear slipping down with the denim.

Then she stands there, looking out at this wild section of Austin, her hands at her sides, her legs slightly parted.

I'm standing behind her, but in the window, I can see that her nipples are tight, and she's biting on her lower lip.

"This excites you," I say, and when she nods, I exhale with relief. Because damned if it doesn't turn me on, too.

"This is my favorite view," I say. "Not the city. Not the trees. Not the river. But you standing in front of me, your skin glowing, your body reflected in the window. Because honestly, how could anything be more lovely?"

"Liar," she says, her mouth curving into a smile. "Nice words, but they're a lie. How can this be your favorite if you've never seen it before?"

I step up behind her and cup her breasts, then slide one hand down between her thighs. She's wet—so damn wet—and all I can think is *mine*.

"I've seen it before. Not specifically, but the idea of it. The idea of you. An innocent beauty standing right in front of me, naked and wanting me." I move the hand on her breast up to her forehead so that I can bend her head backwards, elongating her neck. She draws in a shaky breath, but doesn't move. "Tell me you want me."

"Yes. So much."

I release her, and she sighs, but stays like that, leaning

backwards against me, so that I'm supporting her weight and she's trusting me to keep her upright.

One of my hands is still between her legs, and I tease and stroke her until she's writhing against me, hot and ready. "Take off your clothes," she demands.

"Anything the lady wants," I say, as I hurry to strip.

"Do you mean it?"

I tilt my head, wondering what she has in mind. "Try me."

She slides into my arms, kicking away the last of my clothes, then captures me in a white hot kiss that both surprises and excites me. "Jez, baby," I say, when I pull away, gasping for breath. But she's not giving me a break. Her hand slides between our bodies and she strokes me, making me even harder than I could have imagined, and sending a wild heat coursing through me.

"Now," I say. "Dammit, Jez, I need to be inside you now."

"What floor are we on?" There's a frantic note to her query.

"The twenty-seventh."

"Can anyone see in?"

"I don't know. I don't think so."

"The window," she begs. "Please, take me by the window."

Hell, yes, I will.

"Hands on the glass," I order. "Bend over."

She does, and the view is so hot, I almost come right then. But I want to be inside her. I want to be with her. *Her.* Not just sex, but Jez. And as I move behind her—as I slide my cock deep inside her hot, wet, pussy—as I claim her once and for all—I can't help but wonder what that means.

But right now, I'm too fired up too care. Too lost in passion. Too lost in the waves of pleasure rippling over me.

Most of all, I'm too lost in Jez.

And when she explodes in my arms—when she cries my name and shakes so hard her legs give out—I feel like the most powerful man on the earth.

We've sunk down to the carpet, and I rouse myself long enough to clean us up and get robes. Then I open the door and lead her onto the balcony, settling her on the oversized chaise lounge before I go back inside for two glasses of bourbon.

I'm tending her—and that's a far cry from my usual routine.

But it feels right. Good, even.

And when she smiles up at me as I hand her a glass, it also feels remarkably like home.

"I love this," she says, before I can think too hard about these errant, semi-domestic thoughts skittering through my mind. "Way up in the sky with a balcony. It's like living in the city, but still getting away."

"It is," I say. "I'd like to have a house one day, but only if it has that getaway quality. And that would mean a pretty big yard. And I don't have the time to deal with it."

"You could hire someone."

I shake my head. "Not the same. There's something primal and personal about a yard. What?" I say, catching her look of surprise.

"It's just that I've always felt that way. I want a garden,

and I don't have one for the same reasons. No time to deal with it and I don't want someone else tending what's mine."

I nod, thinking how much we have in common, and how unexpected that is.

She sighs, and takes a sip of the bourbon. "This has been a great few days," she says. "And to be honest, I haven't had a lot of fun lately," she says. "So thank you."

"Because of the scandal?"

"Yeah. But even before that."

I turn toward her, remembering our conversation last night. "You're living a shadow life."

She bristles. "I love my sister."

"I'm not saying you don't. But you need to live your own life. What happens when she's ready to manage her own career?"

"This isn't your problem." Her words are sharp, and painfully true.

Painful because I want to help. I want to pull her into my arms, hold her close, and help her figure it all out.

And damned if I know where I made that left turn, but I did. And now I'm careening toward something with this woman that I don't fully understand. All I know is that it feels right—and that I'm not ready to put on the brakes.

"It is my problem," I tell her. "I don't know why or how or if you'll let me help. But dammit, Jez, you got under my skin. And I can't walk away. Not now. Not without trying."

Her lips press tight together and she holds her eyes wide, obviously fighting tears. But then she pushes out of the chair and hurries inside.

I give her a moment, then follow. She's in the kitchen, the faucet running, her hands clutching the countertop.

"Hey." I put my hand on her shoulder, resisting the urge to turn her around and pull her into my arms, even though that's exactly where I want her to be. "Talk to me."

"I've got this," she says, more to the sink than to me. "I do," she adds, turning to face me. "It's just that sometimes I wish I could hand it all off to someone else. That I could just let go and back away. You know?"

"I do," I say. I take her hand. "Come with me."

She eyes me curiously, but she doesn't protest when I lead her into my bedroom.

"I can't help with Del," I say. "At least not without some research and a few dozen phone calls. But about you handing it off to someone else ... about that, I have a few ideas."

I watch her face. The flicker of interest. The hint of nervousness. "What do you have in mind?" she finally asks.

"Do you trust me?"

"I—"

She hesitates, and in that moment of silence it feels like the ground has fallen out from under me. And fuck, I want to kick myself, because I should not have fallen this hard, this fast. I know better than that.

But what the hell, right? Because all that's going on here is a multi-night stand. And in a few days, she's heading back to LA, and I'll hop back onto 2Nite, and my life will return to stasis.

In the meantime, I have Jez.

And when she nods and says, "Of course I trust you," everything seems sane again.

"Sit on the bed," I order, and when she complies, I go to my dresser.

"What exactly are you doing?" Her voice is amused, but wary.

"Forcing you to give everything over to someone else. Close your eyes. Now," I add, when she hesitates.

She narrows her eyes, but then she complies—and then yelps a little when I put a sleep mask on her, then tighten it to ensure she can't peek.

"Pierce, I don't—"

"Hush. You're giving yourself over. You're letting go. You're putting me in charge. That's the deal. And I promise you'll enjoy it."

She licks her lips, and I hold my breath, afraid she's going to balk. But then she nods.

"Good. Now lay back and put your arms above your head, wrists together." I'm certain she's going to protest again, so I'm surprised when she complies without argument.

I get on the bed beside her, then bind her wrists with an old tie. The headboard has a shelf on it, and since I don't have a better option, I unplug my alarm clock and thread the extension cord though the loop of the tie, effectively binding her wrists near the headboard.

"Pierce…"

"Yes, baby?"

"I don't know," she says. "I guess I just wanted to know you'd answer."

"Always. Now relax. Just breathe."

"What are you going to do?"

"Sweetheart, I'm going to make you come."

"Oh."

I smile, seeing the way her body tightens just from the suggestion, and then I settle in to thoroughly explore this woman. I brush kisses over every inch of her. I oil my hands and massage her breasts. I suck on her tits. I kiss my way up her legs. And I tell her throughout all of it how absolutely fucking beautiful she is.

I lose myself in her pleasure. In watching the way her skin contracts at a touch. In judging the pattern of her breathing. I want to know everything, and I lose myself in the reality of Jezebel.

And only when she is writhing and whimpering, begging for my touch, do I gently slip my fingers between her legs, then hold her still when she tries to grind against me. "Oh, no. That's for me to do," I say, and then I make it my mission to take her to the absolute height of passion.

And since she actually screams when she comes, I think that I did a damn good job.

I hold her body as it shakes in the last throes of the orgasm, then very gently I take off the mask and untie her hands.

Immediately, she curls up against me, then sighs deeply. "That was incredible."

"The orgasm or letting go?"

"That's a trick question," she says, opening her eyes. "I came so hard *because* I let go."

"Listen to you," I tease. "My star pupil."

She reaches out to smack my chest, but I grab her hand and kiss it. "If you can do it in bed," I say, "you can do it in life."

"Have an earth shattering orgasm?"

"Surrender some control."

I think I've proved my point, but she just shakes her head, then props herself up on one elbow. "You're forgetting one thing. I trust you."

CHAPTER TWELVE

I TRUST YOU.

The words rush through me, warm and satisfying—and scary enough that I force them aside. This isn't about me. It's about her. It's about Del. It's about finding an agent or a manager or a partner—someone who can share the burden with Jezebel until Del's ready to take it over herself.

And that's exactly what I tell her.

"And my point's still the same," she says. "I don't have to get naked with them, but I still have to trust them. And after what happened with Simpson..."

She trails off with a shrug, then shifts on the bed so that she's propped up on her knees. "But you, sir, are taking my problem far too seriously. I'll work it out. And in the meantime, we need to get going."

She nods at the clock, and I curse softly. I'd completely lost track of time. We need to be back at the hotel in just under half an hour. "You're a bad influence on me," I say.

"The feeling's entirely mutual."

Fortunately, my condo is only a few blocks from the

Starfire, and soon enough I'm handing the valet my keys and ushering Jez into the elevator with fifteen minutes to spare.

She uses her key to access the floor, and moments later we walk hand-in-hand into her suite—only to find Kerrie sitting at the table, looking directly at us.

Her brows rise, and I see a smug little smile flicker before being replaced by her poker face.

"You're early," I say, releasing Jez's hand. "Where's Del?"

"Remind me never to be a movie star," she says. "Your schedule totally isn't your own."

"Kerrie..."

"She's on the set. Connor took her. Said you could relieve him when you got back."

"The set?" Jez says.

"The producers called while we were in the steam room. I guess they wanted to get started early or something." She takes a gulp from her water bottle and looks at me. "Can you take me home before you go? I've got plans tonight and no car."

"Sure. Grab your stuff." I turn to Jez as Kerrie starts to shove magazines and a pair of flip flops into a tote bag. "You?"

She shakes her head. "I need to sort through a few things here and make a couple of calls to LA." She reaches for my hand, glances at Kerrie, then pulls it back. "I'll see you later, though. When you bring Del home."

"Yes, you will," I say. I step closer, then lower my voice so that only Jez can hear. "You can fire me again tonight."

"Deal."

"I'm ready," Kerrie says.

"Hang on. I want to grab a water bottle." My phone chimes as I head for the fridge in the small kitchen area. I pull it out and set it on the counter, looking at the lock screen notification as I open a bottle of water and take a long swallow.

J from 2Nite has messaged you: Back in town. Let's try again tonight?

I'm about to dismiss it when Kerrie calls for me to bring her a bottle, too. I grab one from the fridge, and head back toward the door, then toss the bottle to my sister. "All set?"

"Let's go."

I wave to Jez, resisting the urge to kiss her goodbye. Not because it would be unprofessional, but because I'd never hear the end of it from my sister.

My sacrifice doesn't pay off, however, because the first thing Kerrie says when we get in my Range Rover is, "You like her."

"Of course I do. She's nice. Smart. Competent."

"That's not what I mean, and you know it. You're falling for her."

"No, I'm not," I lie, because I don't want to get into it with my sister right now.

"It's okay if you are."

"Kerrie..."

"I'm just saying that would be good, that's all. I mean, I know that whole thing with Margie messed you up, but I worry about you. Mom and Dad worry, too. They're just never going to tell you. Or if they do, they'll wait until Thanksgiving and Christmas."

Our parents retired to Nevada five years ago, and while

we stay in touch, the phone calls tend to be pretty bare bones. But my parents are more than happy to meddle when we're together in person for the holidays.

I keep my hands on the wheel and my eyes on the road. "Like I said, I'm fine."

"Maybe. But one of these days you're going to have to realize that only Margie was the asshole and not the entire female population. I mean, some of us are actually loyal, you know? And I love you, is all."

I sigh. "I love you, too." I hesitate, and for a moment I consider telling her everything and letting her help me parse out this mess of emotions that's tangled in my head.

But then her phone rings, and the moment is lost.

"Hey," she says. "What's up?" A pause, then, "Sure, I'll tell him. Bye."

"What's up?"

"You left your phone at the hotel. Jez called Connor so you wouldn't worry when you couldn't find it."

"Oh, good. Thanks."

"And apparently Lisa tried to reach you," she adds. "When your phone and the office line went to voice mail, she called Connor. She's in town and wants to meet you for dinner. She told Connor she has news. And he said he'll cover for you on the set."

"News." I frown slightly, considering, but I don't have any ideas. "I was just telling Jez about her. She was asking about our work."

"You told her about Lisa and the stalker? Did you tell her what happened?"

I understand the surprise in her voice; I don't often share that I killed a man. "I told her."

"Like I said," she says smugly. "You're falling for her."

This time, I don't bother to deny it.

I use Kerrie's phone to call Lisa back, then drop my sister off before going home to change. All of that takes about an hour, but I still manage to arrive right on the dot to meet Lisa. She's already seated, and she stands up and flings her arms around me as I approach the four-top near the front of the restaurant.

"I'm so glad you could come. I know it's horribly short notice, but I'm only in town today. We came in to see Daddy."

"How's your father doing?" I ask. I haven't spoken to her father in months. All I know is that he's living in Salado now, a small town about fifty miles outside of Austin.

"Great," she says. "He's been doing a lot of renovation work, so business is picking up. He uses your recommendation on the website I made for him."

"Good. That's what it was for." I take a sip of my water, then notice the bottle of champagne chilling in a nearby bucket. "Are we celebrating?"

She nods, looking like she's about to overflow with her news. "But you have to wait until—oh! Derek!"

I turn and see a tall, curly-haired man scanning the restaurant. He smiles and hurries toward us, then kisses Lisa's cheek. And, I notice with approval, he doesn't flinch at all when he kisses her right on the jagged scar, a souvenir of her attack.

"This is Derek, my fiancé."

"Lisa, that's wonderful. Congratulations to you both. Derek, a pleasure." I extend my hand, pleased to find that he has a nice, strong grip.

"Sweetheart, Mom just called me back. I'm going to step out so that I can catch her, and I'll let you ask Pierce. Okay?"

She nods, and he shakes my hand again. "I apologize, but my mother retired to Taiwan, and getting in touch with her can be tricky. I'll be back soon."

Lisa waits until he's out of earshot, and then says, "I know this is a little weird, but will you be our best man?"

I sit back in my seat, shocked and flattered. "Lisa, are you sure? Is Derek?"

She nods. "I wouldn't be here to get married if it wasn't for you. And Derek's best friend is a girl, so she's going to be my maid of honor. Would you? The wedding's in June."

"Of course. I'm honored."

She leans back with obvious relief. "Oh, thank goodness. Daddy will be so excited. How about you? Is there anyone you're seeing?"

"Actually," I begin, "there's a woman I—"

"*Pierce.*"

Lisa and I look over at the same time, and while she looks completely confused by the angry woman stalking toward us, I have a sudden flash of comprehension.

My phone. My goddamned phone.

"Is this J?" Jez asks. Her arms are crossed over her chest as she nods toward Lisa, but her furious stare never veers off me. "Is this the woman you left me to come fuck? How the hell could you? I thought we—*Dammit.*"

Lisa's eyes are wide, and I think she's about to ask me what's going on. Instead, her gaze shifts and she calls out, "Derek!"

"I couldn't get the call back to Mom to go through," he

says, hurrying forward. He frowns, looking at Jez. "What's going on?"

"Sit down," I say to Jez as Derek takes the seat opposite to where she's standing.

Her eyes flash with defiance. And then, when she looks at Derek, they flash with confusion.

"This is Lisa," I say gently, indicating her and Derek in turn. "And this is Derek. Her fiancé."

"Oh." All the color drains from her. "Oh, God. I'm so sorry. I—I need—"

She doesn't bother finishing the sentence. Just turns and heads toward the exit.

"Excuse me," I say to the couple. "I need to clear up a little misunderstanding."

I hurry after her, finally catching up to her on the sidewalk outside of the restaurant.

"I'm sorry," she says. "I'm sorry and I'm mortified and I really wish you'd go back inside so that I can feel like an idiot all by myself."

"You don't need to feel like an idiot."

She lifts a brow, and I laugh. "Okay, maybe you do. Because you *are* an idiot if you think that five seconds after I leave you, I'd go to some anonymous girl on the other end of a hook-up app."

After fumbling in her purse, she pulls out my phone and hands it to me. "I went to pick it up, and a message flashed on the lock screen."

"I would have deleted it," I said. "Not even answered it."

"I'm so stupid."

I take her hands. "Come inside. We have an empty place. Join us for dinner."

"Why didn't you tell me you had dinner plans? You said you were going to the set."

I explain about the call, and she frowns. "The universe is conspiring against me."

"Or it's conspiring to get you to dinner with me. Seriously. Join us."

But she can't be convinced. "No, really. I just need to be alone."

"All right." I mentally run through tomorrow's schedule. "Cayden's on deck tomorrow. He's taking Del to the studio for that Sunday morning talk show, and then to the set. I'll come by, too, and we can talk."

"That's okay. Tomorrow's an early afternoon shoot. I'll just see you on the set."

I pause, taking in the bigger meaning of those words: *She doesn't want me coming over.*

"Jez," I say, feeling an unwelcome rush of panic. "You understand that tonight was just dinner with a friend. Right?"

She nods. "I know. I do. And I'm not upset about that."

"Then what?"

But she doesn't say, and I'm left with a hole in my stomach and the feeling that I've lost something, with no idea how to get it back.

CHAPTER THIRTEEN

I GET to the set ridiculously early on Sunday, and I'm pacing Del's trailer when she and Jez arrive. They walk in mid-conversation, and Jez freezes upon seeing me.

I stop cutting a path from the tiny sofa to the tiny kitchen. "Jez, we need to talk."

"Oh, gosh," Del says, looking from me to Jez. "I'm going to be late for make-up."

As she scurries out, I take a step closer to Jez. "Please, baby," I say. "Tell me what's going on. Tell me what happened yesterday. Because I get why you were upset when you had it all wrong. But when we sorted it out—"

"But we didn't," she says. "That's what I realized. We didn't sort anything out at all."

I feel suddenly cold. As if someone has dunked me in a vat of ice water. "What are you talking about?"

"I didn't expect it," she says, moving to sit on the sofa. She has her head down, her forehead pressing against her fingertips.

"What?"

She looks up, and I see the tears in her eyes. "You." A single tear trails down her cheek. "I didn't expect you."

I'm at her side in an instant, my arm around her, pulling her close. My chest is tight, because the words she's saying are the words that have been growing inside me. The words I haven't wanted to examine closely at all. But now ... well, maybe now I should.

"Tell me," I say softly. "Tell me what you mean."

"I realized last night, when I saw that stupid phone notification. It felt like I'd been sliced open." She sits up straighter, moving out of my embrace. I know it's so that she can look at me as she talks, but the loss of contact feels as painful as a kick in the balls.

"I'm feeling too much for you," she goes on. "And I know you're not looking for a relationship, but when I'm with you—"

She cuts herself off and shakes her head, as if trying to knock her thoughts into place. "I want more," she says simply. "More you. More time. More everything. I want to let whatever this thing is between us grow and see what happens."

The wave of relief that sweeps over me is so intense that I'm surprised it doesn't knock me over.

I know I should tell her that I want the same thing. That I want to let this play out. For however long it takes.

I should tell her that she's brought me back to life. That she's a miracle and a surprise and so damned unexpected, and that I never want to let her go.

I should tell her that somehow, someway, we'll make this work. That I know it can work, because in my gut—in my heart—she's already part of me.

I should say all of that. Instead, I say, "We have three more days."

For a moment, she just looks at me, and I want to kick my own ass for being such a pathetic loser. I want to call the words back and tell her the truth. But the words won't come. I've been telling myself so long that I don't do relationships, that I can't make the words come. Because what if I'm wrong about her? About us?

What if I let her in close, and she rips off my balls? What if I need those three days to figure this all out?

"You're right," she says as she pushes off the sofa. "We still have three days. And that's great." She runs her fingers through her hair. "Yeah. So, I, um, need to go meet with the production team. It's going to be a while, I think. So, I'll see you back at the hotel. When you bring Delilah, I mean."

I stand and reach for her, relieved when my hand finds hers. "Jez, please. I don't mean—"

But she pulls her fingers free. "No, it's fine. You're right. This has been fun, and we have three more days. I was just..."

She trails off with a shrug. Then she leans forward and kisses me lightly. "It's all good, really. I'll see you tonight. And this thing we have. It really is fun. It's great, just as it is. But I really have to go," she adds, checking her watch.

Then she practically bolts out of the trailer, and I drop back down on the couch.

Fun.

What a horrible word.

I'm still sitting there thirty minutes later wondering how the hell I managed to turn what was shaping up to be the best thing that had ever happened to me into complete and total shit in under ten minutes. Honestly, I must have some sort of rare power of destruction, because I think that's a fucking record.

And maybe—*maybe*—if I hadn't kept reminding myself how much I didn't want a relationship, I would have grabbed hold of this one and clung on so tightly she could never get away.

Fuck it.

I stand up. Maybe I blew it a few minutes ago, but I can fix it now. I'm not entirely sure how, but I am sure that groveling and honesty—and one hell of a nice dinner—will probably be involved.

I'm just about to go find her and start the groveling part of the equation, when the door to the trailer bursts open and Delilah rushes in, her eyes bloodshot.

"Del, what's going on? Is Jez okay?"

She nods. "She's fine. She went somewhere with the producers."

"So she's not on the set?"

She shakes her head, and I curse the missed opportunity. "Then what's the matter?" I ask.

"They're shutting us down. This was it. We just wrapped the Austin shoot."

I sit back down again. "What the hell are you talking about?"

"They just announced it after we shot the final scene. They've revamped the script. Everything that was supposed to happen under the oak tree or outside the stone house is going to be in a cafe. We're shooting those scenes in LA."

"Los Angeles," I say, as if I've never heard of LA before. "When?"

"Travel tomorrow. Shooting starts up again on Tuesday."

"So much for three days," I murmur. "Fuck."

"Please, Pierce. You have to help me."

I look at her, and realize it's not just the shortened shoot that's bothering her.

"What's going on?"

"Levyl's here already. In town, I mean. He's staying at the Driskill," she adds, mentioning the historic hotel that's across from my office and just a few blocks from the Starfire. "I have to see him. Please, you have to help me get in to see him."

"Are you insane?"

She blinks and tears stream down her face. "Please. Don't you get it? I need to see him. He needs to know that I'm sorry—that I love him, but I did a stupid thing. Maybe he won't forgive me, but I have to let him know I love him, and that I always have. And that even if we're not together, I still want to be his friend, and I never, ever meant to hurt him."

"Del..."

"No, please. I know it's a risk. And I know that maybe he'll push me away or tell his people to not let me in, but I've got to try. I can handle the hurt, Pierce, I really can. But I can't handle knowing I might have missed out on something good. And I really can't handle knowing that I hurt someone I love and didn't try to make it better, you know?"

I sigh. Because, goddammit, I know all of that.

And I know that this kid has a hell of a lot more courage than I do.

"If this ends up on social media, your sister is going to kill both of us," I say, and in response she throws her arms around me and kisses my cheek.

"Thank you, thank you. You're the absolute best. I'm so glad you and my sister—"

"Come on. If we're going to do this, we should get going. Do we even know if he's at the hotel right now?"

"He is. He always holes up for a couple of days before a concert. Sometimes he'll invite the press or a few fans up, but he doesn't go out. He might party after, but never before."

"That makes locating him easy. What about access? If you call, will he tell you the room number? Let you talk to him? In other words, is this just a question of me getting you to him? Or do we have an element of covert ops happening?"

"Um, I think it's kind of a CIA operation," she says, and I have to laugh.

"All right, then. Let me make a few calls."

An hour later, I've called in a half dozen favors, talked to pretty much everyone I've ever met in Austin, and have managed to track down the band's liaison at the hotel, who put me in touch with the band's manager, a woman named Anissa.

"Levyl and I have been friends for years," Anissa tells me. "And I was around during a lot of the drama with Del. I don't know if Levyl will see her, but I think he should. And I can at least get you in the room."

As far as I'm concerned, that's about as good an

outcome as I can hope for, and so Del and I set off for downtown.

I leave my car at the office, and we walk across the street, then follow Anissa's instructions to get to the service entrance that the band has been using to avoid the press.

Anissa's there to meet us, along with the hotel liaison I'd spoken to earlier. "Thank you so much," Del tells her. "It's great seeing you again. But I'm not getting you in trouble, am I?"

Anissa waves a hand dismissively. "If he's pissed, he'll get over it. Like I said, I've known him forever. Trust me when I say this is nothing."

We follow her through a maze of service corridors to the freight elevator, and then finally to the door of Levyl's suite.

"Ready?" Anissa asks.

Del nods, but before Anissa can take her inside, I reach for Del's sleeve. "You're sure about this? If this visit ends up on social media, it could start the whole scandal raging again, especially if it doesn't go well. And if that happens, you might end up off the movie. Not to mention how pissed off your sister will be."

"I get it," she says. "But sometimes you gotta take the risk, you know?"

"All right, then." I release her arm, then step back. "I'll be here. And Del?" I add, as she's crossing the threshold. "Good luck."

Thirty minutes later, I'm pacing the hallway, trying to decide if the fact that this is taking so long is a good thing or a bad thing. Possibly, she's still groveling. Or maybe he's flown into a screaming rage.

But hopefully, they've reconciled and they're catching up. Frankly, I like to think that at least one of the Stuart women will leave this town in a good place.

God, I'm a heel.

I let Jez believe there was something between us because there *was* something. But then when it came down to the wire, I shut down and shut up.

I don't even have the courage of an eighteen-year-old.

And right here and now, I decide that I'm going to fix that.

Because, dammit, I think I'm falling in love with Jezebel Stuart. And it's past time that she knew it.

CHAPTER FOURTEEN

JEZEBEL'S RIGHT inside the door when we enter the hotel suite, and she glares at both of us as she holds out her phone. "What the hell is this?" she demands, shoving the phone between us.

I glance down and see an image showing Delilah and Levyl with their arms around each other, and Levyl pressing a kiss to her temple.

It's posted on Levyl's Instagram page, and the caption reads *Love this girl. #DelilahStuart #stillfriends #shesalwaysgotmyback #IveGotHers #austintexas #NoHaterz #WeGotThis*

"We made up," Delilah says. "It's all good now. And Jason—the band's new drummer—snapped the picture. Levyl said that if he posted it, the fans would chill out." She takes the phone from Jez and starts tapping and scrolling, a hell of a lot faster than I can manage on my phone.

After a moment, she looks to both of us and smiles. "I think he was right. Everything I'm seeing is all thumbs-up. Nothing snarky or mean at all. Not yet, anyway."

"That's great," I say. "It worked."

"But it might not have." Jez's voice is tight, and I know that I'm going to have to double-down on the apology I came here for.

"Oh, come on, Jez," Delilah begins, but Jez just shakes her head, cutting Del off.

"Go on," she says, pointing to Del's room. And then, when Del hesitates, she adds in a softer voice, "Please. I'm glad it worked out with the fans. And I'm glad you and Levyl made up. But right now, I want to talk to Pierce."

Del looks at me, and I can see the solidarity on her face. If I want her to stay, she's not going to leave my side.

"Go on," I say. "I've got this."

She drags her feet, but she goes, shutting the door firmly behind her. And the second the door *snicks* into place, Jez lays into me.

"What the fuck?" she snaps. "I mean, seriously. What. The. Fuck?"

I lift my hands, trying to calm her down and create a break to get a word in. But she's having none of it.

"I told you specifically that I was trusting you with my sister. And you promised. Not only that, but you entered into a contract. And this is how you live up to your obligations? Seriously? This could have blown up. It could have completely destroyed her."

"But it didn't," I finally manage to say.

Now it's her turn to try to get a word in, but I hold up my hand. "No," I say, taking a step toward her. Which is dangerous, frankly, because right now she looks about ready to boil over. "What was destroying her was knowing that she'd never really apologized to him. That he didn't know how she felt."

I try to draw a deep breath, but it's hard. My throat is thick with emotion. "And once I realized that," I continue, "I knew I had to help."

"How altruistic," she snaps. "Why?"

I look at her face. At those eyes now lit with anger. Eyes that used to look at me with heat. And passion. And humor.

"Because of you," I say simply. "Because that's what's been destroying me."

She turns away, looking down so that I can't see her face. "Don't," she whispers. "Don't even go there."

I hear the vulnerability, and I know I should stop. But I can't. I have to make her understand. Because I'm hollow without her, and I'm so desperate to be filled.

"Just go," she says. "Please."

"I can't." I take a step closer. "Jez—everything you said yesterday—"

She interrupts me with a harsh scoffing sound. "How stupid was I to show you my heart?"

"Jez, please."

"I trusted you. With my body. With my secrets. With my sister and her whole career. I thought you were worth it."

"I am. *We* are. But I fucked up."

"Damn right, you did." I hear the thickness in her voice, and I know she's on the verge of tears.

I step closer. I'm right in front of her now, and I have to force my hands to stay at my sides when all I want to do is touch her. Comfort her.

"I let my past get in the way," I admit. "I thought about

Margie and about the way she hurt me. The way she left. But she shouldn't have been anywhere near my head. It should have just been you. Only you."

"Then why wasn't it?"

"Because I'm an asshole."

She lifts her head, her expression wary. "Keep going."

"Because I was scared."

Her brow furrows. "Of what?"

"Of you. Of everything. Of the way you make me feel."

She licks her lips, the anger in her eyes starting to dim. "How do I make you feel?"

"Like maybe I have a chance at forever." I draw a breath for courage. "Like maybe I'm falling in love with you. And I think you're falling with me."

I hear her breath hitch. "Pierce, I—"

"No, let me finish. Jez, I know this has been fast—crazy fast. And maybe we're both wrong, but I don't think so. And I want to put in the time and the work to find out. More than that, I want to make it work. Mostly, I want us to stay us."

A tear trickles down her cheek, and I reach up and gently brush it away. "I was afraid, and I hurt you. And I'm so goddamn sorry. Please, Jez. Please say you forgive me."

She licks her lips and sniffles a little. "Your timing sucks. We don't even have those three days. I'm leaving for LA tomorrow."

I can't help it; I laugh.

Her brow arches up. "That's funny?"

"It's wonderful," I say. "Because you didn't tell me to get lost. All you did was tell me you're leaving. And baby, that's just geography. We can make geography work."

She says nothing, so I take a step closer, then slide my arms around her waist. "Move here. You and Del. You said you want out of LA, right? So come here. Rent a house. Buy a condo. Live with me. But give it a chance. Del's not a struggling actress. She can live wherever she wants."

"She'll want LA," Jez says, and I smile again.

"And she's old enough to live there on her own," I say. "There's this cool invention called the Internet. Texting and video calls and all sorts of magical stuff. And these metal tubes that fly through the sky and get you to LA in only about four hours."

She smacks me playfully on the shoulder.

"You shouldn't hit in anger, you know."

She narrows her eyes. "Maybe I'm not angry anymore."

"Really?" I press a kiss to her jawline. "I'm very glad to hear it. Of course, I still have a lot of apologizing left." My hands cup her waist, then start to slowly slide up, taking her T-shirt with them.

"You hurt me."

"I know," I say, then gently nip her earlobe.

Her body trembles under my hands, and her breath comes out in a shudder. "I think you need to apologize more."

I step back so that I can gently pull her T-shirt over her head. "Sweetheart, I'm going to spend the rest of the night apologizing in every way I know how."

I kiss along her collarbone, then over the swell of her breasts. I tease one of her nipples between my thumb and forefinger, then bend my head to take the other into my mouth, my cock hardening at the sound of her sweet moans of pleasure.

I stay like that, sucking and teasing, soaking in the feel and then scent of her. Then I ease back, releasing her nipple with a wet, erotic popping sound.

I straighten, then look into her lust-glazed eyes. "Enough?" I ask. "Am I forgiven?"

She bites her lower lip, then cocks her head as a tiny smile plays on her lips. "Not even close."

"In that case," I say, as I kiss my way down her abdomen, lower and lower towards heaven. "I'll just have to work a little bit harder…"

EPILOGUE

Eight months later

I'M STANDING in a tux beneath a vine-covered arch at the end of a white, linen runway. Above me, the sky is painted a perfect blue. Behind me, the Pacific stretches to infinity.

From where I'm standing, yards away from the cliff's drop-off, I can't see the crash of the waves against the base of the cliff. But I can hear the roar of the ocean, and I breathe deep, letting the sounds and the sea air settle my nerves as the iconic music begins and the guests in front of me rise from their white, wooden folding chairs.

I look down the aisle, and it's not until I see her that my breath comes easy again. She's walking in time with the music, holding flowers in front of her, looking more beautiful than ever before.

I slide my hand into my pocket and finger the small treasure I've put there. A talisman that I hope will settle my nerves.

Closer and closer she comes until she's standing almost in front of me. She looks straight at me, then steps off to the side, smiling so broadly her eyes crinkle.

Now she's standing opposite me, and we're like two bookends on either side of Delilah and Levyl, who are holding hands now, their eyes not on each other, but on the man holding the Bible and reading their vows.

They each say, "I do," and the guests start to applaud. And as Levyl and Delilah kiss, the director standing off to the left and just out of the range of the camera yells, "Cut!"

Levyl laughs and swings his arm around Delilah's shoulder as she leans into him. "One of my favorite scenes," she teases, and he bends to lightly kiss her.

They're not dating again, but they've rekindled a strong friendship, and their fans—and the studio—love the continuing *will-they-won't-they* drama. The movie actually came about to capitalize on their renewed friendship, and Del urged both me and Jez to be extras in this movie. Supposedly just for fun, but also so that Jez and I would have a reason to fly to LA for a long weekend.

Over the last few months, we've been spending less time in California and more in Texas. At first, Jez was flying back and forth almost weekly so that she could work with Delilah on the basic management of Del's career. But Del's been grabbing the reins more, both by making more of her own decisions and by choosing and hiring a team to pick up the slack.

"Do you miss it?" I ask as I take Jez's hand and lead her away from the crowd. "Hollywood? The ocean? The California traffic? Handling Jez's stuff?"

"I miss the ocean," she says. "And I miss Del. But," she

adds, as she slides into my arms, "I'm very happy with my trade-off."

"You mean the house and the garden," I say, referring to the central Austin house we bought last month, and into which we've been pouring a stream of money, sweat, and elbow grease.

"Absolutely," she says, then rises on her toes to kiss me. "What else could I possibly mean?"

I grin, then step back, still clutching her hand. "Come with me. I want to show you something."

I take her back to the archway. Nearby, Del and Levyl and Anissa are chatting with Connor and Cayden and Kerrie, all of whom think they flew out for my movie debut.

That, however, is only part of it.

"What?" Jez says, looking around the decorative set piece. "If you're showing me the set, I've seen it already."

"But you haven't seen this," I say, dropping to one knee and holding up the ring that's been burning a hole in my pocket.

Jez gasps, her fingers going over her mouth, and I'm not sure if she's holding back tears or laughter. Or maybe she's just in shock.

"I don't think I could ever find a more perfect venue for a proposal," I say. "And since our friends and sisters are here, I'll never hear the end of it if you shut me down. But that's a risk I have to take. Because I love you, Jez. I think I loved you from the first moment I met you. I love your snark and your heat, your warmth and your sense of humor. You're everything to me. You're my soulmate."

She blinks, and though her eyes are watery, her face glows.

"I never thought I would say this again. I never thought I would want to. But Jezebel Stuart, I don't want to go another minute without knowing that you'll be my wife. Baby, will you marry me?"

My heart is pounding so hard I don't even hear her answer. But I do hear the applause and whistles. And when Jez pulls me to my feet—when she flings her arms around my neck and kisses me hard and deep—that's when I know her answer for sure.

It's yes.

And as I kiss her back, surrounded by our friends and family, I can't believe how lucky I am.

PRETTY LITTLE PLAYER

CHAPTER ONE

THERE ARE times in a man's life that can be counted among the best ever. First kiss. First fuck. First taste of caviar and fine champagne.

And the first time he meets the woman of his dreams.

When he sees her across a room, her eyes sparkling. When he holds her in his arms on the dance floor, his thumb brushing the bare skin of her back, revealed by her low-cut dress. When he gets lost inside her the first time they make love.

When she says, "I do."

That should be it, right? The pinnacle of life. The cherry on a sundae.

If you stop the story right there, then it's all about the happy ending. That's where the movies always fade to the credits, right? Those sappy engagement ring commercials? The ads for flower delivery? Every syrupy romance novel?

They all end on the high note.

But turn the page, and guess what? That guy who won

the girl? He's not still singing a love song. On the contrary, he's completely fucked. But not in the literal sense.

Because in the real world, it's some pretentious grad student who's screwing his wife. And the guy wearing the ring—the guy sweating his ass off in fatigues in a foreign desert so his woman can sleep safe at night—that guy's nothing more than a cuckolded fool.

Too bitter?

Maybe. I don't know. Is there a limit to pain when you have a broken heart?

All I know is that I'm not alone. And the truth is, misery really doesn't love company.

But those pleasures in life I mentioned? A man's best moments? One of them is when he catches a cheating woman in the act and completely shuts her down. I ought to know. In my line of work, I've helped out a lot of guys with that particular problem. And I'm good at what I do.

Let's just say I'm highly motivated.

Payback's a bitch, after all.

CHAPTER TWO

THE INTERNET IS AN AMAZING THING.

Not even four hours since I took on my case—a cheating fiancée—and I already have a hefty amount of intel on the two-timing little bitch.

Excuse me—the suspected near-adulterer.

I know her name is Gracie Harmon, although to be fair I learned that fact from my client. She's twenty-nine years old and owns a small house in Travis Heights, although for the past few days, she's been living in the ultra-classy historic Driskill Hotel on Congress Avenue. Convenient, since my office is just across the street, but a bit odd. Her house is only a few miles away, after all, and as far as I can tell there are no renovations or pest treatments or other maintenance-related activities currently underway.

Suspicious? A bit. But maybe she's not camping out in a high-end love nest. Maybe the girl just likes to be pampered. Except I also know she hasn't arranged for the hotel masseuse, and the concierge hasn't booked her time at an off-site spa.

So that's one mystery.

But on the plus side, I know the online address for her Instagram, Facebook, and Twitter accounts. So, if she posts about the hotel, I've got a window. Although she doesn't seem to post much at all, and what she does stays far away from the personal. A bit odd in the share-everything-right-now world we live in, but not condemning.

I know that she makes a decent living as a model—according to her Instagram profile, she primarily models plus-size lingerie and swimsuits—and I know that she's stunning, with golden blond hair, hypnotic blue eyes, and the kind of curves a man appreciates. Granted, that's more a personal preference than a fact, but considering what she does for a living, I also know that my opinion is shared by any number of men.

Maybe that's why she cheats? The temptation is just too hard to resist when so many men see so much of her online?

To which, of course, my response would be "try harder," but in my experience, women often don't. And I have a lot of experience documenting cheating wives for their mostly angry and sometimes baffled husbands.

Usually, I limit myself to cases involving adultery. But once or twice I've been retained by a guy wanting to check out his girlfriend before he pops the question. In those cases, I always point out that the fact they're in my office is a sign that there are some trust issues, and that kneeling at her feet and offering a ring might not be the smartest move under the circumstances.

Most of the time, they take the advice. Occasionally,

they insist I poke my nose in where she really doesn't want it.

Today, I'm working for one of those insistent fellas.

His name is Thomas Peterman, and he's head-over-heels for our little Gracie. Has been for years, apparently. He told me they dated before, when she lived in Los Angeles, but that it ended when he found out that she'd hooked up with another man. He was heartbroken, but they recently crossed paths again in Austin, and now things are sunshine and roses and the tinkle of wedding bells.

Or he wants them to be.

He has concerns, especially since she left him once before. Now, he's afraid that not only does she bump up against a lot of men in her professional career, but that she's also bumping uglies with them. He saw her with another man having a drink at a local bar. Maybe a friend, maybe an innocent after-work thing, but he had a bad feeling. And considering their history, he thought he should trust his gut.

And so Mr. Thomas Peterman called Blackwell-Lyon Security, asked to speak with whoever could best handle a case of possible pre-marital infidelity, and our office manager, Kerrie, told him that yours truly, Cayden Lyon, was the man.

Which brings me back to Gracie. Because after a consult with Mr. Peterman and the delivery of our standard retainer, I'm now holed up in the dark, atmospheric bar of Austin's Driskill Hotel, sipping bourbon on a leather couch and pondering the enigmatic Gracie as she sits at the bar, chats up the bartender—with whom she looks quite cozy—and scrolls through emails on her phone.

This, however, is not a surveillance gig. Or, rather, not yet.

When we talked, I explained to Peterman that in cases like these—when the client is absolutely-sure-but-has-no-solid-proof—the best plan of attack is to get the proof he needs. Forty-eight hours minimum of surveillance. Video and still photography, interviews with shopkeepers and similar civilians to the extent the chats won't tip off the subject, and detailed reports of comings and goings. If possible, phone records and credit card statements are analyzed, though that's rarely possible in a pre-marital situation in such a limited time frame. And sometimes surprisingly difficult even when a couple is in the throes of matrimony.

You want to be cynical? Start diving into other people's marriages. You'd be surprised how much the parties in question don't know about each other. My naïveté was dispelled a long time ago. Trust me when I say that most illusions about the institution of marriage and the concept of fidelity disappear like smoke when you walk in on your naked wife with her feet in the air and another man's face between her legs.

But I digress.

As I explained during that initial call, at the end of the forty-eight hour surveillance period, the investigator—that would be me—and the client—that would be Peterman—would sit down and review the information together.

In my experience, if the subject is cheating, there are clues within those first few days. Then the client decides if he wants additional surveillance to better make his case in court. Or, in a pre-marital situation, to gird his loins for the inevitable cancelation of the wedding.

Usually that's the end of it. But sometimes the results suggest that the client's suspicions are wrong and that the subject is completely faithful. Maybe the client is simply paranoid. Or maybe the subject is doing something outwardly suspicious but actually innocuous. Like the time a client's wife was planning a massive tenth anniversary party. (And, I should note, she filed for divorce less than a week after learning that her husband had the temerity to question her faithfulness.)

In one of those maybe-she's-not situations, I always suggest that the client take a deep breath and take her on faith. I *suggest* it, but I don't necessarily *recommend* it. Because ten-year anniversary parties aside, my personal and professional experience suggests that where there is smoke, there's fire. And if you think she's fucking around on you, she probably is. Just one more pretty little player in a world full of cheaters and liars.

And in that situation, I suggest to the client that we move on to Plan B.

All of which is to explain what happened today. Because I ran through the Plan A process with Peterman. I explained why surveillance made sense. How it was tried and true, and that he'd walk away with real and valuable information. Only after that initial assessment was made, could we decide the next step.

He, however, wanted to jump straight to Plan B.

And while the client isn't necessarily always right, he's definitely the one with the checkbook. And so Plan B it is.

Which explains why I'm here in The Driskill Bar

drinking whiskey and watching a beautiful woman flirt with a bartender.

Not because I'm kicking back during Happy Hour. And not because I'm on the job doing a surveillance shift.

No, I'm drinking and watching because I'm working up a plan. Studying the subject—learning about my mark.

Because in my book the very best way to tell if a woman is the cheating type is to see her in action. And if you can't catch a few snaps of her with the boss or the pool boy, then the next best option is to seduce her yourself.

And that, my friends, is the plan for tonight.

CHAPTER THREE

GRACIE LEANS FORWARD, her elbow on the polished wood bar, as the bartender slides a fresh glass in front of her. A reddish-brown cocktail in a martini glass that I assume is a Manhattan. "So, was I right?" she asks, then props her chin on her fist as she waits for his answer, her ocean-blue eyes full of eager anticipation. I know this because I've abandoned my station on the couch. Now I'm few stools away on Gracie's left, and with the way the bar curves around, following the arc of a circle, that gives me a nice view of her exceptionally pretty face.

"All right, I admit it," the bartender says. "You were dead on. She told me it was the best date ever."

"I'm so psyched for you." Gracie's smile sets the dim room on fire, and as I watch her, I tap out a rhythm with my finger on the bar, mentally revising my earlier assessment. Apparently Gracie isn't getting cozy with the bartender after all. Or at least not the kind of cozy my Mr. Peterman would be interested in. But that doesn't mean she's not on the prowl.

"Need a refill?" the bartender, whose name tag says Jon, asks me. "Or a menu?"

He just freshened my drink and there's a menu within my reach. For a second I'm confused. Then I see my tapping finger and still it. "Sorry. I didn't mean that as a signal for you."

I notice that Gracie is looking curiously in my direction and realize I can shift this potentially awkward situation to my advantage. I lock my gaze onto Gracie as I conjure an enigmatic smile, just enough to highlight the small dimple that Kerrie used to tell my twin, Connor, looks sexy as hell. (For the record, at the time she was talking about *Connor's* dimple, but since we're identical twins, I feel more than justified in using that bit of intelligence.)

"I was thinking about something else entirely," I tell the bartender, still smiling. Still eyeing Gracie.

A hint of a grin struggles onto her lips, but then she looks quickly away, her cheeks blooming pink as she twirls a dark blond strand of hair around one finger.

Bingo.

I'm in.

When I returned from Afghanistan with my left eye blown out, a nasty scar memorializing the incident, and a black eye patch as my new fashion statement, I confess I felt pretty damn sorry for myself. It was Kerrie who kicked my ass and got me looking at reality again.

Kerrie's not only our office manager, she's also my best friend's little sister. And for a short while, she was sleeping with my brother, though they both swear they're just friends now, and insist that's all they'll ever be.

Whatever.

I'm hardly going to push them if they don't want to be pushed, especially knowing how much the fourteen year age difference bothered Connor. But Kerrie's an example of the female sex that I'm happy to put on a pedestal. She's got her quirks and foibles—and her typing is for shit—but I know without a doubt that she would never, *ever*, pull on Connor what Vivien pulled on me.

And in my book, that means a lot.

She is also damned insightful. Which is why it was Kerrie who realized—rightfully so—that my homecoming from the Middle East marked my increased amperage over my brother, at least in the context of attracting female attention.

"It's the patch," Kerrie announced at Happy Hour a few weeks after my return. "You and Connor are both so freaking hot already it's not even fair to mortal men like my brother—"

"Thanks a lot." Pierce, who never lacked for a woman in his bed, tossed a vodka-soaked olive at his little sister.

"Am I the only one who cares about propriety?" she complained, aiming an apologetic smile at the amused bartender.

"Hold on, Princess," Connor said. "You were about to spout some bullshit about how my lump of a brother is hotter than me? Not even possible."

"It's the patch." She shrugged. "Just is. Gives him that pirate attitude on top of the already crazy-awesome movie star looks. And do not even pretend like you two don't know what I'm talking about. You're hotties and you know it. But Cayden's a hottie on overdrive now. Because, you know, the whole fantasy of a pirate tossing her down and ravaging her."

Connor narrowed his eyes at her. "You're serious?"

She tilted her head to the side. "Tossing and ravaging in real life? Not so cool. Fantasy ravaging? I mean, I think pirate and I think Johnny Depp. So, yeah, I'll own up to that. And Cayden's new look gives him lots of fantasy potential. Sorry, Connor. You're just going to have to suck it up. Your brother wins this one."

Which was why, when Peterman pointedly stared at my patch and asked if I thought I was really up to the task of seducing the girl, I assured him that I was the best man for the job.

Considering the way Gracie's cheeks have turned pink from nothing more than my singular stare, I'm going to go out on a limb and say that I made a good call. And when she looks in my direction again, I lift my glass to her in a silent toast, then take a sip. She offers a flash of a smile before her eyes dart quickly away once more.

The couple seated between us downs the last of their drinks. The man, older with graying temples, signs the check to a room, then helps his companion off her stool. She's probably a little younger than him, but not by much. There are lines around her eyes and mouth that suggest a life filled with laughter. And the affection on his face as he gently takes her arm is so profound I find myself staring.

She wears a diamond infinity band. He wears a plain gold ring. I wonder how long they've been married. I have a sudden image of their life together. Mona and Ted. That's what I name them in my imagination, where they live their contented life with two kids and a collie on a tree-lined street where they still walk hand-in-hand at sunset.

I wonder if Ted's ever worried about finding Mona in bed with a co-worker, a friend, the handyman. Probably not—and that's a melancholy thought since it's both happy and sad. Happy because it gives me hope. Sad, because they're a rare specimen. Like a museum display. Something you *might* see in the wild, but probably never will.

I suppose that makes me the rare lucky witness.

I watch as they weave their way through the bar to the hotel lobby, his hand lightly on the small of her back, ostensibly to guide her, but also to make that connection.

That's what I never had with Vivien, of course. A connection.

Connections are another of those rare specimens. Something that lives in the pages of Kerrie's romance novels. Real life is a hell of a lot lonelier.

I draw a breath, then turn back to my drink. It's bourbon-flavored melted ice now, and I toss it back in one swallow, then signal for another. Normally, I nurse one drink for the whole evening when I'm on a job. Tonight, I feel the need for another hit of liquid courage. I'm not sure why, and it's a question I don't want to examine too closely. I don't get tongue-tied around women, and I don't get nervous tailing a subject. Maybe it was the couple. That happy, contented couple with the life I'd expected, but won't ever have.

Maybe I'm sick of chasing their antithesis.

Hell, maybe I'm just a little sad that Gracie, with her brilliant smile and sweet manner, is a Vivien and not a Mona.

Maybe I'm regretting taking this job.

"So what was it?"

It takes me a second to realize that it's Gracie asking the question, and I look up to find that not only has the bartender put a fresh drink in front of me, but Gracie is smiling at me, her head tilted just slightly. Flirtatiously.

Right. Okay.

I'm back in business.

"What was what?" I ask.

"When I was talking to Jon and you were tapping your finger. You seemed so intent. I was just wondering what you were thinking."

Intent. Considering I'd been staring pointedly at her, that one little word is just oozing with meaning. If I were here looking to get laid, I'd be thrilled. Since I'm actually here searching for infidelity, I should be satisfied that the job's on track.

Instead I feel numb, unable to shake that lingering ennui.

I take a long swallow of my drink—the alcoholic equivalent of kicking my own ass—then move over, taking the seat next to her that Ted recently vacated. "I was curious about what he said," I tell her, indicating Jon with a lift of my chin. "That whatever you'd suggested had turned into the best date ever." I stroke my finger lightly along the rim of my glass as I focus on her lips. "I figure that's the kind of information a man should have. Will you share?"

There's a sectioned tray of bar snacks in front of her, and as I ask the question, I take a handful of salted nuts. I pop them in my mouth, then lick the salt off my fingers, my eyes never leaving her face. Everything entirely innocent. Everything completely flirtatious.

I see her throat move as she swallows and know that she's right there with me.

"Planning a hot date?" she asks, then lifts the tiny straw out of her Manhattan and sucks on the end. I notice that she's wearing no rings, engagement or otherwise.

"Always."

As I'd hoped, she laughs. "Well, then my suggestion may not be for you. It's more subtle. More..." She trails off with a shrug.

"Romantic?"

"Friendly," she says. "A getting to know you date."

"Getting to know you," I repeat, holding her eyes with mine. "I think I'd like that."

She turns her head away, her hand going up to cup the back of her neck as her shoulders rise. Her cheeks flush, and I see the reluctant smile on her lips. She looks entirely innocent—shy, even—and I marvel at the duplicitous potential of women.

After a moment, she readjusts, looking at me sideways as she takes a sip of her drink. "I suggested a shopping date," she tells me in an entirely matter-of-fact voice, as if I'd never flirted and she'd never reacted.

"A shopping date?"

"Shopping and cocktails," she clarifies. "There's this fabulous store on North Loop that has all sorts of cool vintage things. Oh, are you local? That's north of downtown, but not far. You just—"

"I'm local," I tell her. "I work across the street. This is one of my favorite places to grab a drink."

"So you know that area? Around North Loop, I mean."

"I've been there a couple of times."

"Lots of artsy small businesses," she says. "Eclectic stuff."

"And that's where you sent Jon?"

"Mmm-hmm. A place called Room Service. It's great for shopping, but it makes for a fun date. Lots of Art Deco. Kitsch. Clothes and dishes and furniture. Some books. Jewelry. A little bit of everything. The kind of stuff that can start a conversation."

I notice Jon watching us, but he doesn't chime in. For a second, I wonder if this is a standard pick-up routine for her. Describe a romantic date. Get close. Suggest a drink in her room...

It's possible. I'll just have to see how it plays out.

"You go there a lot, then?" I ask.

"Oh, yeah. All the time."

"On dates?"

She polishes off the last of her Manhattan as she shakes her head and makes a negative noise. "Not usually. I just like to browse. But what I suggested to Jon was that he take this girl he's interested in to the store, then they could wander down the street to this little bar that makes awesome cocktails. It's called Drink.Well. Ever been there?"

I shake my head, but make it a point to store the name away. I'm always looking for a good bar.

"You should." She lifts a shoulder. "Anyway, I guess it was good advice." She nods toward the bartender, who's at the far end of the circle, out of earshot. "They went out last night after she got off work, and he says it went well." She leans toward me, then lowers her voice. "They're going out again tomorrow."

"Ah, the Friday night date," I say, also leaning in and talking low. "It must have gone well if they're moving on to the big guns."

"My first offer of dating advice," she says. "Clearly I have a knack."

"First? I would have guessed you were a guru."

"Hardly." She makes a scoffing sound as she lifts her hand. I look up to see that Jon has turned around and realize that she's signaling for the check. *Damn.* "What's that saying?" she continues, her brow furrowing. "Those that can't do, teach?"

"I don't believe that for a minute." I keep my voice charming while I'm mentally cursing. Because we aren't nearly far enough along in the flirting and drinking part of the evening.

"Heading up?" Jon says, sliding her a folio, which she opens, then reaches for the pen.

I bite back a frustrated grimace. If I'm going to get any proof for Peterman, I'm going to have to kick it up. I put my hand over the tab. "Let me."

"Oh, I really couldn't."

"It would be my pleasure." I wave to Jon, who nods.

For a moment, Gracie hesitates. Then she says, very politely and simply, "Well, thank you. That's very kind. I'm Gracie, by the way."

"Cayden. Can I walk you out? Are you parked around here?"

"Actually, I'm staying at the hotel."

"Oh." I feign surprise. "With all your talk about that vintage store, I assumed you were a local."

"I am," she says. "I'm just—" She shakes her head as she clears her throat and a blond curl bounces free from where it was tucked behind her ear. I start to reach for it—imagining the silky strands against my fingers—and have to forcibly will my hand to stay where it is.

"I'm just staying here while some work is being done on my place," she finishes, pushing the enticing strand away. "Turns out they had to turn off the water and the electricity for a few days."

"Ah." I force myself to stop imagining her hair against my skin and wrangle my thoughts into some semblance of order. "And your boyfriend? Husband? Fiancé? Did you pick The Driskill so you could turn an unexpected stay into a romantic getaway?"

The blush that had faded blooms again. "Ah, no. Sadly, I'm fresh out of boyfriends, husbands, and fiancés. I just picked The Driskill because it's my favorite hotel in the city."

"Mine, too," I say.

She flashes that sweet smile, and I have to remind myself that this is a job and not a social event.

"It's supposed to be haunted," I add.

"So they say."

"Seen any ghosts on your floor?"

"Not a single one."

"I'm surprised. I would have thought all the ghosts would gather around, just to get a good look at you."

She laughs as she slips off the stool. "If that's a line, it's not a very good one."

I stand as well. "I've had two bourbons, cut me some slack."

"Well, A for effort, then. And it really was nice talking to you. I should say good night."

I should say good night. Magic words, those. It means she *should* but she can be persuaded otherwise. Which, of course, is what I'm here for. "In that case, I should probably see you to your room. Just in case."

"In case?"

"Ghosts," I say, then offer her my arm.

She hesitates, and I wonder if I'm going to have to move up to DefCon 1. But then she slips her arm through mine, and we walk together to the elevator. "Four," she says when we're inside, and as the elevator rises she continues to hold on, and for a moment—just a moment—I actually wish this were real.

But it's not, and it shouldn't be, and I don't need to be wallowing in sentimentality. I'm on the job. And even if I weren't, I'm not looking for any sort of attachment. I'm not setting myself up to get hurt again. And this woman is my subject, which makes her off limits, anyway.

She's not in my life. She's only on my arm. Although, of course, I'm going to try for more. Not that I'll actually sleep with her—there are ethical considerations, after all. But deep, hot kisses? Lingering caresses? A bit of bared, intimate skin? That's not only expected, but arguably required. After all, I have to be able to go back to Peterman with proof.

Usually, that aspect of the job gives me no pause at all. With Gracie...

Well, I can't deny that I want to feel her bare skin under my fingers.

And at the same time, I really don't want her to be the kind of woman who'll let me.

"Cayden? Hey, have I lost you?"

Her voice breaks through my roiling thoughts. "Sorry, what?"

"This is my stop."

"Right," I say as we step out into the alcove. "Sorry. I was thinking about—well, about you, actually."

"Oh." Her smile is tentative, but she seems genuinely pleased. "Um, I can probably get to my room from here. I think the ghouls will leave me alone."

"Nonsense. I provide full-service protection from spooks." My eyes never leave hers.

"Oh." The word is barely an exhalation of breath. "Well, that's very chivalrous of you."

"I promise. I'll do whatever it takes."

"Uh-huh." She glances down, and when her teeth drag over her lower lip, it's my turn to swallow.

"Gracie?"

She looks up, her eyes wide and full of anticipation. And I know right then that this is going to be a cake walk. And that I should be happy about that. Easy money, right? A job well done.

"Cayden?"

"I—I need to know what room you're in."

"Oh. Four-twenty. It's that way," she says, pointing vaguely to the right.

I take her hand and twine our fingers. Her skin is soft, and she holds on as if she trusts me. We walk to the room, and a wave of regret washes over me when we reach the door and she fumbles in her purse for her key.

She looks at me, then at the door. Then she licks her lips and looks down at the carpet before lifting her head and meeting my eyes to invite me inside.

"I'm sorry," she says, and I actually have to rewind her words to make sure I heard her right. "I'm sorry," she repeats, still holding the card.

"Sorry?"

"I—I was going to see if you wanted to come in for—um, you know. To talk. And whatever. But—but I just don't think it's a good idea?"

"No? Sounds like one of the best ideas I've heard in a long time."

She laughs, and the sound squeezes my chest.

"I know—it's only—well, you seem really nice, and I've enjoyed talking to you but..."

I step closer as she trails off, taking advantage of this sign of uncertainty. "Are you sure? I promise I don't bite too hard."

As I'd hoped, she laughs. But then she shakes her head. "I don't know." She taps the side of her eye and grins. "I've heard about you pirates."

I match her grin, surprised and grateful that she acknowledged—even joked—about something that most girls would just politely not mention, even after a wild night in bed.

Her shoulders rise and fall. "Listen, I'm sorry if I—I mean, if you came up here expecting something more."

"More than spending a few extra minutes with you? Believe me, you have nothing to apologize for." I take her hand, then lift it to my mouth and press a gentle kiss to her fingertips. "Say goodnight, Gracie," I say, and she laughs.

"Goodnight, Gracie," she says. "And thanks."

I nod, then turn and head back to the elevator. And though I never would have expected it, I'm actually relieved to be walking away with absolutely no proof whatsoever that Gracie Harmon is cheating on my client.

CHAPTER FOUR

I DON'T USUALLY FEEL at loose ends during a job, but I do tonight. And I'm honestly not sure if that's because I don't have any crystal clear information for Peterman or because I'm legitimately disappointed that Gracie didn't invite me into her room.

Since I have a sneaking suspicion it's the latter, I decide not to think about it. And since the best way not to think is to grab another drink, that's what I do.

An hour later, it's almost ten, I've finished nursing a bourbon, and I've cleared out all the emails on my phone. Absent another brilliant idea to pass the time, I'm about to summon an Uber, head south, then settle in on my couch with the latest *Fast and Furious* movie before giving in and crashing for the night.

I get as far as the hotel lobby before I change my mind. That's when I remember that one of my favorite bands, Seven Percent, is doing a surprise performance at The Fix on Sixth, a local bar and eatery. A surprise because the Austin-based band has become huge over the last few years and an official announcement would draw more people than the place could hold. But their lead singer, Ares, wanted to swing back through town to visit a friend, and so the band decided to do one gig at the bar that gave them their start.

All of which I know only because Pierce, Connor, and I pop into The Fix frequently enough to be considered regulars, and the owner, Tyree, has become a friend.

Now, I head out through The Driskill's main doors on Brazos, then turn left onto Sixth Street. I walk the few blocks until I'm across the street from The Fix, cross against the light, and hurry to the door. Even without an official announcement, the place is packed. I see Tyree in the back, but he's busy and doesn't see me. The bartender, Eric, gives me a shout-out, but since there are no open seats at the bar, I only wave in response as I try to scope out a table.

The band is already on the stage setting up and I'm cursing myself for waiting so long. There's no place to sit, and I'm really not in the mood to stand in the crush that will surely gather right in front of the raised stage that fills the front of the bar.

"Cayden!"

At first, I'm not even sure I've heard my name; the din is so intense it might just be my imagination. But I turn anyway, looking for the source.

And that's when I see her—*Gracie*.

I have absolutely no idea what she's doing there, especially since I saw her to her room over an hour ago. But there she is, like a gorgeous guardian angel, watching over me and offering me the empty seat at her small table.

I make my way that direction, telling myself that my

increasingly good mood is because I don't have to stand during the performance. And that I have a second bite at my investigative answer.

The real reason, of course, is that I'm happy to see her. But I'm not going to think about that.

"Admit it," I say. "You're following me."

"I think that's my line," she counters. "What are you doing here?"

"I was about to head home, and then I remembered that Seven Percent was playing tonight. They're a favorite of mine."

"Mine, too," she says. "But how did you know?"

I swivel in my chair, then point toward Tyree. "Friends with the owner. You didn't know? Why are you here?" Had she ditched me so she could go out and find someone else to cozy up to? The idea leaves a bad taste in my mouth, and I quickly dismiss it. After all, she'd been sitting here alone.

"I ordered room service," she says. "French fries and coffee. And I started talking to the waiter. He's bummed about working tonight and missing the show." She takes a sip of her beer. "I feel no guilt, but if I see him tomorrow, I won't rub it in. It'll be hard, though. I'm a total groupie. I saw them a couple of years ago when they opened for Next Levyl."

"Lucky you," I say. "I missed that one. Although I've met him, you know. Levyl, I mean."

Her eyes widen and she sits back. "You are totally yanking my chain."

"Nope, I swear. He's a friend of a friend." Technically, he's the ex-boyfriend of Pierce's sister-in-law, movie star Delilah Stuart, but I don't mention that part.

"I try not to be a huge celebrity watcher," she says, "but it really irritated me the way Delilah dumped him for Garreth Todd."

I should let it go. I know that. But Del's a sweet girl, and I just can't stay quiet. "They're friends, you know. And in her defense, Garreth seduced her."

She stares at me, her eyes narrowed as she props her chin on her fist. "She's the friend. The one you just mentioned. You're friends with Delilah Stuart."

"That's not something I usually advertise," I tell her honestly. But there's something about this woman that has my brain working at only half-power. I feel charmed. Bewitched. And if it weren't for the fact that she's a subject and Peterman is paying me, that wouldn't be a bad feeling at all.

Under the circumstances, it's more than a little inconvenient.

I'm saved from thinking any more about it when Reece, one of Tyree's partners, climbs on stage, grabs the mike, and introduces the band. Within minutes, the room's hopping, and the music is far too loud for conversation.

And after a few songs and a few Loaded Coronas—a specialty of The Fix that consists of a Corona with the neck filled with rum—I'm feeling pretty good. So much so that when Gracie leans over and shoulder bumps me, whisper-yelling that the song they're playing is her absolute favorite, I don't even think about the fact that my job tonight was to try and seduce her. I'm just having a good time.

In the course of the show, we polish off two Loaded Coronas each, and by the time the band makes its final encore, I'm pretty sure I'll never hear out of my right ear again—it was too close to Gracie's squeals.

"Sorry about that," she teases. "Right ear, left eye. I figured you needed some sort of symmetry."

"Sorry, I can't hear you," I say dryly. "I seem to be deaf in that ear."

She rolls her eyes, then smiles at me. "I'm glad I bumped into you. This was fun."

"Agreed."

"And don't worry. I won't bug you or mention the Delilah-Levyl thing to anyone. Believe me, I know what it's like to be talked about all over the Internet. A much smaller scale, granted, but still."

"Do you? How?"

I know the answer, of course. But since I'm not supposed to know she's a model with a decent following on social media, I have to play ignorant.

She wrinkles her nose. "You know what? I have drunk *way* too much. I shouldn't have said anything. Can we just rewind and pretend I didn't run off at the mouth?"

"That depends. Are we negotiating?"

Her brows rise. "Are we?"

"Have another drink with me, and I'll forget whatever you want me to forget." I cup her chin and hold her head still so that I'm looking deep into her eyes. Ocean eyes. The kind I could float away in. And, yeah, I think I'm a little wasted, too.

I give myself a mental shake, freeing myself from that sensual, hypnotic gaze. "If that's what you want," I continue, "we can even forget tonight. We can just push it into its own little safe space, where anything can happen because there are no memories, no reminders. No souvenirs. Just tonight, and then nothing but fairy dust scattered on the wind."

Her lips part, and I see her swallow. I'm still holding her chin, and I can feel the pulse in her neck, the increased tempo. There's desire here; I feel it, too. I want her to say yes—I want to taste those lips—and at the same time I'm silently begging her to say no.

She sits back, and I reluctantly release her chin. "I—I think I've already had too much to drink," she says. "The way you describe it, that little island sounds almost appealing."

"What's not appealing about a secret?" I ask, because that's the role I'm here to play, and at the end of the day, I'm going to do my job even if sometimes I hate the things I find out. "Something just between you and me? Something nobody else will ever know?"

She picks at the label on her Corona. "Nobody forgets on command."

"Who said anything about command?" I say, this time trying a teasing tone. I take the bottle from her and hold it up. "These babies will handle the forgetting for us."

She laughs, and it's one of the best sounds ever. "You might actually be right about that. And ... well, I'll admit it's tempting. But I should go. I have a job booked tomorrow and I need my beauty sleep."

"I doubt that," I say. "I think you'd look beautiful even with no sleep at all." It's more bait, of course, but the truth is I'd love to test the theory. Love to see how she looks with her face free of make-up and her hair tousled from sleep. Or from not sleeping, for that matter.

"You're sweet," she says, though of course I'm really, really not. "But this time it really is good night."

"Blow to your ego, huh?" I wince as Peterman's deep voice booms out through the speakerphone. I'm sprawled on my office couch, a cold-pack I'd grabbed from the First Aid kit over my eyes. I've got the mother of all hangovers—apparently bourbon, beer, and rum do not a happy combination make—and right now all I really want to do is beg my client to whisper.

"I tell you I think she's cheating on me," he continues, his voice like a mallet on my brain, "and you figured she'd jump right into the sack with you. Sorry, my man. Give the girl some credit."

I wince. It's barely eight in the morning, and I'm only in the office now because we have a status meeting at nine, and Peterman wanted an early morning update before he goes into depositions. I know it's not his fault, but I'm in a foul mood, having stayed out far too late and imbibed far too much with the girl to whom I'm apparently not giving enough credit.

"Look," I say. "I'm giving her credit for not picking up an interested guy in a bar. It's a report, not a wrap-up. And my ego isn't part of the equation. I hit on her pretty hard last night," I tell him. "Even walked her to her door. I made it more than clear that I'd scratch any itch she might have. I got nada."

He makes a disbelieving noise. I haven't met the man yet, but I looked him up online. He's a big guy, probably wrestled in high school. He's a lawyer with one of the bigger firms in town. The kind with a small army of fungible law grads, some of whom love the law and aspire to become Johnny Cochran or the next attorney general, but most of whom just want the respectable paycheck.

Based on the limited amount of information I found doing a quick search, I'm thinking that Peterman falls into the latter category. As far as I can tell, he's the kind of lawyer who spends a lot of time reviewing documents and handling the kind of depositions that have to be done, but aren't going to make-or-break a case.

Normally, I don't sign clients sight-unseen without a referral, but he'd been frantic when he called. Said he'd been on his way to the airport for depositions in Dallas. He'd had to go back to the office, and that's when he saw Gracie with another man. That was two days ago, and it's been eating on him. Especially when he learned from a mutual friend that she was holed up at The Driskill.

What can I say? I sympathized with the guy. And since he didn't want the full-on surveillance right away, I agreed to the Plan B seduction attempt, telling him we'd regroup once he got back in town. Which, as it happens, will be tomorrow, and we've got a ten o'clock meeting on the books.

Meanwhile, he signed the retainer agreement, used a Visa gift card to pay our invoice, something a lot of our investigatory clients do to avoid a paper trail, and forwarded all the pertinent details about Gracie from his personal gmail account—his name, followed by a string of numbers that probably meant something to him. Like the address of the house he grew up in.

Like most clients, he asked that I not contact him at

work, and that's fine. But I did have Kerrie call and ask to speak to him, just as a gut check. His secretary explained that he was in depositions in Dallas, but offered to leave a message. Kerrie told her not to bother, then reported to me that Peterman's story checked out.

"Look," I say now. "She's at a hotel because of the work on her house. And the man you saw her with could just be a friend or a colleague. She seems like a nice girl, and she didn't take the bait. Maybe you don't need me. Maybe you just need to take her out to a nice dinner and have a long talk."

I honestly can't believe I'm saying that. Me, the guy who never discounts a potential cuckold's suspicions of infidelity. But I'm just not feeling it here.

"No. No way. I know what I saw, and I saw my girl on a date."

Who am I to argue with a man scorned? "Fair enough. Let's start surveillance. We can go over the details tomorrow after we meet."

"Wait a sec, back up. She chatted you up, right? Made you think you might get lucky?"

I can't deny it.

"Well, there you go," he says. "And I bet she never once told you she had a boyfriend, much less a fiancé."

Once again, I have to agree. "She wasn't wearing a ring, either."

"That's on me. I'm giving her my grannie's ring, and it's still with the jeweler being sized and cleaned."

"All right. At least we know she's not taking it off and hiding it in her purse every time she goes to a bar."

"Look," he says. "I told you that I think my Gracie's

cheating on me. I didn't say she was a slut. You flirted with her in a bar, but that's not going anywhere. My girl has more class than that."

If he's so certain that Gracie's meeting other men and going out on secret dates while he travels, then I have to debate that whole class thing. Still, I understand his fear.

Frankly, it probably would have been easier on me if Vivien had given in to one afternoon of passion with some anonymous guy she picked up in a bar. But that's not what happened. I'd caught her in bed with her teaching assistant. A guy with whom she discussed the recurring themes in Dumas' novels while sipping red wine and outlining the next week's lectures. They'd had a "thing," she told me later. A connection.

Damn right there'd been a connection, and it wasn't the kind I'd seen with Ted and Mona. No, Vivien had connected to her grad student in a decidedly X-rated kind of way. And I'd had the distinct displeasure of witnessing that connection with my own two eyes.

"Fair enough," I say. "She has to leave the hotel. I'll catch her in a restaurant, a bookstore. Maybe a vintage thrift store."

"Right," he says. "She likes that vintage junk."

I frown, but shake it off. "Point being, I'll find a way to start up a conversation today, do some flirting."

"Right. Okay. She's got a photo shoot," he says. "All day today. It's a whatchacalit. A stock photo shoot."

"Do you know where?"

"Of course. It's at the agency she works with. Moreno-Franklin. Over in East Austin. One of those revitalized artsy areas."

"I'll find it," I say. "And I'll either figure a way in or I'll figure something else out. Either way, I'll give you a full report tomorrow." I pull out my phone and check my calendar. "Ten o'clock. My office. That still work for you?"

"I'll be there." I hear his deep sigh. "It's a pisser of a situation. On the one hand, I want her to jump all over you, because then I'll know I was right. On the other, she's my sweet Gracie. And I want so badly to be wrong."

I just nod, even though he can't see me. Because the truth is, even after only knowing Gracie for a few hours, I feel exactly the same way.

CHAPTER FIVE

"THAT WRAPS UP OLD BUSINESS," I say, looking around the conference table at my partners, Connor and Pierce, and then at Kerrie. She may be our office manager, but I run our Friday morning meetings since I do most of our business development.

Security is a strange bird in the corporate world. Most businesses wouldn't want a guy with an eye patch as the face of their organization. But as Kerrie says, it makes me look like a badass. Gives me that edgy air. Makes people feel like I understand the world. The dangers. And that I—and therefore, my people—are willing to do whatever it takes to get the job done.

That's me, a walking advertisement for Blackwell-Lyon Security, a top-notch, high-end security firm that Connor, Pierce and I started less than two years ago. And we've worked our collective tails off twenty-four/seven to build a solid reputation as a full-service resource. Everything from setting up alarm and monitoring systems to on-site protection for politicians, movie stars, executives. Basically anyone who fears for their safety. Or who wants to make a show of looking like they fear for their safety.

Not that I'm cynical, but I've seen more than one politician's street cred climb when they do a couple of town meetings with very visible security. Ditto up-and-coming rappers and wanna-be teen idols.

Lately, we've started working only half-days on Saturday and taking Sundays off, except when we're on assignment. And now that Pierce has gone and tied the knot, he tends to cut out by six to get home to Jez unless we're on an active detail.

His wife, Jezebel, is one of a kind, and I'm genuinely happy for them. No worries at all that he'll walk in and find her connected to some other man someday. But I confess I was a little bit leery at first. Both for Pierce's personal life, and for the future of our business. But she understands how much the company means to him—to all of us. He works at home when he needs to and, honestly, I think he's getting more done now during the day so that he can head home guilt free at night. Makes for less time shooting the shit in the break room, but I can't fault a guy for that.

I get up and refill my mug with what has turned out to be a never-ending flow of coffee this morning. It's dulled the hangover down to a mild thud that throbs in time with my heartbeat. I tell myself to count my blessings. My head might be pounding, but at least I know I'm alive.

"New business," I say, eyeing Pierce.

"Just finalized the job we talked about last week. The concert in the park. Two weeks from now, Thursday through Saturday."

"Team?" We have a group of vetted freelancers, most of whom the three of us know from our days in the military.

"The usual suspects," Pierce says, running his fingers through his dark blond hair. "I'm getting everyone together for a dry run next Wednesday. We're good."

"And they've already paid the retainer," Kerrie says. "Our bank account is feeling very happy."

"Gotta love celebrities," Connor adds. "And politicians."

"Something to report?" I ask my brother, and he launches in with the news about a Texas senator looking to change her security detail. "That incident in Temple," he says. "Jenson Security really dropped the ball. I'm working on a proposal. I think we have a shot at landing the gig. Her team's coming in next week for a meeting."

"Good work," I say as Kerrie squeals, then leans over as if to give him a hug. She stops herself and backs away, staring down at her hands, her face turning bright red.

I clear my throat. "Kerrie, how about the ad? Any more responses?"

We started running two ads recently. The first in a trade magazine. That one's intended both as a business draw—we're hoping high level managers will see the ad and think about us when they're looking for security for their corporate, political, and celebrity clients—and as a way to simply get our name out there to the industry players.

The second ad is in a local Austin weekly. Its purpose is to advertise our lower-end services such as security installation, short-term protection during contentious custody disputes, that kind of thing.

And, according to Kerrie, both ads have generated calls.

She takes us over the details, and when she wraps, I check the clock. "Okay, folks. I think that's enough for today. Kerrie, can I borrow you for—"

"Um, not quite," she says innocently. "Don't you have new business?"

Shit.

"Nothing we need to bother with."

Pierce and Connor exchange glances. "Give," my brother says.

"Cayden's playing PI again," Kerrie says with a sideways smirk toward me.

"What? You're *tattling* on me? Are we in junior high?"

She stares down her nose at me.

"Fine." I hold my hands up in surrender. "It's just the one case."

"Seriously, Cayden?" Pierce says. "We all agreed. Or did you forget that part?"

"It's just a quick investigation. A cheating fiancée."

"Oh, there's a big surprise," Connor says.

I shoot him a hard glance. "I can't leave the guy hanging. Plus, he contacted us because of the ad. What's the point of advertising if you turn away customers?"

When we'd first formed our company, we'd decided on the name Blackwell-Lyon Security—and not Blackwell-Lyon Security & Investigations—specifically because we'd decided to play to our strengths. And even though I have a dusty PI license that occasionally comes in handy on the security side of things, we developed symbiotic relationships with investigators in town, with whom we refer work back and forth.

Early on, though, when money was tight, we took a few

PI cases that fell across the line. But as things picked up, we made the specific decision to play to our strengths and focus on security.

Fair enough. But while our name in the ad is correct, there's a small mention of investigative work in the body of the text. It was meant to be in the context of security services—investigating who a shooter is, for example—but can I help it how that language is interpreted by the general reader?

"The woman could be stringing him along," I say. "He's convinced she's got a guy or two on the side. I'm doing some more poking around today, then meeting with him tomorrow. I've got the time, my caseload is clear right now. And this guy needs someone on his side who understands."

"Plus, if she is cheating, it justifies Cayden's warped view of the world and relationships," Kerrie says, her smile at odds with the dripping sarcasm in her voice.

"I don't have any illusions about the world," I say. "The world I live in is the world I see. Not some Kumbaya singing, soft-focus view of reality."

"Fine," Connor says with a glance toward Pierce. "Say yes before he gets off on a tirade and we lose a whole day of work."

"Fine," Pierce echoes. "But this is the last."

"Done," I say, then nod toward Kerrie. "Now I'm just going to need to borrow her for today..."

CHAPTER SIX

"A MODEL?" Kerrie says as we cruise down Springdale Road toward the agency. "You want me to pretend to be a model?"

"Why not?" I brake at a red light, then turn and give her the once over. Thin and curvy. Pouty lips. Honey-blond hair. "I hate to break it to you, kid, but you're a looker."

"You are a crazy person. I take terrible photos and the idea of people staring at me like that makes me nuts."

"Then it's a good thing you're only pretending to be a model. And a wanna-be. You don't have to fake experience."

She opens her mouth, huffs a bit, then closes it as she leans back into her seat. "Just in case you were at all unclear on the point, I want to reiterate that you are entirely insane."

"Insane. Check. Got it."

She rolls her eyes and crosses her arms, and I drive on

in peace until she says, "You know, if you're so hyped up to go out with a girl, why not just ask one out?"

I shoot her a sideways glance. "We should be pretending you're a comedian, not a model."

"Just calling them like I see them. It's been five years, you know. Five years, and you never date."

"Eighteen months of that was in the Middle East after I walked in on Viv and found—"

"I know. Heard the story. Move along."

"Three months after I was still recovering and getting used to having absolutely no depth perception whatsoever."

"A fair point, but—"

"Then slogging my way through a dead end job at SecureTech—and those were some crazy hours. Then putting Blackwell-Lyon together. And in case you hadn't noticed, building a business is hard work."

"And yet Pierce managed to find time to get married."

I grimace. I knew she'd throw that back at me.

"You don't even date," she adds, as if that's an indictment on my character. And it isn't true, anyway.

"I do. I've gone out half a dozen times in the last year."

"Drinks with some random woman you never call again doesn't constitute a date. And if you're counting the drink with Gracie last night it definitely doesn't count."

"That—*this*—is work."

"Of course it is. Because work's the only way you see women. The only safe way," she adds with a disgusted little shake of her head.

"Damn right," I say. "I've seen what lies at the end of the path, remember?"

"One woman, and you paint the world that way. It's narrow-minded and stupid."

"Believe me, I've seen a lot more than one woman. Vivien was hardly a solitary example."

"That's because you picked that profession. The world probably looks like it's full of criminals if you're a prison warden."

I just scowl.

"It's bullshit," Kerrie continues. "I mean, honestly. You think that little of Jez?"

"No, of course—"

"Of me?"

"You?" I shoot her a sideways glance. "Who are you in a relationship with?"

She makes a face. "No one. But when I was ... what? Were you going to warn Connor away? Tell him I was a cheating slut?"

"Connor warned himself away," I mutter. "And not because anyone thought you'd cheat. And for the record, my brother was an idiot for cutting you loose."

She lifts her brows. "Are you flirting with me?"

"Most definitely, no. But Connor is an idiot."

She grins. "Not arguing. But are you seeing my point? Have I gotten through at all?"

"I don't need an intervention, Kerrie."

"I beg to differ. I mean, even your client—Peterman?—at least he's trying to have a relationship. All you do is run away. No, scratch that. You don't even start the race."

"I already ran that marathon."

"Bullshit. You entered a sprint, and you tripped over a shoelace."

I turn into the parking lot of the steel and wood building deep in East Austin that is the headquarters of the Moreno-Franklin Talent Agency. "That is probably the worst analogy ever."

"Well, I'm making this up as I go." She groans as I slide into a parking space. "Honestly, Cay. You fought in freaking Afghanistan and survived. You lost an eye, and you survived. But can't pull yourself up and actually have a relationship? I never realized you were such a pussy."

"You know the only reason I put up with you is that you're Pierce's little sister?"

She tilts her head and looks down her nose at me. "At least you have a reason. I don't have a clue why I put up with you."

I kill the engine, then turn in my seat. "We're here."

"Yippee," she says, in the same voice she might use when cleaning out a drain trap.

"Truce?"

"You really think she's cheating on him?"

It takes me a second to downshift back to Peterman and Gracie. I don't know. Considering I like her, I hope not. But since he's planning to marry her, I think he has a right to know, and he's paying for me to help him find out."

She blows out a breath, then opens her door. "Okay. Let's go undercover. At least it's better than answering the phones."

As we head down the bamboo and succulent-lined sidewalk toward the entrance, Kerrie pauses, then asks, "You do know that the odds of seeing her are slim, right? If she's here doing a photo shoot, she's going to be busy."

"Trust me. I've got this."

"Well, now I'm nervous," she says, then smirks as she pulls open the door and steps in ahead of me.

The place is ultra-modern, with a Lucite reception desk that is probably some ridiculously expensive designer piece, but I think is just outright ugly. The girl behind it is pretty, though, as befits a modeling agency.

"Cayden Lyon and Kerrie Blackwell. We have an appointment to see Cecilia Moreno."

"Of course. She's in the studio. I'll just let her know you're here."

"Thanks," I say, leading Kerrie to the waiting area.

"We have an appointment with one of the owners?"

"You want full access, you go to the top. And without full access, I wasn't sure I'd get to see Gracie."

"But—"

"Friend of a friend," I say. "Those half-dozen women I had the singular drink with? I don't just toss them aside. We're still friends. And it's all about connections, right?"

"Show off."

I laugh and am about to sit down when an absolutely stunning woman who looks to be in her early sixties glides into the room, exuding glamour and charm. "You must be Cayden," she says. "And you're the young woman who's interested in modeling?"

"Yes, ma'am," Kerrie says, standing.

"Please, call me Cecilia. Why don't you come with me to my office? I'm happy to answer any questions you might have."

"Um, sure," Kerrie says.

I take a step forward. "We heard you were doing a

photo shoot of some sort. I thought that might be interesting for Kerrie to see."

Cecilia's perfectly plucked brows rise. "Did you? Or did you just want to see the girls in lingerie and swim wear?"

"Well, that too," I say, and thankfully she laughs.

"Of course. We'll go, you'll both look, and then you can stay and keep yourself entertained while Kerrie and I discuss the business."

"Sounds good to me," I say, then fall in step behind them, congratulating myself on how smoothly this is going. She leads the way into a separate building behind the first which is set up as a large photo studio, with well-lit areas, changing stations, and lots and lots of beautiful girls in all shapes and sizes.

I'm gawking—and trying to find Gracie—when I hear her familiar voice saying, "*You?*"

I turn to find her gaping at me, a ratty blue terrycloth robe pulled tight around her. Even tighter since she's holding the neck closed with such an intense grip her knuckles are white. "Gracie?" I say, trying to sound surprised.

"What the hell are you doing here? Are you following me? Because I swear to God—"

"Is there a problem?" Cecilia's firm hand lands on my shoulder, and I watch as Gracie's eyes go wide. "Gracie, dear, what's the matter?"

"Ms. Moreno. I'm sorry. I—I thought…" She shakes her head. "Never mind."

"Mmm." Cecilia smiles pleasantly, then tells me that she's going to show Kerrie around, and do I want to join them?

I glance at Kerrie, see that she seems to be handling herself just fine, then shake my head. "No, no, I'm fine. You go ahead. I know you want to talk shop."

Cecilia looks between me and Gracie, apparently decides we won't kill each other, and takes off with Kerrie.

"I am so sorry," Gracie says, the second they're out of earshot. "I saw you here, and I thought you were—"

"Who?"

She shakes her head, as if shaking away the thought. "Nothing. Never mind."

"No," I say firmly. "When you said *you* to me, you obviously weren't thinking, *Oh, it's you, that incredibly hot guy from The Driskill and The Fix.*"

She laughs. "No, that really doesn't sound like me."

"Didn't think so. Which is why I'll ask again. What were you thinking? Or who were you thinking of?"

Her fingers twist the sash on her robe. "What are you doing here?"

"My, ah, niece is interested in modeling, and Cecilia is a friend of a friend. She heard about the shoot and wanted to get a behind the scenes look, so I arranged a drop-in."

"Oh. That was nice of you." Her smile is quick but genuine. "But, we've got to stop meeting like this."

"I know. It's really embarrassing the way you're following me around."

She laughs. "I can be a huge pest."

"I'm guessing you're a model. Either that or you're part of the crew and forgot to get dressed today."

"Model," she confirms.

"What you said yesterday about being harassed on the internet..."

"Oh. Yeah. I post pictures. On social media, I mean. No personal stuff—not ever. But part of the modeling gig is selling yourself. Most people are nice. But some are crude. And some are just plain creepy."

"So just now? You thought I was, what? One of the creepy ones?"

"Actually, yeah."

I nod, taking that in. "That really must suck. Sorry to have freaked you out."

"No, I'm sorry I jumped to conclusions."

"Perfectly understandable." I feel the sharp twinge of guilt, since the conclusions she jumped to weren't all that far from the truth. I'm not harassing her on the internet, but I am following her. "Can I make it up to you?"

"You seem like a reasonably intelligent man with at least some imagination. I'm going to go out on a limb and say yes."

"Well, it's not very imaginative, but how about dinner?"

"Oh." She narrows her eyes as she looks at me. "You're right. That's not very imaginative."

"I can't reveal all my tricks. You have to say yes to see what's in store."

Her smile is like sunshine. "Well, I guess that's fair. Yes."

"How's seven?"

"Tonight?" Her eyes are wide.

"You're planning on not eating tonight?"

"No. I mean yes. Yes, I'm eating." Her eyes crinkle in what looks like confusion, then her face clears. "Yes, I'm eating. And you know what? Why not? Seven it is. Where should we meet?"

"Are you still at The Driskill? I can come by and pick you up."

"Door to door service? Fancy."

We smile at each other like idiots, and it actually feels nice.

"Yo! Gracie! You're up."

"Oh!" She jumps, then shoots me an apologetic grimace. "Tonight," she says, then sprints across the room.

I watch her go, paying particular attention when she takes off the robe and tosses it over a director's chair, leaving her standing there, curvaceous and lovely, in a red corset, a matching garter belt, and sheer black stockings.

She looks good enough to eat.

And what do you know? I'm the guy who's taking her to dinner.

CHAPTER SEVEN

THE EVENING IS GOING WELL. Magically, even. If it weren't for the lies and deception floating like sewage under our feet, I'd even go out on a limb and say that it's one of the best nights of my life with the sexiest, funniest, most charming woman to ever sneak her way into my world.

Because that's what she's done.

Even though I know that she's some other man's girl—even though I know that she's a Vivien and not a Mona—every second with Gracie is like a bite from a warm cookie. Sweet and delicious and just a little bit bad for me.

And you know what? At this point, I don't even care.

Tonight, I'm going the method acting route. I barely know her. She barely knows me. She's Gracie. I'm Cayden. And the two of us are out on the town, a first date with the snap, crackle, and pop of possibility looming there in front of us.

I can hate my job tomorrow. Tonight, I just want to savor my time with this woman.

A woman who, at this particular moment, is looking at me with a wry grin that brings out the very kissable dimple in her cheek. "You're far, far away," she says. "Want to take me along with you?"

"You already are," I assure her, taking her hand. "I was just ruminating over the metaphysical implications of Esther's Follies." We've just come from the eight o'clock show, where we'd roared with laughter along with the rest of the crowd at the always-sold-out Austin revue that's like the lovechild of vaudeville and *Saturday Night Live*.

"Wow," she says. "You're way more in touch with the universe than I am. I was just contemplating that dinner you promised me."

"I did, didn't I?"

"Mmm," she says. "You don't think I agreed to this date for the witty banter, excellent entertainment, and exceptional company did you? I mean, a girl's got to eat."

"The lady makes a good point," I say, offering her my arm. "I assure you, chivalry is not dead, and dinner is just around the corner. Literally."

We'd veered onto a side street in order to avoid some of the insanity that is Sixth Street on a Friday night. Now, though, I steer her back onto the popular street, which is blocked off for pedestrians only at this time of night. Even so, the crowd is thick with tourists, locals, and boatloads of university students. We meander through the crowd, finally stopping at a pizza place that sells slices to passers by from a case that opens onto the sidewalk.

"Pepperoni work for you?" I ask.

"Always," she says, and I indicate that we want two slices to go to the girl behind the counter—who, with her partially shaved head, facial tattoos, and multiple piercings, fits right into the downtown milieu.

Moments later we've rounded a corner and are perched on a metal step that was probably once part of a fire escape but now just seems like an architectural oddity.

"Good, right?" I say, regretting taking such a big bite, as the cheese is burning my tongue. "I walk down here for lunch some days."

"It's amazing. And without the benefit of that pesky china and those cloth napkins I was expecting to go with dinner."

I wince. "Bad choice on the pizza?"

She takes a bite, and a long string of cheese extends from her lips all the way to the triangle of pizza. She laughs, trying to reel it in, finally twisting the cheese around her finger. "No," she says, with such a bright smile and laughter in her voice that I don't doubt her at all. "This is perfect. Absolutely perfect."

Relief washes over me. "You said to use my imagination. This is how I imagined you."

"Wrangling cheese? Plucking pepperonis?"

I shake my head as she pops a pepperoni into her mouth. "In the moonlight," I say, looking up at the huge full moon that hangs heavy in the sky, its light too much of a match even for the bright downtown glare. "Of course, I also imagined you walking along the river, but now I'm thinking that six blocks is too far to go just so we can stroll hand-in-hand on crushed granite."

"Probably," she says. "How do you feel about three or four blocks—I have no idea where we are—down a crowded sidewalk back to my hotel? And," she adds in a softer voice, "you can still hold my hand."

"Yeah," I say. "I think I'd like that." I take her pizza, guide it to my mouth, and take a bite.

"Oh, now you're in trouble." She laughs, then shoulder bumps me before taking another bite herself, then offering me the last of her slice.

I take it, finish it, then stand. "Shall I see you to your door, m'lady?" I ask, offering her my hand.

She takes it, and as she twines her fingers with mine I have the oddest sense of a fragile permanency. Like the completion of a jigsaw puzzle that's been on a coffee table for years, just waiting for that final piece. But it's never varnished, and if the table's knocked over, the picture it makes will completely disappear again.

"You okay?"

"What? Oh, yeah. Sorry. Just getting my bearings." I look up and down the street as if I've gotten turned around. Then point west, toward Congress Avenue and my office and The Driskill, as if I've only just figured out where I am in this town I grew up in and on this street where I work. "That way," I say. "Shall we?"

She squeezes my hand. "We shall."

We walk in silence for a while, my mind whirring. I have the almost uncontrollable urge to pull her into the shadows and kiss her, but I'm as terrified that she would push me away as I am that she would kiss me back with abandon—and absolutely no thought for the man she's going to marry. I've never experienced such warring thoughts with any woman I've gone out with, and the experience has completely disarmed me. Is she a serial cheater?

Is she unhappy with the man she supposedly loves? Could she be happy with me?

If this were a date, I might gather the courage and ask her. Like Kerrie said, I fought in the Middle East and survived. How much more harrowing could that conversation be?

But this isn't a date, it's a job. And the fact that I keep forgetting this is also messing with my head.

All of which means that I'm a flustered wreck, all the more so since that isn't my usual state.

"You haven't told me what you do," she says, and it's such a dangerous comment it yanks me out of my sappy, befuddled state and straight back into work mode. "Other than escort your niece to photo shoots in the middle of the day, I mean."

"I work in security," I tell her, happy for this tiny sliver of honesty between us. "Installing systems, some protection details, stuff like that."

"Really?" The spark of interest in her eye doesn't surprise me. Most people find the job more glamorous than it is. I mean, it has its moments, but I'm hardly living an action flick. "That's so weird. I just—"

"What?"

She coughs. "Sorry. Dust. Um, I just think that's a really cool job."

It's so obviously not what she was going to say that I don't press her. How can I fault her for being evasive when I'm keeping secrets, too? Instead, I change the subject to one I hope is safer. "How about you? How'd you get into modeling?"

"Fell into it, actually. Almost literally." She laughs at

my incredulous expression. "No, really. In fourth grade, I fell and banged up my knee walking home with my best friend. It hurt like hell to walk and my parents weren't around—I was a latchkey kid. So my friend called her mom to come pick us up. Her mom was high up in an agency and I'd never actually met her before. But she saw me, then asked if I'd like to audition for an ad campaign." She shrugs. "I got it."

"And the rest is history."

"If you're talking literal history—as in complicated and bloody—then it absolutely was."

"Not an easy ride? I'm guessing it's pretty stressful."

She lifts a shoulder. "I was skinny then. But when I hit my teens, the only way I could stay a size two—which is ridiculously tiny, but it's what they expect—was to live on next to no food and work out all the time. I was exhausted and my grades slipped and even though I actually loved the work, I was miserable."

We've reached the intersection of Sixth and Brazos, right across from The Driskill. But I don't lead her there yet. I want to hear what she has to say, and so I pause beside one of the trees that line the sidewalk, then lean against a stone barrier, my hand still tight in hers. "What did you do?"

"I quit my senior year, right when they told me I was on the verge of breaking out big. And then I started eating like a normal person. And biking near the beach—this was in Orange County, I grew up in Southern California—and working out at a gym with my friends. By the time I got to college I was in great shape and a size fourteen—that's what I am now, by the way."

"In that case, a fourteen is perfect, because you're beautiful." I can't imagine her as a two. I don't know shit about women's sizing, but I can count. She must have looked like a skinny little kid, not a woman.

"Not in modeling, it's not. Perfect, I mean. Which is ironic since it's pretty average in the real world. Anyway, I'd walked away from modeling. But then I bumped into my friend's mom again, and she was vile. Told me that I'd thrown away a career with both hands and that I didn't understand how to sacrifice for beauty and that I was lazy and wasn't willing to do the work and on and on and on."

She grins, and it's just a little wicked. "She lit a fire. Seriously, she made me so angry that I blew off my classes for a week—I was at UCLA by that time—and went to every modeling agency that would have me. Turns out that my national average size fourteen is plus size in the modeling world. Which is stupid, but at this point I don't care. Because it got me back in." She pauses, her brow furrowing.

"What?"

"Nothing. I just can't believe I spewed all that out on you. I don't usually do that. My standard answer is that I love my job and I'm honored that I've started making a name for myself."

"Have you?"

She nods. "Yeah. I've got steady work, I'm the face—or body, I guess—of a swimwear line, and I have a fan base. Which is mostly good, but sometimes weird."

"Weird?"

She shakes her head. "Just being on display. That's the part of the job I don't like."

"I'm confused. Isn't being a model all about being on display?"

"Sure. As the representative of something else. But nowadays everyone is on social media, and the line between the ads and my real life has blurred. That's why I—you know what? Never mind. This conversation has gotten way too serious."

I want to hear what she has to say, but I also don't want to push her. "Fair enough." I nod across the street toward her hotel. "Can I buy you a drink?"

She smiles, revealing those dimples. "That depends. Are you planning on getting me drunk and taking advantage of me?"

My mouth goes dry; the idea is far too appealing, and I force myself to remember my job. My mission. "What if I am? Would that be okay?"

She tilts her head, almost shyly, not meeting my eyes. The gesture is sweet. And I'm not sure if I'm charmed by it or infuriated. Since, after all, I know the truth.

Don't I?

I'm no longer sure. Because everything I know about this woman contradicts everything I *know*. Everything I've seen and felt in my time with her.

Is Peterman wrong? Is she completely innocent?

Or is she a Vivien, weaving her spell and keeping her secrets? Showing one version of herself to me and keeping everything else locked secretly away?

I draw in a breath, thinking both about the woman in front of me and also about the job. "About that drink," I say. "How do you feel about room service?"

She licks her lips, and all I want to do is lean in and kiss her. "I—well, I never really do that."

"Drink?"

That earns a laugh. "Invite a man to my room."

"Technically, you didn't."

"Good point." She tugs me toward the crosswalk. "In that case, I guess it's okay."

"You're sure?" I ask as we enter the hotel.

She leads me toward the elevator. And then, when the doors are closing and the elevator rising, she nods and says, "I'm sure."

We don't speak again until we've reached her room, and damned if I'm not as nervous as a teenager on his first date. I want her to push me away—to tell me she made a mistake.

And I want her to pull me close. To slide her hands around my neck so I feel the press of her breasts against my chest as I cup her ass and draw her tight against me. I want to lose myself in her, and I hate that I want what I can't have.

And I hate even more that she can't ever know why.

At her door, she flashes me a nervous smile. "This is me," she says, moving aside the Do Not Disturb sign so that she can press the card key to the handle. I hear the lock click, and she pushes the door open. "Home sweet home. It's kind of a mess."

Books and magazines are strewn about, and I see both a nightgown tossed over the arm of a sofa and a bra dangling from the back of a chair.

It's strangely enticing, and my body tightens as a wave

of desire cuts through me—then tightens even more as she moves to my side, meets my eyes, and kisses me.

It's soft and sweet, and she tastes of pizza and heaven, and this is so much better than my fantasy—and so much worse. Because it's real and I want it—want *her*. But I can't have her, not really, and yet I can't push her away when all I want to do is pull her closer and never let go.

But then she draws back, gasping, her eyes wide, and reality slams back against me. "I'm sorry," she says, her hand over her mouth. "I'm not usually that forward. I just—I just like you. You make me feel safe."

The word hangs oddly in the air between us.

"So, should we order those drinks?" Her smile is both shy and full of possibility, and I can see exactly where this evening is going—along a path I crave and at the same time want to run from.

"Gracie—I'm sorry."

She frowns, blushing a little. "Did I—?"

"No, no. It's just—" *Shit.* "It's just that I really like you, too. But I have to go." Not because of the job—and not because she just came on to someone not her boyfriend, proving my case and all of Peterman's fears—but because I can't deceive Gracie like this. I can't take this any further and not be the man she thinks I am.

"I don't—"

"I know," I say. "I'm sorry. I'm so, so sorry."

And as I walk back out her door into the hallway of the beautiful, old hotel, my heart aches. Because I know that no matter how much I might crave this woman, I'm never going to see her again.

CHAPTER EIGHT

"AT LEAST THE client will be happy," Connor says, then makes a face as he considers his words. "Well, not so much happy as relieved to have the truth before he says his vows."

I nod agreement, but I feel no satisfaction. There's no question but that Gracie was willing to go as far as I wanted to take her, which means that she was diving into that forbidden pool that Peterman feared she was already swimming in.

Congrats to me for a job well done—except I don't feel like celebrating at all. Instead I feel numb.

"I guess we sort of saw it coming," Kerrie says, dipping her spoon into a plastic yogurt cup. "She was pretty flirty at the shoot." I glance at her, frowning, but she just shrugs. "Well, she was. You were, too."

Since she's not wrong, I say nothing. From my side, of course, it was all about the job. And as for Gracie… honestly, I'm tired of even thinking about it. All it does is mess with my head.

We're in the break room as I wait for Peterman to show

up for his ten o'clock appointment. He's fifteen minutes late, and I'm getting antsy. Mostly because I want to get this over with.

And so I sigh with relief when the intercom buzzes and Pierce—who agreed to watch the front desk so that Kerrie could grab a bite—says that I have a client in the reception area.

I hurry out the door, make an immediate left into the hall, walk the short distance to reception, and stop cold.

Because it's not Thomas Peterman I see.

It's Gracie.

"Gracie," I say, then glance around stupidly as if Peterman is hiding behind the furniture. "What are you doing here?"

"I want to hire you," she says, as if I've just asked the most inane question ever. "I saw your ad. I've got a stalker."

A stalker?

Before I can process that unexpected twist, I hear Kerrie. "I can take over the desk again," she says, her voice preceding her into the area. "Thanks for covering for —*Gracie?*"

"Hi, to you, too." Gracie looks between us, her expression confused. "You work with your niece?"

"Niece?" Pierce says, then points between me and Gracie. "You two know each other?"

"We're going to go talk in the conference room," I tell him. "Gracie, right this way. And, ah, let me know when my ten o'clock gets here, okay?"

Kerrie's eyes are wide. Because even if Pierce doesn't

realize who Gracie is, Kerrie is now caught up with the situation. I lead Gracie down the hall to the small, window-lit conference room, then close the door. Both because I want privacy, and because I don't want her to overhear the clusterfuck of a story that Kerrie is undoubtedly sharing with Pierce and Connor at this very moment.

I gesture to a chair, and she sits. I can't seem to manage that, though, so I stand by the window, willing myself not to pace.

"Should I not have come?" Her hands twist in her lap. "I was in the lobby when I realized it was you. I almost didn't come up. Because, you know, of the way you left last night. I wasn't sure if you were leaving for good or just for the night."

"Wait. Wait, back up. What do you mean you were in the lobby when you realized it was me?"

She runs her fingers through her hair, sending golden waves tumbling. She's wearing a retro-style flowered dress, and she runs her palms nervously over her thighs.

"Last night when you mentioned you work in security, I almost told you that I was planning on hiring a security company to help me out. I'd seen an ad for a firm located right across the street from the hotel, and I told myself I was going to do it. I was going to finally take serious steps to get this asshole off my back."

"You didn't say a word."

She shakes her head. "We were having a good time. I thought mentioning some creep who's been harassing me would kill the mood, you know? And I didn't want you to offer to help." Her smile is wistful. "You're a really nice guy, Cayden. And I was sure that you would, and I didn't want you to feel obligated. So I let it go. And then we went to the hotel, and, well, you know the rest."

"And this morning?"

"I walked over here after breakfast and I was in the lobby looking at the directory. Your name's listed. Cayden Lyon. And that's when I realized that the ad was for your company. So I almost walked away."

"I'm glad you didn't," I admit, though under the circumstances, I probably shouldn't say a thing.

She releases a sigh of relief. "Thank goodness."

"What's going on? A stalker?"

She nods. "Creepy gifts left on my door. Phone calls. Angry letters if I so much as have coffee with a guy. He's watching me." She twists her hands together, then looks into my eyes. "So, can you help me?"

I should say no.

Technically, I'm now staring at the very pretty face of a massive conflict of interest. But I also have a niggling suspicion that there's more going on here than I'm seeing yet. So I make the leap and say, "Yes. Of course I will."

Her face glows with relief. "Thank you."

"Let me get my partners in here, and then I want you to tell me the whole story."

She nods, and less than five minutes later, Connor and Pierce have joined us and we're all sitting around the table. Gracie takes a deep breath, then looks at me, and that trust I see in her eyes both humbles me and lances me with a hot cord of guilt.

"Just dive in," I tell her, focusing on her, not me. "However is easiest, just tell us the story."

"It's been going on for a couple of years," she says. "Or,

rather, it started a couple of years ago. I thought it was over. But now he's back."

"Who?"

She shakes her head. "He's tall and skinny and he has dark hair. I—I see him sometimes, watching me. And in LA, where this started, we actually got him on the security camera at my apartment complex. But not his face. Just a view from the back. He—" She licks her lips. "He was peeking in my window while I was sleeping."

She shudders, and I don't blame her.

"When he sends me things—flowers, candy—he signs the notes *Your True Love*. And on my Instagram account, he had the same account name. I blocked him, and now he pops up under different names, but he uses a hashtag—YTL—and even though I can't prove it, I know it's him."

"You have your phone?" Connor asks. "Can you show us?"

She nods, then opens the app on her phone and passes it to him. He scrolls through, frowning. "Lots of posts from men—and lots from him. Racy," he says, looking at me and then Pierce. "And possessive."

She nods, and he keeps scrolling.

"Nothing from you. No replies?"

"No. Years ago I'd interact with fans. Now, not so much. I stay on social media because it's a tool, but now I'm mostly offline."

"And private messages?" Pierce asks.

"Lots," she says. "And ninety percent from him. And I can't block him because he just keeps getting new accounts."

"Obsessive," I say. "Obsession can be dangerous. Was that why you left LA?"

She nods. "The police were sympathetic, but they never made any progress. And after he broke into my apartment—or, at least, I think it was him—I decided to move."

"Why do you think it was him?" I ask. "A gut-feeling? Or did he leave some specific indication?"

"He didn't take anything except my underwear. Every single pair of panties I owned." She shudders, then hugs herself.

"So I moved here. My aunt lived here before she died, so I used to visit in the summers. I've always loved Austin, and I was sick of LA—or, he'd tainted it for me—so I just packed up and came out."

"But you stayed on social media," Connor says.

"I have a job, and it's expected when you're a model. But I don't post anything with locations anymore. Unless it's an out of town job. Then I figure why not? Maybe it'll throw him off the trail." She frowns. "It worked for about a year. But I must have slipped, because he's here. I'm certain he's here."

"Yeah," I say, feeling sick but knowing I have to confess everything. "He is."

CHAPTER NINE

"WHAT ARE YOU TALKING ABOUT?" Gracie asks. "How do you know?"

"I have a hunch," I say. "I want to show you something." I cross to the door, then turn to all of them. "Field trip. Follow me."

All three look baffled, but I'm not in the mood to explain, and when I leave, they follow. I lead them like a trail of ducks down to the basement. I see Connor and Pierce exchange glances, but Gracie just frowns, her forehead creased and her arms crossed tight over her chest.

When we reach the door to the security room, I knock twice, then step in. One of the perks of actually being in security is that you tend to make friends with the building staff. Leroy is sitting in front of the monitors that show the lobby and each floor's elevator alcove and stairwell in a series of rotating images.

"Cayden, guys—and gal—what's up?"

"I need a favor. The lobby. Around ten. Can you pull that up for us?"

"Sure thing. What are we looking for?"

"If he's there, we'll know."

Gracie steps up behind me. "You really think he's—"

"We'll find out."

As we watch, Leroy rewinds the relevant tape. We see a wide shot of the lobby entrance, including the directory on the wall. People come and go, and then Gracie walks in and heads for the directory.

"There," I say, pointing to the skinny man who walks through the glass doors, then stops short, his eyes on Gracie. For a second, I think he's going to turn around and leave right then, but he stays there, his gaze locked on her.

She doesn't notice, but heads into the elevator alcove, leaving this camera's field of vision.

"Want me to follow the girl?" Leroy asks.

"No. Can you pull in closer on his face?"

Leroy cocks his head. "Have you met the landlord? We're lucky the video actually records."

I frown, because even if I have him download the image, I doubt I could pull a good picture of her stalker's face. Blow it up, and it would be way too pixelated.

As we watch, he turns, then hurries toward the door. "Freeze that," I say, then turn to Gracie. "Can you tell? Same guy from LA?"

"I don't know. I think so. Probably. But how did you—"

"He saw you were here. He assumed I figured it out. And so he turned tail and ran. At least, that's my best guess."

"He," she repeats, her voice wary as she takes a step back. "He, who?"

"He called himself Thomas Peterman. And he hired

me," I tell her, my voice lifeless and flat. "He hired me to prove that his fiancée was cheating."

"Oh, God." Her words are barely audible, and she clutches her stomach. "That's why you—" She turns away, and I see Connor and Pierce looking between us, their faces a combination of shock and compassion.

"Why don't we go back upstairs," Pierce begins, but Gracie shakes her head.

"No. No, I think I'll just go." Her eyes cut to mine. "I just need—to go. I really just need to get out of here."

And then she's hurrying out the door, and though I start to rush after her, the guys hold me back. "Give her time," Pierce says. "And then let me go talk to her. I don't think she's in the mood to see your pretty face."

I yank my arm free. "I need to explain. I need to tell her—"

"What?" Connor asks, and I realize that I was about to say, *how I feel*. And that revelation shocks me into silence. Because the truth is, right now it's not Peterman that's on my mind, it's me. And it's Gracie. And it's the horrible fear that I've lost her forever when I've just found her, and where in the *hell* did that thought come from?

"Right," I say, calm now. "Upstairs."

"Good. Come on."

They open the door, and I blast past them, then sprint up the stairs to the lobby. The building's entrance is on Congress, and I blow out the door, hook a right, then an immediate left on Sixth Street. I pause, looking down the block for her. The Driskill is across the street and about a block down, and I'm certain she's heading that way, and I really have to talk to her. I don't see her, but I at least know her room number, and so I jog toward the corner.

That's when I see him. He's rushing out of an alcove toward a group of pedestrians waiting for the light to change. I see a flash of her blond hair, and in the space of an instant I realize that he's planning to push her into traffic.

"*Gracie!*" I shout, and both Peterman and Gracie turn toward me. Her eyes go wide, and she rushes sideways and to safety. Even if he did push her now, she wouldn't end up in the street. Rather, she'd simply be slammed into the side of the delivery truck that fills the loading zone.

But he's not going after her anyway. Instead, he's sprinting eastward, dodging pedestrians, zipping between cars as he crosses Sixth Street, ignoring the squealing of brakes. He races up a side street, turns down an alley, and by the time I reach the corner, he's gone.

I curse, then go back to the corner where I left Gracie, only to see that she's gone, too.

This time, I curse even louder, because, dammit, I do not want her alone right now. Then I hear my name, and when I turn around, I find her leaning against the facade of the Littlefield Building, tears streaking her makeup.

"Was he trying to kill me?"

"Hurt you, for sure. Kill you, maybe."

She nods.

I take a step toward her, and she shrinks back against the stone. I freeze, feeling lower than dirt. "I know a lot of guys in the business. Talented men. Dedicated. Any one of them can keep you safe. Help you track down this guy. And I'll help whoever you choose however I can."

Again, she nods, taking it all in.

"Do you want to come back to the office? We can make a few calls. Or we can go to your room. But I'm not leaving you alone, so you're stuck with me until we find someone else."

"What if I don't want someone else?"

Her voice is so soft, I'm certain I must have misheard her.

"Or, is that not okay?"

"You're serious?" I ask. "I didn't think you'd want me around."

She lifts a shoulder and takes a single step toward me. "Jury's still out. But maybe. I don't know. Start by telling me everything, and we'll go from there."

"I can do that," I say. "I think I can even tell you most of it on the way."

"The way where?"

"The Kleinman, Camp & Richman Law Firm."

"Why are we going there?"

"We're going to go pay a visit to one Mr. Thomas Peterman, Esquire."

Kleinman, Camp & Richman takes up seven floors of the Frost Bank Tower, which is located on Congress Avenue between Fourth and Fifth Streets. It's a pretty quick walk from the intersection where Gracie almost met her demise at Peterman's hand, but we're not going there right away.

First, we're popping into Starbucks.

"I need the caffeine hit," I say when she protests. But

really I want to give her time to catch her breath before we —hopefully—confront the man who's been stalking her.

And I want time for my friend Landon to get here. A detective with the Austin Police Department, Landon Ware is a solid cop with a good bedside manner. If anyone in the police can make Gracie feel safe, he can. And I want him with us when we go find the fucker at Kleinman.

I'm also waiting on a still image from the lobby security cameras, something Leroy assures me he's doing right this second, and will text over as soon as he's pulled the best image.

Most important, though, I want to tell her how Peterman ended up as a client, and I want to do that while we're sitting, not walking. Because I want to see her face as I run her through the details, and I want to watch her eyes when I go back over the parts involving her.

"So that's why you were at the bar that first night," she says after I've told her everything. "You were scoping me out."

I nod. "At first, I thought you might be picking up the bartender."

She laughs, and I consider that a good sign.

"And when you walked me to my room, it was all just part of a job."

"No," I say. "Not all."

"And The Fix?"

"No." The word comes out sharper than I intended. "That was pure coincidence. Totally off the clock."

"No thought at all for your assignment?"

I rub my temples. "It wasn't planned. I was having fun with you. Christ, Gracie I wanted—"

"What?"

"You," I say boldly, though I'd intended to avoid the admission. What the hell, right? Go big or go home.

"Oh. I—well, okay, then."

I'm not sure how to interpret that, but I don't ask. I want to hold onto the fantasy that we're going to move past my royal screw up and return to a world where she wanted me, too.

She frowns, and I wonder for a second if that plan is already blown. Then she meets my eyes and says, "What about the shoot?"

"Peterman told me about it."

"I figured. But how did he know?"

"At the time, I assumed he learned it from you. So, maybe you posted about it on social media?" But even as I speak, I know she'd be too careful for that. "I guess we'll ask him when we see him."

As I speak, my phone dings, and I look down to see that Leroy has sent over the still image. Another piece of ammo in the bag. "And there's Landon," I say, waving from the table we'd grabbed by a window as the tall, black detective comes in, looking like a badass with his scalp close-shaved and just the hint of a beard. His eyes, however, are kind, and when I introduce him to Gracie, I can tell that his confidence and demeanor put her at ease.

"So if he's there, you'll arrest him."

"If we arrest him, the clock starts ticking, and we have to try him quickly. You up for testifying?"

"Oh, yeah," she says.

"You?" he asks me.

"Cayden can testify against him?" she asks. "But

Peterman hired him. Isn't there like a privilege or something?"

"He dragged me unknowingly into his criminal scheme," I tell her. "I can testify. And it will be my pleasure."

"Oh." She sits up a little straighter and smiles at both of us. "Well, this is great." She glances toward the door. "Should we go?" She looks at Landon. "Can you arrest him now?"

Landon meets my eyes with a smile, then returns his attention to her. "Let's go," he says, and we start walking that direction.

When we reach the quiet, wood-paneled reception area for the firm, Landon goes to the pretty girl manning the desk, flashes his badge, and—as her eyes grow wide—asks to see Mr. Thomas Peterman.

"Oh. But, oh. Hold on, please."

She picks up a phone, whispers something, then smiles at Landon. "Ms. Clairmont will be right here."

Gracie and I are standing a few steps behind, and I want to argue that we don't want Ms. Clairmont, and shouldn't someone block the exit stairs? But Landon seems chill, and so I relax, my hand going protectively to Gracie's back.

She tilts her head up, steps away, and my hand falls uselessly to the side.

Apparently we've established a truce, and absolutely nothing more. That reality sits like a rock in my gut, but I'm soon distracted by the arrival of a woman who looks old enough to know shorthand. "I'm Ms. Clairmont, how may I help you?"

"You work for Mr. Peterman?" Landon asks. "We need to see him." Once again, he flashes the badge. "I'm afraid it's urgent."

"Oh, my." She makes a *tsk-tsk* sound. "I can certainly call him, but he's in Dallas in depositions. I suppose he could come back."

I step forward. "How long has he been in Dallas?"

"Several days now. I'm sorry, what is this regarding?"

Landon meets my eyes, and I see the question in his. I pull out my phone, pull up the video image, and hand it to her. "Is that Mr. Peterman?"

"Why no. I'm sorry, but I'm still terribly confused. I believe this is one of the file clerks."

"Is it?" Landon says. "Could you ask him to come up?"

"Well, I—" She cuts herself off as she shows the picture to the receptionist. "I don't recall his name. Do you?"

The receptionist shakes her head, and we agree that I'll email her the picture and she can forward it to the file room. Less than five minutes later, we get an answer. *Daniel Powder*. And he hasn't been to the office in over a week.

He also hasn't been to his apartment, a crappy little studio out near the airport.

"And Daniel Powder was a fake name anyway," Landon tells us at dinner a few hours later. "I'm sorry, but your guy's gone underground."

CHAPTER TEN

"THANKS," she says when we reach her room in The Driskill. "I'll lock the door, keep all the lights on, and hope I can get some sleep."

It's just the two of us, Landon left us after dinner, and now I take the card from her hand, lean past her to open the door, and usher her inside.

"Or I can have you check the place out thoroughly before I crash," she says.

"I'll definitely do that. But you have a decision to make."

"I do?" She has a small suite, and she settles on the sofa in the living area, then hugs a pillow to her chest.

"I can either crash here on your couch, or we can call Pierce or Connor, and they can crash here on your couch. But you're not staying alone."

"I'm in a hotel. I don't think he even knows my room number."

"You don't have a balcony, so there's no way out if he does get in. And he definitely knows you're staying here.

We could move you to another hotel, but even then I'd want someone to stay with you. He attacked you. He tried to kill you. In his fucked up mind, he thinks you spurned him. He's dangerous Gracie."

"I know—I know. But—but what if we never catch him? I have a house. A life. I can't just keep moving to new towns. I don't want—"

I sit, then take her hands, gratified when she not only doesn't yank them away, but squeezes tight. "We will find him," I say. "We will catch him. We will stop him."

She looks up, her eyes shadowed with fear. "Promise?"

I start to lean in, not thinking, simply wanting to seal the words with a kiss, but I stop myself, then nod as if everything's normal and fine. "I promise."

"Well, then, will you stay?"

I try not to show how I'm dancing for joy on the inside. "Are you sure?"

She nods. "I liked you."

I notice her use of the past tense and force myself not to wince.

"I still do," she adds, and now my smile comes easy.

"Good," I say. "Because I like you."

"It was still a dick move."

"Maybe. I thought he was the good guy. Then when I got to know you and you didn't fit with my image of a lying, cheating female..."

"This is an image you keep parked in your brain?"

"Rooted there," I confess. "Has been for quite a while."

She studies me. "Want to tell me why?"

I consider it, then shake my head. "No. I think that we

should order brownie sundaes from room service, drink wine, and watch a movie."

"Yeah?"

"Why do you say it like that?"

She shakes her head, looking slightly bemused, but happier than she has all day. "Because that sounds pretty close to my idea of heaven right now."

And since I'm all about making her happy—and making up for the last couple of days—I call in the order, review our movie possibilities, and get everything set up. Within the hour, we're both on the couch, the remains of a gigantic brownie sundae on the coffee table in front of us and *Arsenic and Old Lace* playing on the screen, a selection from the *Classic Favorites* section of the movie rental system. And since I'm a fan of the classics—Connor and I were practically weaned on Cary Grant—I was thrilled to learn its one of Gracie's favorites.

At one point, when Grant is being particularly slapstick-y, I turn to see if Gracie's enjoying it and find her staring right back at me.

"What—" I begin, but I don't finish.

"You have something," she says, brushing the corner of her mouth. "Brownie crumbs, probably."

I rub my mouth, but apparently rub the wrong side, because she laughs and brushes her thumb over the opposite corner of my mouth.

It's just her thumb against my lips, but it's as if I've been shot through with electricity, and I'm damn sure that she feels it, too, because she's staring at me with such a combination of shock and desire that it would be funny if I didn't want to kiss her so damn badly. But I'm here to protect her, and on shaky ground at that. I don't want to take advantage or push, or—

To hell with it.

"Gracie." My voice is gravely with need as I reach up and close my hand over hers, holding her thumb in place. Her eyes meet mine, and I look for any hint of hesitation as I hold her hand still then turn my head. Just a bit. Just enough so that I can kiss the pad of her thumb.

She exhales, the soft sound filling my head. Firing my senses.

I hold her eyes with mine, still waiting for her to stop me as I draw her thumb into my mouth, slow and deep, and then sucking. Tasting.

And when she tilts her head back—when I see her nipples tighten under her dress and through her bra, then hear her groan with a pleasure that goes straight to my cock —I know that she's not going to call a halt.

And when she whispers, "Oh, God, yes," I cup the back of her neck as I swirl her thumb around my tongue, reveling in the salty sweetness of her skin.

"Gracie," I murmur, when I can't take it any longer. When I have to taste her lips.

I shift on the couch, my body over hers, one hand at the waist of dress she wears. It's a style that buttons from hem to cleavage, with a thick belt at her waist, just beneath my palm. My other hand is behind her head, my fingers twined in her hair, and I hold her body steady as I lift myself up just enough to gaze upon the woman breathing hard beneath me.

"You are so damn pretty," I say, then watch the way her face lights, the dimples in her cheeks appearing like magic.

She has one hand on the back of my neck, and her thumb is stroking my skin in a way that's making me hyper-aware of the touch. The connection.

Slowly, I ease my fingers over the buttons between her breasts. I pop open the first one, then hesitate, giving her the chance to stop me. She bites her lower lip, then closes her eyes as I undo the next four buttons, so that the bodice of her dress falls open, revealing perfect breasts spilling over the top of a pink cotton bra. The kind, I note with interest, that fastens with a front clasp.

I trail my fingertip over the V-shape made by the outline of her bra against her breasts, tracing a path over the heated skin, then down to the clasp, then slowly back up over the mound of her other breast. The cotton is thin enough to see her nipple, hard now and trapped under a blanket of pink.

Her skin is flushed, her lips parted, and her head is tilted back, exposing the smooth, pale skin of her neck. "Gracie," I whisper. "Look at me."

She does, and I see the heat in those sea-blue eyes. "I'm going to kiss you."

She nods, her lips parting in anticipation. But I'm being naughty, teasing her, and I lower my mouth to her breast, dusting a trail of kisses along the line where her skin is revealed at the edge of the cup. She whimpers, and I wonder how long I can go on teasing her when I'm tormenting myself just as much.

Boldly, I shift my kisses, closing my mouth over her nipple, sucking on cotton and feeling that nub harden under the gentle scrape of my teeth.

Then I can't stand it any longer, and I use my fingers to

tug the cup down. She arches up, a strangled, *please* on her lips, followed by a low, deep moan of pleasure when I take her now-bare breast into my mouth and suck as if I want to drink her up. Consume her. Pull her entirely inside me.

And oh, yes, that is exactly what I want.

I play with her other breast with my free hand, and when I can't stand it any longer, I pop open the clasp, freeing her completely. Regretfully, I release her from my mouth so that I can pull back and look at her, bare to the waist, her skin flushed, her lips red and swollen from the way she's been biting them. Her hair tousled, and her eyes dark with lust.

"Cayden," she says. Just my name, but it's a demand. An order, and I follow it eagerly, this time claiming her mouth with my own as my palm cups her breast. Our tongues war, my fingers twisting and tightening on her nipple as our tongues taste and tease. I'm lost in a sensual haze, and as I devour her mouth, I slide my hand down, away from her breast, lower and lower until my fingers can tug up the cotton of her dress, revealing her smooth thighs.

Her low, soft mewls of pleasure encourage me, and I blaze a trail north, easing my way up the inside of her thigh until I reach the band of her panties, and she gasps, her hips rising as if in invitation. Gently, I stroke along the edge of the material, my fingertip grazing her tender skin.

She murmurs my name, and I silence her with a fresh kiss, then suck on her lower lip as I slowly, teasingly, slip my finger under the elastic band, desperate to feel how slick she is.

She whimpers, then shifts, her hand coming from nowhere to close over mine. She holds my fingers in place, just out of reach of heaven, and then she says the word I really don't expect. "No." She tugs my hand away, closing her thighs. "I'm sorry."

She turns away, obviously embarrassed, and I watch, surprised as she sits up and starts to button her dress. "I'm really sorry," she says again, not looking at me as she scoots further into the corner of the couch.

I hesitate, still surprised, then realize that she's afraid I'm pissed.

Well, shit.

"Gracie," I say gently, "it's okay."

"Really? You're not upset?"

I shake my head. "I'll cop to disappointed, but no is no for a reason. I don't want to do anything you're not comfortable with. It's only good if it's good for both of us."

Her smile returns, erasing what I think was embarrassment mixed with fear. "Thank you," she says, then looks down at her hands. "It's, um, not you." She lifts her head and looks straight into my eyes, her cheeks blooming red as she says, "I liked what you were doing. Um, everything you were doing. And, I really do want ... more."

"I'm glad to hear it." And then, because I can be a devilish bastard, I ask, "What kind of more in particular? I want to get it right."

A smile tugs at her mouth. "Everything," she says, and I like the way the hesitancy has faded from her voice. "Tonight is just—it's just too soon. I barely know you."

She's right, of course. But as she gets up off the couch and heads into the connecting bedroom, I can't help but think that it feels like I've known her forever.

I'm pondering that sense of connection when she leans

against the doorframe. "Do you need in the bathroom before me?"

I shake my head. It's the only design flaw I see with the hotel—to get to the bathroom, a guest in the living area has to enter the bedroom.

She nods, then closes the bedroom door, leaving me alone to remember the feel of her skin under my fingers, and the taste of her in my mouth. *Too soon.*

It really didn't feel too soon to me.

A few minutes later, she opens the bedroom door and appears again in the doorway. She's wearing one of the hotel robes over a knee-length nightgown. "There's another robe in the closet, and a spare blanket. Help yourself. And I'll keep this door open so that you can get to the bathroom whenever you need."

"You going to sleep now?"

She nods. "Long day. Um, goodnight, Cayden."

"Goodnight, Gracie."

I wait until I see the light go out, then step into the bedroom and cross to the bathroom, grabbing the robe on my way. I pause long enough to look at her, already asleep and illuminated by the sliver of light coming in through the drapes.

A few minutes later, I'm back on the couch in my boxers, the robe over the back of a chair, and the blanket pulled over me as I lay back against one of the throw pillows. I've just closed my eyes when I hear her voice.

"Cayden?"

I look up to see her standing in the doorway. "You okay?"

"I don't want to be alone."

"You're not. I'm not going anywhere."

"No, I mean..."

"Do you want me to come sleep in there?" I ask gently. "I promise I can behave."

"No. But can I sit with you for a while? Maybe we can watch another movie?"

"Sure," I say, sitting up and offering her half of the couch. She comes, sitting sideways so that her feet are in my lap. And sometime in the middle of *Bringing Up Baby*, we both drift off to sleep.

CHAPTER ELEVEN

I'M BACK in the desert, mortar fire all around, and now my legs are as useless as my eye, and back home, Gracie is in bed with a grad student, and I want to shout at her to not do it. To not ruin everything we could have, and I—

With a start, I come wide awake, breathing hard, and see the ornate interior of the suite all around me. Not smoke and blood and sand and a boiling sun. And my legs are fine, under Gracie's, just as we'd fallen asleep last night.

She's all twisted up on the couch, too, and when I shift, trying to work out some of the kinks that have settled in to all of my muscles, her eyes flutter open.

"Sorry," I whisper. "I didn't mean to wake you."

"It's okay." She stretches and yawns, then runs a finger through her hair. She looks absolutely delicious and I'm so tempted to kiss those sweet lips and continue where we left off.

"Oh, crap," she says. "It's after eight. I need to be in North Austin by eleven."

And there goes my plan for the morning.

She sits up, then rolls her neck, stopping when I reach over and start to knead the tight muscles. "Good thing I don't have a photo shoot today. They'd end up with pictures of a human pretzel."

"Not a shoot?" I ask, focusing my attention on her neck as she moans with pleasure. The kind of noises I'd like to hear when we're both naked, but this will have to do. At least for now. "What's the appointment?"

"It's at an educational facility I work at. Well, sort of," she adds, though I don't know if she means sort of educational or that she only sort of works there. "Oh, yes, right there. Perfect." She sighs. "And I'll be fine. The kinks will be out by then. You've already banished most all of them, kind sir."

"If they're not, I can give you a neck rub any time, any place. My guarantee."

She frowns as she studies me. "You're coming with me today?"

"Security detail, remember? You can consider me your overprotective slave."

"You're really staying. I thought last night—"

"You thought it was a one off?"

"Well, yeah. Kind of."

I shift so that I can cup her chin. "I'm like glue," I say gently. "Until we get this figured out I'm your own personal body guard and masseuse."

She laughs. "I'm freaked enough that I won't argue. But I think tonight I'm sleeping in the bed. My neck can't take too many nights like that."

Neither can mine, but I don't say as much. I'm already

mourning the lack of her warmth against me, aching muscles be damned.

"You're probably stiff this morning, too." Her eyes dip to my lap as she says that, and I can't help but laugh as she blushes bright red. "Oh, my God. That was really not on purpose."

"Well, it's true," I say, working to keep a perfectly straight face. "I could definitely use some, ah, tension relief."

Now she's laughing. "Okay, you blew it. I was going to suggest that you should sleep on a real mattress, but it's the couch for you, mister."

"You were going to invite me into your bed?"

"Well, I was. But forget it. Now I'm thinking a towel on the floor..."

"I accept," I say. "The bed. Not the towel."

"Too late. I rescinded that offer."

I meet her eyes. "Thank you," I say, and then bend over to gently kiss her.

"Oh, man..." Her words are a lament as I break the kiss.

"Problem?"

"Just regretting that I have things to do and places to be," she says.

"And we need to hurry," I add. "We have a stop south of the river before your eleven o'clock. We'll be criss-crossing town, but we'll make it work."

"Do we have time to grab breakfast downstairs? We're going to be skipping lunch."

"It'll be tight. Of course, we could save time and water by showering together..."

"I'll be quick," she says with a smirk, then hurries into

the other room, leaving me with only my fantasies of her naked, soapy body. And my hope that later tonight or tomorrow I can turn that fantasy into reality.

"More coffee?" The waiter in the restaurant downstairs hands me the folio, but directs the question at Gracie, the hand holding the pitcher shaking a little bit. "Or I could grab you a to-go cup."

"No, it's fine. I've had plenty. But it's very sweet of you to offer."

"Oh, it's no problem Ms. Harmon."

He's in his early twenties and completely starstruck.

"Breakfast was great," I say, passing him the folio, into which I've slid the signed credit card receipt. "I think we're done."

"Right. Right. It's just, I'm not supposed to ask, but I've been a fan since you started out in LA. I think it's so cool you're in the hotel. Are you doing a shoot in Austin?"

"Just a short one," I say before Gracie can answer. "Then she goes back home."

"Where's that?" the waiter asks.

Gracie answers before I can, her smile warm and friendly. "If you follow me online, you know that's my best kept secret. But I will say I'm enjoying this hotel very much."

"Would it be okay if I asked for your autograph? I know I shouldn't, but…" He trails off with a shrug.

"Absolutely." She rummages in her purse and comes up with a set of matte cards that are blank on one side and have a picture of her in a retro dress similar to the one she wore last night on the other.

"I'm Joseph. Joe."

"Nice to meet you." She signs, then offers him a wide smile as she pushes back her chair. "You have a great day, okay?"

He beams as we leave, winding our way through the crowd and attracting more than a few stares from a number of the men, many of whom are sitting with their wives. Some even with their children. By the time we're through the restaurant and to the valet stand on the other side of the lobby, my chest is tight, and I'm scowling.

"What's wrong?"

Since I'm not entirely sure, I brush it off. "Just running late. And it bugs me that you can't enjoy a meal in peace."

She shoots me a quizzical look. "It's part of the job. And since I'm online so little, I figure the least I can do is be nice to the fans I meet in public."

I concede the point, especially since the tightness in my chest is conjuring shadows of Vivien. The way her grad students would fawn. The way she'd tell me it was no big deal.

But it was a big deal. Turns out it was a very big deal.

The arrival of the valet with my Grand Cherokee saves me from spiraling down the rabbit hole, and as soon as we're underway, Gracie turns to me, her broad smile suggesting that she either never noticed my mood or has entirely forgiven it.

"Are you always this cheerful?" I tease.

"Why not? Better to go through life smiling than frowning."

"Can't argue with that."

"Will you tell me now where we're going?"

I've been refusing to tell her what our first stop is, and I don't change that position now. "You'll be able to guess pretty soon, I think."

She scowls, but it doesn't erase the smile in her eyes. And as soon as we cross the river, she starts guessing. The Long Center. The Botanical Gardens. Barton Springs. Zachary Scott Theater.

"Peter Pan Miniature Golf," she finally says, and I shake my head, no.

It's not until we're in the maze of streets that make up the quaint—yet expensive—Travis Heights neighborhood of charmingly restored houses that she settles back in the seat and shakes her head. "Seriously?"

"What?"

"You're taking me *home?* Am I supposed to be moving back? Out of the hotel?"

"Not yet. I want to show you something."

"What?"

"Just wait."

She slinks down in her seat, clearly not excited about waiting. But she sits up with more interest and attention as we pull in front of her cute little 1920s bungalow. One of the smaller houses in the historic, popular neighborhood, it has two bedrooms and had been completely refurbished before she bought it. I know, because Connor checked the property records before we started our little surprise project.

Now, Gracie frowns at the array of trucks parked in front of her place and the tech team in Blackwell-Lyon T-shirts moving to and fro over her lawn and roof. "I don't get it," she says. "Who are they?"

"They're installing your security system. Top of the line. No holds barred."

"Um, *whoa*. I didn't hire you for that. And I can't afford it. I may be a model, but I'm hardly a household name."

"I saw you with that waiter—you can be a big name if you want to be."

She rolls her eyes.

"And staying at home will be cheaper than staying at The Driskill. Great hotel. Not cheap."

"Cecilia has a corporate deal. I'm getting a good rate."

"Trust me. Our rate is better."

"Which is?"

I push open my door and start to slide out of the car. "Free."

Since she's still sitting in the passenger seat a moment later, apparently a little shell-shocked, I walk around the car and open the door for her, then give her a hand to help her out.

"Free?" she says once we're on the walkway to her front door. "You're just gifting me an alarm system?"

"Hell, no. It's a security system, not an alarm system."

"But—"

"And it's a prototype. You're getting it for free because you're helping us test out the upgrades."

"Prototype? But it works, right?"

"Oh, yeah. Or it will once we're done with the installation. This is a system we designed with a local company. Well, the local branch of an international company. We partner with a tech genius named Noah over at Stark

Applied Technology's Austin office. You've heard of them?"

She nods.

"Then you know their reputation is stellar. So is ours. Come on."

I give her the quick tour, taking her through all the features, then check in with the head of our installation team. I can tell she's impressed. "You're sure I'm not costing you money?"

"I told you. You're part of our beta team. You're doing us a favor. My house is the same," I tell her. "We test all the new features on my place. It's so small it's easy to get in and do adjustments."

"Smaller than this?"

"Tiny one bedroom in far South Austin," I tell her, and I see the surprise on her face. "My ex and I bought it as a rental. After the divorce, she moved to Indiana and I couldn't stand to be in the same house we used to live in. So I sold it. Never got around to finding a new place and the rental was empty, so I grabbed it. Just under five hundred square feet."

"That is tiny. You probably don't throw a lot of house parties."

"Not too many." I meet her grin, pleased that's her only comment. I've gone out with some women who seem to think that the size of my house has some relationship to the size of my cock. Or my ego. But as far as I can tell, Gracie sees me, not the trappings.

Now that we've gone over the exterior, we head inside the house. She wanders the rooms and chats with my team while I go off to find Pierce, who's overseeing the installation.

"It's looking good," I tell him.

"So are you," he says dryly. "Gracie's looking fresh and perky this morning, too."

I roll my eyes, regretting having such a perceptive best friend. "I haven't slept with her."

"Not yet," he says. "So...care to fill me in?"

"Why bother?" I meet his eyes. "You're doing so good on your own."

He chuckles. "Fair enough. I like her. I approve. You want to talk about it?"

"Really don't," I say. Then add, "She reminds me of Viv."

"Seriously?"

"Just—well..." I trail off, regroup, and relay the morning's drama with Joe.

"So you're bugged by the fact that she has fans?"

I start to deny it, but it's true, and Pierce would see through the lie. "I know it's unfair to compare, but I can't get Viv's grad students out of my head. They worshipped her. And she just took her pick, plucking them off the tree like ripe fruit."

I slide my hands into my pockets "There was more than the one I walked in on."

"You know that?"

"She told me. Not sure if she was feeling guilty or if she was trying to hurt me after the divorce was final. But she told me. Either way, I didn't want to know. But then I couldn't stop seeing them. The men. The easy pickings. And her just tugging them one by one into our bed."

"I'm sorry. I had no idea. But in case you hadn't noticed, Gracie isn't Vivien."

"I know that. Believe me."

"Good. Don't fuck it up, okay?"

Despite myself, I laugh. "I'll do my best."

Those words linger as Gracie and I drive north, me following her directions to a storefront in a strip shopping center off Mesa Drive in the affluent Northwest Hills neighborhood. "That's it," she says, pointing to the unit on the end with a sign that says *Off The Grid*. "Come on," she adds opening her door, as soon as I've put the Jeep into park.

She's lit up like a candle, and I follow, eager to know what's gotten her so excited. But when we walk in, I find no explanation.

The place is cavernous, just a shell of a building. In one corner is a pile of books and some beanbag chairs. A couple of teenagers look up, then dive back into whatever they're reading. On the other side, I see several dining-size tables. One has a game of Risk open on it. The other a half-completed jigsaw puzzle. Further back, I see lab tables and what looks like a rinky-dink chem lab. And on the opposite side is a sewing machine and a kitchen that could be from the nineteen fifties.

"I give up," I say. "Where are we and why are we here?"

"Zombie apocalypse day," she tells me, which really doesn't answer the question. "Come on," she adds. "Everyone's in the back." She turns toward the kids in the beanbag chairs. "Laura, Craig. You guys coming?"

"One more chapter," Laura says as Craig grunts.

"Uh-huh." Gracie's tone is dubious. "I can't really complain. They both had massive phone withdrawal when they first started coming. Now we can't get their noses out of books."

"Oh." It's all I can think of to say. Mostly because I'm completely clueless.

A tinted back door opens, flooding the dingy interior with light, and a tall man steps in, looking harried. "There you are, Gorgeous," he says, pulling her into a hug and sending me into a jealous snit for which I'm not proud, but can't deny. "We're just about to start."

"Great, Frank. This is Cayden. I wanted to show him what we've got going."

"Well, come on," Frank says. "I think you'll be impressed."

He swings an arm around Gracie's waist and my jealousy spikes again. At least until we get outside and a ginger-haired man comes over and gives him a kiss, then tugs Gracie into a hug. "Anson, this is Cayden. Cayden, Anson is Frank's boyfriend. They're getting married next month."

"Congrats," I say, taking Gracie's hand even though my competition has just fizzled.

Across the parking lot I see an area where the asphalt has been removed, replaced by what looks like an urban garden. Nearby, about a dozen kids are standing around with compasses. They look to be in middle school, and one of the girls raises her hand and calls for Gracie. "We've been waiting *forever*," she says, even though Gracie assures me that we arrived on time. "They're just eager," she says as she hurries that way.

"For what?" I ask Frank.

"She didn't tell you?"

I shake my head and he rolls his eyes. "She gets caught up when she's here. I'm guessing that in her head she's already run through the whole deal."

"Feel free to take care of that oversight. I'm feeling a little lost."

"This whole place is Gracie's idea," he said. "The ironic thing is that she and I met online. I'm a photographer and I was following one of the women who'd shot some pics of Gracie."

"Why is that ironic?"

"Because this whole place is an internet free zone. The way Gracie tells it, she got tired of feeling like she was on social media all day, and at the beck and call of whoever emailed her or texted her, wanting an answer right then. And I think she was getting harassed a bit, though she never talks much about that, but some of her followers can be pigs."

"So I've noticed."

"Anyway, one day she was reading a book—some time travel romance—and she thought about how she'd be in pretty bad shape if she was the one getting sent back to the Scottish Highlands."

I can't help but laugh. "She has a point."

"She does. Always be prepared, right?" He nods in agreement with his own wisdom. "And then she was watching *The Walking Dead*."

"Zombie apocalypse," I say. "I get it now."

"She and I started talking. Our grandparents knew how to can vegetables. They memorized poetry and entire speeches from great orators. They knew how to hold a conversation." He shrugs. "And the amazing thing is not only did she pull this place together from scratch, but it's actually turning a profit. Parents love the idea and kids love the activities. There's a non-profit arm, too. Purely educational. Right now, the place is almost like after school care. Parents pay a monthly fee and the kids hang out here. And we have weekend activities, obviously."

"And what's that all about?" I ask, nodding to where Gracie and the kids are scurrying around the parking lot.

"Compass skills. We've hidden prizes around the parking lot. And you can see the vegetable garden. The kids tend it and then do their own canning."

"How long has this been around?"

"Going on a year now. I've been involved from the start, so I feel proprietary, but it's Gracie's baby. She's here most of the time, except when she has a shoot. And lately she's been coming less," he adds with a scowl.

"You know about that."

His eyes narrow. "Do you?"

I hand him my card. "I'm security. I'm not leaving her side until we catch the guy who's harassing her."

"Well, hurry up about it," he says. "We all want her back."

CHAPTER TWELVE

"HARD TO SURVIVE a zombie apocalypse without combat skills," I say, glancing sideways at Gracie as I exit MoPac—the western-most north/south highway that runs through Austin. We're almost back to The Driskill and I've spent the drive thinking about Off The Grid.

She twists in her seat. "Oh, definitely. Those zombies can fight."

"They seem like nice kids. I'd hate to see their brains get eaten. Yours, too, for that matter."

"Couldn't agree more. I'm all about keeping my brains from being someone else's lunch."

"I should probably set up some time to pop in regularly. Make a training schedule. Help you out." I flash her a grin. "In the interest of saving the human race in a post-apocalyptic world, of course."

"Just doing your part, Mr. Lyon?"

"Always."

She presses her lips tight together, but reaches out and

takes my right hand. I drive that way until I need it again, then reluctantly release her. "Thanks," she says.

"You're welcome. I was really impressed."

"In that case, thanks again. It's kind of my dream."

"It shows."

Her smile lights up the car.

We spent the entire afternoon at Off The Grid, so we've decided on a lazy evening catching up on paperwork and eating a room service dinner. We park at my office so I can grab my laptop and some case files, then we walk across the street to the hotel. We're about to take the elevator up when one of the desk clerks recognizes Gracie and hurries over.

"I was just about to send the bellman up to slide this under your door," she says, handing Gracie a plain brown envelope with her name on it.

"What is this?" I ask. "Hotel receipts or something?"

"No, sir. It was left for Ms. Harmon at the front desk."

"Oh." Gracie's drops the envelope as if it's a burning coal.

"I've got it," I say, as the clerk bends to retrieve it. "Thanks so much for delivering it personally."

She gives us a friendly, helpful smile, then turns away. I take Gracie's elbow and guide her onto the elevator. I don't say that it might not be from him. Of course we both know that it is.

"Do you want me to open it?" I ask once we're back in the room.

She hesitates, then shakes her head, making a face. "My stalker. My responsibility."

I consider arguing, but I know she won't give in. So instead I move beside her once I give her the envelope so that I can see everything at the same moment she does.

Everything turns out to be one thing, but that doesn't make it any less effective. Or horrible. And the moment Gracie pulls out the photograph, she sucks in air, then drops it and buries her head against my chest.

"Please," she says. "Please."

I know the part that she's not saying—*Please find him. Please stop him.*

I look down at the photo that has landed on the table with the image up. The two of us outside of Off The Grid, with Gracie in my arms, my fingers in her hair, and her face tilted up to kiss me. Written across it in ominous red ink is a giant red X.

I look at it, my blood boiling. And all I can think is *Hell yes, I will.*

I order wine to take the edge off, and we spend the evening not thinking about Peterman or photographs or anything at all. I put on another movie, but Gracie only half-watches, more interested in a book. I'm only half-watching, too, as I'm on my laptop playing catch-up on a variety of lingering projects.

I'm trying to work out a scheduling conflict for an upcoming job in San Antonio, when Gracie's soft voice interrupts me.

"Busy?"

"Nothing that can't wait. What's up?" Her head is tilted and she looks a little embarrassed. I frown. "Gracie?"

"Nothing. I just—I got sidetracked because of the photo. But there was something I wanted to tell you when we got back here."

"Okay." I hear the wariness in my voice. "Tell me now."

"I just wanted to say thanks for today. For installing the security at my house. And for being so supportive about Off The Grid." She lifts her glass. "For ordering wine. You're taking really good care of me."

"That's the job."

"Just a job?"

I cock my head, studying her. "You know it's not just a job."

She nods, twisting a lock of hair around her finger. "So I was wondering. About last night...."

She trails off, but I stay silent. If she's going where I think she's going, the only way this will work is if she gets there on her own.

For a moment, there's silence. Then she clears her throat and says, "I was thinking I'd like a do-over."

"Were you? What does that mean, exactly?"

I watch as the blush rises on her cheeks. "What do you think?"

I brush my forefinger over her lower lip. "I think I want to hear you say it. I think I'd like hearing you tell me what that means."

"I guess that's fair. I—I mean, I was the one who stopped."

"And if we'd kept going? Tell me what you liked."

"I liked the way you kissed me."

I tap her lip gently. "Here?"

"I—I like being kissed there. But that's not what I meant."

"I see." I lean back a bit. She's changed into a nightgown over which she wears the hotel robe. I reach out and untie the sash, then push the robe open and off her shoulders, relishing the soft little whimpering noise she makes.

The nightgown is soft cotton with a wide, elastic neckline, and I use both hands to tug it down, so it resembles an off-the-shoulder summer dress. Then I lower one side even more until I've exposed a breast.

I put my finger back to her lips and whisper for her to suck, then I tug my finger free, feeling the corresponding ache in my cock, before circling my wet fingertip around her nipple as she arches back, her breath coming faster.

"Here? Is this where you want to be kissed?"

"Yes. Oh, yes, please."

I stand, and she blinks up at me, clearly confused. Then I hold out my hand to her. "Come with me if you want to be thoroughly kissed."

The corner of her mouth twitches, and she takes my hand. I tug her to her feet and lead her into the bedroom, then nod at the bed. "Leave the robe," I say. "And get on the bed."

"Just the robe?"

"Oh, baby."

She holds my gaze as she reaches down and pulls the gown up over her head, then drops it on the floor with her robe.

"You're perfect." I draw a shaky breath, relishing her smooth skin, her delicious curves. She wears pale pink panties that hug her hips, and when she crawls onto the bed, I run my hand over the fabulous curve of her ass.

"Uh-uh," she says, with a definite tease. "Not yet. Finish what you started."

I follow her onto the bed, then straddle her waist, my cock straining against the athletic pants I'd tugged on once we'd settled in for the night. I bend forward, blatantly rubbing myself against her as I close my mouth over her nipple, one hand cupping her breast as the other slides down the length of her body, then eases up the inside of her thigh.

As I had last night, I find the edge of her panties, and as I stroke along the length of the elastic, I tug my mouth free of her breast and look into her eyes. Slowly, I slip my finger under the silk and cotton as her hands slide up under my T-shirt, her nails scraping my back.

She arches up, sucking in a shaky breath as I skim my finger over her slick labia.

"Baby," I say, slipping my finger inside her sweet pussy, "this is where I want to kiss you."

"Yes. Oh, yes, please."

I kiss my way down her body, reveling in the taste of her, in the way that she squirms with pleasure and twines her fingers in my hair.

I slip my fingers under the band of her panties, then tug them off as she lifts her hips, then boldly spreads her legs for me, her obvious desire making me even harder. I want to bury myself in her—I want to look into her eyes and fuck her hard, then slow down and make love to her all night long.

First, though, I want to taste her, and as her hand in my hair guides me, I kiss my way from her hip down to the landing strip that leads the way to her bare, wet pussy.

I run my tongue from her core to her clit, then slip my fingers under her ass cheeks to raise her up. Her hips rock as I eat her out, and as I close my mouth over her clit, I thrust two fingers inside, then almost shoot my wad when her body clenches around my fingers, her orgasm coming hard and fast and unexpected.

"Baby," I say, licking her, sucking her, tasting all of her as the last throes of the explosion run like shudders through her body.

I ease up and kiss her deep, telling her how good she tastes. And telling her how much I want to be inside her.

"Yes. Please." She lifts her knees, opening herself for me, and I kick myself for not having brought a condom in from the other room. I hurry back, find my wallet, then strip and sheath myself. "Like this?" I say, kneeling between her legs, wide and open to me. "Or do you want to ride me?"

"You tell me."

"Like this," I say. Because right now, she's mine, laid out like a feast for me.

I lean forward as I bend over, kissing her deep as she cups my ass, silently urging me inside her, but I wait, my cock poised at her core. "Tell me you want me," I say.

"I do. Please, Cayden. I want to feel you inside me. Please. Please, take me."

And since that's exactly what I want, too, I do, thrusting deep inside her core, so hot and slick and tight. We rock together, the bed squeaking, the headboard knocking against the wall. I'm sure they can hear us in the next room, and I don't care. Hell, I want them to. I want to make Gracie scream. I want to own her. I want to claim her.

I want to come with her.

And when she trembles beneath me as I explode into a million pieces, all I can think is that she gave me exactly what I wanted...and everything that I needed.

We spoon together, my hand cupping her breast as I bury my face in her hair, completely content.

So content, in fact, that I'm not quite sure why I say what I do. But the words that come out are, "I caught her in bed with another man. My wife. You asked me last night about why I was so quick to assume you were the cheater rather than Peterman being a stalker. That's why."

"I'm sorry."

"She was a professor. I'd been overseas. I was home on leave. I thought things were fine. I went out one day, came back early, and found the two of them in bed. I learned later it wasn't a one off."

"That's horrible," she says. "But thank you for telling me."

"It messed me up," I admit. "I thought you should know."

She snuggles closer, and I hold her tight. And I'm just

starting to drift off when she says one more thing.

"Cayden?"

"Mmm?"

"Your wife. She was a freaking idiot."

I smile against her shoulder, and I fall asleep holding her tight.

CHAPTER THIRTEEN

GRACIE'S WORK schedule is thankfully light. She has some sort of show Friday night at a boutique on South Congress, but other than that, she's working at Off The Grid.

Since my schedule is also light—I made it so once Gracie ended up on my itinerary— we end up dividing the time between Blackwell-Lyon downtown and Off The Grid up north.

By Wednesday, I'm cursing traffic even more than usual as we head south back toward the hotel.

"I'd say we could stay at my house," Gracie says, "but it's not quite ready. And it's further away from Off The Grid than the hotel."

"And my house is all the way in hell," I say, resisting the urge to honk at the asshole in front of me who's going forty in a seventy zone. "That's okay. I love traffic. It's my happy place."

"Liar," she says and puts in a Lyle Lovett CD. We

listen for a while and then she turns the volume down. "What are we going to do?"

I don't have to ask what she means. As much as we're enjoying each other, we both have jobs that need more than our partial attention. More important, Gracie needs to feel safe.

Which means I need to catch Peterman.

"Working on it," I say. "I promise."

"I know. I just…" She trails off and looks out her window. "I just don't like knowing he's watching me."

"I know, baby."

She smiles at the endearment, and I reach for her hand.

"Anything on the cameras?"

"No." After we received the photo outside Off The Grid, I had a team install an array of cameras to cover the parking lot, back alley, and the facade. So far, no sign of Peterman, though. Presumably he witnessed the installation and is staying away. "If we could just figure out a way to ensure that he would be somewhere…"

"The show on Friday?"

"We're working under that assumption, but I have a feeling he's going to be a no-show." It's a fashion show that's been advertised to customers and also several of the models' fans. And while getting lost in a crowd might appeal to Peterman, I think he may stay away simply because that many people mean too many variables. He may have gone off the deep end, but at the same time, he's not stupid.

I hold out hope that we'll randomly run across Peterman as we're walking down a street. I can take him out fast in an alley, and we can leave him to rot in a Dumpster. But of course it doesn't happen. Instead, we pass the week at our various jobs with breaks for shopping, sex, drinking, sex, friends, and more sex.

Despite the lingering threat, I really can't complain.

Wednesday night, we have dinner at Pierce and Jezebel's house at a stone table in the beautiful garden that Jez has been tending.

"She's wonderful," Jez tells me in the kitchen where I'm filling a tub with fresh ice. "Is it serious?"

"Oh. You know. It's all so up in the air." The words seem to fall from my lips, staccato and strange. I have an odd desire to kick my own ass. It should be serious. Hell, it probably *is* serious. Gracie is amazing. Smart and funny and beautiful and there's that connection. That Mona and Ted thing. I feel it; I'm certain of it.

And yet I can't just say yes. Can't admit that I want it to be serious. That I want Gracie.

Can't admit that I want to commit. Because what if that's the wrong move? What if I get burned all over again?

I look away from Jez, who's openly contemplating me. "It's hard being with someone in the spotlight," she says, and while Jez isn't famous, her little sister Delilah is.

"Gracie's very down to earth," I say, which is both true and entirely irrelevant.

Jez sighs. "Well, if you ever need to talk..."

I'm saved from answering by Kerrie bursting through the door with Gracie right behind her.

"Instagram," Kerrie says. "That's the answer."

I frown at her and Gracie in turn, then look to Jez who shrugs.

"Okay," I say as Connor and Pierce join us in the small, now cramped kitchen. "What's the question?"

"How he found her and how we'll catch him."

Kerrie tosses her arm around Gracie's shoulder and pulls her close. "We are brilliant."

"Not arguing," I say. "Why?"

"Pierce took a picture of me and Jez and Kerrie earlier this evening. And I was saying to Kerrie that if I wasn't so private, I'd post it on Instagram."

"But she is private," Kerrie says. "Because, hello?" She passes me Gracie's phone, and I scroll through all the comments to the various images she's posted over the last few months. Lots of positive thoughts from women. Quite a few nice and not overtly creepy posts from men, some of which lead into requests for dates or online conversations. And more than a few sleazy, suggestive posts that bump up against an NC-17 rating.

That tightness in my gut ramps up again. The idea that these men are there. Watching her. *Wanting* her.

I glance at her and see that she's watching me, her expression like a question mark. I conjure a smile and shake it off as Kerrie rushes on.

"And then we started talking about how a lot of the other models aren't private at all. And we started poking around, seeing who's posted what and who's tagged Gracie and—"

"Sheila," Gracie says. "My good friends know not to mention me. But I hardly know her. She's sweet, but we don't really talk."

My head is swimming, but I keep listening, assuming they're building up to something.

"*She's* the one who posted about the shoot at Cecilia's

studio," Gracie says. "That's how Peterman was able to tell you to go there to meet me."

"And we all know this guy is out of his head, right?" Kerrie says, stating the obvious. "I mean, he is seriously living in a fantasy world."

"Kerrie..." Connor's voice is low and firm, and his eyes are on Gracie. "Just get on with the story."

"Sorry," she says, but of course she's right. And the fact that he's stepped over into non-reality only makes him more dangerous.

"Go on," I tell her. "You're leading up to something."

"She also mentioned that I was at The Driskill. Just a passing *my friend is staying at my favorite hotel* kind of post. But he knew that, too. He told you where I was hold up."

"And she's posted about Friday night's show at the boutique," I guess, but Gracie shakes her head.

"Not a word. She's not doing that show. So I'm betting he's not going to be there. I didn't advertise to my fans. Not with everything going on."

"We can't rely on that," Pierce says. "Nothing changes on Friday. We have security lined up. It stays lined up."

"Sure," Gracie says, "but what about Saturday?"

She and Kerrie are both grinning wide, so I know they have a plan. "And Saturday is...?"

"Our engagement party, of course," she says, batting her eyes at me as Kerrie bursts out laughing.

For a second, I'm befuddled. Then lightning strikes and I look at both women in turn. "You're right," I say. "You really are brilliant."

"Well, I'm not," Jez says. "Explanation, please?"

"They're suggesting we have Sheila post about Gracie.

About how she's excited for the small engagement party and her friend's whirlwind romance. Peterman—sorry, Daniel—will see it, he'll crash it, and we'll catch him."

"Sounds dangerous," Jez says, then looks around at all of us. "And it also sounds like a great idea."

"It's both," I say, taking Gracie's hand. "But I'll keep you safe. That's a promise.

The store is called Bliss, and the fact that they have a local distiller serving free whiskey makes me think that it was aptly named. We have a ten-person team from Blackwell-Lyon working the show, including five women, three of whom are undercover as salesgirls while the other two are in the back of the store, which is being used as a makeshift dressing room for the product the girls will be modeling.

It's a decent-sized space, and the racks have been rearranged to make way for an open area that acts as a runway. When the show begins, I have a ringside seat as Gracie and a half-dozen other woman of all shapes and sizes model a range of everything from business attire to underwear for the mostly female audience.

The owner was kind enough to let us put up temporary cameras, and whenever Gracie's not on the runway, I'm looking at my screen, constantly checking the feed. So far, no sign of our guy. That's expected, but unfortunate. I want him caught. And I don't want to have to rely on tomorrow's fake engagement party as our last hope.

Not last. Latest. Latest hope.

Because no matter what, I'm going to make sure that Gracie is safe and that she stays that way.

The show ends with the underwear, and now Gracie and the others mingle with the whiskey-drinking crowd while wearing Smart Vixen lingerie, the brand that the store carries and which sponsored the event.

I hang back, just watching, that tightness in my chest returning as dozens of Joe-the-Waiter clones fawn all over her. I watch each face, searching for any sign that one might be Peterman in disguise. But I don't see her stalker. All I see are men who are fascinated by her. In lust with her.

Men who want her.

Seriously, I fear for drool.

"You look jealous." Kerrie's familiar voice comes from behind me, and I turn to find her with Pierce.

"Any sign of him?" I ask, ignoring Kerrie.

"None," Pierce says. "I think our theory is right. He's tracking her using Sheila's social media posts."

"At least we know," I say.

"And we'll catch him tomorrow," Kerrie says loyally as Gracie comes over to join us.

"Nothing?" she asks, and we all shake our heads.

"You were amazing," Kerrie tells her. "On stage, and the way you handled those guys."

"Why *do* you handle them?" I ask.

Both women turn to me, their expressions equally baffled.

"They're her fans," Kerrie says.

"And I'm part of the reason they're here," Gracie adds.

"That doesn't bother you? You don't interact online. Why do it now?"

Kerrie stares down her nose at me. "What bug crawled up your butt?"

Gracie ignores her. She doesn't ignore me. Her response is level and overly reasonable. As if she's talking to a child. "I don't get into it on social media because I made a decision not to. But I still have a fan base, and these men aren't Peterman. Maybe they're here for the lingerie, but maybe they just like the glamour. Maybe they want a tiny escape from their ordinary lives. They aren't bothering me—every man here was perfectly polite, just like the waiter you got so touchy about."

I wince. I hadn't realized she'd picked up on that.

"Besides," she adds, "I'm not going to completely shut down my life because Peterman has an obsession. Do that, and he's won."

I rub my temples, trying to dial back this foul mood. "You're right. Sorry. I just don't understand it. Why does the store even want them here? They're not going to buy the clothes."

"They might," Pierce says. "I was thinking about getting that little number Gracie modeled first for Jezebel."

"And the owner has an interest in the distillery. I bet some of these guys buy a bottle or two."

"Fine. You're all right."

Kerrie's eyes narrow, but I ignore her. I know I'm being defensive and prickly. I don't need her narrow-eyed stare to remind me.

"I saw you talking to Cecilia," I say to her, because I think I need to change the subject.

"Yeah, I didn't realize the women are all her models. She said if I ever want to try my chops at something like this to let her know."

"Really?" Gracie smiles. "That's great."

"Maybe. I didn't think I'd like it, but maybe I was wrong."

I fight a grin. I can't help but wonder how Connor would react. He says there's nothing between them any more, but would he be willing to sit here like me and watch her parade in front of other men in her underwear?

"Just let me change and we can go," Gracie tells me, interrupting my musing.

"Sure," I say, falling in step as she walks toward the back. It takes forever, because most of her fans are still lingering, and she's stopped every few steps by another man who wants her autograph or wants to tell her how he follows her and has her picture as a screensaver. None go so far as to say they jerk off to her picture, but I think it's implied.

And Gracie of course is lovely to each and every one of them. Smiling and chatting and telling them how nice it was that they interrupted their busy day to come to the show.

By the time we get to the door to the back room I feel like putting my fist through a wall.

"You okay? You look tense."

"A little bit," I admit.

"I have an idea," she says. "Tomorrow, after it's all over —whether we catch Peterman or not—lets go to Fredericksburg for an overnighter. Just you and me and no drama."

I want to say yes. Hell, I want to grab her hand and race

down the street with her. I want to hop in my Jeep and drive until we can't stand it anymore and then make love under the stars.

But we live in the real world. A world where wives cheat. Where temptations are dangled day and night. Where husbands get jealous.

Where boyfriends have to admit that they can't handle the thought of men pawing all over their girl, fantasizing about her.

And where sometimes you have to know when to walk away.

"I don't think so," I say softly, then watch as she stiffens.

"This is about today? About the fans. The comments on my posts. The things they said. You can't deal with it. The big tough guy who fought in the Middle East can't handle a few lonely guys looking at his girl. Is that it?"

It is. Of course it is. But all I say is, "You deserve better, Gracie,"

She looks me up and down, anger and hurt shining in her eyes. "Yeah," she says softly. "I do."

CHAPTER FOURTEEN

WE RENTED the Dufresne Mansion near the Capitol for our faux engagement party, and we were lucky to get the stately southern mansion on such short notice. A frequent location for weddings and anniversaries, it has an excellent set up for our sting. Although, if we'd had more time to look, I would have preferred someplace slightly smaller so we could control and monitor the crowd a bit better.

Because we had to, we put the announcement out on social media, and not just through Sheila. And though it would be too obvious for Gracie to make an out-of-character announcement of the place and time, we did have her post a picture of herself holding up a new dress, and say in the comments that it was for her "special day tomorrow."

Sheila also mentioned the party would be a "crush" so that our ballsy, psychopathic stalker would feel comfortable infiltrating the place.

In fact, it's not that crowded, and most of the guests are colleagues from other security firms, off-duty cops who Landon wrangled, and other handpicked friends.

We even have last minute catering arranged by yours truly. As much because we need it to seem real, but also because I needed to keep busy. And last night was the first night in over a week that I've slept alone.

I stayed in my tiny, quiet, empty house. Connor stayed with Gracie. And on the whole, it sucked.

We arrived together, of course, presenting the image of the happy couple, but after a few circuits, Gracie gave me a chaste kiss and said loudly that she needed to go gossip with her girlfriends. Then she clung to Kerrie's arm and slipped into the crowd, with Pierce texting me immediately that she was in his sights.

Now I grab a sparkling cider, wishing I wasn't on the job and could slam back a few glasses of champagne, and start to head outside. I'm intercepted by Kerrie, who approaches me with such a stern face that I know I'm in for a lecture.

"I'm not in the mood," I tell her, then start walking away.

"Fine. Whatever. I was just going to say that I was wrong."

I pause and look back over my shoulder.

"I thought Connor was the idiot for dumping me. But it's you."

"Thanks. Appreciate the support and understanding." I turn away again.

"Oh, I understand. I understand that you're a chickenshit."

Her words follow me, but I don't turn back again. Instead, I keep walking until I reach the flagstone patio. I'm on a mission, but even so, I'm looking at every face, examining every pair of eyes. I'll know him when I see him—but he's not here yet.

Then I see her.

Gracie.

And maybe it's a mistake—maybe I need to wait until wounds are healed and we don't risk causing a scene. But I can't. I have to talk to her. Have to find forgiveness—or at least understanding—in those beautiful blue eyes.

She's talking with one of her modeling friends, and I step up, telling the girl that I need my fiancée for a moment.

"Is he here?" she asks once I've steered her to a cordoned-off room, because under the circumstances, I have no other reason to talk to her. "Did you see Peterman?"

"I need to talk to you."

I see her body crumple under her false facade of strength. "No," she says. "Please, Cayden. Just, no."

I should walk away, but I don't want to lose this chance. I'm not sure, however, if I'm looking for the chance to fix things or the chance to make her understand.

Mostly, I know that I want to apologize. To make it right. But I really don't know how.

"I didn't mean to hurt you," I say, and she laughs. An ugly sound that makes me wince.

"Did you think that I'd be happy?"

"No, of course not. I—"

"This isn't about me, anyway. Or, actually, it is. Because you're jealous, and I'm right there in the center of it."

"I am," I confess, more relieved than I expected to have

it out in the open like that. "I'm jealous of all of those men who want you."

"Why?" she demands. "Tell me why that matters to you. Why?"

The words hang between us, and I see the answer. It flashes in my mind as clear as it had been all those years ago. My wife with another man. A man who was fascinated. Who desired her. And whose desire she wanted.

Gracie shakes her head sadly, and I know that she's understood all along what I'm only now seeing. "Maybe she wanted that, but I don't. Those men that look at me? That desire me? I don't care about them. Don't you get it, Cayden? I only want you. But I'm not going to be the woman you look at that way. It's not love—it's not trust—if you're just waiting for the other shoe to drop. And I—" She breaks off, her voice cracking. "I can't live like that."

I want to argue. To tell her that's not how I feel.

Except she's right. Of course she is. I don't give a flip what those men do.

All I care about is her.

All I'm scared of is having my heart broken again.

I take a step toward her, searching for the words, but we're interrupted by Jez who's come to tell us it's time for our toast.

I start to tell her we'll be there soon, but Gracie nods and follows her out, leaving me to hurry and catch up so that I can take her hand and we can walk in together, the happy couple.

My insides would be in tatters if it weren't for the job. Because instead of focusing on Gracie and my mangled heart, I can focus on all the faces in front of me. And while the crowd applauds and Connor says they all need to raise a glass to his brother—I'm scouring every person looking back at us.

And I'm seeing nothing.

Beside me, Gracie smiles at the crowd. "We decided not to make a speech so that all our friends could get back to the important business of drinking," she says, as we'd planned. But then she continues, and I turn to her in surprise. "But I want to say a couple of words. Just a few. To memorialize how I feel right now."

She draws in a breath and faces me. "When I first met Cayden Lyon, I thought, wow. This is a man I could love." Her smile is watery, her eyes glistening with tears. "And here we are now."

She lifts herself up on her toes and kisses me so softly it feels like goodbye. Then she raises her glass to applause, even though almost everyone in the room knows our engagement is fake.

And I'm the only one who knows that her speech was real. *Here we are now* indeed.

As soon as the applause dies down, we mingle, and cake is served, and I lose sight of Gracie. "Where is she?" I ask Sheila, the owner of the magical Instagram page that made all this possible.

She points vaguely toward the stairs. "Dressing room. She said her shoes were hurting her."

More like her heart. And even though I'm certain she wants to be alone, I head to the back and climb the carpeted stairs. If nothing else, I can tell her I came to let her know we're calling the operation a bust. It's been two hours with not a sign of Peterman.

But at least we had some decent cake.

There's a hall at the top of the stairs with three doors, the one at the far end being a giant bathroom that is used during weddings as a dressing room. As I step into the hall from the stairs, I see a frail woman in a loose flowered dress, practical shoes, and frizzy red hair step into the room.

For a moment, I assume she's just there to use the facilities. But, of course, there are bathrooms downstairs.

I'm running even before I think about what I'm doing. And maybe I'm being paranoid—maybe I'm about to give an old lady a heart attack—but I'm not willing to slow down and take that gamble.

I throw myself against the door and, sure enough, someone had latched it. But the wood shatters under the force of my impact, and in the second that I burst in, Peterman looks up, his red wig now lopsided from where I assume Gracie grabbed it.

She shoves him, and as she falls backward, he drops a knife. Gracie scrambles out of his way on hands and knees as I pull out the gun I've had holstered inside my waistband all night and aim it at the fucker's chest. "Just try it," I say. "Just try it and I will end you."

He stands there frozen, a dangerous man in a comical wig and a flowery dress.

"Call Landon," I tell Gracie, but she already has her phone out, and though she's shaking, her voice is strong when she tells him to come upstairs.

He arrives in a minute, Landon and Connor and Pierce. And while I holster my gun and move over to sit on the floor and pull Gracie against me, Landon takes point in clearing the bastard out of our sight.

It seems to take forever. And, at the same time, it feels like we're in that little room for no time at all.

"He's gone?" Gracie asks Landon when he returns to the dressing room. Though we've moved to a small velvet divan, her hand is still tight in mine, her normally pale skin almost translucent.

"In cuffs with four of my best men," Landon assures her. "He'll get a full psychiatric evaluation and the district attorney will get involved, too. No matter what, I don't see him getting out of confinement for a long, long time."

"Thank you." She releases me to hug him, and when they break apart, my fingers itch for her touch again. But it never comes. Instead, she says goodbye to him, then to Pierce and my brother.

They all leave, knowing that we need a moment alone.

"Well," she finally says. "I guess this is goodbye."

The word feels like a kick to my heart. "Gracie, please. I never meant to hurt you. Do you have any idea how special you are to me?"

They are, I think, the truest words I've ever spoken. And also the most useless. Because the woman standing in front of me is shaking her head. Not in denial of my words, but in denial of *me*.

"Don't," she says, and I can see the tears pricking her eyes. "You saved my life, and that's amazing. But don't try and be sweet to me. Not you, Cayden. You already told me why it can't work. And I told you why you're right. I won't sit around waiting for you to think I'm cheating. And I don't want to spend my life nursing your jealousy. I can't. I won't. And I need to go now, because thinking of what we've lost hurts too damn much."

I watch her leave, my body and soul aching. And as she disappears down the stairs, all I can think is that I fucked up royally. And I don't have a clue how to fix it.

CHAPTER FIFTEEN

IT'S a terrible feeling to walk through a gray world and know that you're the one who made it that way. Worse, to know that although you brought it on yourself, there is nothing you can do to fix it. Because it all boils down to trust.

You trusting her.

And her trusting that you're finally over the bullshit jealousy that you've been wallowing in for years.

There's no switch to flip. No fight to win.

No bang, no whimper.

There is simply no way.

That's what I've been telling myself since the engagement party. And I know it's true. But it's been two weeks now, and even though I *know* it, I don't *believe* it.

There has to be a way. There has to be a way to get Gracie back.

"I don't know how," Connor says when I gather the troops in the break room.

"I'd like to figure it out though," Pierce adds. "Because you've been distracted as shit."

I glare at him, because he's right—but only during my off time. Professionally, I'm still on my game. It's killing me, but I'm still on.

"Fine," he says, when I demand that retraction. "But honestly, you need to figure it out. Not only because you're a miserable fuck without her, but because you two were good together."

"What does Jez say?" Kerrie asks, and I turn my attention sharply to her.

"What does Jez have to do with this?"

"They hit it off," Kerrie says. "And from what Jez tells me, Gracie isn't much perkier than you are."

That news doesn't particularly make me happy—I don't want her to be miserable—but it does give me a strange sort of hope.

"I've called her. Several times. She won't return the calls." And I can't call anymore. She already battled off one stalker. I'm not going to step into that role. If she really wants me gone, I'll go. But not until I'm sure I've done everything in my power to convince her she's wrong.

I catch Kerrie later at the elevator as she's about to leave for the day, then slip on and ride down with her. "I called Jez," I tell her.

"And?"

"I got voicemail."

She steps to me, puts her arms around me, and gives me a hug.

"What was that for?" I ask when she's back on her side of the elevator.

She shrugs. "Just seems like you could use it. Look, just call her. Not Jez. Gracie. Tell her you want to meet someplace neutral and talk like adults. And somewhere in all of that, tell her you're sorry. And maybe even tell her you love her. I'm not sure. That might scare her off."

"Would it scare you off?"

"Love? Hell, yeah." Her smile is wide. "That's scary shit."

I laugh, but the truth is she's right, and I'm still thinking about that as I pull into the driveway of my crappy, tiny house. A house that is now officially on the market because I'm tired of living in a place that feels temporary. I want a home.

I want it with Gracie, but either way, I'm finding a real place. With room to grow, to have a family. To have the life I want and not just mourn the one I lost. Because the truth is I never lost it because I never had it. Because Vivien never really loved me. We never connected.

She was never Mona to my Ted.

The memory of that couple—of that night—makes me smile, and I'm grinning as I put my key in the lock. Then I step into the boring, boxy living area and see her. *Gracie.* Sitting right there on my couch.

"Hi."

"Um, hey." I step inside, treading carefully so I don't accidentally crush the possibility that is laid out in front of me. "How did you get in?"

"Jez said you called. And she said I was being stupid. And she gave me your spare key."

"Stupid?"

"Not her words, but the sentiment was the same."

I sit tentatively on the coffee table facing her. "Ah, was she talking about, say, your skill at calculus?"

"More like my skill at interpersonal relationships."

"Then you must have misunderstood. I promise you, I've been the stupid one."

"I'm going to give up modeling," she says at the same time I say, "I was so busy painting everyone with the Vivien brush I forgot that most women are Monas."

Her brows rise. "Who the hell is Mona?"

I explain about the couple from the bar the first night we met.

"You asked her name?"

"That part's made up. But the affection, the trust..." I trail off with a shrug. "They had a connection. You could see it. Hell, I could almost feel it. It's what Jez has with Pierce. And though I won't ever tell my brother, I think he and Kerrie have it, too."

"Oh. I get it."

"I never had it with Vivien. Not ever."

She nods, then looks up at me. "You had it with me," she whispers, and the word is like a knife through my heart. *Had.*

I drop down on my knees in front of her and take her hands in mine. "Can I get it back?"

"I don't want to lose you," she says. "But I can't live like that. I told you. And if that means I have to quit modeling, then—"

"No."

"Hear me out. Off The Grid is doing well. I have plenty of work there. I'd be cutting back on my modeling hours anyway."

"No," I repeat, then hold her chin so she has to look at me. "You can't live waiting for the other shoe to drop. And I can't live knowing that I took that away from you. Because you're good at it and you enjoy it."

"But if it makes you crazy..." she says, and I burst out laughing.

"It did, didn't it?"

"Did?" Her brows rise.

"Will I ever like men staring at my girl? Probably not. But it's some consolation that you're *my* girl and not theirs. And it's even more consolation knowing that it doesn't matter to you." I lift a shoulder. "You're a Mona."

"No," she says sliding off the couch and into my arms. "I'm a Gracie."

"But the real question is, are you mine?"

"Yeah," she says nodding. "Yeah, I really am."

And then, even though there's more to say, I kiss her. Because right then I know that there will be plenty of time for talking.

All the time in the world.

EPILOGUE

"HEY, LAURA," I say to the girl on the beanbag as I walk into Off The Grid.

The teen raises a hand, but doesn't take her nose out of her book. I chuckle. I've been coming here almost daily for over six months now, and I don't think I've ever seen her without a paperback in her hand.

"Frank," I say, when the tall man looks over from where he's rewiring a lamp with the help of his husband. "Gracie around?"

He points vaguely toward the back. "Office. Paperwork. We've got a shot at a grant, so she's got her nose in a legal pad making notes."

I find her back there, scowling, although it disappears when she looks up and sees me. "Hey, stranger."

"Trouble?"

"Only the kind I made myself. All these grant forms are online. I don't allow computers on the premises." She sighs. "Guess who's bringing home a ton of files and notes tonight?"

"Frank?"

"Ha. I wish."

"Home, huh? All that glorious traffic?"

"You're cruel."

My place sold within a month, and we've been living in her Travis Heights house ever since. She wants to rent it, though, and then we can move closer to Off The Grid. Close enough where she can run home if she needs to work on the computer. I'll still get to commute downtown, but I consider that a small price to pay.

"I'm not cruel at all. In fact, I think I found us the perfect place."

"Really?" She shoves back her chair and bolts to her feet. "Can we go see it?"

I dangle the keys. "I'm friends with the agent. Let's go."

It's only a couple of miles away, and we don't have to get on a highway. It's a four-bedroom house with two living areas, a huge yard, and a pool. And when we pull into the driveway, Gracie gasps. "I love this place. I've always loved this place."

"I know. It went on the market last week."

"We can really go in?"

"We can."

I lead her in, and she makes the kind of noises I hear during sex, which clues me in to how much she loves it.

"It's spectacular," she says.

"Wait until you see the bedroom."

A set of floating stairs rise from the foyer to this half of a split second story, which consists entirely of the master suite and bath, a small bedroom suite that could be a nursery, and a well-lit reading area.

The doors to the master are closed, and she opens them and then gasps in wonder.

I step up behind her, but I already know what I'm going to see. After all, I'm the one that set it up. A king size bed with a bookcase headboard. No books yet, but it's topped with dozens of faux candles that flicker and glow, filling the room with golden light.

A bluetooth speaker is playing Billie Holiday, and when Gracie turns around to look at me in wonder, I'm on one knee and holding a ring.

Her hand flies to her mouth, and her eyes are wide.

"Gracie Harmon," I say, "I'm madly in love with you. Do me the honor of being my wife, the mother of my children, my best friend forever?"

She doesn't say yes right away, but that's okay. I can see that her throat is clogged from the tears. Then she nods and says yes and tells me she loves me, all while tugging me to my feet, sliding on the ring, and then wrapping her arms around me.

"If you want the house," I say through laughter, "we close on Monday. Otherwise—"

"I want it," she says eagerly, her voice full of joy. "And do you know what else I want?"

"Tell me," I say as she tugs me into the room, then tumbles me onto the bed.

"You," she whispers, then straddles me, her fingers dancing over the buttons of my shirt.

And there, in the house that will become our home, I make love to the woman who is my heart, and will very soon be my wife.

SEXY LITTLE SINNER

CHAPTER ONE

I'M SO COMPLETELY SCREWED.

The thought rattles around in my head, and I try to shove it away. Smother it. Silence it. Because that really isn't the kind of thought a guy wants screaming at him while his tongue is in a woman's mouth. Or when her hot, little body is writhing against him. Or when his cock is harder than he thought possible and all he can think about is sliding his hands up her thighs and under her skirt, then ripping off her panties and letting her ride him until they both see stars.

But, dammit, the thought looms: *Screwed. Totally, completely, one-hundred-percent screwed.*

Because this woman is off-limits to me. Big time. No excuses. Hands-off territory.

Not that you could tell from a snapshot of the moment, because now I've got my hand on her breast, and she's arching back as I use my thumb and forefinger to tease her nipple while she bites her lower lip and makes that sexy little whimpering sound that used to drive me wild.

Apparently it still does.

Did I mention that I'm screwed?

I break the kiss, knowing we both need to take a few deep breaths, otherwise I'll end up fucking her right here against the washing machine, the smell of fabric softener mixing with the scent of sex and desire as I claim her fast and hard, just the way I want to. The way I know *she* wants me to.

"Connor, *please*."

My name on her lips is a demand, and so help me I give in, claiming her mouth with my own. Anything to sneak in a few more moments of stolen bliss.

"Oh, hell, *yes*," she murmurs as she tightens her fingers in my hair. Then she practically crawls up my body, releasing her grip only long enough to settle her ass on the washer lid so that she can wrap her legs around my waist.

One of my hands cups the back of her neck, but the other is on the smooth skin of her thigh, and as I briefly open my eyes, I see that her skirt has ridden up high enough to reveal a swatch of pink panties, a dark spot revealing just how wet she is.

I groan—could the woman torture me any more?—and force myself not to slide my finger up her thigh even though all I can think about is the way she'd feel naked and beneath me, her pussy hot and slick and tight as I thrust inside her.

I recall the way she bites her lower lip when she's about to come. The way her body would tighten around me, as if she could pop me like an overripe cherry.

I remember the way it feels to explode inside her, and then pull her close and breathe in the fresh, clean scent of her hair as we both drift off to sleep, her skin warm and soft against mine.

Oh, holy hell...

I'm not just screwed. I'm fucked. Completely and totally fucked.

Because this woman is my best friend's little sister.

More than that, she's the office manager of the business I own with Pierce and my brother. And won't this make for an awkward Monday morning?

But the real cherry on my screwed up sundae is that she's my ex. The woman *I* broke up with. The girl I said goodbye to for a litany of excellent reasons, not the least of which being a fourteen year age difference that couldn't be bridged simply by mind-blowing sex.

We'd admitted there was still an attraction, but we'd agreed it was over. And ever since, we've been pretty damn mature about the whole thing.

And then I'd gone and let two martinis, celebratory champagne, and a generous pour of bourbon on the rocks lead me straight into this utility room, and right into my own personal hell, all the more so because it feels so much like heaven.

I guess that's the point of forbidden fruit.

"Kerrie—" Gently, I push her away, a fresh round of desire rising when I see her kiss-swollen lips and the flush of sensual heat on her cheeks.

"Just this once," she whispers. "Then we walk away and never mention it again." She takes my hand, then slides it under her skirt until my fingertips are rubbing her pussy. "Please, Connor," she whispers. "For old time's sake? I'm so damn horny."

"We said we wouldn't—"

I don't get the rest of the thought out, because she puts her hand over mine and tugs aside her panties. So now it's just my fingers on her core, her clit swollen and sensitive beneath my finger. "Don't think about us. Just think of it as a public service. And I'm your adoring public."

"They'll know," I say, because I know damn well she'll cry out when she comes, and our friends are just one room away, gathered in the living room to celebrate my brother Cayden's engagement.

But the protest is only for show. Hell, I'm just a guy. A guy who maybe could hold his own against the flood of alcohol that has washed away my better judgment, but who is absolutely no match for this hot little spitfire of a woman. And she damn well knows it.

My thumb is already busy on her clit, and my fingers are thrusting rhythmically inside her. If she screams, she's just going to have to stifle the sound herself, because, oh, Christ, I have to taste her. Have to see if she's as sweet as I remember, though I know she will be. How could she not? After all, she's goddamned forbidden fruit, and as I start to lower myself to my knees, all I can think is how much I crave one more bite of that apple.

"We shouldn't," I whisper. One last, lonely, futile protest.

"I know." Her voice is tight. Desperate. "I know," she repeats. "We'll think of it as another ending. The final nail in the coffin. I know you said it's over, and I get that. But for right now, let's pretend it's not."

I don't know if I should embrace those words or run

from them. All I know is Kerrie. All I know is this deep, violent need.

And so as my twin brother and his fiancée play host and hostess to a houseful of their closest friends, I slide my palms along Kerrie's inner thighs, then ease her legs further apart. Then, for what is absolutely, positively going to be the very last time, I bury my face between the legs of the woman who once upon a time belonged entirely to me.

CHAPTER TWO

One month later

"LEO CALLED," my brother Cayden says, referring to an Army buddy we're hoping to entice into signing on as the newest employee at Blackwell-Lyon Security. Cayden and I are the Lyon part of the equation, and our buddy Pierce is the Blackwell part. "He's running about fifteen minutes late."

"Not a problem. I just updated the client list and the calendar. That'll give me time to run a clean set of copies before the meeting."

"Hmm," he says, as I head toward the file room where we keep the monster of a copy machine that does everything except make espresso and warm your croissant.

I pause, glancing back at my scowling brother, who looks all the more intense with his pirate-style eyepatch, a souvenir of an injury in Afghanistan. "Problem?" I ask, though I know I shouldn't. Because that one question will undoubtedly open the can of worms that I've been doing my best to avoid for the last four weeks.

"I didn't say a thing," he assures me.

"True, you didn't. But you were thinking pretty damn loud."

He lifts a shoulder in a casual shrug. "I've got a big ass brain, brother. Can I help it if my thoughts can move mountains?"

I flip him the bird, consider myself lucky for avoiding a conversation I really don't want to have, and take a step toward the file room.

"Just wondering why you don't ask Kerrie to make the copies for the meeting." His words follow me. "Seems like a better use of your time, what with her being the office manager, and you needing to log last night's surveillance report."

I ignore him—and his suggestion that I'm avoiding Kerrie. I'm not.

Okay, that's a lie.

I am avoiding her, but with good reason. Because after you drink a little too much, then go down on your ex-girlfriend/co-worker/best friend's sister while hiding in a laundry room during your brother's engagement party, things tend to get a little uncomfortable. Or so I'm told.

But this isn't about that. It's about logistics. I passed the open door to Kerrie's office not two minutes ago, and she wasn't at her desk. Which means it's just plain easier for me to run off the five copies before returning to my office to write up my reports.

I'm not avoiding shit. And despite what you might have

read in *Popular Psychology*, just because he's my twin, Cayden can't actually read my mind.

All of which I tell myself as I turn the knob on the file room door, step inside, and register two salient facts. First, the room is filled with the mechanical *whirrrr* of the machine. And second, Kerrie is the one operating it.

Her back is to me, and she's leaning forward to staple some papers, which is giving me the kind of view I really don't need at the moment. Nothing X-rated. Not even NC-17. But PG is enough to get my blood pumping. The erotic silhouette of her ankles and calves, both accentuated by four-inch heels. The soft skin behind her knees—which I happen to know is one of her most erogenous zones. Her lean, strong thighs courtesy of a daily routine of yoga or biking or swimming. And, of course, the curve of that perfect, heart-shaped ass.

How many sunrises had I greeted, morning wood nestled against that perfect rear? How many times have I cupped those round cheeks on a dance floor or held on tight as she straddled my cock, riding me all the way to heaven?

Dammit.

I'm getting hard just from the memories, and since that is definitely not the direction my thoughts need to be going at the moment, I take a step backward, intending to slip out through the still-open door before she notices me.

"Connor. Oh. Hey."

Too late.

I freeze, then gesture stupidly at the copy machine. "I needed to make some copies. It can wait."

"It's okay, I'm almost—"

But I don't hear the rest of it because I've already

backed out of the room. I'm five steps down the hall when I feel her hand on my back. I'm a big guy, former Special Forces, and I hit the gym every morning, run at least two miles daily, and treat myself to a forty or fifty mile bicycle ride in the Hill Country most weekends. Even so, it only takes her one hard and fast shove to land me in one of our three empty offices. She follows me inside, slams the door behind her, then stands there glowering.

"What the hell, Kerrie?"

She crosses her arms over her chest and stays silent. Kerrie is stunning—and I'm not just saying that because she used to be mine. She is a one-hundred percent looker who even went undercover for us not that long ago as a model. Now, those huge brown eyes are soaking me up, and damned if it doesn't feel like I'm melting.

I move to the desk and lean against it, not saying a word. Maybe we're having it out and maybe we're not. But I'm not going to be the one who pushes the launch button.

There's an electrical tension in the room that both disturbs and excites me. Excites, because that's the way it is between the two of us. Always has been. And that, of course, is the disturbing part. Because how the hell are we supposed to get over each other and slide back into being just friends if the air crackles every time we're in close proximity?

"I'm sorry," she finally says, which really isn't what I expected.

"Wait. What?"

"You heard me. I screwed up." She runs her fingers through her dark blond hair, the color of local honey, then simply sighs. Kerrie has a gorgeous mouth, with full, pouty lips, and I can remember only to well how delicious they taste. Right now, though, her mouth is a thin line, the corners tugging down into a frown.

I take a step toward her. I want to reach out, to touch her. But with all the electricity zinging around the room, I can't risk the explosion.

"It's okay," I assure her, wondering if she somehow gave a client wrong information or messed up one of our corporate filings. Considering she works full time, is pursuing an MBA, and barely has time to sleep, I'm amazed she doesn't drop the ball more often. "Whatever it is, we can fix it."

"Can we? Because honestly, if I'd known you'd be like this, I would have escaped through the garage that night at the party. I would never have kissed you, much less—well, you know. No matter how much I wanted it or how amazing it felt."

Everything inside me sags with her words. "Kerrie, you know we can't—"

"Dammit, I know." She moves toward me, and now we're less than an arms-length away from each other. "I know we can't be together. Believe me, Connor, you've made that more than clear. We had just shy of a year, and then we moved on. No strings, no drama. When you told me you wanted to break up, that was the deal we made, right? We swore we'd still be friends."

"That was the deal." My voice sounds tight, and I try not to anticipate where she's going with this.

"Right. That was the deal. What we both agreed to. Even though I thought you were a complete dumb ass for breaking up with me, I didn't throw a fit or whine or turn into a raging bitch, did I?"

I can't help but smile. "No, you definitely didn't."

"Our break-up was calm and rational. As neat and tidy as that kind of thing can be. And afterwards, we were still friends. Still co-workers. And everything was cool, right?"

"It was."

"Yeah," she says. "*Was.*" She surprises me with another shove to my chest. "Hello, past tense. Because now everything has changed. So why in the name of little green goblins have you been acting like a total jerk ever since Cayden and Gracie's engagement party?"

"Whoa," I said. "How exactly am I acting like a jerk?"

"You're avoiding me," she says, because Kerrie has never been one to beat around the bush. I knew she'd call me out. That, of course, only made me put more effort into avoiding her.

"Even after we ended our fling," she continues, "which was what *you* called it, not me, you never avoided me. But then we both got a little drunk and took advantage of the utility room, and suddenly—"

"You're imagining things," I tell her, because I'm a complete ass. Of course she's not imagining things.

"Don't even."

"Fine. You're not imagining things. And the answer is that I'm a jerk. Just like you said."

"No argument there. But why the sudden case of jerk-itis? More important, do you need oral antibiotics or a cream to cure what ails you?"

"Kerrie..."

"Do not *Kerrie* me. You're being an idiot. I will totally cop to having had a crush on you for years, but once we actually got together, all that changed. It wasn't just a school girl fantasy any more, and I wasn't thirteen with a crush on the soldier who came home on leave with my brother. I was twenty-three and working as a paralegal when we started going out right before my birthday, and I was twenty-four when we broke it off, remember?"

"You think I could forget?"

"Maybe. I'm twenty-five now. Or did you forget that? Because I'm all grown up. It's been over a year since you —*you*—put on the brakes. And during all that time, did I ever badger you for more? Did I whine that I wanted anything beyond what you were willing to give? Did I complain that you were a delusional loon who didn't know a good thing when it was staring him in the face?"

"No. Not until—"

"Exactly. All that time we've been friends—good friends, obviously. Friends who know each other pretty damn intimately, and that was okay. And we've been co-workers, too. And that never caused a problem until—"

"Exactly. *Until*."

"*Until*," she says, mimicking the way I stressed the word, "we got good and friendly at the party. And after that, I told you I missed you. Missed us."

"You told me you wanted to get back together," I remind her. Which is exactly what she'd said later that night as we shared an Uber to our respective homes.

"Yeah. And I meant it. But you said no. And I didn't press, did I? Not once, Connor. Not once, because even though I want you so bad I sometimes think it's going to drive me mad, I still value our friendship."

I want to get a word in, but honestly I don't know what to say. Besides, she's talking at the speed of light, so I'm not sure I could even manage to squeeze a syllable in, much less a coherent sentence.

"Don't you get it? If I can't have you in my bed, I still want you in my life." She blinks rapidly, and I know her well enough to know that she's fighting back tears, and my heart squeezes tight as she says, "But you're acting like one hot night in a utility room means we can't even be friends anymore."

"Maybe we can't," I say, then want to kick myself. I don't want to hurt her—that's the last thing I want—but I've been thinking about this a lot. Thinking about *her* a lot. We can't have a relationship, for all the reasons that existed when we broke up. Fourteen good, solid reasons. And then some. But after the utility room, I have my doubts about the friendship route, too. "Maybe 'just friends' won't work for us. Because we weren't *just* friends. If we'd just been friends, you wouldn't have been so quick to say you want to get back together."

"So you're saying I blew it. I opened my mouth, told you the truth, and screwed us up forever? Well, fuck you, Connor."

I rub my temples. This is not going well. "All I'm saying is that—"

"You know what?" Her words cut me off, and I'm grateful. Because I have no clue what I intended to say. "You're right. We'll play it your way."

"My way? What do you mean we'll play it my way?" I didn't even realize I had a way.

"You say we can't be friends?" She inches forward, and I take a corresponding step back, only to find myself pressed up against the desk. "Fine. We won't be."

"What are you talking—"

I don't get the rest of the question out, because suddenly she's pressed up against me. "Forget friends. If we're going to tumble down into the land of awkward acquaintances, I want it to be because of more than fifteen minutes in a laundry room. I don't get you as a friend or a boyfriend anymore? Then I think I deserve a fuck buddy. At least then I'll feel smug and not pissed when you can't look at me in the conference room."

I know she's kidding. Kerrie is the kind who will always try to bring some levity to an awkward situation. But before I can even grin, she shocks me by sliding her hand down to cup my package.

I jump, my entire body fried from the ten thousand volts of raw electricity that shoot through me with the contact, then I push her away, thrusting my hands into the air in a gesture of self defense.

"Whoa there, woman. Let's leave some room for the Holy Spirit."

As I'd hoped, she laughs at the reference to what had been my grandmother's favorite expression when Cayden and I were growing up in East Texas. For Gran, it had been more than a trite saying; it had been the essential rule for living that we boys and all the other boys in town were expected to follow at any and all school functions. Not to mention every other moment of the day until we resigned ourselves to wedded bliss.

Naturally, every boy in the county lost his virginity well before college. With that kind of carrot dangling, we had to see what all the fuss was about.

"I'm serious," she says, and when I meet her eyes, I

realize that she means it. What I'd thought was an attempt at levity was an actual, authentic proposition.

"Fuck buddies?" I can hear the disbelief in my voice. "Sweetheart, you're insane."

"No, I'm not. And don't call me that. Not unless you're agreeing, and then only in bed. You walked away. You can damn well call me Kerrie. Or Ms. Blackwell."

"In case it escaped your attention, Ms. Blackwell, the reason we broke up was that it made no sense to be together. We didn't have a future."

"Said you."

"Damn right. Somebody had to face reality. I'm fifteen years older than you. That's a decade and a half. I'll be drawing Social Security before you even subscribe to AARP."

"Since when did you start letting government pensions and magazine publications dictate your life? And it's *fourteen* years. Not fifteen."

"I'm forty. You're twenty-five. Do the math."

She rolls her eyes. We both know that for most of the year, the difference is fourteen years. But until her birthday, I win. The victory gives me little satisfaction.

"Can we not do this again?" She drags her fingers through her hair, leaving it tousled, which on Kerrie is a very good look, indeed. "I think your reasons were bullshit, but I'm not arguing them. I'm not asking to be your girlfriend. I've moved on, Connor."

Even though that was the point of our break up, I can't deny that her words are like a spike to my heart. "I didn't realize you were seeing someone." I mentally congratulate myself on keeping my voice steady and level.

"Why would I tell you? That's not really your business anymore."

"If you're seeing someone, then why do you want us to—"

"Dammit, Connor, I'm not seeing anyone, okay? And I'm not asking you to marry me, either. I'm just saying that we had something good, then we put it away in a box and shoved it under the bed. But it didn't stay there and when we set it free at the party, we destroyed something. So let's fix it. Can't we do that? Can't we go back to the way we were, only with both of us knowing that the relationship isn't going to go anywhere? But that—for right here and right now—we're both going to enjoy this intense attraction. Because I know you feel it, too."

Every atom in my body wants to do a fist pump, shout with joy, then bend her over the desk and seal the deal with a hot, dirty, fast fuck. That, however, I can't do.

Because even though a thousand green-eyed monsters gnawed on my kidneys simply from the thought that she'd found someone else, I know that it's just jealousy, not rationality, running the show. She needs to move on. She needs someone her own age. What's between us might be fun, but it can't last. And I can't be the guy stealing her focus when she should be looking for the real thing.

She deserves more.

And I'm going to make sure she finds it, even if it kills us both.

"Connor," she presses. "You have to at least answer me."

"I want to. Christ, Kerrie, you have to know I want to."

I watch as she licks her lips, then swallows. "That means there's a *but* coming."

"But we can't."

"Yes, we can. All we have to do—"

"*No.* Dammit, Kay," I say, calling up the nickname that only I use. "Do you have any idea how hard it is to find someone in this world you connect with? Right now, you're meeting all sorts of people through work and through school. Now's your time to meet the guy you're going to end up with. And that's good, because it just gets harder as you get older. But if we're fucking like bunnies, you won't pay attention." I feel a twist in my heart, but ignore it as I press on. "You won't find that special guy if you're with me."

"Won't I?" she says, her head cocked sideways as she studies me. For so long, in fact, that I start to get antsy.

"What?" I demand, when I can't take it any longer.

"Nothing." Her smile is both resigned and melancholy as she gets up and goes to the door. "I'm just trying to figure out how a man I know to be smart as a whip can be so goddamn stupid."

And as I stand there wondering what the hell she's talking about, she tugs open the door, slips into the hallway, and pulls it firmly closed behind her.

CHAPTER THREE

MY INSTINCT IS to follow her. I want to smooth out the bumps and make everything better for her. Hell, if I'm being honest with myself—and where Kerrie is concerned I've sacrificed both of us on the altar of my honesty—I have to admit that what I really want is to hold her and soothe her.

That, however, would be highly counterproductive.

Still, I'm not going to hide from the truth. I want her. That's the thesis of my fucked up personal essay, all the more wretched since she wants me, too.

It's like we're living in our own personal O. Henry story, complete with an utterly wretched, melancholy ending. Apropos, maybe, since the famous writer—William Sydney Porter to his friends—used to live just a few blocks away from this very office. A small house where he penned those ironic twists.

I don't know if he ever wrote a story with characters like Kerrie and me, but if he didn't, he should have. Two people, desperately attracted to each other, who can't be together. And who, if they give in to desire, will end up paying for the pleasure of the now with the inevitable, inescapable pain of the future.

That might make for a classic short story, but that's not a future I want for her. Not Kerrie.

Being with me might be fun at first, but I've known since childhood that a relationship can't survive that kind of age gap. As the years marched on, our relationship would become a prison, and I don't want to see Kerrie ending up like my grandmother, a vibrant sixty-five-year-old who lost a decade of active life to the yoke of obligation.

Growing up, my grandmother had been a force of nature in our family, taking up much of the slack after our mother left and our dad spiraled down into depression and drink. She ran our house, volunteered all over the city, and traveled the world with her friends and my grandfather.

But that came to a screeching halt when a heart attack landed Grandpa permanently bedridden. She spent the next decade as a shadow of herself, her vibrancy erased by long hours at the side of a man she adored, but whose slow, bedridden decline stole her life.

My grandmother always told me and Cayden that it was no hardship to stay home with him, but how could she say otherwise? Once she'd made that choice, she had to make herself believe it. Hell, she had to make him believe it.

And even if that's truly how she felt, how can I move forward with Kerrie knowing that this might be her fate? I may be in stellar shape now, but combat strains a man's body, and even though I have all my limbs, I took plenty of hits, and have the scars to prove it. Maybe I'll be fine until the end of my days. But it's more likely that some injury will flare up or some unknown toxin embedded in my cells will rear its head, and I'll end up like my grandfather, trapped in a bed under a blanket of guilt because the woman I adore is there beside me, handcuffed by the obligation of a love we should have never succumbed to.

How can I risk burdening Kerrie that way?

And what if it goes the other way? Instead of being like my grandmother—trapped by the burden of love—she follows in my mother's footsteps and grows to resent the discrepancy between us. What if, craving freedom and youth, she simply walks away from the man who is almost two decades older than her, leaving me in the same way my mother left my father. A lonely, bitter man who drowned his pain in a bottle, abandoned his eight-year-old sons to their aunt and grandmother's care, and moved ghostlike through the next few years until he finally passed out after one of his benders and never woke up.

Either way, Kerrie and I are fucked.

I know it, and she won't accept it.

But I'm not giving her a choice. I love her too much to risk destroying her.

So, yeah. I'm gonna have to RSVP "no" to the fuck buddy plan. With regrets, of course.

I stifle a frustrated sigh, then push away from the desk. Leo must be here by now, which means I need to get to the meeting, sit across a conference table from Kerrie, and try to look like none of this just went down.

Should be simple enough, but I'm foiled the second I

pull open the door and find my erstwhile brother leaning against the opposite wall, his head tilted, and the brow of his visible eye cocked in something that's either amusement or consternation. Possibly both.

"What the fuck?" he asks.

Apparently, it's consternation.

"Problem?" I turn right out the door and start heading toward the conference room. "Are Pierce and Leo already in there?"

"Leo just texted. He's parking. Should be up in five." His large hand—so like my own—closes over my upper arm, urging me to a stop. "Don't you think it's time to officially tell me what's going on with you and Kerrie?"

"Going on?"

He just gives me *the* look. Because he knows. Of course he knows. Not only do we have the twin thing going on, but the man works in security. He notices when people disappear. He notices when they return. And he notices the way they interact.

I, however, am not giving an inch.

Cayden clears his throat. "Let me rephrase," my brother says. "Don't you think it's time you told me what the devil went on with you and Kerrie at my engagement party? Because unless Gracie, Pierce, Jez, and I are all completely off-base, that's when you started acting like she was Kryptonite to your Superman."

"Gracie and Jez?" Gracie is Cayden's fiancée, and Jezebel is Pierce's wife. And I've been intentionally keeping so busy over the last month that I don't think I've spent more than ten minutes at any given time with either one of them.

"You can try to avoid us," he says in a demonstration of twin-related mind-reading, "but it's pretty damned obvious. For that matter, I don't even really need to know what went on at the party, because that's pretty obvious to. And can I just say that it's breaching the boundaries of etiquette to fuck on someone else's washing machine? Just pointing that out in case you missed that lesson in finishing school."

"Cute. And I didn't fuck her. Not technically," I add when he cocks his visible eyebrow. Cayden lost an eye in the Middle East, and while I've never been intimidated by my twin, even I have to admit that it makes him look like a bad ass. Honestly, it comes in handy for the job.

"Well, hell, maybe that's the problem. Maybe we need to lock you two in the penthouse at The Driskill and let you go at it like bunnies until you get it out of your system. Because honestly, Con, you can't keep avoiding her. In case you forgot, she works here, too."

"I'm not avoiding her," I lie, pointing to the office behind me. "Talking. Just now. You watched her leave."

He meets my eyes, and except for the patch it's like looking into a goddamn mirror. Only the reflection staring back at me is centered, together, and completely content for the first time in a very long time. I'm happy for him and Gracie, I truly am.

But I can't deny the green serpent of jealousy twisting in my gut.

"Work it out," he says. "And do it fast. If we want to entice Leo to join us and not the competition, we need to make sure he sees us as a razor sharp security company with a stellar reputation and an increasingly elite client base. He's not looking to sign up at Payton Place. Got it?"

I hold up my hands in surrender, and for the first time in a long time, I really do feel like the younger brother being schooled by his elder.

Even if there is only a nine minute difference between us.

CHAPTER FOUR

AS SOON AS I step inside the large conference room, I see Leonardo Vincent Palermo standing by the windows, a huge smile lighting up his face as we all greet each other with firm handshakes and slaps on the back. Leo did a tour with Pierce, and Cayden and I met him a couple of times when we were all on leave. Born of an Italian mother with a love of art, he was named after Da Vinci and Van Gogh. "But I can't paint worth a damn," he assured us. "I don't think my mother ever forgave me."

In all the time I've known him, I never thought about the way he looks. But now, as Kerrie breaks stride when she enters the room with a sheath full of copies, I take full stock of the guy. He's dark, like Cayden and me, but whereas Cayden and I look like we grew up on a ranch, Leo looks like a cross between European royalty and a classic film star.

"Leo!" I watch, not sure if I'm amused, pissed, or jealous, as Kerrie bounds across the room into Leo's outstretched arms.

Jealous.

Yeah. Definitely jealous.

What the hell, right? I might as well own it. Because at the moment, there's really no other way to describe the dark, storm-green maelstrom of emotions roiling inside me.

"It's so great to see you again," she squeals. "It's been, what? At least two years, right?" She grinning so wide she's practically giddy, and, damn me, my first instinct is to sidle up next to her, put my arm around her shoulder, and lay claim to her.

My second impulse is to punch Leo in his smug, youthful face. Because the man's more than a decade younger than Pierce, Cayden, and me. Which means he's right there in Kerrie's target range. Or, at least, in the range I defined for her.

And I'm so lost in trying not to show on my face everything that's going on in my head that I completely miss how he responds. But if his expression is any indication, he's just as happy to see her.

Fuck me.

"Don't leave us in suspense," Pierce says, as we all finally settle into our seats. "Are you accepting our offer? Or are you going to move all the way to Austin only to sign on with some lame ass competitor?"

Leo chuckles. "When you put it like that, I guess I don't have much of a choice. When can I start?"

His words raise a chorus of welcomes, from myself included. I may have felt the bite of jealousy looking at him with Kerrie, but the truth is that Leo is a stand-up guy with a good head on his shoulders. He's competent, has a solid work ethic, and he's one of the nicest guys I've ever met. He's going to make one hell of an addition to the team.

And if there is something brewing between him and Kerrie, well, at least he's the right age. And didn't I just tell Kerrie that one of the reasons we couldn't be together was because she needed to be free to go out with eligible guys? And Leo's not only eligible, but vetted by me, Cayden, and Pierce.

That's a good thing, right?

I lean back in my chair, my head telling me it's a very good thing while my heart wants to land a quick, hard punch right in Leo's gut. That, however, is an urge that will dissipate once I get my shit together and my heart and gut catch up to the truth I already know—that Kerrie will be better off in another man's arms.

I swallow a sigh. Why the hell does being reasonable and doing the right thing have to be so goddamn painful?

"—but Connor's worked with the senator quite a bit," Pierce says, and I drag my attention back to the meeting at hand, confirming which of the names on the list are clients I brought in, answering other questions Leo has related to our processes, and generally diving into the business of growing our company.

"You mentioned that you're coming to us with an active investigation?" I say, recalling the phone meeting we had last week. Leo was still debating between joining us or accepting an offer with another company in town. But either way, he intended to retain a long-term corporate client.

Leo nods. "Carrington-Kohl Energy," he says. "Brody Carrington and I have been friends since high school, and he took over as CEO after his father retired a few years ago. About four months ago, he realized that someone in the company had been stealing proprietary information and selling it. We know who was siphoning off the information," Leo continues, pulling a file folder out of his briefcase, then passing us each a copy of a thick report. "Unfortunately, he's dead."

"Foul play?" I ask.

Leo shakes his head. "Suicide. Apparently he had aggressive cancer. He knew he was dying and decided to sell corporate secrets so that his family would have some cash after he was gone. Personally, I think more traditional life insurance would have been a better option. As it is, his family's got nothing."

"So you plugged the leak," Cayden says. "But you don't know if he managed to pass the information on to the buyer. Or even who the buyer was."

"But we have a suspect," Leo tells us. "And we're pretty confident he's holding onto the information, waiting to sell it to the highest bidder." He looks at all of us in turn, his expression underscoring the import of what he's about to say. "Michael Rollins."

Pierce whistles, and Cayden mutters a mild curse.

"Rollins." I lean back in my chair. "Would be one hell of a coup to catch that man with his hands dirty." Based two hundred miles away in Dallas, Rollins is a constant fixture in the world of high finance. A man who has a reputation of having a deal with the devil since he always seems to be two steps ahead of the market. An incredible skill if it's legit. A criminal offense if he's using spies and other nefarious means to collect pertinent data on competitors and various industrial players like Carrington-Kohl.

"So far, no one has been able to nail Rollins for playing dirty, but that's partly because no one in his organization is willing to talk," Leo says. "I have some friends in the Justice Department, and they're all panting for him to make a mistake. There's no solid proof, but they're all certain that he's not only dirty, but that he's dangerous. The kind of man who kills if it suits his needs."

"Would be quite a feather in the Blackwell-Lyon cap if we can catch Rollins with his hand in the cookie jar," Cayden says.

"And not a bad launch for my career with you guys," Leo says.

Pierce chuckles. "That sounds like you have a plan."

"I do. I just need a little help." His eyes cut to Kerrie. "Of the feminine variety."

I stiffen, every protective urge in my body flaring. "What do you mean by that?" I ask, unable to keep the possessive tinge out of my voice.

"My sister went to school with Rollins' girlfriend, Amy, who's apparently been trying to lose that particular title for over a year now, but Rollins' is a possessive, vengeful son-of-a-bitch, and the girl's scared to leave him. I won't bore you with the details, but after much back and forth, we came up with a plan. Rollins hosts a lot of house parties, and next weekend should be a doozy, since it's his yearly extravaganza. For the last month, I've been corresponding with Rollins as a high-rolling ex-Pat living in Dubai looking for a risk-free investment. He's been pitching some bullshit deal to me, and when he heard I was going to be in town with my girlfriend, he invited us to the party."

I meet Cayden's eyes and can see he's equally impressed. That's exactly the kind of resourcefulness that Blackwell-Lyon is becoming known for.

"The plan was that I'd go in with a date, and while Rollins is busy flirting with my lovely companion, Amy and I would infiltrate his system and gather enough proof to take him down. But I've hit a snag."

"What snag?" Kerrie asks.

"The woman I usually work with on this kind of job broke her leg in a skiing accident. The job should be an easy in and out—Amy has access to Rollins' home office and I know you guys can get whatever tech we need—but I can't risk taking in a partner who's not completely mobile, just in case."

"Makes sense," Pierce says. "I'm guessing you're looking at Kerrie as an alternate?"

"Ah, yeah." His eyes dart to Kerrie. "You know the score, you're at least somewhat familiar with the tech, and you're definitely Rollins' type. You corner him for a drink, and I'm sure Amy and I will have enough time to get the data."

"I thought this guy was dangerous," I say, my chest constricting.

"Like I said, this should be an easy in and out."

"I can totally handle that," Kerrie says, shooting me a sharp glance.

I scowl, but nod. I'm not happy, but I know I won't win this one.

"Right. Good." Leo tugs at his collar, and I actually see a hint of red creep up his neck.

"What aren't you telling us?" I ask.

"Ah, right." He swallows. "The thing is, Rollins is famous for his parties. Not because they're extravagant—they are—but because they're risqué. And when I say that, I'm being polite. I won't say that we'd be walking onto the set of *Eyes Wide Shut*, but my, um, partner and I are going to have to be convincing. And play along."

His words are like a roar in my head. "Wait a second," I say, noting Cayden's amused expression as I try to process this. "You're saying that it's a sex party?"

"Yeah," Leo says, shooting an apologetic glance toward Kerrie. "That's exactly what it is."

"Hell, no," I say at the exact same time that Kerrie smiles, flips her hair, and says, "I'm in. Hell, it'll be an adventure."

CHAPTER FIVE

AN ADVENTURE.

It's been more than twenty-four hours, and Kerrie's words still ring in my head ... along with the conversation between her and Leo that followed.

"Were you serious about it being a sex party?"

"Intrigued or mortified?"

A blush rose on her cheeks and she actually giggled. "You know me. Always up for a new kind of adventure. At least we've been friends for years. That'll make it easier."

"But we have to look like more than friends." Leo's smile was warm, not leering or suggestive. Even so, I wanted to punch him in the face. "Wanna grab dinner and a drink soon? We can share our secrets and practice looking like a couple."

That's when she'd shot me a tight little smile. "That sounds just about perfect."

Perfect my ass.

But considering I'm the one slamming on the brakes and pushing her away, I know I can't say anything. Especially since every rational bone in my body is telling me that she and Leo really would make a solid couple.

Unfortunately, the boneless parts—like my heart and another major organ to the south—aren't feeling too rational at the moment.

That's okay. I know I'm doing the right thing. The smart thing. Staying with Kerrie might be fun for a while, but the longer we let it go on, the more she'd lose. Better to take our pain now and get on with our lives. Even if that pain, by definition, hurts like hell.

I know that. I believe it.

And yet here I am parked outside her tiny South Austin house. Why? Well, that really is the question of the hour. The real answer is that my car pretty much drove itself over here. Which means that I should put the car back in gear, pull away from the curb, head down the street, and leave her alone.

Instead, I kill the engine and get out of the car, justifying the visit by telling myself that it's my responsibility to make sure she's comfortable going undercover. One afternoon pretending to be a model around people who weren't even remotely dangerous is one thing. Attending a party hosted by Michael Rollins under false pretenses is entirely different. I want to make sure she understands the potential danger. And that she's prepared for anything that might go down.

As I head up the drive toward her front porch, my hand goes automatically into my pocket for my keys. Not because I'm in the habit of walking into Kerrie's place uninvited—that privilege evaporated long ago—but because I still half-think of this place as Cayden's house. Once a rental property, he'd lived here after his divorce and before he and Gracie got together. It's a tiny place—just one bedroom and not even five-hundred square feet—but Kerrie jumped all over it when Cayden put it on the market.

I pull my hand out of my pocket without the key and rap on the front door. *Nothing.*

I knock again.

Still nothing.

With a frown, I look back over my shoulder to the driveway. Sure enough, her car is right there. Of course, she could have walked down the block to the convenience store on Brodie Lane. Or she could have taken an Uber to go meet her girlfriends at the bars on Rainey Street. It is a Friday night, after all, and since I spent the entire workday in Waco going over the details of an upcoming protection gig with our part-time McLennan County team, I haven't seen Kerrie since yesterday. No chatter in the break room about her plans. No laughing over a stupid joke while we wait for the Keurig to brew.

No cringing as she tells me about how she and Leo are going make such a convincing couple while they're on the Dallas job next weekend.

Shit.

I really should just turn around and go home. Because Cayden is right. This woman is my Kryptonite, and under the circumstances I should stay away until I've managed to flush her from my system.

I start to turn, but the lock clicks as I do, and the door opens to reveal Kerrie with her hair piled up under a towel, her skin dewy from what I'm certain was a scalding hot shower. She's in a pair of fleece shorts that accentuate her well-toned thighs and a white tank top that clings to her breasts, the material thin enough to reveal the outline of her dark brown nipples.

My entire body clenches, and my mouth goes dry.

Yeah, I probably should have driven away. Far and fast. And yet...

"Connor?" There's no mistaking the surprise in her voice. "I thought it was..." She trails off with a wave of her hand and ushers me inside.

"Sorry," I say. "I just got back from Waco. I had a few thoughts about next weekend for you to keep in mind while you're prepping."

She studies my face as if she's looking for signs that I'm bullshitting her. I am—well, partly—but I hide it well. After a moment, she sighs. "This really isn't a good time. Couldn't you tell me Monday at the office? Or send me an email?"

Ouch.

"I thought—"

"That you can just pop in like nothing's changed. Like we're just friends and all is hunky-dory and peachy-keen?" She glances down, frowns, then crosses her arms over her breasts. "It's not."

"I know that. But next weekend is a new situation for you."

"And I'll have Leo to help me out. He may not have been at Blackwell-Lyon, but he's been in the business for years. Or, what? Are you saying we just hired a guy who's not up to your standards?"

"Come on, Kerrie. Don't play that game. You know that's not what I'm saying."

For a moment, I think she's going to argue. Then she turns on her heel and disappears into the bedroom. A moment later she reappears, her damp hair hanging limp around her face, her body wrapped in a fluffy pink robe that's all-too-familiar to me. I rub my fingers together, the visceral memory of the soft material torturing me.

"Fine," she says. "You're right." She leans casually against the back of the couch, the robe opening to reveal the hem of the shorts and her thigh. Before, it was just skin. Granted, it was Kerrie's skin, and therefore exceptional. But now that she's taken the effort to cover it, this unintended peek seems that much more naughty, especially since I can so easily imagine what her skin feels like under my fingertips.

Probably not the reaction she'd intended...

A few more moments pass, then she pushes a lock of hair out of her eyes and sighs. "Look, I know you care about me. I know you worry about me. I know you think that breaking up was the right thing to. I get it. I do. And for a while I was handling it just fine. But things changed at the party, right? We both know that. I mean, weren't you the one who wasn't even sure we could be friends? So what are you doing here on a Friday night, Connor? Are you trying to make this harder on me?"

Her voice is tight with emotion, and for the first time in my life I'm not that chivalrous guy who always tries to do right by a woman. Dammit, my grandma taught me better. "Shit, Kerrie, you're right. I'm sorry. I swear I wasn't thinking about anything except making sure you're well-prepped."

"That's not your job. And this isn't the time."

"This is Michael Rollins we're talking about." I say the words, but I'm hating myself as I do. Because even as they're rolling out in all their efficient, reasonable, truthful-sounding glory, the man I'm really concerned about isn't the potentially dangerous scumbag of the financial world. No, I'm worrying about the hot-blooded, Italian, former Marine who's escorting my ex-girlfriend to a sex party.

When you put it that way...

"You need to be careful." My words are stern.

She cocks her head, her mouth curving into a knowing grin as she asks, "Are we talking Rollins, the situation, or Leo?"

I want to retort, but considering she's nailed me, there's not much to say.

Kerrie, however, is not similarly stymied. "I never wanted to break up with you. But now you're making me think that maybe your lame ass decision was the right one. I mean, you must be too old for me, right? Because I swear, you're acting more like my father than a boyfriend."

"I'm not your boyfriend."

A muscle in her cheek twitches. "No, you've made that clear. You're not acting like a co-worker, either. A co-worker would call or email or wait until Monday."

"Is it a crime for me to still care?"

"*Yes*. No. Hell, I don't know." She meets my eyes, and I see something that might be sympathy reflected back at me. "Listen, Connor, I know you're worried, but I'm going to be fine. I'm just a prop, just the girl Leo needs on his arm. You know that as well as I do. Leo's the one who'll be doing the heavy lifting, and we both know he's well-trained. Really," she adds gently, "I'll be fine."

My heart twists from nothing more than the tone of her voice, and I feel like a heel again. I didn't come here to remind her that she cares for me or to make it harder on her.

Which begs the question of why I came at all. Because she's right. Everything I came to say could easily wait until Monday.

I'm trying to decide if I should own up and tell her that I was wrong. That we *can* be friends. More, I want to. Yesterday in the office was a stumbling block, but despite what I said, even though I've pushed her out of my bed, I don't want to push her out of my life.

That's what I *want* to say. But I don't get the words out because as I'm still playing the tune in my head, she clears her throat, then nudges me with her voice. "Um, listen, can we talk on Monday? Or later this weekend if you think we need to. It's just that I need to go get ready, so..."

She trails off with a slight nod toward the door.

I glance at my watch—almost seven. Kerrie habitually spends her nights at home in PJs and a robe. "You're going out?"

"Well, um, yes. *Yes.* I am. It's Friday, and I have a date." She licks her lips. "So if you could go, that would be great. It would be kind of awkward for the two of you to bump into each other, don't you think?"

"Who is he?" I tell myself I'm happy she's dating again. I force myself to believe that the only reason I'm asking the little prick's identity is so that I can run a quick check on lover boy. For Kerrie's safety, of course.

I can tell from the look on her face that she knows exactly what I'm planning.

"We're not playing this game." Her voice broaches no argument.

"Right. I know. I'm sorry." I move to her front door and rest my hand on the knob. "I'll get out of your hair." I want to tell her she looks great, but considering where this relationship needs to go—specifically, nowhere—I keep my mouth shut and tug open the door.

And standing right there, his hand raised to knock, is Leo.

CHAPTER SIX

"CONNOR! Hey, buddy, good to see you."

Leo gives my shoulder a friendly pat as he steps past me to enter the house, either not caring or not knowing that his date's ex-boyfriend is standing right in front of him.

Is this a date-date, I wonder. Or are they just doing what they'd talked about and getting comfortable with each other so that they can pass themselves off as intimate.

I glance over in time to see Leo brush a kiss over her lips without appearing the slightest bit self-conscious.

That, I think, *is clue number one.*

"Sorry I'm not ready," Kerrie says. "Connor and I got to talking."

"No worries. We have time before the reservation."

Reservation. That sounds like more than a rehearsal to me. Let's call that *clue number two.*

Fucking, Lame-ass Clue Number Two.

I shake my head like a dog, warding off these damnable thoughts.

"You okay?" Leo's squinting at me.

"Fine. Just a lot of stuff on my plate." I toss my thumb over my shoulder to indicate the door. "I should head out. And I know you two need time to, ah, rehearse."

"Oh," Leo says. He looks up at Kerrie's beaming face, then murmurs. "Rehearse. Yeah." He takes her hand. "That's a good word for it."

My stomach twists, but I remind myself that this is good. Leo's a stand-up guy. This is what I want.

My brain knows that. The rest of me just hasn't caught up with reality.

Which is why I need to leave before I kill the son-of-a-bitch. "Right," I say, my voice brisk and cheerful. "I'm out of here."

I'm at the door when he calls out, "Actually, can you stay a bit longer? There's something we need to discuss. About the Rollins case, I mean."

My brow furrows as I look to Kerrie, who shrugs. Obviously she doesn't know what's going on any more than I do.

I follow both of them to the living area, which isn't a long trek in the tiny house. As Kerrie settles onto the floor, her back against the sofa, I cop an armrest. Leo stands in front of us, his hands shoved deep into his pockets, his expression unreadable.

"Just spit it out," I say, curious now.

He draws in a breath, and I see a flicker of consternation cross his face. "As much as I'd enjoy this assignment, there's been a change in plans."

I turn to Kerrie, only to find her looking back at me, clearly just as confused.

"What are you talking about?" I ask.

"Remember how I told you that my sister went to

school with Rollins girlfriend, Amy? The one who's been helping us? Well, turns out there's a picture of me in Rollins' office."

"How?" I ask. "According to the briefing notes, Amy and Rollins weren't together until well after she graduated."

"True," Leo says. "And that's part of why it never occurred to me that this might be a problem. But apparently Amy had a photo collage of her made for Rollins about seven months ago. To celebrate the anniversary of their first date. Back when she didn't realize that Rollins was the spawn of Satan."

"I still don't understand what the problem is," Kerrie says.

"The problem is that Leo's picture is part of that collage." I meet his eyes. "Isn't it?"

"Afraid so." His hands are still in his pockets, but now his shoulders rise and fall in an expression of frustration. "Mae and I went with Amy to a concert in Zilker Park. We were all screwing around, and someone took a picture of the three of us. I'm right in the middle, larger than life, an arm around both girls' shoulders."

"Which means that Rollins might recognize you," Kerrie says.

"He probably won't, but we can't take the risk. If we'd known, I could have shifted my cover story. Worked Amy in as an old friend. But changing it up now is too risky."

Kerrie's brow furrows. "So what do we do?"

"Same plan, different players," Leo says. "I just got off the phone with Cayden and Pierce. Called you," he adds, looking at me, "but it rolled to voicemail."

I pull out my phone. Sure enough, there's a missed call.

"Consensus was, as the only single guy in the company not on Rollins' radar, you're our man. And Kerrie, of course, is still the girl. And you two have been friends forever, right? So the fake relationship thing won't be a problem."

"No," I say, my chest suddenly tight, but whether with dread or anticipation, I really don't know. "That won't be a problem at all."

"Wait, wait," Kerrie says. "Won't Rollins realize that Connor's voice is different?"

Leo shakes his head. "I doubt it. Our voices are pretty close in timbre. And most of the time, Rollins and I communicated by email. Made it easier, what with the time difference. The one time we did talk, it was on speaker and I turned on a static generator. We could barely hear each other." He grins, looking pleased with himself. "I like to plan for all contingencies. Guess this time that practice came in handy."

"No kidding," I say.

"So that's the plan," Leo says, looking between Kerrie and me. "All good?"

I know that I should object. Right now really isn't the best time for Kerrie and me to be undercover at a sex party. But all I say is, "Yeah. Sure."

I am, after all, a professional.

Besides, this might turn dangerous. And in that case, I'm the only one I truly trust to keep Kerrie safe.

"Excellent," Leo says. "So we've got about a week before the party. We can start briefing tomorrow, and I'll get you access to my fake Dubai email account, all our correspondence, and the rest of it."

I nod, not worried about getting up to speed. I've taken on more complicated personas for undercover work. No, my only concern is sitting right next to me. But—again—*professional*.

And that, of course, is going to be my buzzword for the entire operation.

Leo reaches down and offers Kerrie his hand, helping her up. "Rain check okay?" He's still holding her hand. "I want to make sure everything in my head is in a brief for Connor."

"Of course. We can do dinner some other time."

"And you two should probably go out," he adds, nodding at me. "Play the boyfriend/girlfriend game. You want it to look convincing."

"Yeah," I say, acknowledging that despite my best efforts to stay away from this woman and give her the space to move on, Leo Palermo has just shoved both of us into the rabbit hole.

CHAPTER SEVEN

ALTHOUGH THE IMAGE of Kerrie's hand intertwined with Leo's stays in my head for the next few days, I get no further clues as to whether or not there's anything brewing between the two of them. Maybe it was just a friendly, casual gesture. Or maybe they're both damn fine actors in the office who fuck like bunnies once the workday is over.

I tell myself that would be just fine. Great in fact. They'd make a cute couple.

I am, of course, a lying son-of-a-bitch.

Fortunately, I don't have much time to ponder. Instead, I'm focusing on the role I'll be playing. John London. An ex-Pat high roller looking to pad his pocketbook even more. Back in the states for a whirlwind trip to see friends and business advisors, his young and pretty trophy girlfriend—Lydia—at his side.

And no, I'm not blind to the irony. For this particular assignment, the fifteen years between us works to our advantage.

One week is pretty tight prep time for a Thursday-to-Sunday, no-respite undercover assignment. But Leo's a consummate professional, and he's been working closely with both me and Kerrie, drilling us over and over again on our cover stories, the details of how I made my fortune, a description of my office in Dubai, the backstory of how I ended up living and working in that part of the world, how I met Kerrie—sorry, *Lydia*—and on and on and on.

The three of us have been more or less attached at the hip for days. Certainly, we've been locked in close quarters, having commandeered the bigger of the office's two conference rooms as our own. The downside is that I never have a moment to myself as we cram, study, and stay in character. The upside is that we've thoroughly trounced whatever insecure demon had me avoiding Kerrie.

"I guess my evil plan worked," she says as we're taking a break to wolf down a quick lunch, and Leo had stepped out to take a phone call.

I grin. "I always knew there was a touch of evil inside you. Those wicked, wicked ways of yours."

"Not wicked," she retorts in that silky tone I know so well. "Naughty." For a moment, I'm caught in her sultry gaze. Then she grins broadly, laughs, and says, "Isn't this so much better?"

It takes me a moment to mentally switch gears, and longer for my body to drop back to a normal temperature. I, however, reveal none of that as I say, "Better?"

"Than you avoiding me. It's been nice working side-by-side with you again. I've missed you."

My gut twists. "Kerrie..."

"No, no. It's okay." She lays her hand on mine. "This is what I meant. My evil plan. I mean, I didn't really have a plan, of course. But I think this job will be good for us. I feel like it's already repairing our friendship. Don't you?"

I glance at where her hand rests on mine. She's right, of course. We'd been friends for years before we were lovers, and I've always respected the hell out of her. She's smart and loyal and sweet and funny. She's never met a stranger, and she goes after what she wants. I should know—she went after me, didn't she?

Not that I put up much of a fight. Hell, once I saw her as a woman and not the thirteen-year-old girl she'd been when we met years before, I wanted her, too. For that matter, I still do. Only now I'm exercising the self-control that I didn't have back then.

And, yes, I regret the month I spent avoiding her. I blame it on Adult Onset Adolescence caused by an unexpected make-out session. Which is to say that I got lucky in the utility room, and like a thirteen year old boy who doesn't have a clue how to deal, I basically hid under the metaphorical covers and tried to pretend the world—or at least the girl—away.

Which is especially ironic considering that we broke up because I'm so much older. Apparently *older* doesn't always translate to maturity. Who knew?

"Connor?"

I hear the worry in her voice and look up, realizing I'm still staring at our hands.

"You do agree, right? That this has been good for us."

"Yes. Yes, sorry. My mind is all over the place, but I do. I absolutely do."

"Good." She gives my hand a quick squeeze, and I wish that I didn't feel the contact so deeply. But I do, and I hate myself for the fantasies that whip through my head, each and every one flying by on guilt-ridden wings. Because what right do I have to fantasize? I'm the one who called it quits, after all.

Kerrie, however doesn't seem to notice my mood shift. And when Leo returns she snatches her hand off mine, flashes him a wide smile, and offers him her bag of potato chips.

Jealousy, thy name is Connor.

I force the green monster back into his pen and knuckle down, trying to ignore my growing suspicion. And as more hours turn into more days, it becomes easier. Because Leo is a relentless taskmaster, and there's no room to think about anything other than the operation.

Hopefully all our intensive prep is overkill, but the alcohol will surely be flowing at the party, which means that tongues will be loose. And while we can try to limit how much we drink, we can't refuse to imbibe without causing suspicion.

Considering the nature of the party, there are other things we can't avoid doing without causing suspicion. And, damn me, I can't deny the unwelcome anticipation growing inside me.

I shouldn't want it. I should tell Kerrie that no matter what, we're going to fake it.

But faking it could put us both in danger. And—hell, I have to at least admit it to myself, right?—I do want it. I want *her*. Despite everything I know is right and every solid reason I have for not ever touching her again, this job feels like a gift. A strings-free way to have Kerrie beside me—*with* me—one last time

And that, of course, is what makes this mission truly dangerous.

For days, I've been expecting Kerrie to make some comment—a tease about how we're fated and there's no way I can truly walk away from her because the universe will just draw us back together. But that comment doesn't come.

I tell myself that's good. That she's healing. That I want her to move on.

Sure, there's still a dull ache that surrounds my heart, like the phantom pain of an amputated limb. But that's okay. I survived multiple tours in the Middle East. I can survive heartache.

Hell, yeah, I can.

The party is Friday to Sunday, and I work late Thursday to clear my plate of all my other work. We're both taking burner phones—Pierce, Cayden, and Leo have the contact info — but nothing that gives away our true identities. We don't want any identifying information on us if we're caught red-handed, but I wouldn't put it past a man like Rollins to ransack his guests' belongings looking for ammo to fuel a blackmail scheme.

It's almost seven by the time I finish. Leo left just after noon for a lunch meeting with a client who's in town on other business. Before that, we went over the tech one last time—we got some seriously cool new gadgets for this job from our most innovative supplier, Noah Carter over at the Austin Division of Stark Applied Technology—then Leo wished me luck and told me to watch out for Kerrie. And to nail Rollins.

I assured him that was my plan.

Cayden and Pierce left later after another quick debrief. They're both serving as backup, but they're as up to speed on the job as Kerrie and I are.

Now, I'm heading home for a quick workout and a full night's sleep. Considering the reputation of Rollins' parties, I'm not sure I'll be getting much shut-eye until Sunday night.

Although she's our office manager, lately, Kerrie's been working more from the reception desk in our small lobby than from her office. We've had four receptionists over the last six months and at this point, we're all pretty convinced that the post is cursed.

I expect to see her there, buried in either briefs for the operation or spreadsheets for the business. But the computer is shut down and the desk is locked tight.

Which means that Kerrie left for the night without even a goodbye.

I tell myself she probably didn't want to disturb me, but the truth is that her silent departure bothers me more than any interruption would. It's just not like her.

Still, I don't want to read too much into it. She undoubtedly still needs to pack. And I'm sure she wants to get a full night's sleep, too.

I lock the office, then take the elevator to the lobby, feeling a little bit hollow and oddly alone.

The plan is for me to pick up Kerrie at ten tomorrow morning. It's about a three-hour drive to Rollins' ranch in

North Dallas, and if we stop for lunch along the way, we should get there right at the appointed hour of two. That gives us time to get settled in our room, possibly meet up with Amy, and become familiarized with the layout of the place before the welcome cocktails at five.

We have the blueprints and Amy's description, of course. But I'm not willing to take anything for granted. Especially since Kerrie is with me, and no matter how much of an in-and-out job this is supposed to be, her presence on an operation means that her safety is on the line. And that's not something I'll ever take lightly.

I cross the lobby, then step out onto the sidewalk that runs in front of our building at Sixth and Congress. The street is bustling, and I join the fray, eager to get home.

Like Kerrie, I moved not too long ago. When I first came to Austin, I lived in a small house in Central Austin, but used some of my trust fund to buy one of Austin's early downtown condos as a rental property. An investment banker, our dad might have spiraled down after our mom left, but he was always careful with his money, and after his death, our grandmother managed the trusts until Cayden and I were old enough. Not a huge sum, but enough for a nice down payment on the condo, which I turned into a shiny profit a few months ago when I sold it, then upsized to a bigger condo in a nicer building.

Now I'm living the downtown urban lifestyle in a fabulous two story corner condo with a view of the river. And my original Crestview bungalow has been converted from my primary address to a rental that brings in a tidy monthly income.

Dad may not have had the wherewithal to survive

heartache, but he left his sons a nice legacy. His grandkids, too, since I'm one-hundred-percent certain that Cayden is waiting for kids before spending a penny of his still-untouched trust.

Unlike my brother who prefers a sprawling house with a yard that requires constant upkeep, I love my condo and its location. My view is exceptional and requires no effort from me. The lobby is always tidy, and if there's no food in the refrigerator, all I have to do is go out through the lobby door, turn left, and I can grab some supplies at the nearby Royal Blue Grocery. Turn right, and I can eschew cooking all together and grab a sandwich at my favorite deli. Not to mention all the options open to me if I walk even a few blocks.

My usual after-work routine is to head south down Congress Avenue, popping into Brew for coffee before I head home. They know me there, and I kick back, log onto my favorite news app, and spend half an hour catching up on the world outside my little circle.

Then I head home, change into shorts, and go for a quick run around the river. After that, my routine gets fuzzy. Before, I tended to stay in with Kerrie. We'd cook, maybe watch a movie, maybe read. Often we'd take nighttime strolls along the river. And we always ended up in bed. Sometimes wild and desperate. Others times, slow and easy. Hell, sometimes we just held hands and talked.

Now, I tend to watch a lot of reality TV. What can I say? I sacrificed the bliss of those nights for the promise of her future. I don't regret it. But if I'm being honest, I have to admit that I don't like it.

Scowling, I cross the street and head toward Brew.

Really not the kind of thoughts I want in my head while I'm trying to make a clean break. Especially since that break just got messier. Because even if we can fake what happens behind closed doors, we can't pull off even pretend intimacy without physical contact.

Damn Leo and his sister and Amy.

But at the same time, I'm glad it's me and Kerrie going, and not her and Leo. I'd be a jealous fool waiting behind in Austin for them to complete this operation. This way, at least, I have a few more moments with her. A few more touches and kisses. A few more memories.

Just a little bit more to hold onto after we get back and finally, truly, cut the lingering ties between us.

I've hit Brew at just the wrong time, and the line for coffee is out the door. I wait, using the time to scroll through messages on my phone. Once the line moves enough for me to enter, I glance automatically around the room. Occupational hazard—I'm always assessing my surroundings.

Right now, my assessment reveals Kerrie. And, fuck me, she's sitting at a table with Leo, deep in conversation.

Obviously, they're doing prep work, and the green demon in my gut needs to chill. I'm trying to tame the jealous beast, when Kerrie pushes a strand of hair out of her eyes, and in the process turns in my direction. She's looking right at me, but her eyes are unfocused, and though I lift a hand in greeting, she turns away as if I'm nothing more than a shimmer in the air, then takes Leo's hand as she laughs at something he's said.

My gut tightens, and in that brief moment, I have a

sense of what it will really feel like when there's a new man in her life. I don't like it, but I can't change it.

Because I know that my decision is the right one.

I just never expected that doing the right thing was going to hurt like hell.

CHAPTER EIGHT

"WE'LL STOP at George's for lunch, right?" Kerrie asks as the soundtrack to *Wicked* blares from the Mercedes S-Class sedan I rented for the trip.

Correction: The Mercedes that John London rented upon his arrival in Austin last night.

I reach over and turn down the volume. Kerrie's musical taste runs to Broadway musicals, classic country, and hip-hop. My girl is nothing if not eclectic.

We've been driving north on Interstate 35 for the last forty-five minutes and we're about halfway to Waco. We've already run through *Into the Woods*, and Kerrie's already downed half a bag of jelly beans.

As I glance over at the bag in her lap, she flashes a grin, then grabs a handful of the candy and holds it out to me. "Share?"

"Keep eating those and you won't want George's." The long-established Waco dive is famous for its burgers and beer. And for good reason.

"It's not the burger I want," she says, adding a sultry lilt to her voice. "It's the Big O."

"Kerrie..."

She laughs. "That's Lydia to you, bud. And I think that under the circumstances I'm entitled to a little naughty talk. Gotta stay in character, right? Besides, all I want is a beer."

"Uh-huh." The Big O at George's is a glass of beer. A very big glass of beer that has sustained many Baylor University students over the years.

She rolls her eyes. "Your mind is *so* in the gutter."

"Fine. Lunch it is. And you can have all the Big Os you want."

She reaches over and gently presses her palm on my thigh. "Now you're talking."

"Kerrie..."

"I'm just teasing," she says, but she pulls her hand back. "I mean, we are still friends, right?"

"Of course we are." As hard as it is, I can't imagine not being her friend, no matter what I might have said in desperation a few days ago.

"Well, I'm Cayden's friend, too, and we flirt."

"Yeah, but you never slept with Cayden. Did you?"

I get her eye roll in response. "All I'm saying is that I don't want to lose your friendship. Am I attracted to you? Of course. Would I jump all over you and dive head first into my fuck buddy plan if you said go? Absolutely. Am I going to push you on it? No."

She shifts in her seat so that she's facing me more directly. "I'm all grown up, Con, and I'm moving on. And I'm mature enough to talk about this reasonably."

She's still talking, but my mind stopped processing after *moving on*. Is she?

I can't help but think of Leo and the image of the two of them laughing and talking in the coffee shop. And me, right there, but completely apart.

I don't like it. But what the hell am I supposed to do about it? Especially considering I'm the one who told her to move on in the first place.

When I tune back in, I realize I've lost the thread of the conversation. "Sorry. What?"

"I said that I don't want to lose having you in my life. You weren't just my boyfriend, you were my friend. Probably my best friend. We're not going to toss that all away just because we're going through an awkward period, are we? We can get past this. And in a few years when I have kids, I want them to adore their uncle Connor as much as I do."

Mentally, I cringe. And despite the fact that her last bit really twisted the knife, I can't deny that her speech makes sense, and I tell her so.

What I don't tell her is that her words only emphasize all the reasons I love her. Kerrie is one of those people who sees the world with crystal clarity. And for a man who works in a world where people usually aren't who they seem, that's a pretty damn refreshing trait.

"I'm sorry," I say as we speed north on the highway, leaving Belton and Temple in our wake.

"For what?"

"For knowing that what you just said is true. For believing it since the first moment I walked away. And for still acting like an asshole and avoiding you."

"Oh." She breaks into a wide smile, looking happier than I've seen her in days. "You're forgiven," she says. "On one condition."

"Buy you a beer?"

"Buy me two."

I don't know about Kerrie, but I'm still stuffed when we reach the turn off to Michael Rollin's North Dallas ranch, over a hundred miles from where we grabbed lunch.

Kerrie's been dozing—she's a lightweight with alcohol anyway, and two beers did her in—and I've been cruising along dead cold sober with only my racing thoughts to occupy me. Everything from memories to past drives with Kerrie to worries about how the hell we're going to share a room without her ending up naked and hot beneath me.

Be strong, Connor.

That's all well and good. But tonight, I'm John. And God only knows how much willpower *that* man has.

I turn off the asphalt and onto the crushed stone drive leading up to the huge mansion that sits on what I'm guessing is a four-hundred-acre ranch. The land is flat and raw and beautiful, green from the frequent summer thunderstorms, and dotted with color from wild flowers. I see horses and cattle and goats and a few critters I can't identify from this distance.

I drive slowly, taking it all in and giving Kerrie a chance to wake up beside me.

"It's pretty," she says. "And that house…"

"I'm not sure that's a house. I'm thinking it's an

embassy."

She laughs, but it's true. The red brick and white-column two-story ranch house is huge and stately and looks like it could house the key players of a small country. Michael Rollins clearly has the kind of money that normal peons like me can't even wrap their heads around. John London, however ... well, to him this is old hat.

I force my face into a bland expression as I glide the Mercedes to a stop in front of the door. A young valet in jeans, cowboy boots, and a starched white button down hurries to my door as another opens the door for Kerrie. Or, rather, for Lydia.

"Ready, Lydia?"

"Ready, John."

I give the keys to the valet and pop the trunk. Our bags are whisked efficiently away, presumably to be searched before they arrive in our room. Ditto the car. I'm not worried. We packed and traveled in character.

I doubt they'll run prints since the car is so obviously a rental and must have quite a variety of prints on the interior, but if they do, they'll come up empty. Prior to setting out, we wiped down our luggage and then both used liquid latex and a thin layer of powder on our fingertips to conceal our prints during the drive.

I take Kerrie's hand as we walk together toward the door. Both because I imagine she wants the support, but also because I want to confirm that she remembered to rub off the telltale latex. She has, and I presume the remnants are now unrecognizable in her purse or pockets.

Probably overkill, but I'd rather overdo caution than find myself screwed.

The front door opens as we're walking up the steps, and Michael Rollins steps out, tall and commanding, with blonde hair, piercing blue eyes, and a wide mouth. He stands with his feet just slightly apart, and one hand behind his back. He looks like a king about to give a speech, and I have a feeling that's the way he thinks of himself. He's the man in charge, and the rest of us need to just fall in line.

This weekend, that's the plan. Get in, make nice, and draw absolutely no suspicion.

"John London," he says, extending his hand to shake. "I would recognize you anywhere."

I make it a point not to react. Leo had already papered the John London persona for anyone who might be searching the internet. But he'd included no pictures. Last weekend, we had our media-tech consultants upload some fake files and images for Rollins to find on the chance he was looking. Apparently he was.

"And you must be Lydia," he adds, his voice full of charm and charisma.

"I sure am," Kerrie says, letting her natural Texas twang shine through. "I just love your place. I've been to Dallas many times, but I never even knew there was so much ranch land this close to the city."

"Most of it's been developed. I'm holding out," Rollins says, still clutching Kerrie's hand as he looks into her eyes. "I like my privacy."

She giggles, and I want to punch him. A reaction that doesn't really bother me. I do my best work when I think the mark is an asshole. Clearly, I'm going to excel at this job.

Rollins leads us over the threshold and into an elegant

foyer. It pushes toward garish—hell, it crosses the line—as does what little of the rest of the house I can see through the archways leading to the adjoining rooms. But none of it seems erotic or decadent or remotely like what I imagined the forum for a sex party would look like.

Apparently Kerrie is thinking the same thing, because she smiles, revealing a dimple, and says, "It's a lovely home, but not what I was expecting."

"No?"

She lifts a shoulder. "I guess I was picturing it with ropes and chains. Or at least red satin sashes. I've never been to this kind of party before."

She's flirting with him—which is what she's supposed to do. The plan is for her to distract Rollins to give Amy and me time at his computer. But even so, that flirtatious lilt aimed in his direction acts on me like fingernails scraping a chalkboard.

He hooks his arm through hers and leads us into a living area. "I'm honored to be the one popping your party cherry," he says, making me roll my eyes and Kerrie titter. "But I assure you that by this evening the house will have a much more sensual allure."

"I can't wait."

He starts to put his arm over her shoulder, but Kerrie gently breaks away and returns to my side. I slide my arm around her waist and pull her close, feeling ridiculously smug.

"What's the dress code tonight?" Kerrie asks. She's already chastised me for not thinking to find out from Amy, forcing her to pack for contingencies ranging from slutty to sensually formal.

"Elegant," Rollins says, going to a wet bar and offering us each a drink. We both take a bourbon, and when he puts Kerrie's in her hand, Rollins adds, "Of course, we will undoubtedly loosen up later in the evening. If formal wear seems too restricting."

"Right." Kerrie smiles, her cheeks going red.

"My Lydia is an innocent," I say, brushing the pad of my thumb over her lips.

"That's deliciously sweet." He runs his gaze possessively over her, and though she smiles, I see the fire in her eyes. Under other circumstances, she'd slap his face.

"So, do we have to wear masks?" she asks.

"Not at all, though you certainly can if you want to. Just think of it as a cocktail party where everyone skips the social niceties and goes straight to getting to know one another. Intimately. The idea is to be comfortable. Play. Explore. Or just watch, if that's your particular predilection." He steps closer, then trails his fingertip down her arm. "But I do hope you play."

Kerrie's bright smile is tightening into a grimace, but the click of high heels on the marble floor thankfully draws Rollins' attention.

"Amy, darling. Come meet John and Lydia." He turns back to us. "May I introduce my fiancée and your hostess?"

Fiancée?

Amy is tall and curvy and blonde, with eyes that are just a little too wide and a mouth that's a bit too small, making her appear meek and naive, an assessment I know to be false if her earlier interactions with Leo are any indication.

I notice that she does indeed wear an engagement ring,

and she's twisting it nervously. This is a new development, and a potentially dangerous one. She might have been pressured into the engagement, making her even more of an asset as she'll want to ensure our help extricating her from Rollins. Or she may be so desperate to get away that she takes unnecessary risks.

Alternatively, she may have decided that she does love Rollins and that she doesn't want to betray him. I've seen it happen. A woman with scruples who loses them once she realizes the lifestyle she'll be landing in once he kicks her out.

I study Amy, trying to decide which side of that line she stands on, but I just can't get a read.

Meanwhile, Kerrie is playing the game the way it should be, gazing at the stone with a drippy expression and effusing, "Oh my gosh, that is beyond gorgeous. Have you set a date?"

"Soon," Amy says, and I hear the quiver in her voice. Amy must hear it, too, because her eyes widen with what I'm certain is fear.

"You must be so nervous," Kerrie says, once again stepping in and transforming an awkward, suspicious moment into stereotypical bridal jitters. "I mean, Johnny hasn't asked me—yet," she adds, with a Scarlett O'Hara smile in my direction. "But just knowing that I was going to be marrying such a powerful man? That must be a lot to process."

She beams at Rollins, looking at him as if he could walk on water, and undoubtedly feeding the man the kind of tripe his ego needs to thrive.

"Oh, it is," Amy agrees, her eyes going wide and her

face painted with relief. "It's great to meet someone who gets it. Everyone just says how lucky I am, and I really am. But they don't understand the pressure of being married to a man like Michael. He's as sweet as pie, but I'm always afraid I won't live up to his expectations."

"Never," Rollins says, taking her hand and kissing it. "You're perfect, my sweet. How could you do anything but make me proud?"

Again, Amy's smile wavers, but I'm no longer worried that Rollins will notice. This time, it just looks like she's overcome with emotion.

"Darling, I put them in the Magnolia Suite," Rollins says to her. "Would you mind showing them the way? Another guest has arrived and I should see to them."

"I'd be happy to," Amy says. "Magnolia is my favorite," she adds in a chipper hostess voice as we fall in step behind her.

As we walk, Amy chitters on about the house as if her head was full of soap bubbles. Maybe it is, but that would surprise me, because I saw a sharpness in her eyes.

The moment we enter the suite, Amy puts a finger to her lips. "The closet is over there," she says, pointing to a vase and then touching her ear. "And the bathroom is through those French doors." She indicates the television that sits on the dresser and surreptitiously taps her eyes.

Great. Audio and video surveillance. Isn't that just peachy? We brought countermeasures, of course, but I don't want to use them if the loss of signal will draw suspicion.

"Let me show you the tub," Amy says as we follow her once more. "The spigot's a little tricky, see?"

As she speaks, she easily turns on the water, then lowers her voice. "There's no surveillance in here. He tried, but the video would fog up and the water messed with the sound, so he eventually gave up."

I nod, and though I believe her, I'll still do a sweep after she leaves, just in case Rollins added bugs without telling her.

"Video in the TV and audio in the vase? Nothing else?" I want confirmation.

"That's it. And don't feel singled out. All the guests are bugged. Michael's not above blackmail. In fact, I think payouts are a pretty large percentage of his annual income."

"That fucker," Kerrie says, to which Amy just shrugs and nods.

"So tell me exactly what y'all need."

"Five minutes minimum at his computer. Fifteen is better in case someone is monitoring usage."

"That shouldn't be a problem. But I don't know his passwords."

I shake my head. "Don't worry about that. We've got it covered."

Her eyes go wide. "How?"

"If I understood that, I'd be in R&D and someone else would be here risking his neck."

In truth, I do understand it. Sort of. Okay, not really. The way Noah described it, we're accomplishing the electronic equivalent of stealing the entire safe when all we're really after is the brick of gold inside. But we'll take the safe back home and crack it after we're free and clear. Only with a safe, the bad guy will notice that it's missing. With digital information, our larceny should go undetected.

That's the plan, anyway.

Hopefully it will work like Noah said. Not that I doubt him. The man's a genius, and now that he has billions of dollars in R&D money thanks to Damien Stark's worldwide conglomerate, he has the scratch to make the crazy things his brilliant mind conceives.

"So are we moving in tonight?"

I can tell by Kerrie's voice that she hopes so. Most of her nervousness is because of anticipation. Get the job over with and she can relax.

But Amy shakes her head. "He's always keyed up on the first night, making sure everyone's having a good time, that kind of thing. He'll notice if you wander. But he never stops drinking at these things. So by tomorrow, you could pop into Dallas and spend the day shopping and the odds are he wouldn't even blink."

"That works," I say. "Plus it gives me time to get a feel for his patterns. Will you be able to get away from him to go with me?" I ask Amy.

"I don't think that will be a problem at all. He likes to say we're exclusive except when we're not." She smiles at Kerrie. "And I'm sure he'll be more than happy keeping you company."

"Great," Kerrie says.

I think about the man and the way he leered at her. And I know right then that as simple as this assignment may look on paper, it's still going to rank as the hardest in my career.

CHAPTER NINE

YES, I know that the plan was for Kerrie to cozy up to Rollins so that Amy and I could get away.

And yes, I know what's riding on the plan working out.

Moreover, I know that Kerrie is perfectly capable of taking care of herself with that arrogant fucktard of a human.

I know all of that; I do.

And at the same time when I see the way Rollins' hand slides over her ass as he moves behind her, I pretty much want to rip his balls off. The man's dangerous, after all. And the thought of him touching her makes me ill.

At the same time, I can't really blame him for being so handsy. Kerrie looks incredible.

We'd been unsure about the dress code, a problem that I solved by bringing jeans and a Henley as one option and a tailored silk suit as the other.

To this, Kerrie informed me that I was not only cheating, but that as a man I didn't realize how difficult it is to maneuver in her world. When she unpacked in our room, I understood what she meant. Being careful to remain in character as Lydia and John, she showed me the options she'd brought. A tube style gown you might see on a hooker trolling for tricks in Hollywood. A denim miniskirt and a midriff-revealing top that accentuated her assets in a way that I thoroughly approved of, but which didn't come under the umbrella of elegant. A sexy cocktail dress that I thought would be just fine, but that she insisted was too "pearls and snobbery."

"I have a few other things, too," she said. "But nothing that feels right."

I just stood there in my suit and thanked my parents for providing me with my particular pair of chromosomes.

Finally, she remembered that there were outfits in the closet. And that's where she found the shimmery gold gown with the plunging back, equally revealing neckline, and a slit up her left thigh that made no allowance for underwear.

She's wearing it now and looks good enough to eat, and from the stares she's getting from both men and women as they mingle in the ballroom, I know that I'm not the only one who thinks so.

The material has some stretch to it, and it clings to the curve of her ass, which is where Rollins' hand dallies before sliding over a bit so that his fingertips caress the bare skin of her thigh.

She turns, ostensibly to talk to him more directly, but it has the effect of shifting his hand away from her bare thigh and back to her ass. Under the circumstances, I consider that an improvement.

At least I do until his fingers creep up. And when I see

him brush the pad of his thumb on the skin at the base of her spine, I realize I have to intervene. Not for me, but for her. She's going to have to deal with him all alone tomorrow when Amy and I make our escape. Tonight, she deserves to relax with me.

A waiter glides by with a tray of champagne, and I grab two glasses, then join them. "Lydia," I say, handing her a flute, then sliding my free hand around her waist as I nod to Rollins, claiming what's mine.

She turns to me, and I see the trust—and the gratitude—in her eyes. I want to pull her close and kiss her. And since Rollins is watching us—and since it's that kind of party—that's exactly what I do.

She's just sipped her champagne, and I can still taste the tingle of tiny bubbles on her lips. She gasps in surprise, but doesn't pull away, instead she deepens the kiss, her body going soft in my arms, her mouth opening to me. I close my eyes, wishing we were anywhere but here and at the same time grateful that this is exactly where we are, because under what other circumstances would I have done this?

I know better, after all. I know exactly what kind of door I'm opening.

And I know damn well that once this fantasy of John and Lydia is over, I'm going to have to close it tight again.

I pull away gently, breaking the kiss. Her lips are parted, her skin flushed, and her nipples are hard against the soft, clingy material. I take a step back, sucking in air to get my own body under control. Because right now, all I can think about is ripping that dress off of her and tasting every delicious inch of her sweet little body.

I meet Rollins' eyes and note the way he's watching us, his own face flush with desire. "I think Lydia and I are going to go explore. There must be a dark corner around here somewhere."

The corner of his mouth quirks up, and I'm quite certain that his eyes are following us. If I were to take her into a dark corner and do all the things I want, I'm absolutely positive that Rollins would follow.

"Thank you," she whispers as we move away.

"For the kiss?"

"Yes." Her smile teases me. "And for rescuing me. At least until tomorrow. Tomorrow, I guess there's no rescue allowed." She sighs, and I have to join in. Because she's right.

Great.

"Then again, maybe it won't be so bad." She glances around the room. "Considering this is supposed to be a sex party, it seems rather tame. Maybe all he'll want to do tomorrow is play chess."

"I wouldn't count on that. But you're right about the party."

I look around, too. There are couples and clusters everywhere. Amy told us the house has twenty bedrooms and all are occupied by two people at a minimum. There are also a dozen or so people staying in a guest-house about half a mile away on the property. So the place is teeming. But it's not like we're in a porn film. Hell, it's not even like we're at a Vegas strip club.

"I'd conjured up a lot more risqué things in my imagination," she says.

"Oh, really?" We're in the dining room now, standing in a corner near the food-laden table.

She takes a step toward me, then cups her hands on my ass as she eases against me. I watch as she bites her lower lip, and I know that she can tell exactly what kind of effect the feel of her is having on me.

"Lydia..."

The corner of her mouth twitches. "Hmm?"

But I say nothing. Instead, my hand glides around to trace the plunging edge of her dress, my fingertip warm against her soft skin. I watch as she closes her eyes, as her breath comes in short, stuttering gasps. Her teeth drag across her lower lip, and she opens her eyes, soft with a desire so familiar to me it makes my heart ache.

"John." She swallows. "Please."

"Please what?" I want to hear it. I want her to beg for my touch. I want to close my eyes and imagine all of our nights, remembering the feel of her in my arms, the joy of knowing that this incredible woman belonged to me.

"Please don't start something you're not willing to finish."

Crash!

And just like that, the moment shatters. Because what the hell am I doing? Where am I taking this? How can I justify this moment—or where this moment was going—knowing that it can't go anywhere?

I take a step back. "I'm sorry."

She licks her lips, then nods. "Yeah. Me, too."

I take her hand. "Come on." This time, I lead her outside. The backyard is like a fairy land with twinkling lights, intimate seating areas, a steaming hot tub, a crystal clear pool, and walking paths through the kind of garden that usually isn't found on North Texas ranch land. Presumably, Rollins pays a fortune for irrigation and landscaping.

"Should we sue for false advertising?"

I shoot her a questioning glance.

"The party. Not really as expected."

"Disappointed?"

I'm teasing, but she considers the question. "I'll admit to being curious. But if a bunch of people standing around talking while a few more make out in corners constitutes a sex party, then I went to at least half a dozen my senior year of high school."

I chuckle. "Guess I've been to quite a few sex parties myself if that's the definition."

I love the way she laughs. None of that ridiculous attempt to pull back. When she finds something amusing, she doesn't try to hide it. With Kerrie, what you see is what you get, and I've always admired the hell out of her for that.

Casually, she reaches over and takes my hand. I glance down, more affected by her touch than I want to let on.

"I want to talk to you. It's easier if I'm holding your hand."

My chest constricts with apprehension, but I simply nod. "All right."

"I just want to say that I get it. Why we broke up, I mean."

I turn just enough to see her face, trying to ascertain where she's going with this.

"I don't agree with it," she adds, with enough humor in

her voice that I know she's not looking for an argument, "but I do understand."

She pauses, as if making sure that *I* understand. So I nod and say, "I'm glad to hear it."

"And I really do want to stay friends."

"So do I. If you're still worried about what I said in the office—about that not being possible, I mean—I was just—"

"No, no, I get it. I cornered you and it was weird and we're fine." She draws a breath. "But you are right that it can be awkward. And I don't want things to be awkward between us."

"Oh, Ke-Lydia." I wince, then watch her fight not to laugh. It's not as if we think that there's surveillance out here. I'm actually pretty sure there's not, as I have a bug detector in my pocket. Any mics, and it should be vibrating. But I also don't want to drop character too much. "I don't want that either," I assure her.

She draws a breath. "That's why I'm thinking about taking another job."

We've been walking through a young maze, not too tricky since the hedge is only about shoulder height. Now, I pull her to a stop. "What are you talking about? What job?"

She starts to rub her chin with her thumb, something she does only when she's nervous.

"Lydia..."

"I'm thinking of moving to Los Angeles, okay?"

The words hit me with the force of a wrecking ball, and I take a step back, stunned. "What? Why?"

"Delilah asked me to come work for her. Like a manager, but not. I'd basically help run her life. All the stuff that a star needs except for the actual Hollywood part, which I know nothing about. But her finances and organizing her life and arranging her travel and overseeing security and on and on."

I stand there in shock. "Does Pierce know about this?" Delilah is Pierce's sister-in-law. He and Jezebel met when Delilah, a young movie star, was in town and needed protection from some truly rabid fans.

"Not yet. I was talking to Del about us, and one thing led to another. I'm seriously considering the job. The title is executive assistant, and the woman who did have the job recently married and moved to Chicago."

"You're really thinking about leaving?"

Her shoulders rise and fall. "I'd miss you. But the thing is, I already miss you, you know? And I do think that we can go back to the way things were before the utility room. But I also know that in the back of my mind, I'm always going to be wondering if history will repeat itself. And the real kicker—the thing that lets me know that leaving is right—is that I want it to."

"I don't know what to say," I admit. I can't tell her I want that as well. It was my decision to break up, and I know it was the right one. I have to at least give the illusion of being strong.

"Age really is just a number, you know."

"We've had this conversation. You know my reasons. We both know I'm right."

She shakes her head. "No, I don't know that at all. In fact, I think you're dead wrong. You're grandmother loved your grandfather. It wasn't an imposition when his health declined. And your mother was an idiot. I'm not an idiot. And just because you're older doesn't mean you're going to get old and feeble before me. And just because you were in combat and exposed to all sorts of weird shit doesn't mean you're going to fall down dead tomorrow."

She sucks in air. "I get it. I do. But don't put words in my mouth. I think you're wrong. Hell, I'm certain you're wrong. But that doesn't matter. Because while couples can have disagreements, whether or not to be together can't be a subject that's up for debate. So I respect your decision. I do. And I want to be your friend. Truly. But I just think that it will be easier from fifteen hundred miles away."

I swallow. Then nod. Then slide my hands into my pockets. "I get it."

"Do you?"

"Same as you. I don't like it. But I get it."

She flashes me a wide, side smile. "See? We really are compatible."

Despite myself, I laugh.

"I didn't mean to lay all of this on you, tonight. I mean, if there was any sort of bondage or wild fondling going on in there, I never would have brought it up."

At that, we both laugh. We also decide that we've escaped the party long enough, and so we head back to the sex party that lacks sex, only to find out that we made our assessment far too early. Because as soon as we enter the house, it's clear that things have changed.

The lights are off, and now the interior is illuminated only by candlelight, the orange light flickering over bare flesh. It's as if our departure was everyone's cue to get busy. From where we stand in the kitchen, we can see that there are couples and threesomes and foursomes on sofas and on the floor of the room beyond. And just a few feet away, a woman on her knees is giving a blowjob to a man leaning back against the counter. To our left, in the dining room, a woman is strapped naked and spread-eagled to the table as another woman brushes the soft end of a flail over her body, then snaps it, making the woman cry out in a mixture of pain and bliss.

"Oh," Kerrie says, and for a second I think that's a reaction to what we're seeing. Then I realize that she's seen Rollins. He's heading toward us, though I don't think he's seen us yet. Nor do I want him to. She's going to be with him—in this environment—tomorrow. As far as I'm concerned, that's more time with her than he deserves.

I tug her sideways until we end up in a narrow butler's pantry. I put my finger over her lips, and she nods. We can't see him now, but I can hear someone walking. I can also hear the sounds of sex all around us.

"Does it turn you on?" I whisper, then immediately regret my words.

She meets my eyes. "Yes. And no."

I wait, silently inviting her to explain. For a moment, we just look at each other. Then she steps forward, her arms sliding around my neck, her mouth brushing my ear as she speaks.

"It's hot, like when we'd watch porn. Remember?"

I do, and the feel of her lips and the whisper of breath are as arousing as her words.

"But I never wanted to be in the movie, and I don't want to be on display here. Public group sex isn't my thing. I just wanted—I *want*—to be with you." She runs her tongue along the edge of my ear, and I stifle a moan.

I should put a stop to this. Weren't we just having the friends-only talk? "We shouldn't," I manage.

"Probably not. But I'm leaving anyway. The utility room was hardly a good send off. There's a bedroom here. And a shower with jets."

Her hand slides down to stroke me. I'm already as hard as steel. "What about Leo?"

Her hand stills. "Huh?"

"Aren't you two seeing each other?"

Again, her tongue teases me. "Would that be a problem?"

"Hell, yes."

Her laugh is like the tinkling of bells. "We're not dating. What gave you that idea?"

I don't bother answering. They're friends, of course. And I wished a relationship on her because I want her happy. Because I didn't want to be the asshole who loved her and left her.

Still...

"We shouldn't. You know we shouldn't."

But she just shakes her head. "No, John, you're wrong. It's a sex party, remember? And we're not Kerrie and Connor," she adds, her voice so soft I can barely hear it, even with her lips against my ear. "We're Lydia and John. And they're hot and heavy. So isn't that what we need to be? Isn't that how to not only survive undercover, but to excel at it? To get fully and completely into character? To embrace the role?"

She slides around my body until her ass is pressed against me. "So let's embrace it." She takes my hand and rests it on her thigh. Then she takes my other hand and cups it over her breast. And God help me I let her. For that matter, it's all I can do not to yank her skirt up and fuck her right there. Hell, it's private enough.

And when she eases her hand onto mine, then starts to inch our way up her thigh, I know that whatever battle I've been fighting is a lost cause. I take control, easing my fingers up, teasing the soft skin between her thigh and her pussy, and then slowly—so deliciously slowly—teasing my finger along her slit, reveling in how damn wet she is for me.

"John?" Her voice is rough. Needy.

"Yes?"

"Now," she demands. "Please, please fuck me now."

CHAPTER TEN

THAT IS an invitation I'm not prepared to ignore, especially when her low, sensual groan entices me as I ease my finger inside her, my cock now painfully hard.

"God, yes," she murmurs, her hips moving as I finger fuck her fast and deep. "More," she demands. "Con—*John*. Please. Please, I want more. I want everything. *You*," she says, making my heart swell. "I want you."

"Upstairs," I say, but she shakes her head. "Now. Here." It's a demand, and oh, Christ, how the hell do I say no to that? "Are there doors?"

I glance to both sides. "No." Apparently it's not a butler's pantry after all. More like a damn butler's hallway, and I don't care what kind of party we're at, I can't fuck her here where anyone can walk in, anyone can see. I'm not that guy.

But at the same time, who am I to ignore her demands. Maybe I can't fuck her, but I can make her come. *That* I want to do. To hold her here in the dark in her slinky gold dress. To play my fingers over her clit. To listen as her sensual sounds join the moans and sighs filling the air around us.

Yeah, I'm all over that.

"Just relax, baby," I whisper, as I tease her clit, stroking and playing with her pussy as my other hand slides inside that low-cut dress to find her nipple and squeeze it hard between my thumb and forefinger.

I know Kerrie's body as well as I know my own, and I can tell that she's already close. Her nipple is tight under my fingers, her breasts full and heavy. And her core is slick and hot, her clit hard and sensitive.

Usually, she's a slow build, and I'll take my time, playing and teasing and coaxing an explosive orgasm out of her. But now I'm thinking that she likes the hint of danger. The possibility that we're being watched. Because I can tell how turned on she is, how much this whole kinky scenario has revved her up. And damned if it doesn't make me even harder.

So, yeah. I want to fuck her. Want to sink myself deep inside her. But not here. And not yet.

Right now, this is all about her.

Her hips move in the kind of rhythm that lets me know that what I'm doing is exactly what she wants, and damned if the whole scene isn't erotic as hell. Me getting her off, her on the knife-edge of what promises to be an explosive orgasm, and the sounds of sex all around us.

"That's it, baby. Come for me," I order. "Explode for me, so I can take you upstairs and fuck you all over again."

She moans, then reaches up, cupping her hand over mine and forcing me to squeeze her breast harder as she arches back, her entire body shaking as she goes completely over the edge, her core tightening so hard around my fingers I fear for my circulation.

She grinds against my hand, her body on overdrive, as I continue thrusting, wanting to keep her on edge as her climax explodes in wave after delicious wave that almost sends me over as well, until finally her legs sag and she starts to sink, her little body utterly worn out.

I catch her as she goes down, scooping her up and holding her close as she hooks her arms around my neck. "That was incredible." Her voice caresses me, the sound like liquid sex.

"It really was," I agree. "Want more?"

Her laugh delights me. "I want you to take me to our room and fuck me so deep they can hear me scream all the way down here."

Considering how hard her words make me, I think that may actually be possible. Assuming I can get us to the room. Carrying her and walking with my cock this hard is no easy task. But I wasn't a soldier for nothing, and soon enough we reach the room.

I gently put her on the bed, then turn on the music in defense against the microphone. I'm tempted to let whoever's tuned in get a thrill by listening to us, but I figure they probably get enough of that. Plus, I don't want them to hear our real names if one of us makes a mistake in bed.

As for the television, I'm not sure about that. The one thing I know for certain is that I have no interest in starring in a sex tape. There's always the bathroom, but I've never been one for making love in a whirlpool tub. Call me old fashioned, but I like a bed.

I can tell that Kerrie is thinking along the same lines,

and after a moment, she sits up, then slides off the bed. Then she indicates that she wants me to sit.

"Showtime," she says, taking my phone off the dresser and scrolling through the streaming app until she finds a playlist of sexy, sultry songs.

I watch, mesmerized, as she dances in front of me, her hands going to the side zipper of her dress. She wriggles her hips and shoulders and the entire garment slithers down, leaving her completely naked.

Whoever's at the other end of that video feed is getting quite a show, but since I know Kerrie's aware of that, too, I don't say a word. Instead, I watch as she bends over, picks up the dress, then tosses it over the television, taking care to cover the top middle where the camera would be embedded. "I'll hang it up later," she says loudly, obviously for the benefit of our undoubtedly disappointed audience. "Right now, I just want you."

Then she turns up the volume on the speaker, tosses my phone onto a nearby chair, and moves to stand in front of me.

"Okay?" She asks, and she pushes me back, then climbs onto the bed. Now I'm leaning back on my elbows, still fully clothed, and she's riding me, her hot little body enticing me, and her slick core leaving a wet patch on the silk blend of my pants where she's rubbing herself against my thigh.

It's ridiculously sexy, and part of me wants to stay like that, watching her use my body to get herself off. But it's just not enough, and when I can't take it anymore, I grab her waist, flip her onto her back, and close my mouth over hers.

I kiss her long and deep, and she responds with wild enthusiasm, arms and legs clutching me tight, pulling me to her. "Too many clothes," she murmurs. "I want you naked."

That's easy enough to remedy, and soon my clothes are on the floor, my skin warm against hers. "Please," she begs. "I don't want to go slow. I just want you inside me."

"Oh, baby." I meet her eyes, looking deep. This is more than just the eroticism of the weekend. It's more than play-acting Lydia and John. This is the desire that has always burned between us. A desire I know well. That I wish we could nurture. But we both know that this weekend is going to be the end. Our last hurrah.

And dammit, we're going to make the most of it.

I lower my mouth to hers, wanting the kiss to start slowly. But I'm too aroused, too lost in the scent and taste of her. Instead of slow and sensual, our mouths clash violently, a wild kiss. A claiming. A demand.

We devour each other, and then I move down, tasting her neck, teasing her collar bone, sucking on her sensitive breasts as she arches up, squirming beneath me, taking more and more until she twines her fingers in my hair and urges me down lower.

I go eagerly, wanting the taste of her. Wanting to tease her all the way to the edge with my tongue. She's soft and sweet and she moves against me in a way that always takes me to the brink. There's no question with Kerrie that she likes what I'm doing. With her, sex is an all-in proposition; something that I've always found so damned arousing.

"Yes," she cries as I suck on her swollen clit, her hips bucking with passion as another orgasm washes over her and she grinds against my mouth, riding it out until she's gasping and begging for more. Begging for me to thrust deep inside of her.

"Hard," she begs. "Fast."

And that's what I give her. Thrusting in deep and riding her, our bodies slamming together in a wild frenzy until I clench up, frozen for that sweet moment before I explode, filling her, and then collapsing, spent, on top of her.

She strokes my hair, sighing with contentment. "That was incredible," she says. And then, even though I've barely had time to catch my breath, she asks sweetly, "Can we do it again?"

And, honestly, how the hell can I say no to that?

CHAPTER ELEVEN

I WAKE to the familiar feel of Kerrie beside me, her naked body pressed against mine, her leg thrown over me as if to keep me beside her. She's a possessive sleeper, and I used to revel in that, knowing that even deep in sleep she wanted to be near me.

I feel no different now, and I pull her close, breathing in the fresh scent of her hair and the musky smell of sex that lingers on our bodies and the sheets. Today's the day, and I don't want to let her go. Because what if something goes wrong and Rollins realizes our game? What if she gets caught or hurt or worse? How the hell could I live with myself?

You broke her heart. You're living with that.

I push the thought away. She understands. And she's doing fine.

She's leaving. Moving away from her family and friends because of you.

"Del is family," I mutter, only realizing I've spoken aloud when she stirs.

"Did you say something?"

"I said good morning," I lie, then kiss her, glowing with warmth when she rolls over so that she can wrap her arms around me.

"Can we just stay here all day?"

"I can't think of anything I'd like better," I admit.

"But?"

I laugh. "But if we did that, I couldn't make love to you in the shower."

She studies my face, then props herself up on her elbow. "I need some music to help me wake up." She grabs my phone off the windowsill above us. Then she opens a music app, connects my speaker to Bluetooth, and blares the music just loud enough to ensure we can talk in privacy.

"I thought last night was a one off." She's whispering, but I can hear the note of eagerness in her voice.

"Did you want it to be?"

I see her throat move as she swallows. "You know what I want." She meets my eyes, her gaze steady. "I've wanted it since the first day Pierce dragged your sorry ass home with him when you guys were on leave."

"And you know I can't offer that."

She nods. "I know. I do. If memory serves, I was the one who convinced you that last night would be a good idea. And I was right, wasn't I?"

"Last night was incredible."

She nods firmly. "Okay."

"Okay, what?"

"Last night wasn't a one-off, but it also wasn't a beginning. It was the Lydia and John show. A limited run. No touring production. Call it a bubble or an anomaly, it doesn't matter. Hell, we can call it a glorious send-off, because once we get back, I really am giving notice. I can't do this with you and stay. I wish I could be that girl—I thought I could. Before the utility room, I think I even was. There was a dull ache when I was around you, but I handled it. I don't think I can handle it any more."

I nod. I know exactly what she means.

"So John and Lydia?" Her voice rises in question.

"Is that a yes?" I think it is, but I want to be absolutely clear that we're on the same page.

Her smile is wide and a little bit devious. "It's not only a yes, it's a hell yes. Because if this is our last run, *John*, I want to go out wild. I want everything. And then I'm going to store it in my heart, a dirty sweet memory that I can pull out whenever I need to. Deal?"

I slide out of bed and stand up, my hand held out to her. "Deal," I say. "Now let's go make it official with a fast fuck in the shower."

She laughs as I pull her to her feet. "I'll say one thing. You sure do know how to romance a girl."

If last night's atmosphere could be described as darkly raunchy, today's is steamy and sticky.

The Texas sun beats down on the back yard, and dozens of naked men and women sprawl on the cushioned chaises that surround the huge, rectangular pool.

Another dozen or so float or swim in the water. And a few rebellious types even wear bathing suits.

One couple is fucking languorously under a giant umbrella, the woman's loud moans acting as a counterpoint to the wet smack of the volleyball that two well-endowed women are batting back and forth over a net.

It's all very surreal and not my scene at all. Though I can't deny that I'm enjoying stealing glances at Kerrie beside me. She's topless, but she drew the line at removing her bikini bottoms. A decision I heartily approve of. I'm not the sharing type.

Unlike last night, which apparently got even wilder after Kerrie and I moved our private party to our room, today feels like we've time traveled to the sixties and stumbled upon a nudist commune.

Tamer, but still not my scene. And while I can't deny that fucking Kerrie in the butler's pantry was seriously hot, this assignment has driven home that public sex and sex parties aren't my thing at all.

On the contrary, I'm a one-woman man, and I don't like to share.

For a moment, I let myself acknowledge that the *one woman* in that equation is Kerrie. But that's false reasoning. The one woman *in this moment* is Kerrie. And I just need to keep reminding myself of that.

This weekend, that woman is Kerrie.

Right now, that woman is Kerrie.

But moving forward? That's a different story altogether.

I glance over at the woman beside me, soaking up the sun. She's lithe and lovely, and I'm not the only one who thinks so. That much I can tell by the attention she's drawing from everyone who passes in front of the area we've staked out.

Kerrie, of course, notices none of it, as her eyes are not only closed, but covered with cucumber slices. She's been that way for the last fifteen minutes, and I'm under strict orders to wake her at thirty so that she can turn over. "Especially since my tits aren't used to the sun," she'd added.

When I asked why she didn't keep her top on if she was worried, she shrugged. "When in Rome. Besides, who wants tan lines if you can avoid them? And what's the big deal anyway? They're just breasts."

I almost countered that I was feeling proprietary about them and didn't want to share with the entire party. But considering the limitations of our weekend arrangement, I decided I didn't have the right.

As I study her now, I notice Rollins heading our way. "I didn't see much of you two last night," he says as he pauses beside Kerrie's lounge chair.

"We had our own private party," I confess, since with the surveillance in our room, he must know that anyway. "You might say the atmosphere downstairs inspired us."

"In that case I won't be insulted. But now that you've got that out of your system, I expect we'll see you downstairs tonight." His gaze cuts to Kerrie. "I want to claim my dance with Lydia. And anything else I can persuade you to give me." His words are directed to me but his gaze is on Kerrie as she sits up, peeling the cucumbers off her eyes.

She smiles at him, not self-conscious at all as he stares at her breasts.

"She'll need to be in on that negotiation," I say. "Unlike some of your guests, I can't claim ownership of the woman I'm with."

She turns a wide, genuine smile on me before returning her attention to Rollins. "Well, you know that Johnny has my heart. But I suppose there are parts of me that are available for sharing. The three of us could make some sort of deal, don't you think, darling?"

"I do," I say, deliberately looking toward Amy, who's standing by the bar chatting with the bartender.

Rollins follows my gaze, then chuckles. "Oh, yes. That can definitely be arranged."

"You can speak for her?" Kerrie asks innocently.

"Of course," he says, then tilts his head in dismissal before continuing down the path, chatting with the other guests sunbathing by the pool.

I meet Kerrie's eyes, and it's clear that we're both fighting the urge to laugh. "Come on," I say. "Let's go get cleaned up before cocktails."

"I've got a better idea," she says, falling in step beside me as she pulls on a T-shirt. "Why don't we go up to the room, get dirty, and *then* get cleaned up?"

"Dirty, huh?"

She grins, and I laugh.

"Aren't you a sexy little sinner?"

"Absolutely," she says. "And you know you like it."

CHAPTER TWELVE

THERE'S a lot to be said for lazy, afternoon sex, and I'm feeling relaxed and highly confident about tonight's mission when we finally roll out of bed to shower and dress for both tonight's party and tonight's adventure.

"So we're clear, right?" I ask, after cranking up the volume on our music. "You'll be his charming little side-piece, and Amy and I will head to the study. I can't imagine he'll follow but if he does, text me the moment he steps away from you."

"Will do. And if he insists I come with him, I'll pretend I'm checking a text from my sister. I'll text you a heart emoji, so that if he sees it, I can say I was just telling you how much I missed you."

I nod. "Perfect."

As we talk, I've been taking the device out of its small case. Barely bigger than a business card, the gizmo hooks into a computer by port or Bluetooth. We'll be using a port, and I have the adaptor already attached to the tiny thing.

Once attached, it goes in and essentially downloads the computer's equivalent of DNA. Then its counterpart at Noah's office takes that data, applies a billion to the nth byte of processing power, and does a Watson and Crick number on the information, unraveling that computer DNA strand so that it can then rebuild the guts of the information. How it does that without requiring a password, I have no idea. But Noah assures me it will.

All of which means that if Carrington-Kohl's proprietary information is in there, we'll know Rollins' people stole it, and Brody Carrington can decide what his next move is.

"Hard to believe it's so simple," she says after I've run through all of that.

I don't disagree. But since it's backed by both Noah and the Stark name, I'm confident it's going to work.

I skim my eyes over her outfit, another low-cut number that accentuates her cleavage and her ass. "And you? How's your confidence level?"

"I can handle it," she says. "I can't say I'm looking forward to being touched by that man, but I can take one for the team. I just hope he doesn't expect…"

She trails off with a shudder, and I don't blame her.

"He can expect whatever he wants," I say. "But that doesn't mean he gets. You have your secret weapon?"

She grins and nods, then reaches into her cleavage and extracts the tiny bottle she's tucked into the hidden pocket. It's Ipecac syrup, and it's a last resort in case she needs to escape. Because Ipecac induces vomiting, and surely that will destroy even a man like Rollins' amorous edge.

"Good," I say. "Don't hesitate to use it if he pushes too hard."

"Believe me. I won't."

I watch as she takes a deep breath, then nods. "Ready," she says, and we head down to join the party.

Tonight, things have heated up earlier than before. It's the last night, after all, and I assume everyone wants to indulge as much as possible. That's fine with me. It means the liquor's been flowing for hours, and everyone—Rollins included—is already well lubricated. That can only help our mission.

When we see Rollins, though, my stomach twists into knots. He practically licks his lips as he stares at her tits. And when he follows that class act up with, "Oh, yes, my dear. You're definitely the cherry on tonight's sundae," I consider calling abort and getting the hell out of there.

Kerrie, however, is completely professional. She sidles up to him, smiles, and says, well if you've got me, where's Amy for John?"

Immediately, he signals for her, and she hurries over, looking both submissive and annoyed, which is exactly what we'd rehearsed. "You're with John tonight, baby," he says, then turns away in dismissal before she even acknowledges his words.

I meet Amy's eyes, see the flare of anger, and any lingering doubt as to her loyalty to me and Kerrie flies out the window. She takes my hand, then coos, "I know just the place for us," before leading me toward a back service hall where I happen to know Rollins' private office is hidden in a high-security room to which Amy has full access.

Maybe that's Rollins' one redeeming quality—he trusts the women he takes into his bed.

I glance back to make sure Rollins isn't paying attention to us before we duck into the hall. He's not. How could he be? Every ounce of his attention is focused on Kerrie, including the hand that's slowly creeping up her thigh. She's sitting rigid, and I know she hates this. She wants to nail him, and she's making the sacrifice for the good of our operation, but she hates it.

So do I. Because how can I do this to a woman I love?

Love. Yeah, there's that word. And it's true. I do love her. But where the two of us are concerned, I don't know what that means in the larger context. All I know is that right here, right now, it means that I can't let her go through with this.

There has to be another way.

"Change of plans," I say to Amy, who eyes me as if I'm crazy while I lay out the revised approach. Hell, I probably am.

Moments later, Kerrie gapes at me as I hurry across the room, but her stare isn't as bold and confused as Rollins'. He, however, recovers quickly. "Problem?" he asks.

"More like a proposition." Amy's caught up with me, and I meet Kerrie's eyes, then scratch my chest, right about where the Ipecac would be if I were her.

For a moment she looks confused, but when I turn my attention to Rollins, I realize she gets it. I'm afraid she's going to argue, but she has to know I have a new plan. I'm not going to sacrifice the mission. I'm just going to save her.

Thankfully, that reality must dawn on her. Because as I

start to talk, she surreptitiously takes out the small bottle, opens it, and quickly swallows the contents.

Meanwhile, I've moved behind Amy so that my hands are on her breasts. "We want to watch," I say, amused when Kerrie's eyes go wide with shock. But it's not shock on Rollins' face. It's excitement.

"Do you?"

I trace Amy's lower lip with my fingertip until she starts to suck, playing the role we'd quickly discussed. Beside Rollins, I see Kerrie start to retch.

Rollins hasn't noticed. He's too intrigued by my proposition. "I like the way you think, Mr. London. Perhaps we should—"

But I don't know what he was going to suggest, because that's when Kerrie vomits all over his fine Oriental carpet.

"I'm so sorry," she says. "I don't usually drink, and—"

"It's okay, honey," Amy says, sliding into maternal mode and helping Kerrie to her feet. Let's go get you cleaned up."

The women escape before Rollins manages to gather himself. I study his face, looking for signs that he saw through the charade or that he's going to take out his frustration on Amy later. But all he does is look at me soberly and say, "Well, if watching is your kink, let's see who else I can find so we can get you off good and proper."

Does this guy have his host duties down pat, or what?

He heads out, leaving me alone for a good half hour as he presumably searches out a companion. Fortunately, before he finds the lucky woman to pair with him for my entertainment, Amy returns. I relax immediately, understanding that the girls were able to run the tap and gather the computer DNA.

"I tucked her into bed," she says as Rollins returns with a tall, thin blonde. "She's got a little bit of a fever, so I don't think it's alcohol. She really wants you with her."

I try to look disappointed. "I'll be back once she falls asleep," I lie. Then I nod to Amy and head upstairs, my body practically dripping with relief.

I don't relax until I get into the room, though. The music is playing and there's a robe over the television. I want to cry out with joy at our success. I want her to tell me exactly how it went down, and from the way her eyes are shining, I know she wants to tell me, too.

Mostly, though I want to pull her close and fuck her until she explodes with long, passionate cries.

But she's sick, or she's supposed to be. Which means we can't have whoever is monitoring the mics and cameras wondering why the sick girl is suddenly having wild sex.

That's okay, though, I think as I strip and climb into bed with her. "You did great," I whisper. "How's your stomach?"

"Getting better."

"Yeah? I should check." I slide back the covers and see that she's wearing only a tank top and tiny panties. I lift up the tank and press a kiss to her belly. "Better?"

She doesn't actually answer, but I interpret her soft moan of pleasure as a yes.

I lift my head and meet her eyes. "You were amazing," I say.

"I would have stayed with him," she whispers, then

tangles her fingers in my hair. "But I would have hated it. Thank you so much for rescuing me."

"I couldn't stand the thought of him touching you," I say. "That's my job. For this weekend at least, I'm the only one who has that privilege."

"In that case," she says, "quit talking and start touching."

I eagerly do as ordered, pulling her roughly to me and closing my mouth over hers. She tastes like sin and strawberries, and I could kiss her all night. Enjoying the softness of her lips, the wild exploration of her tongue against mine. The way our passion ramps up as our kisses mimic sex, growing in need and desire. In wildness and heat.

Soon, though, it's not enough. I need more. I need all of her. I need to claim her. To have her. I suck on her breast through the tank as my fingers slip down under her panties. She's hot and slick, and I want more than my fingers inside her. I want all of her. All of us.

Gently, I peel off her panties, but leave on the tank. We still have to be quiet—just in case—but right now I can't turn back. I have to be inside her.

I meet her eyes, see the way she bites her lower lip, and know that I can't wait any longer. I ease between her legs, taking it slow and easy, going deeper with each thrust, biting back my own moans of pleasure and covering her mouth when she forgets and starts to cry out.

Our eyes meet, and I see the humor there. And that moment is everything to me. Because this is *us*, not just sex. It's friendship and fun and heat and lust, and that drives me harder and harder, until we're staring into each others eyes, both of us right on the edge.

Then her body tightens around me, and as she bites her lip to keep from crying out, she pulls me over the edge with her, and we tumble off into space together

It's magic, I think. This thing between us. This intensity. This attraction. This need. Magic, pure and simple.

But the real trick is going to be surviving once we get out into the real world again. Once we walk away from what we've rebuilt, and everything we've shared between us this weekend disappears into the mist of memory.

CHAPTER THIRTEEN

WHEN WE RETURN to Austin on Sunday afternoon, we're greeted with much praise and applause, the bulk of which is aimed at Kerrie in congratulations of her first real undercover operation.

"Modeling doesn't count," Gracie tells her, leaning against Cayden as we all gather in Pierce and Jezebel's backyard garden. "You're such a natural, it was hardly a stretch. And I wasn't evil." A stunning woman, Gracie has made a successful career as a plus-size model.

"Maybe a little evil," Cayden teases, making Gracie roll her eyes.

"Who's evil?" Jez asks, joining us with a tray of coffee, wine, cookies, and cheese. "Did Noah call? Did we catch Rollins?" The weekend get together is part of our regular routine, but today is slightly different as we're waiting to hear back from Noah, with whom we left the device on our way in from town.

"Oh, he's evil," Pierce tells her. "We just don't have the

proof yet." He glances at his watch, then frowns. "It's only been a few hours."

Kerrie shrugs as she takes a glass of wine, passing me one, too. I bite back a smile; she knows me well. After our adventure, this just isn't a coffee kind of afternoon. "When we dropped it off with him," she says, "Noah told us it could be fast or it might take until tomorrow. Or longer." She lifts a shoulder. "Lots of factors, I guess."

"It's all good," Leo says. "Gives us more time to just enjoy hanging out, and to celebrate Connor and Kerrie's safe return from the jaws of hell." This is his first weekend to chill with us, and when he casually grabs a cookie from the tray, I know he'll fit right in.

"So how was it?" Jez asks. Glancing sideways toward Pierce. "I've never been to a sex party."

"Nonsense," he scoffs. "We host private parties pretty much nightly."

Jez shoots him a scowl, but I can tell she's fighting a smile.

"You didn't run across that kind of thing in Hollywood?" Kerrie asks, which makes the jealous green monsters in my belly start hopping. Is *that* what she'll get up to when she moves west to work with Del?

Jez's brows rise. "With my sister's schedule? Who had time for that? Not that I was ever invited. Or would go. But no. No invitations. No hints. And no regrets."

"Good," Pierce says, kissing her forehead.

"I've heard of them in the modeling world," Gracie puts in. "Not really my thing."

Cayden releases an exaggerated sigh. "Damn," he says, earning him a shove from his wife-to-be.

We all look to Leo, who holds up his hands and shakes his head. "I take the Fifth," he says, but I can't tell whether he's being serious or pulling our legs.

Soon enough, we shift gears, moving off the topic of work to general weekend chatter. As Pierce tells me about their new sprinkler system—and I remind myself why I prefer condo living—I can't help but notice that Kerrie and Leo are sitting on the glider, deep in conversation about something.

An unwelcome bolt of jealousy stabs at my gut, and though I try to ignore it, I can still feel those nasty green claws in my gut an hour later when Kerrie flops down next to me on the double chaise lounge. "I saw you with Leo," I say, the words coming of their own accord even though I know I'm indulging in word vomit. "You two looked cozy."

She smiles brightly. "He's a nice guy. I was thinking about what you said. That you thought we were dating." She lifts a shoulder, looking at me innocently. "I could see that."

My insides tighten up. "Not much sense starting something if you're leaving for California." I swallow. "Are you still planning on going?"

She tilts her head and crosses her arms as she looks down her nose at me. "Gee, Connor, I don't know. Should I stay here and date Leo? Or should I go take a fabulous job in LA with Delilah?"

"Kay…"

"Don't even," she says, lowering her voice so the others can't hear. "Do not play those games with me."

My shoulders sag. "I'm sorry. I really don't mean to."

Her mouth twists. "I believe you. I get it. And that's

why I have to leave. Besides, there's no point staying. Leo's great, but he's not my guy."

"How do you know?"

She meets my eyes. "I know," she says aloud, but her tone says, "You're an idiot."

I stand up, suddenly feeling as if I've lost my grip on this conversation. "So when are you going to tell them?" I ask. "About LA, I mean."

She frowns, then sighs. "What the hell? I guess I should go ahead and tell them now."

Fifteen minutes later, I'm looking around the garden at a group of shocked faces, Pierce's most of all. "I'm going to miss you," he tells his little sister. "We've never lived that far apart."

"Um, Middle East?"

"That was a tour of duty," he tells her. "Not an address change."

"Maybe," she counters. "All I knew was that you were gone." At ten years younger than Pierce, I know she felt his absence deeply as a kid.

"We'll miss you," Jez puts in. "But if you're leaving us, I'm thrilled you'll be out there with Del. I miss her. More than that, I worry about her."

Kerrie waves a dismissive hand. "Worry no more. We'll have a blast. Girls gone wild in Hollywood."

Jez just stifles a laugh. It's Pierce who scowls and says, "How about we nix that idea?"

"Yeah," I say before I can stop myself. "Why don't we?"

Kerrie rolls her eyes. "Um, guys? It was a joke. That's not my thing. Or Del's."

"Kidding," I say, though of course I wasn't. Jealousy is an ugly mistress. And from the way Cayden is looking at me, I'm certain he knows that something's up.

"What?" I demand when we're standing together a few moments later.

For a moment, I think he's going to say something, but then Kerrie's phone rings.

She grabs it out of her back pocket, meets my eyes, and smiles.

For a minute or two, she just listens, her grin growing wider and wider. Then she ends the call and looks at all of us. "That was Noah," she says. "Not only does his gadget work like a charm, but he found the Carrington-Kohl information—and lots of other proprietor corporate files that he doubts were handed over voluntarily."

In other words, Michael Rollins is going down.

CHAPTER FOURTEEN

THE ROLLINS SITUATION is too big for Blackwell-Lyon to handle, which is why the Justice Department took over two weeks ago. Noah, Leo, and I are consulting, but the Feds are on it, with constant surveillance on Rollins as they build the case, and an exit plan for Amy.

Moreover, the agents we're working with were impressed enough with the job we did that I expect we'll be getting some referrals for both on and off-book jobs.

All of which is great.

And which begs the question of why I've been in such a pissy mood for the last week. Except, of course, I know why. It's because Kerrie flew to LA eight days ago to find an apartment, and the cold hard reality of her move is hitting me for the first time.

I don't want her to go. But I can't ask her to stay. Not unless I'm going to take our relationship further, and I can't do that. Nothing has changed. I wanted her before; I want her still. I was older than her before; I'm older still.

I know the downside of that kind of age difference, and

not one goddamn thing has changed. Nothing, that is, except this pit of loss and longing that's growing in my gut. But that's selfish. And where Kerrie is concerned I can't be selfish. I have to think about what's best for her.

"You really think you're doing this for her?" Cayden asks me when he finally calls me out on being a moribund ass who's dragging down the mood of everyone around me.

"I know I am. Do you think I'd let her out of my sight if I wasn't positive?"

"Doing the right thing shouldn't make you so miserable," he says. "Maybe you need to take another look at the evidence. Maybe what you think is right is all fucked up."

"It's not." I'm nothing if not firm in my resolve.

"You really think you're doing this for her?" he asks again. This time, I don't bother answering.

He sighs. "So, what? That means there's someone else out there for you, too? Someone who fits you better than Kerrie? Because I've seen the two of you together, and you guys click."

We do. We really do.

"That's not the point," I tell him. "You know why we can't be together. I can't do that to her even if I love her. We're star-crossed."

"That is such bullshit." We're in my living room, and he's pacing in front of the window, a glorious panorama spread out behind him.

"How can you say that? You were there when Grandpa went downhill. You saw how much Gran gave up."

"*You* saw that," Cayden retorts. "You remembered how active Grandpa was and how much fun you two used to have throwing a ball around while I was off doing martial arts."

It's true. Cayden loved Grandpa, but I was the one who really spent time with him.

"You missed him and hated seeing him forced into bed after being so vibrant. And so you assumed that Gran was as laid flat by his decline as you were."

"Of course she was. The man had a heart attack. He was bedridden for years. How could you not see that?"

"I did," Cayden assures me. "I also saw a woman who loved her husband. Who read to him and laughed with him. Who watched movies and shared her life. I saw love, Connor. Do you think the fact that she couldn't hop on a plane and pop over to Rome changed that? For that matter, he never stopped her. She could have gone. She *chose* not to. She chose him. Because she loved him."

I say nothing.

He exhales, clearly frustrated. For a minute, I think he's done haranguing me. Then he narrows his eyes, studying me.

"What?"

"If I asked Kerrie if she thought there was someone out in the world better for you than her, what do you think she'd say?"

I scowl, but I also answer honestly. "She'd say no. But she's not thinking clearly."

"What gives you the right to decide for her?"

"Because I don't want her to be miserable."

He rubs his temples. "I love you, bro. But you know you're an idiot, right?"

"Dammit, Cay—"

"Should I sell my shares of Microsoft?" he blurts.

"What?" I'm completely baffled.

"How about Facebook? What should I buy this year if I want to grow my savings by 150% in the next nine months?"

"Have you gone completely insane? What the hell are you talking about? How should I know what to do with your portfolio?"

"Oh, sorry." He flashes me a smug grin. "I thought you could see the future."

"It's not the same."

"Yeah," he says simply as he heads for my door. "It really is."

He leaves me alone, and though I know I should get up and do something—anything—all I can manage is to sit in my favorite chair and stare out at my view, watching as the sun sinks lower and lower in the sky.

A thousand thoughts race through my mind, but I can't wrap my head around any particular one. All I know is that I'm miserable. And that I love Kerrie. And that suddenly my phone is in my hand, and I'm dialing her number even though I have no idea what I'm going to say.

She answers on the first ring, her voice like a balm. "Hey, I was just thinking about you."

"I like the sound of that. Where are you?"

"I just got back in town."

"How was Los Angeles? Did you have fun?" I clutch my phone tighter. I really hope she hated it.

"I did. I think I'll like it out there. And Del and I have always gotten along fabulously, so work should be good."

I have to clear my throat before I can speak. "That's

great," I finally manage to say, but my voice is flat. I can't conjure even an ounce of enthusiasm.

There's a pause. Then her voice comes across the line, soft and tentative. "Are you okay?"

"Sure. Just tired. The Feds. Work. Lots of stuff going on."

"Oh."

"You know what?" I blurt out before I even have time to think about my words. "Fuck that. I'm not tired and it's not work." The words flow like water, coming unbidden and unedited. But I don't want to stop them. They feel right. Like I've finally gotten out of my own way.

"Oh," she says again, but this time the word doesn't sound flat. It sounds hopeful.

"Don't go." I pour my heart and soul into those two words. "I know Del will be disappointed, and I know that LA might be fun, but we need you here. Who else is going to run the office? And keep us all in line?"

"Connor, please." Her voice is heavy. The sweet lilt fading.

I barrel on. "But that's only part of it. *I* need you. Hell, Kerrie, I love you."

Silence.

"Kerrie?"

"What are you saying?"

"I'm saying I've been an idiot. I'm saying I don't want to live without you." The words rush out of my heart and past my lips. "I'm saying that if you don't care about the years between us, then neither do I. What the hell is a number anyway? I was never good at math."

She laughs, the sound strangled, as if she's holding back tears.

"Kerrie? I know my timing sucks and Del will probably hate me. But please stay."

Again, there's silence. Except for a soft sound that might be crying.

"Kerrie? Baby, say something please."

"I love you, too," she whispers, her words melting my heart. "Now get your ass over here and kiss me."

CHAPTER FIFTEEN

I'M out the door in minutes, hauling ass toward her place. Now that I've made my decision—now that I've gotten my head out of my ass—I'm all in. Kerrie is mine, dammit, and we're moving forward together.

And as far as I'm concerned, together needs to start as soon as humanly possible.

It's not that far mileage-wise to her South Austin house from downtown, but traffic is a bitch in this town, and on top of that, I seem to hit every red light along the way.

I'm cursing Austin, city planners, and cars in general when my phone rings. I hit the button on my in-dash display to take it on speaker, assuming it's Kerrie.

It's not.

"Where are you?" Cayden asks, his voice tight.

"Heading to Kerrie's," I tell him. "I owe you a thanks. You were right. I've been an idiot. I'm—"

"Shut up and listen," he says. "I just sent you a text. Have you seen this?"

"I'm driving, remember?"

"It's important."

"Fuck." Since I'm at one of the damn red lights, I glance down at my phone, see that he's texted me an image, and push the button to transfer the picture to my console screen.

"Kerrie and Del," I say, glancing at the image of my girlfriend and her sister-in-law. "Not a bad picture." They're by the ocean, but traffic is moving again, so I take my eyes off the screen and continue down South First Street.

"Del sent it out over her Instagram feed," he says. "Some entertainment news agencies picked it up."

"This is all fascinating. Why do I care?"

"Because this is what she wrote." He starts to read. "So excited that my sister-in-law, Kerrie Blackwell, will be joining Team Delilah soon as my executive assistant, which pretty much means she'll be the boss of me. I'm so excited and can't wait for her to finish packing up her Austin house and move out here. And in case she looks familiar, Kerrie has been working for Blackwell-Lyon for years. That's the security company that helped me out a few years ago in Austin. So she's a tough cookie. Plus, her brother is the best. He'd have to be to be married to my sister. I'm so thrilled. Love you, K, and see you soon."

He stops reading and for a second there's silence. Honestly, I'm not sure what I'm supposed to say.

And then it hits me.

"The story was picked up?"

"Afraid so," my brother says.

"Where's Rollins?"

"The FBI went to pick him up, but he's bolted."

"Amy?"

"She's safe," Cayden says. "And when she poked around on his computer, she saw the picture. He's on his way to Austin. I'm certain of it."

"Fuck. Where are you? Where's Pierce? Leo?"

"Same as you. We're all heading to Kerrie's."

"You warned her?"

"Her phone's going straight to voicemail."

I bite back another curse. Hopefully she's just in the shower, and Rollins is still miles away. But I have a bad feeling.

"See you there."

I run the next three lights, pissing off the other drivers but not causing an accident, and when I screech to a halt in front of Kerrie's house, I'm relieved to see that there's no other car around. Pierce arrives only moments after me, looking as scared as I feel. I get it. She's my girlfriend, but she's his little sister. "She'll be fine," I say. Any other outcome is unacceptable.

"Any sign of Rollins?"

I shake my head. "I'm going in."

"I'm going around back," Pierce says. "Just in case."

I nod, then head to the front door. It's unlocked, which isn't a good sign, but when I step inside, my gun at the ready, Kerrie is alone.

"Thank God," I say, hurrying to her side as her eyes go wide. "Rollins—"

"—is very happy you're here." The voice is familiar, and I turn in time to see him emerge from the kitchen, his own weapon aimed at Kerrie. "You're just in time to watch her die."

I react without thinking, launching myself at her and knocking her to the ground just a split second before he fires. I hear the sharp report of the gun, then feel the burning impact in my leg. I smell gunpowder and blood, and I hear Kerrie's scream.

But I'm alive. For the moment. And so is Kerrie.

"Nobody screws me," Rollins growls, his voice seeming to come from underwater. I try to move, but it's not possible. But in my periphery, I can see him coming toward us, gun outstretched. I try to cover Kerrie, but I can't manage it. And then he raises his gun, and all I can think is that I can't let her die. But there's not a goddamn thing I can do except pray.

And then there's a loud *crack* and he flinches. Red blooms on his chest and he falls backward.

I hear Kerrie scream Pierce's name at the same time I see my friend burst in through the back door.

Everything blurs as a fresh wave of pain envelops me, but in the rising gray, I see Pierce take off his belt and tighten it around my leg. I hear the word *thigh*. I hear a siren.

Most of all, I hear Kerrie's voice telling me to stay with her.

"I love you," I whisper.

And as the world starts to turn gray, I see the fear on her face. I try to tell her it will be fine. No way am I leaving her now that we're together again. But somehow I can't make the words come.

That's okay, though. I know this isn't the end. On the contrary, it's just the beginning.

Because I'm not going anywhere. Not even if I end up an old man with only one leg. No way am I pushing her away.

Not ever again.

EPILOGUE

Two months later

"HAPPY BIRTHDAY TO YOU! Happy birthday to you! Happy birthday, dear Kerrie ... Happy birthday to you!"

The horribly out of tune birthday serenade ends as I stand behind Kerrie, leaning on my cane as she makes a wish and blows out the candles. The cake is still in the nine-by-thirteen inch pan. A Betty Crocker yellow cake with Betty Crocker chocolate frosting. I made it myself, although according to Del I can't really say that I *made* it since it wasn't from scratch.

"You *combined* it," she'd insisted this morning when she stepped in as my much-needed kitchen assistant. Only slightly younger than Kerrie, Delilah has the bearing and sophistication of someone who's grown up in the public eye. "And you baked it," she added. "But you didn't make it."

She'd shrugged philosophically. "But you still get credit for effort."

After the drama with Rollins—who died in the hospital after falling into a coma—Kerrie had given Del her regrets, electing to stay in Austin as our office manager. And my girlfriend. As of today, we've been living together for seven weeks and five days.

Today, I'm hoping to lock her in for a bit longer. Like, say, a lifetime.

And I'm as nervous as a cat at a dog show.

As soon as the candles wink out, Kerrie beams first at me, and then at the family and friends gathered around us. Del, Cayden, Gracie, Jez, Pierce, and Leo. Not to mention Amy, Noah Carter and his wife Kiki, and at least a dozen more friends that Pierce and I knew she'd want to celebrate this day with.

At least, I hope that's the case.

"Can I cut the cake now?" She directs the question at me, and I nod. Then immediately hold up my hand and tell her to wait.

"Champagne," I say, then lean my cane against the table as I limp toward the refrigerator. I should only need it for another month or two—the bullet did a number on my leg, but it's healing nicely—but in the meantime, Kerrie amuses herself by remarking what an old man I am every time I pass by.

I retaliate by threatening to withhold sex. At which point she has nothing but good things to say about my youth and prowess.

I return from the fridge with the champagne, which I open with a loud *pop*, followed by universal applause. Gracie passes around plastic flutes, and I pour for everyone.

"Fancy," Kerrie says with a grin. "Usually chocolate cake calls for cold milk."

"My girl deserves champagne," I say, moving beside her and kissing her head. I meet Del's eyes and find her grinning.

As for me, my stomach is in knots.

Kerrie seems entirely oblivious.

"Shall I just slice anywhere?" she asks. The cake is decorated with the words *Happy Birthday* over the number 26. Beneath the number is a little candy heart.

"That's your birthday girl slice," I say, pointing to the heart. "Cut a slice around that."

I hold my breath as she does, then slides it neatly out and puts it on her plate.

She starts to cut another slice, but I stop her. "Go ahead and see if you like it."

She frowns, looking around at the group. "I thought you were supposed to pass it around first."

I shake my head, looking at Del and Pierce for confirmation.

"He's right," Del says. "The birthday girl takes her wish-bite, then serves everyone else."

I watch as Kerrie looks at her brother, obviously confused. Pierce just shrugs. "I don't know the rules, and they sound pretty convinced."

"Family tradition," I say.

"Whatever." She takes her fork and starts to dig in, only to be stymied by something hard. "What the—"

I watch her face, seeing the exact moment when she realizes something is hidden in the cake. And then I see it go completely blank as she excavates the small metal box.

My stomach twists, suddenly fearful, because why isn't she smiling?

Then she opens the box, and I watch as joy floods her face, the emotion so palpable it makes me weak at the knees.

She looks at me, her lips moving, but she can't seem to form words.

I take the ring from her hand, then hold it out. A silent request for her ring finger.

When she extends her hand, I slip it on. The room is hushed, the silence rich with anticipation. "Yesterday we were fifteen years apart," I say. "But now it's only fourteen. So I had to pick today to ask you, Kerrie Blackwell, if you'll be my wife."

Tears trail down her cheeks as she nods. "Yes." Her voice is thick, and she tries again. "Oh, yes."

"I love you, Kay," I say as she launches herself into my arms.

"Love you, too, Old Man," she replies, then kisses me hard as our friends and family laugh and cheer, and I hold her tight, knowing that we're going to face our future together.

Want more?

Keep reading for a peek at Leo in Tempting Little Tease!

TEMPTING LITTLE TEASE
SNEAK PEEK

**TEMPTING
LITTLE
TEASE**

J. KENNER

TEMPTING LITTLE TEASE

PLEASE ENJOY THIS EXCERPT!

A MAN IS nothing without a code.

And he's less than nothing if he breaks his own code.

That's what my father always told me, and with his chest full of medals and an office papered with commendations, General Christopher Anthony Palermo knew a thing or two about honor.

I like to think that I do, too.

My whole life, I've walked the straight and narrow, following but never crossing those lines in the sand. The lines called trust and ethics and good old-fashioned decency.

I respect the law and the system. I don't break my friends' trust or toy with a woman's heart. I don't stand by doing nothing when I see injustice, and I'm willing to get my hands dirty for something I believe in.

I won't stand for being used, and I don't tolerate those who prey on misfortune. I fight fair, but anyone who comes after me or mine better expect to get knocked down.

School. War. Work. Family. Doesn't matter. I've held fast to those tenets my entire life.

Then she slips into my bed, and suddenly I can't keep my code without breaking my code. Around her, everything I know about my life and myself flips completely upside down.

And I honestly can't even tell if that's a bad thing, or something very, very good.

"In other words, you stopped this thief with your ass." Brody Carrington grins at me. "I'm impressed, Leo. You always were resourceful."

"What can I say? I go the extra mile for my clients."

He holds out his beer bottle. "To Leonardo Vincent Palermo. Fastest ass in the West."

I raise mine in response, then clink. "Aw, shucks," I drawl. "You'll make me blush."

He laughs, then takes a long swallow. We're drinking Loaded Coronas, a specialty drink at The Fix on Sixth, a favorite Austin bar that's just a few blocks from my office.

My best friend, Brody Carrington was the first client I brought over to Blackwell-Lyon Security after I started working there about six months ago, and last night I was working a case he'd referred to us.

Simple enough, really. The client was Brody's friend, the right hand of one of the United States' senators from Texas. The Senator's ramping up for re-election, and he suspected that there was someone on his staff selling his secrets and strategies.

It only took a few weeks to confirm the breach and finger the thief. The team and I outlined a plan. We had the Senator plant some cheese, and I lurked in the darkened office, waiting for our rat.

Of course, none of us expected that the rat would break a fifth floor window and try to escape by shimmying down the drainpipe. And since I'm nothing if not devoted to my work, I took off after him, leaping onto the pipe myself, then loosened my grip about halfway down so that I'd slide the rest of the way fast enough to catch him.

To be clear, I hadn't actually planned to knock the prick unconscious with my butt, but you can't argue with success. And I'll be sure to thank my trainer the next time he loads up the barbell for a fresh set of squats. Buns of steel. That's me.

"That's twice you've come through for me." Brody takes a long swig of his drink, then asks, "Want to try for three out of three?"

I lean back in my chair, chuckling. "You've got another job? Brody, my friend, you're attracting assholes like flies."

"Nah, this one's a gimme. Seriously. Pure escort duty, nothing more."

"I can't believe I'm turning down the chance to take you to the prom, my friend, but I've been going non-stop for months. I'm taking a couple of weeks for some R and R."

"Yeah? Where are you heading?"

"Not far. Just South Austin and my house. I've been in this town almost half a year, and the garage is still full of boxes."

He shakes his head in mock reproach. "You are a sad specimen, my friend. Where's your sense of adventure?"

"I get enough adventure on the job," I remind him. "To be honest, I'd originally planned to head up to Dallas and see my folks, but Mom talked Dad into one of those Alaskan cruises." My mother loves to travel, but Dad says he saw enough of the world bouncing all over it during his years in the service. Now, he just wants to stay at home, spending time with his friends, the dogs, and the woman he adores.

He loves my mom too much to stick to his guns, though. And they compromised with Alaska. "Because a cruise is the only way to go to multiple destinations without having to repack your damn suitcase," he'd told me.

"He'll enjoy it," Brody says. "That was the last trip Karen and I took."

"I'm sorry," I say, feeling like an ass. "I didn't know. I wouldn't have mentioned Alaska at all if—"

"I know. It's fine. And it's a good memory. There will always be things that remind me of her. And one of these days, the memories will be happy." He lifts his beer bottle with a shrug. "At least that's what everyone tells me."

I flounder a bit, wishing I had some way to erase the sorry from my friend's eyes. Karen passed away just over three years ago, the victim of a late diagnosed brain tumor. The speed with which she had declined had been a blessing and a curse. She suffered less, but Brody barely had time to wrap his head around what was happening before she was gone.

A few months later, he'd quit his job as a detective with the Dallas Police Department to take over as CEO of the family business after his father retired. He's consistently said that he made the switch for his dad, but I have my own theories. I think he loved his work so much that it was a painful, daily reminder of how much he'd loved Karen. And how much he'd lost when she passed away.

I also think he regrets leaving, though he'll probably never admit it. Brody's not the desk jockey type. Nor does he like playing office politics. So far, though, he's shown no sign that he's thinking about pulling up stakes.

"You've got that apologetic look in your eye," he chides me. "Seriously, it's okay. Buy the next round and hear me out about this job, and we'll call it even."

"Fair enough," I say, then signal for Eric, the bartender, to send over another round.

"You remember Sam, right?"

"Sure," I say, smiling at the memory of his kid sister. "Remember ninth grade? She was, what? In sixth? I thought your mom was going to skin us alive when she learned we ordered Sam to do all your chores so you could come over to my house." The very well-built Myers twins lived behind my house, and my room had an excellent view of their pool.

"It was worth it, though," Brody said. "I wonder what the twins are up to these days..."

"I haven't thought about them in years. Sam, either, to tell you the truth. I don't think I've seen her since we graduated."

Technically Brody's stepsister, Samantha Watson had moved in with Brody when her mom married Brody's dad. She was two and he was five. By the time I met Brody freshman year, there was nothing "step" about their relationship; they were siblings, through and through, and he was the big brother who both harassed and looked after his kid sister. She'd been a gawky pre-teen, and I don't think I ever saw her when she wasn't either buried in a book or a computer game.

And since Brody and I were as close as brothers, Sam became my pseudo-sister, complete with arguments and teasing and sass.

She was a good kid with a snarky sense of humor, and the fact that she needs help from a guy who works in the security business worries me.

"No, no," Brody says when I tell him as much. "Nothing like that. She needs an escort to a wedding."

"That's it?"

Brody shrugs. "I told you it was no big deal. She was planning on going stag, then she found out her ex is going to be there. She's—well, honestly, she wants to go with someone who'll pretend to be her fiancé."

I sit back, amused. "She trying to make this guy jealous?"

"No, no. Unless she's totally bullshitting me, she's not interested in him anymore. But I guess he said some nasty things when they broke up and she wants to take him down a peg. Show him that he was just a stepping stone to the real thing."

He holds up his hands as if in surrender. "It's stupid game-playing, but Sam doesn't date much, and this guy hurt her. It's not socially acceptable for me to beat him up in a dark alley, so I decided I'd back her plan."

"And rope me in," I add with a smile.

"That was her idea, buddy, not mine."

"Really?" A waiter I haven't seen before delivers our second round, and I take a long swallow, enjoying the burn from that first hit of rum filling the neck of the bottle. "Why?"

Brody shrugs. "I'm guessing it's because you're the second best thing to me."

I raise my brows, and he laughs. "I mean that she's not looking for a fling, just someone who'll play the part. Obviously, she can't drag along her real brother, so she wants the runner-up."

"A guy she can trust."

He nods. "She always thought of you as safe, but she doesn't know you like I do." He spreads his hands, as if asking *what can you do?*

I cross my arms over my chest, trying not to let Brody rankle me. Especially since he speaks the truth.

"I promised her I'd ask. But dammit, Leo, don't agree unless you can handle the job. And by that I mean not handling my sister."

Anger flares inside me, red and ripe. "Pull it back a notch," I say, my voice low and edging toward dangerous. I can see in his eyes that he knows he pushed me a little too close to the line. "Do you really think I'd go there?"

For a moment, we just look at each other. Two men who know each other better than most brothers, and sometimes that can be a dangerous thing. For a moment, it seems as if the whole bar has fallen silent. Then Brody shakes his head. More of a twitch, really, but it's enough. Then tension shatters like glass, and we both pick up our bottles.

"Fuck, man," he says. "She's my kid sister."

"She's an adult now," I remind him. "And I am, too."

He cocks his head and says nothing.

I lift my upper lip. "Asshole. I may not be a monk, but I can keep it in my pants when I want to."

"Can? Or will?"

"What the fuck, Brody?" I mean, come on. Brody's supposed to be my best friend. Which, I guess, does mean he knows me better than anybody. So maybe his concerns are legitimate.

Or maybe they're not. Lately, I've gotten a bit tired of riding the hook-up train. I haven't fucked a woman in over two months. And I'm not sure if I'm getting bored with the whole damn thing, or if I'm just ready to settle down.

Honestly, both options scare the shit out of me.

"What?" I say, realizing that Brody's been rattling on about something.

"I said I'm sorry. I was being an ass. But she's my sister, so just promise me, okay? Make me feel better about asking you this, because I swear I'm only doing it because Sam asked me to. I know you, man."

"If you did, you'd know there's no way in hell I'd make a pass. She's like a little sister to me, too."

"So is that a yes? I can tell her you're in for this crazy scheme?"

I shake my head, not in response, but in bewilderment. "Crazy is right. Honestly, Bro, it's a little off the wall."

"Can't argue with that, but if you get past the crazy, it sounds like a great deal. It's a destination wedding. A long weekend in Fredericksburg," he adds, referring to a charming town in the Texas Hill Country that has become famous for its local vineyards, restaurants, and shopping. "Go up Friday. Come back Monday morning after the wedding. You drink. You eat. You sit around and read. You've been going a million miles an hour since you moved to Austin, right? And you can unpack anytime. How often do you get the chance to go on an all-expense paid vacation where the alcohol is included?"

It's a fair point. And I've been managing just fine without all the crap that's still in those boxes.

"Remember her freshman formal right before we graduated?" he prompts.

I scowl. "Now you're playing dirty." She'd worn a denim jumper over a long-sleeve T-shirt and Doc Martin shoes. A more confident girl could have pulled it off, but Sam was the geeky, shy girl.

I never knew exactly what happened that night, but when she couldn't track down her parents or Brody, she'd called me, begging me to come pick her up. I did. I'd taken her home, but not before taking her into the center of the gym for one dance. It had been a slow song—Aerosmith's *I Don't Want To Miss A Thing*—and she'd practically shaken in my arms as everyone watched us.

Then I kissed her, walked her off the dance floor, and took her to Whataburger for fries and a shake.

"You were like her knight," Brody says. "A knight who flipped off the rest of the freshman class."

"She was a good kid who didn't deserve to be teased."

"True that," Brody says. "She was such a gawky thing back then."

"From what I saw last Halloween on your feed, she still is." I'm rarely on social media, so I miss a lot, but from what

I can tell, Sam hardly ever posts pictures. Or maybe Brody just never shares them. Last year, though, he'd shared one of her posts after a Halloween party. Honestly, she'd looked pretty much the same. Adorable, but gawky.

Brody chuckles. "I forget you haven't seen her since senior year. But seriously, you changed her life that night. Because of you, she had a much better sophomore year. People remembered that hot shit Leo Palermo was her date that night. It mattered."

I suppose it did. By senior year, I was definitely up there in the high school social strata. I was into sports, made solid grades, and was on the Student Council. Plus, it didn't hurt that I've got my dad's dark, Italian looks and a decent build.

"You know, that formal was the last time I saw her." I'd gone to college out of state, and by the time I moved back to Texas, she was in Seattle working at some video game company. "Has it really been that long?"

"Time flies," Brody says. "Remember after you brought her home? I'd just pulled up from a date with somebody, and she told me what happened and how you were her hero, and I said—"

"That one or the other of us would always be there for her. I remember."

"And then we went off to college and abandoned her," Brody adds. "Pretty shitty of us really."

"Is this your way of guilting me into helping her now?"

"Hell, yes."

I have to laugh. "Okay, give me her phone number. I'm not saying yes, but I'll at least get her take on this scam."

"You should talk to her in person."

"When's she flying in for this shindig?"
"She's not," he says. "She's already here."

Want more?
Grab your copy of Tempting Little Tease from your favorite book store!

DOWN ON ME SNEAK PEEK

DOWN ON ME

PLEASE ENJOY THIS EXCERPT!

REECE WALKER RAN his palms over the slick, soapy ass of the woman in his arms and knew that he was going straight to hell.

Not because he'd slept with a woman he barely knew. Not because he'd enticed her into bed with a series of well-timed bourbons and particularly inventive half-truths. Not even because he'd lied to his best friend Brent about why Reece couldn't drive with him to the airport to pick up Jenna, the third player in their trifecta of lifelong friendship.

No, Reece was staring at the fiery pit because he was a lame, horny asshole without the balls to tell the naked beauty standing in the shower with him that she wasn't the woman he'd been thinking about for the last four hours.

And if that wasn't one of the pathways to hell, it damn sure ought to be.

He let out a sigh of frustration, and Megan tilted her head, one eyebrow rising in question as she slid her hand down to stroke his cock, which was demonstrating no guilt whatsoever about the whole going to hell issue. "Am I boring you?"

"Hardly." That, at least, was the truth. He felt like a prick, yes. But he was a well-satisfied one. "I was just thinking that you're beautiful."

She smiled, looking both shy and pleased—and Reece felt even more like a heel. What the devil was wrong with him? She *was* beautiful. And hot and funny and easy to talk to. Not to mention good in bed.

But she wasn't Jenna, which was a ridiculous comparison. Because Megan qualified as fair game, whereas Jenna was one of his two best friends. She trusted him. Loved him. And despite the way his cock perked up at the thought of doing all sorts of delicious things with her in bed, Reece knew damn well that would never happen. No way was he risking their friendship. Besides, Jenna didn't love him like that. Never had, never would.

And that—plus about a billion more reasons—meant that Jenna was entirely off-limits.

Too bad his vivid imagination hadn't yet gotten the memo.

Fuck it.

He tightened his grip, squeezing Megan's perfect rear. "Forget the shower," he murmured. "I'm taking you back to bed." He needed this. Wild. Hot. Demanding. And dirty enough to keep him from thinking.

Hell, he'd scorch the earth if that's what it took to burn Jenna from his mind—and he'd leave Megan limp, whimpering, and very, very satisfied. His guilt. Her pleasure. At least it would be a win for one of them.

And who knows? Maybe he'd manage to fuck the fantasies of his best friend right out of his head.

It didn't work.

Reece sprawled on his back, eyes closed, as Megan's gentle fingers traced the intricate outline of the tattoos inked across his pecs and down his arms. Her touch was warm and tender, in stark contrast to the way he'd just fucked her—a little too wild, a little too hard, as if he were fighting a battle, not making love.

Well, that was true, wasn't it?

But it was a battle he'd lost. Victory would have brought oblivion. Yet here he was, a naked woman beside him, and his thoughts still on Jenna, as wild and intense and impossible as they'd been since that night eight months ago when the earth had shifted beneath him, and he'd let himself look at her as a woman and not as a friend.

One breathtaking, transformative night, and Jenna didn't even realize it. And he'd be damned if he'd ever let her figure it out.

Beside him, Megan continued her exploration, one fingertip tracing the outline of a star. "No names? No wife or girlfriend's initials hidden in the design?"

He turned his head sharply, and she burst out laughing.

"Oh, don't look at me like that." She pulled the sheet up to cover her breasts as she rose to her knees beside him. "I'm just making conversation. No hidden agenda at all. Believe me, the last thing I'm interested in is a relationship." She scooted away, then sat on the edge of the bed, giving him an enticing view of her bare back. "I don't even do overnights."

As if to prove her point, she bent over, grabbed her bra off the floor, and started getting dressed.

"Then that's one more thing we have in common." He pushed himself up, rested his back against the headboard, and enjoyed the view as she wiggled into her jeans.

"Good," she said, with such force that he knew she meant it, and for a moment he wondered what had soured her on relationships.

As for himself, he hadn't soured so much as fizzled. He'd had a few serious girlfriends over the years, but it never worked out. No matter how good it started, invariably the relationship crumbled. Eventually, he had to acknowledge that he simply wasn't relationship material. But that didn't mean he was a monk, the last eight months notwithstanding.

She put on her blouse and glanced around, then slipped her feet into her shoes. Taking the hint, he got up and pulled on his jeans and T-shirt. "Yes?" he asked, noticing the way she was eying him speculatively.

"The truth is, I was starting to think you might be in a relationship."

"What? Why?"

She shrugged. "You were so quiet there for a while, I wondered if maybe I'd misjudged you. I thought you might be married and feeling guilty."

Guilty.

The word rattled around in his head, and he groaned. "Yeah, you could say that."

"Oh, *hell*. Seriously?"

"No," he said hurriedly. "Not that. I'm not cheating on my non-existent wife. I wouldn't. Not ever." Not in small part because Reece wouldn't ever have a wife since he thought the institution of marriage was a crock, but he didn't see the need to explain that to Megan.

"But as for guilt?" he continued. "Yeah, tonight I've got that in spades."

She relaxed slightly. "Hmm. Well, sorry about the guilt, but I'm glad about the rest. I have rules, and I consider myself a good judge of character. It makes me cranky when I'm wrong."

"Wouldn't want to make you cranky."

"Oh, you really wouldn't. I can be a total bitch." She sat on the edge of the bed and watched as he tugged on his boots. "But if you're not hiding a wife in your attic, what are you feeling guilty about? I assure you, if it has anything to do with my satisfaction, you needn't feel guilty at all." She flashed a mischievous grin, and he couldn't help but smile back. He hadn't invited a woman into his bed for eight long months. At least he'd had the good fortune to pick one he actually liked.

"It's just that I'm a crappy friend," he admitted.

"I doubt that's true."

"Oh, it is," he assured her as he tucked his wallet into his back pocket. The irony, of course, was that as far as Jenna knew, he was an excellent friend. The best. One of her two pseudo-brothers with whom she'd sworn a blood oath the summer after sixth grade, almost twenty years ago.

From Jenna's perspective, Reece was at least as good as Brent, even if the latter scored bonus points because he was picking Jenna up at the airport while Reece was trying to fuck his personal demons into oblivion. Trying anything, in fact, that would exorcise the memory of how she'd clung to him that night, her curves enticing and her breath intoxicating, and not just because of the scent of too much alcohol.

She'd trusted him to be the white knight, her noble rescuer, and all he'd been able to think about was the feel of her body, soft and warm against his, as he carried her up the stairs to her apartment.

A wild craving had hit him that night, like a tidal wave of emotion crashing over him, washing away the outer shell of friendship and leaving nothing but raw desire and a longing so potent it nearly brought him to his knees.

It had taken all his strength to keep his distance when the only thing he'd wanted was to cover every inch of her naked body with kisses. To stroke her skin and watch her writhe with pleasure.

He'd won a hard-fought battle when he reined in his desire that night. But his victory wasn't without its wounds. She'd pierced his heart when she'd drifted to sleep in his arms, whispering that she loved him—and he knew that she meant it only as a friend.

More than that, he knew that he was the biggest asshole to ever walk the earth.

Thankfully, Jenna remembered nothing of that night. The liquor had stolen her memories, leaving her with a monster hangover, and him with a Jenna-shaped hole in his heart.

"Well?" Megan pressed. "Are you going to tell me? Or do I have to guess?"

"I blew off a friend."

"Yeah? That probably won't score you points in the

Friend of the Year competition, but it doesn't sound too dire. Unless you were the best man and blew off the wedding? Left someone stranded at the side of the road somewhere in West Texas? Or promised to feed their cat and totally forgot? Oh, God. Please tell me you didn't kill Fluffy."

He bit back a laugh, feeling slightly better. "A friend came in tonight, and I feel like a complete shit for not meeting her plane."

"Well, there are taxis. And I assume she's an adult?"

"She is, and another friend is there to pick her up."

"I see," she said, and the way she slowly nodded suggested that she saw too much. "I'm guessing that *friend* means *girlfriend*? Or, no. You wouldn't do that. So she must be an ex."

"Really not," he assured her. "Just a friend. Lifelong, since sixth grade."

"Oh, I get it. Longtime friend. High expectations. She's going to be pissed."

"Nah. She's cool. Besides, she knows I usually work nights."

"Then what's the problem?"

He ran his hand over his shaved head, the bristles from the day's growth like sandpaper against his palm. "Hell if I know," he lied, then forced a smile, because whether his problem was guilt or lust or just plain stupidity, she hardly deserved to be on the receiving end of his bullshit.

He rattled his car keys. "How about I buy you one last drink before I take you home?"

"You're sure you don't mind a working drink?" Reece asked as he helped Megan out of his cherished baby blue vintage Chevy pickup. "Normally I wouldn't take you to my job, but we just hired a new bar back, and I want to see how it's going."

He'd snagged one of the coveted parking spots on Sixth Street, about a block down from The Fix, and he glanced automatically toward the bar, the glow from the windows relaxing him. He didn't own the place, but it was like a second home to him and had been for one hell of a long time.

"There's a new guy in training, and you're not there? I thought you told me you were the manager?"

"I did, and I am, but Tyree's there. The owner, I mean. He's always on site when someone new is starting. Says it's his job, not mine. Besides, Sunday's my day off, and Tyree's a stickler for keeping to the schedule."

"Okay, but why are you going then?"

"Honestly? The new guy's my cousin. He'll probably give me shit for checking in on him, but old habits die hard." Michael had been almost four when Vincent died, and the loss of his dad hit him hard. At sixteen, Reece had tried to be stoic, but Uncle Vincent had been like a second father to him, and he'd always thought of Mike as more brother than cousin. Either way, from that day on, he'd made it his job to watch out for the kid.

"Nah, he'll appreciate it," Megan said. "I've got a little sister, and she gripes when I check up on her, but it's all for show. She likes knowing I have her back. And as for getting a drink where you work, I don't mind at all."

As a general rule, late nights on Sunday were dead,

both in the bar and on Sixth Street, the popular downtown Austin street that had been a focal point of the city's nightlife for decades. Tonight was no exception. At half-past one in the morning, the street was mostly deserted. Just a few cars moving slowly, their headlights shining toward the west, and a smattering of couples, stumbling and laughing. Probably tourists on their way back to one of the downtown hotels.

It was late April, though, and the spring weather was drawing both locals and tourists. Soon, the area—and the bar—would be bursting at the seams. Even on a slow Sunday night.

Situated just a few blocks down from Congress Avenue, the main downtown artery, The Fix on Sixth attracted a healthy mix of tourists and locals. The bar had existed in one form or another for decades, becoming a local staple, albeit one that had been falling deeper and deeper into disrepair until Tyree had bought the place six years ago and started it on much-needed life support.

"You've never been here before?" Reece asked as he paused in front of the oak and glass doors etched with the bar's familiar logo.

"I only moved downtown last month. I was in Los Angeles before."

The words hit Reece with unexpected force. Jenna had been in LA, and a wave of both longing and regret crashed over him. He should have gone with Brent. What the hell kind of friend was he, punishing Jenna because he couldn't control his own damn libido?

With effort, he forced the thoughts back. He'd already beaten that horse to death.

"Come on," he said, sliding one arm around her shoulder and pulling open the door with his other. "You're going to love it."

He led her inside, breathing in the familiar mix of alcohol, southern cooking, and something indiscernible he liked to think of as the scent of a damn good time. As he expected, the place was mostly empty. There was no live music on Sunday nights, and at less than an hour to closing, there were only three customers in the front room.

"Megan, meet Cameron," Reece said, pulling out a stool for her as he nodded to the bartender in introduction. Down the bar, he saw Griffin Draper, a regular, lift his head, his face obscured by his hoodie, but his attention on Megan as she chatted with Cam about the house wines.

Reece nodded hello, but Griffin turned back to his notebook so smoothly and nonchalantly that Reece wondered if maybe he'd just been staring into space, thinking, and hadn't seen Reece or Megan at all. That was probably the case, actually. Griff wrote a popular podcast that had been turned into an even more popular web series, and when he wasn't recording the dialogue, he was usually writing a script.

"So where's Mike? With Tyree?"

Cameron made a face, looking younger than his twenty-four years. "Tyree's gone."

"You're kidding. Did something happen with Mike?" His cousin was a responsible kid. Surely he hadn't somehow screwed up his first day on the job.

"No, Mike's great." Cam slid a Scotch in front of Reece. "Sharp, quick, hard worker. He went off the clock about an hour ago, though. So you just missed him."

"Tyree shortened his shift?"

Cam shrugged. "Guess so. Was he supposed to be on until closing?"

"Yeah." Reece frowned. "He was. Tyree say why he cut him loose?"

"No, but don't sweat it. Your cousin's fitting right in. Probably just because it's Sunday and slow." He made a face. "And since Tyree followed him out, guess who's closing for the first time alone."

"So you're in the hot seat, huh?" Reece tried to sound casual. He was standing behind Megan's stool, but now he moved to lean against the bar, hoping his casual posture suggested that he wasn't worried at all. He was, but he didn't want Cam to realize it. Tyree didn't leave employees to close on their own. Not until he'd spent weeks training them.

"I told him I want the weekend assistant manager position. I'm guessing this is his way of seeing how I work under pressure."

"Probably," Reece agreed half-heartedly. "What did he say?"

"Honestly, not much. He took a call in the office, told Mike he could head home, then about fifteen minutes later said he needed to take off, too, and that I was the man for the night."

"Trouble?" Megan asked.

"No. Just chatting up my boy," Reece said, surprised at how casual his voice sounded. Because the scenario had trouble printed all over it. He just wasn't sure what kind of trouble.

He focused again on Cam. "What about the waitstaff?"

Normally, Tiffany would be in the main bar taking care of the customers who sat at tables. "He didn't send them home, too, did he?"

"Oh, no," Cam said. "Tiffany and Aly are scheduled to be on until closing, and they're in the back with—"

But his last words were drowned out by a high-pitched squeal of *"You're here!"* and Reece looked up to find Jenna Montgomery—the woman he craved—barreling across the room and flinging herself into his arms.

"With each novel featuring a favorite romance trope—beauty and the beast, billionaire bad boys, friends to lovers, second chance romance, secret baby, and more—this series hits the heart and soul of romance." — *New York Times* bestselling author Carly Phillips

Who's Your Man of the Month?
Down On Me
Hold On Tight
Need You Now
Start Me Up
Get It On
In Your Eyes
Turn Me On
Shake It Up
All Night Long
In Too Deep
Light My Fire
Walk The Line

MEET DAMIEN STARK

Only his passion could set her free...

The Original Trilogy
Release Me
Claim Me
Complete Me
And Beyond...
Anchor Me
Lost With Me
DAMIEN

Meet Damien Stark in the award-winning & international bestselling series that started it all.

The Stark Saga by J. Kenner

STARK SECURITY

Stark Security, a high-end, high-tech, no-holds barred security firm founded by billionaire Damien Stark and security specialist Ryan Hunter has one mission: Do whatever it takes to protect the innocent. Only the best in the business are good enough for Stark Security.

A team with dangerous skills.

A team with something to prove.

Brilliant, charismatic, sexy as hell, they have no time for softness—they work hard and they play harder. They'll take any risk to get the job done.

But what they won't do is lose their hearts.

Charismatic. Dangerous. Sexy as hell.
Meet the elite team of Stark Security.

Shattered With You
Broken With You
Ruined With You
Wrecked With You

ABOUT THE AUTHOR

J. Kenner (aka Julie Kenner) is the *New York Times, USA Today, Publishers Weekly, Wall Street Journal* and #1 International bestselling author of over one hundred novels, novellas and short stories in a variety of genres.

Stay in touch with JK and be the first to know about new releases: Just text: JKenner to 21000 to subscribe to JK's text alerts.

www.jkenner.com

Printed in Great Britain
by Amazon